IF YOU WERE THE ONLY GIRL

When Lucy's father dies, she is forced to take a job in service as a scullery maid at Windthorpe House, home to the aristocratic Hetheringtons, who lost three of their sons in the Great War. When their only remaining son, Clive, returns home, he and Lucy strike up an immediate bond but Clive, much to his family's alarm, decides to volunteer in the Spanish Civil War, though when he returns, he is injured. With the outbreak of war ever more certain, the two fall in love. But Hitler's troops are gathering and fate has something very different in store for both of them...

IF YOU WERE THE ONLY GIRL

IF YOU WERE THE ONLY GIRL

by

Anne Bennett

Magna Large Print Books
Long Preston, North Yorkshire,
BD23 4ND, England.

British Library Cataloguing in Publication Data.

Bennett, Anne
If you were the only girl.

A catalogue record of this book is
available from the British Library

ISBN   978-0-7505-3808-4

First published in Great Britain in 2012 by
HarperCollins*Publishers*

Copyright © Anne Bennett 2012

Cover illustration © Gordon Crabb by arrangement with
Alison Eldred

Anne Bennett asserts the moral right to be identified as the author of
this work

Published in Large Print 2013 by arrangement with
HarperCollins Publishers

Magna Large Print is an imprint of Library Magna Books Ltd.

Printed and bound in Great Britain by
T.J. (International) Ltd., Cornwall, PL28 8RW

I would like this book dedicated to Judith Kendal in recognition of the many things she has done for me in our twenty year friendship.

ACKNOWLEDGEMENTS

As always, thanks must go to the fabulous team behind me at Harper Collins, my editor Kate Bradley, my publicist Elinor Fewster, Amy Winchester her assistant and Yvonne who does the second edits. Special thanks must also go to Susan Opie who does such a marvellous job copy editing my work and my agent Judith Murdoch for she is always there for me should I need her help. It is very comforting for a writer to have such a strong team at their back and I owe a debt of gratitude to you all.

I can also always rely on the support of the family, my husband, Denis, my three daughters, Nikki, Beth and Tamsin, my son Simon, the out-laws Steve, Carol and Mark and the five grand-children. Briony, Kynan, Jake, Theo and Catrin who help to keep me grounded.

But the most important people are the readers – you out there who buy the books or borrow them from the Library for without you there would be no point to what I do. And when you write and tell me what you think of the books it means an awful lot and I am immensely grateful to all of you. One thing I am always asked is how I get the ideas for the books and sometimes there is something that sparks it off, but for this one I cannot claim any Damascus moment, it just popped into my head.

As always I did a lot of work on research. The internet is a wonderful tool and I could not manage without it, but I also use books such as Niall Noi-gallach's book 'Our Town', which is a history of Letterkenny. I also used 'Sutton Coldfield in the Forties' by John Bassett, 'Catholics in Birmingham' by Christine Ward Penny, 'Life on the Home Front', which is a Reader's Digest publication and the book that helped me so much in writing 'To Have and To Hold,'. 'Q E Nurse 1938–1957' compiled by Doreen Tennant, Jeffrey Wood and Ann-Carol Carrington and edited by Collette Clifford, which I once more found an invaluable resource. Last but no means least I used 'Brum Undaunted' by Carl Chinn which details Birmingham through the War and I was forced to buy another copy as the original fell apart through overuse.

My editor came up with the title, 'If You Were The Only Girl' and I didn't like it. Every month I meet for lunch with fellow writers and I told them of the proposed title, expecting them to agree with the unsuitability of it and maybe between us come up with something better. However, to my amazement, they not only loved it but burst spontaneously into 'If you were the only girl In the world.' They sang it right through and then we sang it all together again, much to the astonishment of the hotel staff. In fact so positive were my friends that I began to see the title in a different light entirely and now I love it, so thank you Kate.

I particularly like the fact that it tells the story of the novel very well indeed and researching it, I found that it was written by a man called Nat D. Ayer with lyrics by Clifford Grey. As it was first published in April 1916 with the war raging and just before the bloodiest battle in the First World War at the Somme, in July that same year, I could imagine any soldier being ripped from his girl by war might also wish they were the only two in the world.

So that's it really. Another one to hit the shelves and if you would like to hear a little more about me and mine and more about the books too, please sign up for my newsletter. Contact details on my website. Look forward to hearing from you.

ONE

Lucy Cassidy saw Clara O'Leary for the first time that she could remember that dull Sunday morning in late October as they were leaving the Sacred Heart church in Mountcharles, County Donegal, after early Mass. Clara was her mother, Minnie's, oldest friend.

'Since we were girls,' her mother had told Lucy. 'Even after we married we were friends, and then when you were born just a fortnight after her daughter, Therese, we were so happy to be young mothers together.'

Then Clara's husband, Sean, developed typhus. He was a strong man, however, and was fighting the illness, but Therese caught it from him, quickly grew very ill and died on Lucy's birthday.

'Every year I think of that,' Minnie said. 'Sean had got over the worst and was recovering, but at the death of his small daughter it was as if he had given up and a fortnight later he died too.'

'And that's when her brothers took Clara O'Leary back to England?' Lucy would prompt, though she knew the story well.

'After Sean's funeral,' Minnie said with a nod. 'And she's never been back until now. Of course, it was a terrible tragedy and I don't think you ever really get over a thing like that.'

Lucy thought privately that Clara O'Leary looked as if she had got over it well enough, for

15

she was so elegant. Only the few very rich in Mountcharles's parish could afford such clothes as she wore. She even had fur mittens to match her hat. How Lucy, whose gloveless fingers would throb painfully in the winter months, envied her those. Clara's grey melton coat had the same black fur around the collar and cuffs, and Lucy gave a little gasp when she caught sight of Clara's warm-looking, snug-fitting boots. Any boots Lucy had were either too large or toe-pinchingly small, often leaky and always heavily cobbled. She looked down with a sigh at the battered boots that she had thrust her benumbed and stockingless feet into that morning before Mass.

Lucy could hardly believe that this woman was the same age as her mother. She looked years younger. She was a little plumper, and she had a kindly face with pink-tinged cheeks and bright blue eyes. Her hair wasn't grey-streaked but dark blonde and caught up in an elaborately woven bun at the nape of her neck, fitting so tidily under the hat.

As Clara drew nearer, Lucy saw her blue eyes widen with surprise as her mother introduced all of them: Lucy herself, and Danny, who was two years younger than she was, her nine-year-old sister, Grainne, and her two young brothers, Liam and Sam, who were seven and five.

Clara, observing her friend's eldest, wasn't merely surprised, she was totally shocked because Lucy was so thin and small, the size of a child of ten or eleven. She had seen her standing with the others, but had assumed she was a younger sister to the child she remembered. Lucy's tawny-

16

coloured hair was thin and straggly, and her deep brown eyes stood out in a face that was so gaunt it was like looking at a very old woman.

Lucy shifted her feet a little at Clara's scrutiny, well aware that though she was wearing the smartest clothes that she possessed, her coat was far too short, the sleeves barely reaching her bony wrists, and she had a struggle to fasten it across her chest. Beneath the coat was a thin dress, which was also far too short, and with all the goodness washed out of it, totally unsuitable for the weather, even with the threadbare, darned cardigan she wore over it.

Clara took all this in, noting as well how the arms and legs of all of the Cassidy children were stick thin, and pity washed over her. But she pushed it away before she addressed herself to Lucy in a cheery way. 'Well, well, Lucy, I last saw you as a toddler, running and tumbling about the place, and here you are, almost a young lady. You will be fourteen now, won't you, my dear?'

Lucy gave a little bob of her knee and tried to smile at the woman her mother set such store by, and it tore at Clara's heartstrings as she said, 'Yes, Mrs O'Leary, just last week.'

Clara knew that Minnie's husband, Seamus, had died six months before, for the old friends wrote to each other often, and Clara knew too that she should have come home and not just sent a Mass card, but she never dreamt that the family would be reduced to such penury so quickly. She also had a sense of unease when she saw the shabby state of the sparse cottage, which was none too warm, though Minnie soon poked new life into the fire and threw on more turf, causing a flickering glow to develop under the porridge she had left cooking in a large double pan.

'Take off your coat,' she said to Clara, 'or you'll not feel the benefit when you go out – Lucy will lay it on the bed in the room – and then come up and sit here before the fire. I will have it ablaze in a moment.'

Clara did as she was bid and watched Minnie swinging the kettle above the heat of the fire as she took the porridge pan off the hook. Clara was shaken by how little of the thin porridge was ladled into the children's bowls laid ready. Minnie had none herself but she made tea for them both.

'And I have some soda bread too,' she said. 'It would be a poor day altogether when someone is offered a bare cup of tea in my house.'

Lucy's mouth watered at the thought of soda bread spread with butter, for the porridge did little to fill her up. She knew that's all there was, though, and she suppressed the sigh and watched her mother making tea and slicing and buttering the precious loaf.

Clara heard the slight release of breath and saw the children watching her, the younger ones, eyes alive with hunger, but when she tried to refuse the bread, Minnie turned from the fire and looked at her friend steadily.

'Leave me some pride, for pity's sake,' she said. 'God knows, I haven't much else.'

Clara dropped her gaze as she mumbled, 'I'm sorry, and you're right. A cup of tea and some soda bread would be lovely.'

She said nothing more until this was set before her. Then she said, 'First of all, Minnie, let me say how sad I was to hear of the death of Seamus. It must have been a heavy blow for you with five children to provide for.'

Lucy caught her breath. She still grieved for her father and her heart had an ache in it whenever she thought of him.

Her mother replied in a thin, watery voice, 'It was, but, you know, in the end his death was a blessing because he was suffering so much. And he had been ill for such a long time.'

Lucy knew that only too well.

Casting her mind back while Clara and her mother spoke together, Lucy remembered that when she had been a small child, her father had seemed to be the strongest man in the world. He worked for Farmer Haycock and he was a hard worker and always gave of his best. He was made up to head cowman, and would have been given a cottage too, but Minnie had inherited one from her parents when they died and as it was only a couple of miles away from the farm they decided to stay there. Many times Minnie was thankful for that decision, for once Seamus grew too sick to work, they would have had to leave any farm cottage so another cowman could live in it.

Lucy was not aware of this at the time; she came to that realisation as she grew. As a young child she knew only that when her father came home from work the house became alive. She would fall upon him as soon as he was through the door, and in time Danny did too. Their father would toss the children in the air with ease and they would scream with delight. There was a lot of laughter in their house then, and a lot of singing. Both Seamus and Minnie loved the old songs they had learnt from their parents, and Lucy loved to hear them because it made her feel happy, safe and secure.

'It was when I was expecting Sam that I first realised that the cough Seamus developed after a bad cold was still bothering him,' Minnie said. 'I didn't take that much notice at first. Seamus always claimed he was fine and, as he said, everyone has a cough now and again, but his didn't clear up and he would be grey-faced when he came home from work. The children were confused because he wasn't able to play with them any more. All you could hear in the evening was the rasping sound of his chest and the relentless cough but we had no money to spend on doctors. I started to grow vegetables in the back garden because I couldn't think what else to do. My priority was feeding the children and keeping the lot of us out of the poorhouse. By the time Sam was born, Seamus was too ill to work and in the end I had to find the money to have the doctor in.'

Lucy remembered the night the sounds from her parents' bedroom wakened her and she had slipped out of the bed that she shared with her sister and ran across the landing, soon joined by Danny, still flushed from sleep, his hair tousled. Minnie was standing in the bedroom doorway, her hand to her mouth, her eyes wide with shock, and Lucy saw there were splashes of blood on her threadbare nightgown. Then she saw her father on the bed making guttural noises as the blood pumped from him in a scarlet stream. The spasm was over when the doctor arrived, but the evidence was there for him to see.

Lucy heard him tell her mother that her father's first haemorrhage was unlikely to be his last because he had TB, which was highly infectious.

'Keeping him at home any longer is madness,' the doctor had barked. 'You are risking your own life and that of your children. You must agree that Seamus is taken to the sanatorium immediately or you are risking your whole family being wiped out with it.'

'Seamus said he must go when he heard what the doctor said,' Minnie told Clara now. 'None of the children saw him again and he lasted only six months after that.'

'Ah, yes,' Clara said in agreement. 'It's hard to see them suffer.'

'Well, you would know about that, of course.'

'Yes,' Clara agreed, 'and the memories were raw in the beginning, but I wasn't the only one to suffer a loss. There is only one thing to do and that is to go on as you are doing and fulfill your intention of keeping the children alive and out of the poorhouse.'

'Aye, so far,' Minnie said. 'Sometimes, though, I feel as if I'm balanced on a knife edge. You went to Birmingham and made a new life for yourself – made up from lady's maid to housekeeper within three years.'

'The aftermath of the Great War helped me there,' Clara said. 'The war had given women and girls greater opportunities and after it fewer girls were looking for "in service" work.'

'Did you not mind going to live with strangers?'

'Not really,' Clara said. 'My brothers were very kind to me but I knew I couldn't be beholden to them and their wives for ever. By taking a job in service I had a roof over my head, clothes on my back and plenty to eat, and though the wages weren't much to start with, they have improved with time. And that is where I can help you, Minnie, I am looking for a new scullery maid and your Lucy is of an age to work.'

'In Birmingham?' Minnie cried. 'I could never countenance her being so far away.'

'Now would I ask you to?' Clara said. 'I know how precious daughters are. But this is the beauty of it. The Master of the house where I work, Lord Charles Heatherington, was a general in the army and was recently badly hurt in a skirmish in India. He spent months in hospital and eventually insisted on being shipped home where he said he could be nursed just as well. I would say he was right, too, because he is cared for by his batman, a man called Rory Green, a taciturn Scot who is devoted to the Master. Anyway, the Mistress decided that a change of scene and peace and quiet are what her husband needs now and they have taken charge of a large house in its own grounds, a place called Windthorpe Lodge, just outside Letterkenny.'

'Donegal Town is a long way from there.'

'That doesn't really matter,' Clara said. 'All the positions are "live in", you see. I have a house-maid and a kitchen maid, both a bit older than

Lucy, and I am short of a scullery maid.'

Clara knew that she didn't need to be short of a scullery maid, that she could have filled the post ten times over, but though in her letters Minnie never moaned, Clara had known things would be tight after Seamus died and she often worried that she could offer her friend no help. Then Lady Heatherington started making plans to decamp to the North of Ireland for a while and Clara thought straight away of helping her old friend by offering Lucy employment.

'I never thought of Lucy doing that kind of thing,' Minnie said.

Clara hid her impatience and asked instead, 'What had you in mind?'

Minnie shook her head. 'You lived here,' she cried, distressed. 'You know there is little employment for young girls.'

Clara put her hands over Minnie's agitated ones and said, 'Please, listen to me, Minnie. Lucy's job could lift you out of the extreme poverty you are in at the moment. You would have one less child to feed or find clothes for, and she will be paid eight shillings a week, a goodly portion of which I know she will want to send to you.'

Minnie cast an anguished glance at Lucy as if she could hardly believe what she was hearing. 'But when will I see her?' she cried.

'Well,' said Clara, 'in Birmingham the scullery maid has two half-days a week off and one full day every month. It will probably be the same here. Not that she'll be able to see you on her half-days.'

'Not on her full day either,' Minnie said. 'Letterkenny is a fair step from here.'

'But the rail bus goes all the way,' Clara said.

Lucy knew what she was talking about: the little bus that ran on rails, which she had seen many a time, though she never thought that she would ever have the opportunity to ride on it.

'Lucy's never been on a rail bus,' Minnie said. 'None of us has.'

'Well, that can be remedied,' said Clara with a smile. 'That's how I travelled down and how I will go back in a day or so. And remember that while Lucy will be far from home, I will be there to look after her as if she were my own daughter. What d'you say, Lucy?'

Lucy knew what she wanted to say: that she didn't want to go so far away from home to work. What Clara said was a shock and not just to her but to all her siblings.

Sam's eyes had filled with tears because Lucy had done a lot of the rearing of him. 'Lucy's not to go anywhere,' he cried to Clara in protest. 'She's not to. She lives here with us.'

Danny thought the same. He and Lucy were very close, but he knew when adults decided something that was that. Grainne was dismayed that she would be losing the big sister that she looked up to so much and left with just the boys for company, and even Liam felt a bit sniffy at the thought of Lucy going away.

Clara looked at the saddened faces around her, Sam's still red with temper and Lucy's eyes sparkling with unshed tears, and she said, 'I see that wasn't a very popular thing to say.'

'You shan't take Lucy away,' Sam said belligerently. 'You shan't because I'll not let you.'

'That will do, Sam,' Minnie said.

'But–'

'Enough, I said. You are being rude.'

'Lucy must work someplace, you know, now her school days are over,' Clara said to the children. She went on to describe the big house just outside Letterkenny and the benefits for them all if Lucy were to take a job there.

As Clara spoke, things became much clearer to Lucy too. She was no keener to leave home but she knew that for all their sakes she must go and be a scullery maid at this house and lift some of the burden from her mother.

For years Lucy had listened to Minnie in the garden from early morning till late at night, digging, planting, hoeing, weeding, watering and then harvesting. Any surplus was exchanged for oatmeal, flour and fats and candles at the shop, and Lucy knew that it was time now for her to contribute to the family. She nodded her head to Clara. The younger children stared at her open-mouthed, but Danny had known all along what the outcome would be.

Then Clara asked Lucy, 'Is that your best dress?' She knew the answer really. She had seen how the others were dressed.

Minnie's face flamed with embarrassment but she answered firmly enough. 'Sometimes there is barely enough money to put food on the table and there is none to spare for new clothes. St Vincent de Paul come round with a bundle of things sometimes, but ours is not the only poor family in Mountcharles. There has been nothing suitable for Lucy in the bundles lately.'

Clara knew that she would have to tread carefully. Minnie set a great store by pride. 'Don't fret about it,' she said. 'The family will provide Lucy's uniform – a grey dress and various aprons – though they will have to be altered to fit.'

'She's handy with her needle,' Minnie said. 'I have taught her that much. But if her uniform is provided why does her normal dress matter?'

'Lady Heatherington expects a certain standard of dress among her staff,' said Clara. 'So that if they should choose to walk about the town on their time off and certainly on Sundays when we go to Mass we shall not disgrace the house.'

'Then I don't know what is to be done.'

'Let me buy Lucy a couple of dresses.'

Lucy caught her breath in a gasp of pleasure, for she could never remember having new clothes before. However, Minnie was shaking her head. 'I couldn't possibly let you do that.'

'Why not?' Clara demanded. 'Stiff-necked pride again?'

'As I said before, it's all I have.'

'You are denying Lucy a chance in life,' Clara said angrily. 'And denying all of them the opportunity to make their lives even the tiniest bit easier because of some crackpot notion you have. Have you the right to do that?'

Lucy saw her mother was wavering and so did Clara, and she went on more gently, 'Minnie, you said you will miss Lucy sorely when she is gone from you and I am sure you will, but I would give my eyeteeth to be in that position and able to see my daughter every month. Now you are my dearest friend, and it would ease my soul to buy the clothes needed for your daughter. Surely we have been friends too long for you to feel awkward about it?'

There was only one way to respond to that, and when Minnie inclined her head, Lucy let out the breath she was unaware she had been holding.

'But how will you get the things so quickly?' Minnie asked. 'You'll have to choose the material and contact the dressmaker.'

'There is no need for that now,' said Clara. 'You can buy things off the peg.'

'Not in Mountcharles, you can't.'

'No, but we'll probably be able to in Donegal Town,' said Clara. 'There is a large store called Magee not far from the Abbey Hotel where I am staying.'

The whole family looked at her, stunned. Though Donegal Town was only three or four miles away, none of them had ever been there. In fact, Lucy hadn't been further than Mountcharles all the days of her life, and here was Clara talking blithely about a hotel in the town where she was staying and taking her to a big store to buy her clothes. It was totally beyond her understanding.

'How will you get there?' Minnie asked. 'Walk?'

'No,' Clara said, 'I thought we'd take the rail bus. They have really opened up the North of Ireland. We can pick one up at the halt in the village and be in Donegal Town in no time at all. Now,' she said to Lucy, 'I will be here bright and early tomorrow because I must leave on Tuesday. The family are arriving at the weekend and it's my job to make sure everything is ready for them.'

Lucy knew Danny would have given his eyeteeth to be the one travelling on the rail bus the following morning. She would never admit it to him or anyone else, but at first she had been a bit worried that the rail bus would jump off the tracks and that she would be thrown out of it, especially as it seemed to go at such speed.

However, she soon got used to it and watched the countryside flashing past as Clara told her all about the people she would be working with.

'It's not a large household,' Clara said, 'and some have come with us from the house in Birmingham, like the General's batman, and the butler and footman. Now, the footman goes by the name of Jerry Kilroy. He has a shock of ginger hair, and green eyes like a cat, and he usually has a large grin on his face, remembering some devilment he has been at. He is an impudent scamp, not averse to pinching the girls' bottoms.'

Lucy's eyes opened wider. Clara said, 'I think we won't tell your mother that and I'm sure you can deal with him very effectively. You may have to join forces with Clodagh Murray – she's the new kitchen maid that I have engaged – or Evie McMillan, the housemaid. Between you all I'm sure you will teach him a lesson he will not forget in a hurry.'

'Yes,' Lucy said, but she said it uncertainly; then added, 'So, Evie is new too?'

Clara nodded. 'The parents of the younger girls didn't want them so far away,' she explained. 'The cook, Ada Murphy, came with us, of course, and Norah Callaghan, Lady Heatherington's personal maid. But come on,' she said as the rail bus pulled into Donegal station, 'we're here.'

Lucy knew straight away that Magee was the type of establishment that wouldn't welcome the likes of her through the doors. She saw one saleswoman's sidelong look at another as Clara pushed open the big glass doors and stepped inside. Their attitude turned completely, however, when they realised that Clara was actually going to spend money. She soon chose two winter-weight dresses for Lucy. One was in a plaid design with fancy buttons up the bodice and what the assistant described as a Peter Pan collar, and the other was navy blue with a cream trim and the skirt pleated all the way round. To wear underneath she bought two flannelette petticoats and three sets of underwear, also three nightgowns and three pairs of stockings, and a navy cardigan because she said the attics in the big house could get very cold.

'Oh, Mrs O'Leary...' Lucy gasped, almost overcome with pleasure.

However, Clara wasn't finished, for she bought Lucy boots made of the softest leather, which fitted snugly around her ankles, and a navy-blue coat and matching bonnet, scarf and gloves. She insisted Lucy wear the new coat and the bonnet, scarf and gloves while the assistant wrapped up the old shabby old coat and packed it with the other things into the new case that she had also bought. She had known that there wouldn't be one in the house because the Cassidys would have had no need to buy one and, as she said to Lucy, she couldn't go to her new place of work with her new clothes wrapped up in newspaper.

'Now,' Clara said, standing Lucy in front of one

of the many mirrors in the shop, 'don't you look a picture?'

And Lucy did look a picture. In fact, she couldn't believe that the figure in the mirror was her, and she turned to Clara with her eyes shining. 'I ... I don't really know what to say,' she said. 'I mean, thank you, of course, but that doesn't seem half enough for what you have done for me.'

'All I've done is buy you a few clothes,' Clara said as they left the store. 'And I have enjoyed it probably as much as you have. Now, I don't know about you but I am starving and so I say we find some place to have dinner. That all right by you?'

Lucy's mouth had dropped agape, for she had never eaten out before. 'You ... you mean dinner in a café somewhere?'

'That was the idea, yes.' Clara's smile was warm.

Lucy felt as if she had died and gone to Heaven a little later, after a meal of steak-and-kidney pie, with potatoes, carrots and cabbage and lots of gravy, followed by treacle tart and custard. Clara thought she had never treated anyone who was so appreciative, and she smiled with satisfaction.

Before they made for the rail bus, she bought a large cooked ham at the butcher's, two loaves of bread, creamery butter, a pot of jam, a huge slab of cheese, proper milk and tea.

Minnie cried when she saw all Clara had bought – the bountiful food on the table and the clothes and suitcase – and when Lucy tried on the clothes for them all to see, she cried afresh and burnt with shame that she had not been able to dress her own daughter or any of them half as well.

'Now, that will do,' Clara chided Minnie gently. 'I have no daughter of my own to spoil and it's the God's honest truth that I enjoyed every minute of the time I spent with yours. Now, are we going to sit here weeping, or eat this fine food, for the children's eyes are standing out of their heads as if on stalks?'

The young Cassidys had never smelt, never mind tasted, such wonderful food, and they did give full justice to the meal.

'Now remember, I return tomorrow,' Clara said to Minnie as she prepared to leave. 'And Lucy must be on the first rail bus next Monday morning. The other two girls are starting this Wednesday because we really want them licked into some sort of shape before starting anyone else new.'

Lucy nodded but, when Clara had left, she was filled with doubt that she would be able to do the job of scullery maid. But she also knew that she had do her best, for the family would be relying on her, and she sighed, suddenly feeling the burden a heavy one.

TWO

The last days at home seemed to fly past and at last it was Monday morning, bleak and icy. Lucy woke early as she usually did. She lit the stub of the candle that was stuck in a saucer and began

31

to dress in the clothes Clara had bought her, which she had laid ready on the rickety chair by her bed. It was the first time she had worn them, wanting to keep them all nice for her first day at Windthorpe Lodge, and she loved the feel of the new vests and knickers next to her skin, and the delicious warmth of the flannel petticoats, followed by the plaid dress and cardigan. Then she donned the stockings and boots, brushed her hair with the old ragged brush with very few bristles and took the candle up to look at her reflection in the mirror.

'You look lovely,' Grainne suddenly said from the bed, and Lucy saw that she had woken and was staring at her with her large dark brown eyes. She sighed. 'Those clothes Mrs O'Leary bought you are so beautiful. I wish I had something half as good.'

Lucy did feel guilty about being dressed so well, but to say so would not help. Instead, she said, 'I know, but don't fret. By the time it's your turn, I will have been working some time and I will get your clothes together and I will make sure they are just as lovely as these.'

'Will you, really, Lucy?'

'I promise.'

Grainne sighed again. 'I wish you didn't have to go away, though. I'm going to miss you ever so much.'

Lucy crossed the room and gave her sister a hug. 'I'm going to miss all of you, but, however we feel, all the moaning and whining in the world will make no difference. Now,' she said briskly, 'as you're awake you may as well get up and I will go and help Mammy with the breakfast.'

'I was going to anyway,' Grainne said. 'This is your last breakfast at home probably for ages and ages so I wanted to share it.'

The others felt the same, Lucy realised as she went into the kitchen to find the boys already there, Danny doing up the buttons on Sam's shirt, which had defeated his small hands. When he saw Lucy he tore away from Danny, buried his face in Lucy's dress and burst into tears. Lucy hugged the child tight, urging him not to get upset, though her own stomach had given a lurch when she had seen her case packed ready, and knew when she next opened it she would be far from home.

Minnie, coming into the kitchen at that moment, gently pulled Sam from Lucy as she said, 'Now, now, you will mess up all Lucy's good clothes with your carry-on. And dry your eyes, too, because she doesn't want to remember a row of mournful faces when she thinks of her home.'

Lucy swallowed the lump in her own throat while Sam scrubbed at his face with his knuckles and made a valiant effort to stem his tears, but it was a dismal group that sat down at the table a little later. They were too miserable to keep any sort of conversation going, although as a treat for Lucy's last morning, Minnie had made soda bread for the children to eat after their porridge, and they fell upon the extra food eagerly.

'Have a slice,' Minnie urged her eldest daughter. 'I don't want you arriving starving at the place.'

But Lucy shook her head. She had seen the

33

faces of her siblings and she couldn't take any of the bread, knowing they would have less, so she answered, 'I have butterflies in my stomach, from nerves, I suppose, and couldn't eat anything else.' She didn't know whether her mother believed her or not, but she didn't press her again and Lucy knew she wouldn't because she had allowed herself only a meagre amount of porridge and had no bread either.

There were many tears at the parting, and even Danny's voice was choked as he submitted to a hug from his sister.

'Look after yourself and don't worry about us back here. I will see to Mammy and all,' he said.

'I know,' Lucy replied. 'Goodbye, Dan.'

Despite the cold they all stood at the cottage door, and the sorry sight of them brought tears to Lucy's own eyes, but with great resolve she refused to let them fall. She shivered despite her good clothes because the thin porridge had done little to warm her.

She hadn't long to wait for the rail bus. She was the only passenger to get on at Mountcharles and she was so glad of the trip to Donegal with Clara because she was able to board the rail bus confidently as if she had been doing it for years.

By the time Lucy reached the level crossing just before Donegal Town she was able to see the gates tightly shut because the gatekeeper, swinging his lantern, came out to wave as the rail bus passed. Clara had told her that just the other side of Donegal Town the track ran along the side of Lough Esk, but she could see nothing outside and the rail bus was approaching Barnes Gap before

34

Lucy noticed the sky had lightened just a little. As the rail bus chugged its way through the Gap, the austere and craggy hills loomed upwards on each side like threatening, grey monstrosities. Lucy remembered the tales she had been told as a child, of the highwaymen who used to hide in the hills and swoop down on the coaches in bygone years.

The darkness receded further so the journey became less tedious as she was able to see more. When the track ran alongside Lough Mourne, Lucy could see the gleam of water. She knew that Letterkenny was still some distance away, and Clara had warned her that before that she would have to leave the rail bus at Lifford because it was a border post, and that sometimes they opened people's cases.

'Why?' Lucy asked. 'What are they looking for?'

'In case you are carrying something you shouldn't, I suppose,' Clara said. 'But you won't be doing that, so there will be no problem.'

Although it was full daylight when they eventually pulled to a stop at Lifford station, heavy grey clouds made the day a gloomy one. There were not that many passengers, Lucy noted, and she followed the others to the customs shed, which was down the platform, next to the stationmaster's house. The unsmiling customs officer asked Lucy where she was coming from and where she was going to and then whether she had anything to declare.

'Like what?' Lucy might have said. However, she thought it more sensible to say nothing and so she just shook her head, was signed through and was glad to get back to the relative warmth of the rail bus.

Clara had told her that Letterkenny wasn't all that far from Lifford, and Lucy was glad because nerves had driven sleep away the previous night and she suddenly felt very weary. She leant back against the seat and closed her eyes, and when she opened them again the train was stopping. She sat up straighter and read the name: Letter-kenny. She climbed out onto the platform.

It was a very busy station with many people milling around, but Lucy was intent only on fol-lowing Clara's instructions, which were to go up the hill she would see on leaving the station and then cross over Main Street and on down the road leading out of the town. She remembered Clara saying that Windthorpe Lodge was only about one and a half miles out. 'Not far,' she'd reassured Lucy, 'and you won't be able to miss it.'

As Lucy trudged along she reflected that places not far away seemed much further when a person was carrying a case, and she really hoped Clara was right about not being able to miss it.

Windthorpe Lodge was set back from the road, but the name was written on a plaque in huge golden letters attached to black-and-silver steel gates with spikes on top. These were supported by two massive honey-coloured stone pillars with a lion atop each one. Lucy knew she never would have the courage to walk through those gates, but luckily she didn't have to because Clara had said that set into the wall on the right-hand side, but well away from the main entrance, was a door to the path the servants used.

She located it and stood for a moment in front of it. It was Monday, 4 November 1935 and she knew she was beginning a new phase in her life, that once through that door nothing would ever be quite the same again. She swallowed the lump that had risen in her throat and she resolutely turned the handle. She was so glad to see Clara O'Leary there, waiting for her, wearing a thick woollen shawl over a shiny black dress, and she gave her a hug.

'You got here all right then?' she said unnecessarily. 'And you made good time because I have just got here myself. Let's away in, for they are all looking forward to meeting you.'

Clara led the way along the track to the house and Lucy, behind her, did her best to avoid the puddles caused by the recent rain, not wishing to arrive with excessively muddy boots. She thought she might catch sight of the house, but it was partially hidden from view behind a high hedge.

'How do we get in?' she asked, for the hedge seemed impregnable.

'Well, not through the front door,' Clara said. 'Oh, dear me, no, that would never do. In houses such as these, Lucy, servants always go in to the back of the house and always use the back stairs.'

'They have two sets of stairs?' Lucy asked incredulously.

'Oh, yes,' Clara said with a wry smile. 'You will find people like the Heatheringtons like to have everything done for them, but never like to see much of the servants that do it. Still, as long as they stay as lazy as that we all have jobs – that's how I look at it, anyhow. Now here we are at the kitchen door and this is the way we go into the house.'

She swung open the door as she spoke and Lucy noted with surprise that only the bottom half of it was wood, while the top was two panes of frosted glass. However, when she stepped inside that enormous kitchen, where rows and rows of copper pots and pans gleamed on the shelves, welcome warmth enveloped her. So did delicious smells, and Lucy's nose wrinkled in appreciation as she realised how hungry she was.

'Leave the case here and it can be dealt with later,' Clara said, pulling off her shawl. 'And take off your coat or you will cook in here. There are hooks behind the door for the moment, though it must go up to your room later.'

Lucy nodded, laying down the case with a small sigh of relief and taking off her outer clothes. As she descended the three steps after Clara she realised that the warmth was coming from the long shiny black range that ran almost the entire length of one of the walls. There was a sink fitted in beside it, where a girl was washing pots, a huge, very solid-looking scrubbed table in the middle of the room, and a range of wooden cupboards along the side wall.

'Now, Ada, here's the help in the kitchen I was telling you about,' Clara said.

The woman turned from the range where she had been stirring something. She still had the long tasting spoon in her hand, and Lucy couldn't help feeling that if it tasted as good as it smelt it would be delicious.

'This is the cook, Mrs Murphy, Lucy, and she

will explain your duties to you.'

Cook's eyes widened as she surveyed Lucy, but she didn't speak, and Lucy was little unnerved by her stare and her stance because she was a hefty-looking woman. A stained apron was tied around her ample waist and the sleeves of the striped dress that she wore beneath it were pushed up to reveal forearms bulging like two pink hams. Added to that, her round and slightly podgy face was more than pink, and above her bulbous lips, brown eyes like two currants sank into her face. A white cap sat on the top of her mop of brown frizzy hair, which was liberally streaked with grey.

Clara went on, 'Her name is Lucy Cassidy. Now, Lucy,' she said, indicating the girl at the sink, 'this is Clodagh Murray, and you will see a lot of her because you will be working together in the kitchen.'

Clodagh gave Lucy a tentative smile as Clara continued, 'If you will excuse me, I must see her ladyship. I said that I would let her know immediately Lucy arrived.'

Barely had the door closed behind Clara than Cook almost barked at Lucy, 'Are you sure you are fourteen?'

'Yes,' Lucy said.

'Yes, Cook,' Ada snapped. 'That's how you answer me.'

Lucy gulped. 'Sorry, Cook.'

'So when were you fourteen?'

'Nearly a month ago, Cook,' Lucy said. 'The school said I could leave if I had a job, and I have brought my birth and baptismal certificate for you to see, er, Cook,' Lucy went on, glad that

Clara had advised her to bring these with her just in case. She wished wholeheartedly that Clara had not left her in the kitchen with this woman to go and speak with her mistress.

'Well, I have never seen a child of fourteen as small as you are,' Ada said to Lucy. 'And Clara had no right to have it all signed and sealed you working here without me even being consulted. She might think she is in charge here, but let me tell you, I make the decisions as regards the kitchen and I'm not at all sure that a person so small would be capable of the work here, whatever age you are.'

'I'm very strong, Cook,' Lucy said. 'Much stronger than I look.'

She knew that wasn't true, strictly speaking, for she often felt weak and faint, but that was usually because she was so hungry, and she was suddenly apprehensive because she didn't know whether the disapproving and formidable cook had more sway than Clara. Her eyes suddenly met Clodagh's sympathetic ones across the kitchen.

In the few days Clodagh had been there she had learnt that Cook's bark was far worse than her bite, as long as you were prepared to work hard.

Lucy, however, didn't know that yet. She felt tears stinging her eyes just as Clara O'Leary opened the door she had gone out of at the opposite end of the kitchen and beckoned to Lucy.

'The Mistress wants to see you,' she said. 'Come along.' Lucy followed Clara through the first door, along a small corridor that she was to find led to the butler's pantry and back stairs, and through another door covered in green cloth that closed with a sort of sigh. 'This is the door that leads to the other part of the house where the Family live,' Clara said, and she pulled out a comb she had secreted up her sleeve and set about tidying Lucy's hair, retied the bow on her dress and pulled the bodice straighter. Her attentions made Lucy more nervous than ever.

'What's the matter?' she cried.

Clara smiled. 'Nothing,' she said. 'You'll do.'

Lucy wasn't at all sure if she was right, and she could feel her stomach churning as they walked along the corridor.

'Lady Heatherington is seeing you in the library,' Clara said.

'Do I call her "Lady Heatherington"?' Lucy asked.

'No, you will just call her "my lady".' Lucy looked up at her apprehensively. 'Now come on,' Clara said. 'That's not so hard, is it?'

'S'pose not.'

'And she doesn't bite,' Clara said. 'Well, not on Mondays, anyway.'

A ghost of a smile touched Lucy's lips as she said, 'I don't think that cook, Mrs Murphy, likes me very much.'

'Oh, I'll deal with Cook,' Clara said. 'Now, I have recommended you to the Mistress and she values my opinion, but the final decision is hers and she wants to meet you as she does with most of the staff, the indoor ones, anyway. It's not unreasonable.'

Lucy shook her head. No, none of it was unreasonable except for the fact that Lucy didn't

41

want to be here at all. And then Clara was knocking on a cream door with a shiny brass handle. They were bade enter and as Clara stepped into the room, Lucy, following behind her, felt as if a leaden weight had settled in her stomach.

'I've brought the girl, my lady,' Clara said, ushering Lucy forward, bobbing a curtsy and bidding Lucy do the same.

As she was doing this, Lucy had a swift look around. A great many polished wooden shelves were fitted floor to ceiling and filled with books of every shape and size, yet the room was light and airy with the light coming from the large windows at the back.

'Thank you, Mrs O'Leary,' Lady Heatherington said.

At her words, spoken in a languid, almost bored way, Lucy swung her eyes away from the books to study the woman in front of her, who sat in a black leather chair behind a gleaming wooden desk. 'You can leave us,' she said with an imperious wave in Clara's direction and her eyes met Lucy's as she looked her up and down.

For Lucy's part, she saw a very beautiful woman, which surprised her because Lady Hetherington wasn't young. Yet her dark brown hair was dressed beautifully with combs and ribbons, and though most of it was caught up, curls still framed her oval face, which was as white and smooth as alabaster. Her dark eyes matched the colour of her hair, her long nose looked quite haughty and her mouth was like a perfect rosebud.

Amelia Heatherington, on the other hand, saw an undersized, stick-thin girl who looked far younger than fourteen and far too frail to be of any use to anyone. She smiled at Lucy, though the smile didn't reach her eyes, and she fingered the mother-of-pearl brooch at the neck of her navy-blue woollen dress as she said, 'Well, Mrs O'Leary said you were small and I must say I agree with her.'

Lucy thought it better to agree with the woman. 'Yes, my lady.'

'Mrs O'Leary also said you have trouble at home. That your father is dead.'

Lucy nodded. 'He had TB, my lady,' she said. 'But he had been ill a long time before he was taken to the sanatorium.'

Her eyes clouded suddenly at the memory of him and Lady Heatherington saw this. 'I understand that things have been very difficult, but yours is not the only family to have hit hard times,' she said.

'No, my lady.'

'And I am not running a charity.'

'No, my lady.'

'Mrs O'Leary has said that you come from a hardworking family and that you are respectable and honest.'

Lucy didn't know how to answer this so she stayed silent and Lady Heatherington continued, 'And while they are honourable qualities and ones I would expect of all those in my employ, I am worried that one of your stature would be unequal to the work in the kitchen. Are you not concerned about that?'

Lucy was very concerned, but for her family's sake she had to have this job and so she answered firmly, 'No, I'm not, my lady, because I am a lot stronger than I look.'

'Hmm,' Lady Heatherington said. 'I am not at all sure.' She sighed and stared at Lucy as if deliberating, and she then burst out, 'Oh, all right then. For Mrs O'Leary's sake I am willing to give you a trial, but I will be getting regular reports from our cook, Mrs Murphy, and if she's not happy then you must leave.' A faint smile touched her lips for a moment as she said, 'I have learnt to my cost it doesn't do to offend one's cook.'

Lucy suppressed her sigh of relief and said, 'No, my lady. Thank you, my lady.'

'Now, you will take your orders from Mrs Murphy direct and you must do whatever she tells you. She is in charge in the kitchen and you are under her jurisdiction.'

Lucy nodded 'Yes, my lady.' She had no intention of doing anything to upset the woman she was already nervous of.

'Now, as for uniform,' Lady Heatherington said, 'you will be given a grey dress and apron that you will wear at all times, and any we have will have to be altered to fit you. Can you sew?'

'Oh, yes, my lady.'

'Good,' said Lady Heatherington. 'Then you will attend to your uniform immediately in your spare time, for I will not have anyone slovenly attired in my household.'

'No, my lady.'

'All right, Cassidy. You may return to the kitchen.'

'Thank you, my lady,' Lucy said, bobbing another curtsy before she made for the door. She was glad to find Clara outside ready to escort her back. Lucy told her what had transpired in the library and she nodded.

'You'll soon settle in,' she said, 'and if you work hard you and Cook will soon be the best of friends. Now, first things first,' she continued as they reached the kitchen again. 'Young Jerry here will take your case up to the attic you will share with Evie and Clodagh.'

Lucy remembered what Clara had said about Jerry Kilroy and so she wasn't surprised when, catching her eye, he winked at her. A man had never winked at Lucy before and she blushed slightly and was suddenly glad she had a decent case for she would have hated to have been shown up in front of this cocky footman.

Clodagh, though, was different altogether. She was sixteen and Lucy thought she looked really pretty with tight brown curls framing her face and a smile of welcome shining out from her brown eyes, and she was glad that she would see a lot of her. She had come from Ballintra, outside Donegal Town, a place not that much bigger than Mountcharles, which made another thing they had in common.

Evie, who was seventeen, came from the Donegal Town itself and she was just as pleasant as Clodagh, and as pretty, with her dark blonde hair and eyes of deepest blue.

'You won't see quite so much of me because my duties are in the house, you see, and so I don't need to come into the kitchen much,' she explained to Lucy. 'I came in today to meet you when Mrs O'Leary told me you had arrived.'

45

'You'll see her at mealtimes,' Clodagh said. 'All the servants eat together.'

'Yes, and we will all share the attic, though I don't suppose that will bother you.'

Lucy shook her head, for she had never had a room or even a bed to herself in the whole of her life. 'No. Not at all.'

'Well, there you are, then, and in no time at all I'm sure we will be the best of friends.'

Lucy hoped so, for she had never really had a friend before and after meeting both girls she felt far more positive about working in Windthorpe Lodge.

Even Cook spoke to her far more civilly when she said, 'Clara was saying that your father died six months ago, but she said he had been bad for some time.'

Lucy nodded. 'Ages. He had TB.'

Cook knew about TB, that insidious illness that could wipe out whole families. Clara had told her of the poverty the family lived in because Seamus hadn't been able to work for some years before he died, and certainly, Lucy Cassidy didn't look as though she had ever had a decent meal in her life. So Cook said, 'Well, though we will all eat later, I will not put anyone to work on an empty stomach. So how about you go to the attic with Clodagh and put your uniform on, for all it will drown you for now, and I will cook you some eggs and bacon to keep you going?'

Eggs and bacon! Lucy's mouth watered at the very thought of it and she nodded vigorously. 'Yes, oh, yes. Thank you.'

The cook smiled at Lucy's enthusiasm, and

Clodagh said, 'Come on, then.'

She led the way up the back stairs and as she did so she said, 'Your face was a picture when Cook mentioned cooking you bacon and eggs.'

'That's because I can't really remember what either tastes like,' Lucy said.

Clodagh stopped on the stairs and looked into Lucy's face. 'Honestly?'

'Honestly,' Lucy answered. 'When Daddy was first sick, Mammy turned the garden over to grow vegetables, and we have hens as well, but the eggs are not for us to eat. Mammy needed them and the surplus vegetables that she barters at the shop in exchange for flour, oatmeal, candles and other things she couldn't grow.'

'Oh, that's awful,' Clodagh said. 'Well, you needn't worry here. Cook keeps a good table and now she probably sees it as her life's work to feed you up because that's the type of person she is. She is much kinder than she appears. But now we'd better get you dressed up properly for the kitchen or, despite what I just said, if we take too long we'll get the rough edge of her tongue. She can't abide slacking.'

Suddenly Clodagh stopped on a sort of landing. 'Our bedroom is up those stairs,' she said, indicating another flight. 'This is the linen press where our overalls and uniforms are kept.' She opened the door set into the wall as she spoke, and Lucy saw the overalls folded in piles and uniforms hung on hangers at the back. 'Cook says the Mistress is a stickler about uniform if you are ever to be seen by the family, and even more so if they have guests for dinner, but I doubt we have a uniform to fit you.' She held aloft a light grey dress as she spoke and went on, 'This seems to be about the smallest. Let's pop upstairs and you can try it on.'

Lucy was agreeable to that because she was anxious at any rate to see what the room was like, and in that, too, she was pleasantly surprised. It had whitewashed walls, which Lucy thought a good idea when the only light came from the skylight, and though the room was small, good use had been made of the available space, which housed four iron bedsteads, a dressing table, rag rugs on the floor and a small wardrobe behind the door.

The dress swamped Lucy's frail frame and the skirts reached nearly to her ankles, as did the coarse apron that Evie tied around her waist. 'You'll have to turn them up, that's all,' Clodagh said, surveying her critically. 'Can you sew?'

When Lucy nodded, Clodagh said, 'And me. Mammy taught me. She said every housewife should be able to sew. So we'll do it together. It would be quicker and it wouldn't do me any harm to get some practice in.'

'Oh, that is kind of you,' Lucy said. 'Are you sure?'

'Course I am,' Clodagh said. 'Now, let's put your hat on. We'll need to put your hair up. You got any Kirbigrips?'

Lucy shook her head.

'Never mind,' Clodagh said. 'I have tons, and a band to gather it altogether. You'll have to have it piled up on top of your head somehow, see, or the hat won't go on.' She coiled up Lucy's hair as

48

she spoke. 'Golly, Lucy, you have got lovely hair. It's like a reddish-brown colour.' In fact, Clodagh thought if Lucy were to put more meat on her she would be a very beautiful girl. Her eyes were large, a lovely colour and ringed by long black lashes, and she had a classic nose, high cheek-bones and a beautiful mouth. Even her neck, she noticed with a stab of envy, was long and slender. It was a shame that the skin on her face was a muddy-grey colour and her pale cheeks sunken in slightly.

'That will have to do,' Clodagh said, stepping back from Lucy and surveying her handiwork. 'Come on, let's go and see Cook. I can almost smell the bacon and eggs sizzling.'

THREE

By Sunday, 1 December, Lucy had been at Windthorpe Lodge for four weeks and was ready for her first full Sunday off. She had hardly slept the night before because she had been too excited, but though she had the whole day to herself she had to rise earlier than anyone, as she did every morning, to clean the range, then light it, fill the large kettle with water and put it on the range to heat for the tea.

She would not be staying for the servants' breakfast because she would be taking communion that morning and, if she caught the rail bus at seven, she would be at Mountcharles in

49

plenty of time to make nine o'clock Mass, the one her family always went to. She was so excited to be seeing them all again and to tell them of her new life.

She wouldn't mention the fact that there was always plenty of food because Cook always maintained that no one worked well on an empty stomach. She had porridge every morning with plenty of sugar and as much milk as she wanted to pour over it, followed by bread and butter and jam, and several cups of tea. On Sunday mornings she would go with Evie, Clodagh and Clara to early Mass in Letterkenny, and Cook would have porridge ready for their return, followed by bacon and eggs. Then at midday they would sit down to a meal of roast or boiled meat and vegetables, followed by something sweet, usually with custard, and there was similar fare taken just before the family dinner. Since she had come to work in the house the only time she had been the slightest bit hungry was before Mass on a Sunday morning.

Lucy wrote to her mother every week but she never told her any of this because she didn't think it would help. It was enough for her mother to know that she was being adequately fed and she resolved she wouldn't go on about it when she got home either. There were plenty of other things she could tell them about and she fair rattled through her jobs that morning.

Lucy only wished she had something to take to cheer the family, for she knew she wouldn't get to see them over Christmas. She could spend hardly any of her wages because her mother needed every penny and she had retained only two shillings for herself, and one and six of that she spent on the fare home so she would have thirty shillings to give her mother. She had that ready, wrapped in a little cloth bag and pushed right down to the bottom of the big bag that Clara had loaned her.

Clara had called Lucy into her quarters just after she had finished scouring the pots used for the family dinner the previous evening, and asked her to wait a moment in the housekeeper's snug and well-furnished parlour as she had something for her.

Lucy was pleased to be asked to wait because it gave her a chance to look around. She had never been asked in here before. She noted the brightly coloured rugs covering most of the floor, and the small beige settee and two chairs, covered with soft brown cushions, which were drawn up before the fireplace where a small fire burned in the grate. There was also a small table drawn up between the chairs, with a matching sideboard against the wall, full of pretty ornaments that she would have loved to examine.

Clara came in at that moment, carrying a big bag in one hand and holding a pair of boots in the other, a collection of garments draped over her arms.

'Now,' she said as she began to sort through the garments, 'these are just some old clothes your mother might find a use for.' Lucy smiled, for she had never seen Clara wear any of the things she was packing away neatly in the bag.

'What's wrong with the boots?' Lucy said as

51

Clara put them on top. 'They hardly look worn. Mammy will go on about pride.'

'Well, let her,' Clara said. 'Pride doesn't keep a person's feet warm.' And then, as Lucy still looked apprehensive, she continued, 'Look, Lucy, if the boot was on the other foot, your mother would be the first to stretch out a helping hand, I know she would. She is my oldest friend and if I can make life a little easier then I feel I should. I would think myself less of a person if I didn't.'

Lucy couldn't think of a reply to that and Clara added, 'There is an envelope there, too, with a Christmas card in it.'

'Won't you get home at all before Christmas?'

'It isn't home to me now,' Clara reminded her. 'No one belonging to me lives there. I will go to see your family if I can, but if the weather worsens I wouldn't go as far as Donegal by choice, that is, if the rail buses would be running at all.'

'I hope the weather or anything else doesn't stop me.'

'It won't,' Clara assured her. 'Not this time, anyway. It's fine and dry, and the forecast is for more of the same tomorrow.'

'Oh, good.'

'It'll be cold, though,' Clara told her. 'It always is when the night's a clear one.'

'I don't care about cold,' Lucy declared stoutly. 'The thought of seeing the family will warm me, and I can't wait to see Mammy's face when she sees all this stuff.'

However, the clothes and boots weren't all. After leaving Clara, Lucy found Mrs Murphy waiting for her as she packed a basket for her to take home. 'Now, Clodagh was telling me that though you have chickens you don't get to eat the eggs.'

'No, we don't.'

'Well, in this box here,' Cook said, opening it up, 'see, I have put six fresh eggs and these are not for giving away. They are for eating.' She placed the box in the basket alongside a loaf and butter wrapped in greaseproof paper. 'Now, you can have what was left of the pork joint the family had for their dinner last night, and some cheese, and I will put you in a twist of tea and another of sugar.'

'Oh, Cook, Mrs Murphy, I don't know how to thank you,' Lucy said, very close to tears.

'Then don't try,' Cook advised. 'Your face says it all.'

'It's just that my mother... I mean, I can just imagine her face, and my sister and my brothers. They will all be over the moon, I know.'

'Well, that's all the thanks I want,' Cook said.

Now that the bag and basket were standing packed and ready at the top of the stairs by the kitchen door, Lucy buttoned up her coat, pulled her hat over her ears, put on her gloves and wound the scarf around her neck so that only her nose and mouth were visible. The day was icy and there was no warmth in the winter sun shining in a pale blue sky. Lucy picked the bag up in one hand, held the basket with the other, stepped out into a frost-rimmed world and felt the ice crunching beneath her feet as she made for the rail bus.

The journey home seemed tedious because she was so anxious to be there. At Mountcharles station, looking anxiously through the windows, she was delighted to see all the family assembled to meet her. The rail bus had barely stopped before Lucy was out of it and, putting the bag and basket down on the platform, she hugged them all as if her life depended on it.

'What you got?' Danny said, indicating the baggage.

'Oh, lots of stuff,' Lucy replied.

'Yes, but it will have to wait,' Minnie said. 'And so will any questions. We will just have time to put the stuff in at the cottage and then we will need to hightail it to Mass or we will be late.' And so saying she caught up the bag, and Danny got the basket so that Sam and Liam could hold Lucy's hands, and she swung the young boys along the road, Grainne hurrying along beside them. They arrived at the Sacred Heart church just a couple of minutes before Mass began. During the service, Lucy felt peace steal over her; she was so glad to be home again even if it was just for a few hours.

After Mass many greeted Lucy and said how much she had been missed and asked how was she liking the fine job in Letterkenny; and although she was polite she answered as briefly as possible. She was anxious to get home but no one lingered long because most had taken Communion and were ready for their breakfasts.

In the cottage there was the smell of the peat fire and the porridge cooking in the embers of it in the familiar double pan.

'I have extra sugar in, and milk, for I thought you may be used to that now,' Minnie said.

'Yes, I am,' Lucy admitted. 'But that is what I'll have tomorrow morning so today the others should have their share. And you can have the sugar without worrying too much about it because Cook has put some in the basket, and there is tea too.'

'Oh, that was kind of her,' Minnie said, 'though I am careful with tea and often use the leaves twice, so I still have some left from when Clara was here.'

'Mammy, you haven't kept it all this time?' Lucy cried in surprise, and remembered a trifle guiltily how many cups she consumed in an average day.

'Like I said, I am careful, but now I can relax a little more, so, after we have cleared away after breakfast, I will make a big pot and we'll all have a cup.'

'Even me?' Sam asked, and Minnie smiled.

'Even you.'

'With three sugars?'

'Don't push your luck, my lad,' Minnie warned him grimly. 'You are only having tea at all because of the kindness of the cook at the place where Lucy works.'

'She is kind,' Lucy said, 'though she didn't seem so that first day. She was worried because I was so small. She wasn't sure that I was even fourteen. Good job Mrs O'Leary advised me to take my certificates with me.'

'But she is all right with you now?'

'She's grand, Mammy, don't worry. One thing she can't abide is slacking. Not that you get much opportunity to do that, though Jerry Kilroy seems to have more time on his hands than we girls do.'

'Who's he?'

'A footman, and so under the jurisdiction of the butler, Mr Carlisle,' Lucy said. 'Cook said in most houses she has worked in the butler has more to do with the Master of the house, but his batman, a man called Rory Green, came to care for him.'

'So the butler hasn't that much to do either?'

'No, not really, I suppose,' Lucy said. 'He looks after the Master's clothes, presses them and things like that, but Rory helps him bath and dress and gives him a shave.'

'Goodness,' Minnie said. 'They seem to take an awful lot of looking after.'

'They do,' Lucy agreed. 'Lady Heatherington has got a personal maid as well, called Norah Callaghan, and she's been with her years, so I heard. Anyway, she doesn't sleep in the attics like the rest of us do. She has a little room close to the Mistress in case she needs her in the night.'

'Why would she need her?'

'I don't know,' Lucy admitted. 'They do proper daft things at times. And Mrs O'Leary's right when she said that they want everything done, but they don't want to see anyone doing it unless it's waiting on or something, I suppose. Like, after I have cleaned the range, I have to light it and then boil water for the tea and take a cup to Cook and Mrs O'Leary. Then I have to get the steps to the front door scrubbed and all the brass polished before anyone would need to go in and out the door, and then make sure I have tidied everything away before I lay the table for the servants' breakfast at eight.'

'When do the family eat?'

'Lady Heatherington comes down at nine and Rory carries Lord Heatherington down the stairs and they have a wheelchair for him to sit in. Anyway, talking of breakfast, has everyone had enough? There's a large loaf and butter in that basket. In fact, Mammy, now that we've all eaten the porridge, you had better see what else there is.'

Lucy stacked the bowls while Minnie collected the basket from the settle, and as she uncovered one delight after the other there were 'ooh's and 'aah's from the watching children. When it was all displayed on the table, Minnie said, her voice husky with unshed tears, 'She is a kind and thoughtful lady, that cook. Tell her thank you a thousand times from me.'

'I will, Mammy,' Lucy promised, as Sam broke in with, 'Is the bag filled with food as well?'

Lucy laughed. ''Fraid not, Sam. That's filled with boring old clothes.'

'Oh,' said Sam. 'Are they from this cook as well?'

'No, they're from Mrs O'Leary.'

'Clara?'

'Yes,' Lucy said. 'And for you, Mammy. But let's decide what to do with the food before we see what's in the bag.'

'I've a good idea,' Danny said. 'Why don't we just eat it?'

They didn't eat it all, but Minnie cut all the children slices of bread from the loaf, which she

57

spread with the creamy butter. The rest she put away: she said, so she could have something wholesome to make a good meal for Lucy before she would have to return to Letterkenny.

'Don't worry about me, Mammy,' Lucy protested, as she poured water from the kettle above the fire into the bowl Grainne had got ready, and began to wash the bowls. 'I didn't come here to eat the food I brought. That was done to help all of you.'

'You will have a good feed before you leave here,' Minnie said determinedly. 'God knows, I do little enough for you now.'

'Ah, Mammy!'

'No, Lucy,' Minnie said. 'Please, let me speak. When I saw you get off the rail bus I could hardly believe my eyes. In the short time that you've been away you have grown and there's far more meat on your bones. I didn't expect that. For all Clara said, I thought that they would have you run ragged.'

'And let me tell you, Mammy, there are few minutes in the day when I can sit down,' Lucy said. 'I am on the go from when I rise in the morning till I go to bed, after I have everything washed up, cleaned the kitchen and scrubbed the floor. When I first went there, I found the days long and the whole of my body ached. I couldn't lift the heaviest and biggest pots that I had to scour and Clodagh would have to help me. However, I am used to the hours now, and the work, and although the pots are just as heavy, I can lift them up with the best of them.'

She dried her hands, went over to the settle,

58

picked up the bag and gave it to her mother. She said, 'At the bottom of the clothes you will find a cloth bag and inside there are thirty shillings. I only wish it was more, but that is yours, and every month I will bring the same. But look at the things Clara has sent first. She said she had no use for them.'

Minnie lifted the things out one by one. The warm black boots on the top had hardly any wear, and there were two winter-weight dresses: one in navy with cream trimmings, similar to the one Clara bought for Lucy, and the other dark red with navy collar and cuffs. There was a cosy, woolly blue cardigan, a cream blouse and a brown skirt, and wrapped up in the skirt a pair of lisle stockings unopened. The children stared open-mouthed, but it was Lucy that Minnie was looking at. Her eyes were very bright and her voice choked as she repeated, 'No use for?'

Lucy shrugged. 'That's all she told me, and she sent a Christmas card as well.'

'I know,' Minnie said, and she lifted out the envelope and slit it open to reveal a beautiful card with a snow scene on the front. When she opened it up, a five-pound note fell out and the children let out a gasp.

'"Have a very happy Christmas, all of you. Lots of love, Clara,"' Minnie read out, and she picked the note up from the floor and said to Lucy, almost angrily, 'Is this something else Clara had no use for?'

Lucy shook her head. 'Oh, I don't know. I truly didn't know about the money. To be honest, when it first fluttered out I was a bit annoyed myself

59

because it makes my contribution look so small and unimportant, and then I thought that that was a selfish way to think. She doesn't know whether she will get to see you before Christmas – travel in the winter is so dependent on the weather – and she wanted to make sure that you didn't go without at Christmas. Can't you see it in that light?'

'I don't think she meant it as any sort of insult,' Danny said. 'You know her better than I do, of course, but from what I saw of her she was a sort of kindly person. Wouldn't you say so, Lucy?'

'Aye, I would, Danny, definitely.'

Minnie was thinking hard. She wanted to return the money because to her it was as if her friend was looking down her nose at her, playing the Lady Bountiful.

Lucy watched her mother's face and guessed her thoughts. 'You accept clothes from St Vincent de Paul for all of us,' she said, 'so what's the difference to you accepting the clothes and money that Mrs O'Leary has given with a good heart?'

'Things from St Vincent de Paul are different, and they have never given me money.'

'You've had food vouchers, which is the same thing,' Danny put in.

'That's right,' said Lucy. 'And just because there is plenty of wear in the boots and clothes and all doesn't mean that Mrs O'Leary will ever wear them again. I would say that it's wrong to have clothes just hanging in the wardrobe that you know you will never wear when others are in need. If she had given them to St Vincent de Paul and they had made a gift of them here you wouldn't have found a problem with that.'

'Yeah,' Danny said enthusiastically. 'This Mrs O'Leary is just cutting out the middle man.'

'And as for the money,' Lucy continued, 'can you put your hand on your heart and say that you don't need it?'

Minnie looked at the family grouped around her, their hollowed faces white and anxious, and she knew she couldn't. For some time she had been worried about the children's footwear and had known that unless St Vincent de Paul came soon with boots in their bundles, Danny and Grainne at least would have to go barefoot, winter or not, because their boots were so small they were crippling them. Grainne, anyway, was near walking on the uppers. With the money, Minnie could have her old boots soled and heeled for Danny, and get Danny's fixed for Grainne. A knot of worry fell from her shoulders and she knew she had to accept the money, and with good grace. 'You're right, both of you,' she said to Danny and Lucy. 'This was meant to help us all.'

'So is this,' Lucy said as she withdrew the bag that she had put her money in and placed it in her mother's hands.

Minnie held it out to her. 'You must have something for yourself,' she said. 'I have no need of it all now I have Clara's Christmas box.'

'No, Mammy,' Lucy said, closing her mother's hand over the small bag. 'I don't want any back, for I need very little. I kept back enough for the fare to come here and I needed sixpence to put together with Clodagh and Evie so that we can buy some nice soap and shampoo for our hair.'

'Is that what it is?' Grainne said. 'I have never seen your hair so nice and shiny.'

'And it smells nice, too,' Liam said. 'I noticed that.'

'Yes, that's the shampoo,' Lucy said. 'I had been used to using soap, but Clodagh stopped me and gave me some of her shampoo and I saw the difference straight away, so now we share the buying of things like that because we all sleep in the attic – Clodagh, Evie and me – and we have our own bathroom with a flush toilet and a bath, too, when we ever get time to use it.'

'Are they nice girls?'

'Lovely,' Lucy said enthusiastically. 'And it helped to have them there when I was suffering homesickness.'

'*Were* you homesick?' Danny asked.

'Course I was,' Lucy said, and then grinned at her brother. 'Missed seeing your ugly mug, for a start.'

'We missed you, too,' Sam said, before Danny had time to reply. 'I cried loads, and Liam did.'

'No, I never.'

'Yes, you did.'

'No, I never.'

Grainne raised her eyes to the ceiling. 'Here we go again,' she said.

'Boys,' Minnie cut in, 'I am ashamed of you arguing the first time that Lucy has been able to get home to see us, and over nothing at all.'

Though Minnie told the boys off and they subsided and looked thoroughly chastened, Lucy had been pleased to hear her young brothers arguing because it was what they did and it was familiar.

She realised then that that was what she missed most – just family life. Seeing them once a month was not going to be enough to be part of it. She would be the absent sister, the one they spoke about and remembered in their prayers but hardly knew. She realised, though, that she had to hide how she felt from her mother at all costs. The family's survival depended on her.

Fortunately, Minnie's attention was still on her obstreperous sons and so she didn't see the shadow flit across Lucy's face, and though Danny did, he said nothing.

Minnie continued, 'We all missed Lucy a great deal – it would have been strange if we hadn't – and every one deals with that differently.' She got to her feet and added, 'Now, I am going to make that tea I promised you while Lucy tells us more about the life she is living now.'

Lucy looked around at the family she loved, which she must leave again in another few hours, and for a moment couldn't think of a thing to say. Danny, guessing her state of mind, prompted gently, 'What about the other girl you mentioned that shares the attic? Evie, was it?'

'Yeah, Evie.'

'Well, what does she do?' Danny asked. 'Is she in the kitchen, too?'

'No, she's a housemaid,' Lucy said. 'She hasn't to touch the Master's room, though, unless she is asked to, because Rory does everything needed in there, as Norah does for Lady Heatherington, but she has to dust, polish and run a carpet sweeper over every other room in the house. As well as this she has to lay and light fires in all the rooms and keep all the scuttles filled up. She lays the table with a fresh cloth and napkins for every meal apart from breakfast, and often serves afternoon tea.'

'Well, I'd say she's kept busy.'

'She is always at it,' Lucy said. 'And Jerry is supposed to fill up the coal scuttles for her in the morning and chop up the kindling, but often Evie has to fill the scuttles herself and search for Jerry to find out where he's put the kindling.'

'Is that all he does, this Jerry?'

'Well, he cleans the shoes for the family as well,' Lucy said, 'though it's only Lady Heatherington and the Master in the house at the moment. They put the shoes they want polished out at night and he has to see to them and replace them the following morning and he has to lay up the table for breakfast and then serve it later. I don't touch any crockery or glassware used by the Family. That's all stored in the butler's pantry, and each day Jerry has to clean the silver before it's used and wash it up afterwards. He sharpens the knives for Cook as well.'

'And Clara, what does she do?'

'Oh, she is sort of in charge of everything,' Lucy said. 'She wears a shiny black dress all the time with a white collar and cuffs. And she has always got a pile of keys attached to her belt because she is in charge of the storeroom, and the china, and the linen cupboard. Every day she discusses the menu for the day with Cook and then sees Lady Heatherington to check if it meets with her approval and if there is anything she needs to know, like people coming to dinner or to take afternoon tea, I suppose. Anyway, then Cook phones through to a big grocer's and greengrocer's or whatever in Letterkenny to order anything she needs.'

'Phones?' Minnie repeated with awe. 'They have a telephone?'

'Oh, yes,' said Lucy. 'Cook finds it very handy.'

'Have you ever used it?' Grainne asked, as impressed as her mother.

'No,' Lucy admitted. 'I've never had reason to, but I'm not as scared of it as I was when I went there first. Anyway, when all the stuff Cook ordered is delivered later that morning, I help Clodagh pack it away and Mrs O'Leary takes the receipts and enters the figures in a big ledger, or so Cook says. They send tons of stuff to the laundry, too, and Mrs O'Leary checks it out and the returned stuff back in again.'

'She doesn't do any of the cooking then?' Minnie asked. 'She used to like cooking, as I remember, but then I don't suppose the cook would like that.'

'Oh, she cooks most days,' Lucy said. 'But it's all special stuff like little delicate cakes and pastries. She usually comes to cook after we have eaten our midday meal at twelve o'clock and Cook is usually pleased to see Clara because it takes the pressure off her and she can get on with preparations for dinner.'

'So who eats the cakes Clara makes?'

'People who call to take tea with Lady Heatherington,' Lucy said. 'Or some come to see the Master – army types, many of them – and Rory said they are all more than partial to the cakes

65

and fancies made by Mrs O'Leary. We, of course, don't get much of a look-in, but the odd one I have tried was delicious.'

'She always had a light hand,' Minnie said as she gave out cups of tea. 'But I think it a lot of fuss and palaver to have all of you employed to cook and clean for two people who choose to live in a house far too big for them.'

'I couldn't agree more,' Lucy said. 'But if I wasn't there what would I be doing all day? And where else would I earn the money I do, and all found? As Mrs O'Leary is fond of saying, "Every cloud has a silver lining."'

Far too soon after that they were all walking down to the station for Lucy to catch the rail bus back to Windthorpe Lodge. Mist swirled in front of them as they walked in the deepening dusk. 'It will be full dark when you reach your place,' Minnie said.

'That's all right, Mammy,' Lucy said with a smile. 'I'm not afraid of the dark.'

'I forget how grown up you are now,' Minnie said almost wistfully, and Lucy put her arms around her.

'Not too big for a hug,' she said, and Minnie hugged her as if she would never let her go.

'Ah, my darling girl.'

Lucy fought for control as she broke from her mother's embrace to hug Danny, Grainne and the two younger boys, quickly, as the rail bus was ready to leave. As it chugged out of the station, she watched until her family were like little dots before taking her seat with a sigh.

66

FOUR

Lucy felt even more homesick after her visit home, and Clodagh and Evie were full of sympathy.

'I suppose it helps that we are kept too busy to brood much,' Clodagh said one morning as they were getting dressed.

'Yes, and set to get busier,' Evie said, 'because the Heatheringtons are having guests for Christmas.'

'Are they?'

'So it seems. I overheard Mrs O'Leary talking to Cook,' Evie said. 'Two couples: the Mattersons and the Farrandykes. People of importance around here, it seems.'

Lucy and Clodagh soon found out that Evie was right. Cook was complaining about it over breakfast.

'It will mean extra work for all of us,' she said. 'And that's the trouble with trying to run an establishment like this with such few staff.'

'Well, they're hardly likely to ask our permission, are they?' Clara said.

'Not likely,' Norah said with a wry smile. 'As far as I can see, we must like it or lump it, but I must say that it has perked up Lady Heatherington no end knowing that there will be company over the festive season.'

'Oh, I suppose the poor lady must be fair lonely at times with Lord Heatherington keeping to his room so much,' Cook conceded.

'Well, that will soon be changed,' Rory said. 'When Master Clive is home for Christmas, the General intends to be much more active. He says he doesn't want Master Clive to think of him as some old crock.'

Lucy knew Clive was the Heatheringtons' only son. 'The only one they have left,' Clara had told her the day she had bought Lucy the new clothes.

'The only one left?' she repeated.

'Yes,' Clara said with a sigh. 'Their three elder sons were killed in the Great War. It was Cook told me about the tragedy of it not long after I started working in the Heatherington household. And, as you know, I'd had my share of tragedy and loss in my own life then, and I knew what they had been going through and felt some sympathy because money and influence cannot make up for the loss of a loved one.'

Lucy nodded. 'I didn't know that it hurt so much when someone you love dies,' she said. 'The night Daddy was taken to the sanatorium was the first time I faced the fact that he was dying. I knew I would miss him greatly and I did. But it hurt so much. I had an almost unbearable ache in my heart and sometimes was doubled over with the stabbing pains in my stomach. At times even now it catches me.'

'I know.' Clara nodded. 'After Sean's funeral, in November 1924, which my two brothers arranged, for I was in no fit state to do anything much, they took me back to England with them. They looked after me so well, and so did their wives, but I was like a zombie and the pain too

68

deep for any tears to ease, though I shed many of them. For a time I really didn't want to go on because I felt that I had no one to go on for. I think my brothers were aware of that for I was seldom left alone. Eventually, and slowly, as the spring of 1925 gave way to the summer, I knew I had to leave. Times were hard and my brothers' families had little enough to eat themselves, without providing for me as well. I also found it hard to be around my young nieces and nephews. It wasn't their fault but the sight of them was sometimes like a knife twisted in my heart.

'When I applied to be lady's maid to Lady Heatherington, in June 1925, I was initially dismayed to hear that there was a child in the house. Clive had just turned seven. I knew, though, that he would almost certainly be sent off to school before he was much older, and I was surprised when his mother was against the whole idea. It was Cook, who had been with the family since she was a child of twelve, who told me why. And she said the two eldest sons had been killed when the youngest, Clifford, enlisted, and shortly afterwards Lord Heatherington was invalided home, having been wounded in the arm. By the time he was drafted overseas again, Lady Heatherington found herself pregnant. For many that would have been an unwelcome shock, but Lady Heatherington was delighted.'

'Oh, I can see that, can't you?'

'I can, Lucy,' Clara said. 'But Ada said Lady Heatherington was two months from giving birth in April 1918 when the telegram came telling her of her youngest son's death and the shock of that

69

caused her to go into labour. When Clive was born he was so small and puny the doctor thought he had little chance of survival. However, Clive did survive, but he was doubly precious to his mother. Cook said he was cosseted and spoilt and that was why she didn't want him to go away to school. Lord and Lady Heatherington used to have up and downers about it. I heard them myself. She maintained Clive was delicate, not strong enough for the rough and tumble of school, and he would say that was poppycock and that the lad was turning into a mother's boy.'

'And was he?'

'I think he was a bit,' Clara said. 'Lady Heatherington certainly pampered him more than was good for him. Anyway, Lord Heatherington won and the boy was sent away to school the following year.'

'So where's this Clive now?'

'Still at school in England, sitting for his Higher Certificate,' Clara said. 'Then he will go to Oxford University where his brothers were all due to go. Mind you,' she added with a smile, 'he's a cheeky young pup, and certainly has a way with him, but you'll see that for yourself soon.'

Intrigued by what she had heard, Lucy looked forward to that.

It was time to decorate the house for Christmas. Clara told Lucy that the attics at Maxted Hall, the Heatheringtons' proper home in Sutton Coldfield, near Birmingham, had been filled with decorations, but they hadn't thought of them when they had packed up to leave. So Jerry and Mr Carlisle

70

had to travel to Letterkenny to buy more, and Lucy and Clodagh sneaked out to have a look in the sitting room when Evie told them how beautiful it was. Lucy stood at the doorway, entranced. Garlands of ivy, yew and laurel fell in swags around the room, interwoven with twinkling lights, and holly wreaths with bright red berries decorated the doors. The ceiling was festooned with streamers and paper lanterns that, Evie told them, spun round in the heat from the fires.

'What's that?' Lucy asked, pointing to a rather mundane piece of greenery pinned to the ceiling.

'That's mistletoe,' Evie said. 'And Mrs O'Leary told me that if a girl stands under that a man can kiss her, and if a man stands under then he is inviting a girl to kiss him.'

'Goodness,' said Lucy. 'If that's true I would take care not to go near it.'

'You wouldn't get the chance,' Clodagh laughed.

'And that suits me,' Lucy replied.

The kitchen became a hive of activity. Delicious spicy smells wafted in the air as Cook weighed, pounded and kneaded ingredients. The family still had to be fed, too, and Cook's temper often got the better of her, especially when she was forced to forego the little snooze she often had in the chair after the family's midday meal.

The Christmas cakes had been made weeks before and Cook kept dribbling sherry over them and promised they would look the business when she had them iced. They would all have to have a stir of the pudding, Cook told the staff, and when they did that they could make a wish.

'What will you wish for?' Lucy asked Clodagh.

'Oh, you can't say,' Clodagh answered. 'If you tell, it won't come true.'

Well, Lucy decided, she wouldn't risk that. She would wish for something to happen so that she could move back home again. As Christmas drew nearer she missed her family more than ever, and that was the only thing she really wanted.

They all heard the van chugging up the drive and drawing to a halt in front of the house on the evening of 22 December. As they sat down for tea, Mrs O'Leary told them all that Master Clive had arrived home, bringing with him from Letterkenny a huge tree and a big box of baubles and lights to decorate it.

'What sort of tree?' Lucy asked.

'A Christmas tree, of course,' Clara said. 'You must have seen Christmas trees. They have one in the Diamond in Donegal Town every year, and in the church.'

Lucy nodded. 'Yes, but I've never seen a tree inside anyone's house.'

'Well, they certainly have one here,' Clara said. 'I always think that once the tree is up and decorated then Christmas is just around the corner.'

The others began to talk about Christmases past. Though Lucy said nothing, her own memories were stirred back to the blissful time when her father had been alive and healthy, a time she had thought would go on for ever. He had made Christmas exciting then, taking her and Danny into the woods to search for holly with lots of red berries to brighten up the cottage, and he had shown them how to make streamers with scraps of coloured paper that he would string around the room. Their mother had laughed at his foolishness and said he was worse than any wean, but her voice had been soft when she said this, and her eyes would be very bright, and the smell in the cottage was fragrant as the goodies that Minnie cooked for the festive season overrode the smell from the turf fire.

On Christmas Day itself, Lucy's toes would curl with excitement when she woke to find the bulging stocking hanging on the end of her bed. And there were such delights in store: always an orange and an apple, a small bar of chocolate, a bag of sweets and a toy or two. This might be a tin whistle, mouth organ or puzzle, and maybe tin soldiers for Danny and a whip and top for Lucy. One Christmas Day, she remembered with a rush of pleasure she had a rag doll pushed into hers and she had been speechless with delight.

They would greet friends and neighbours on their way to Mass and 'Happy Christmas' seemed to be on everybody's lips. Back home the cottage would be filled with the smell of the fowl roasting above the fire, and the plum duff that was bubbling away in its own pot above the smouldering turf.

If the weather was up to it after that delicious dinner, Seamus would take them all for a brisk walk, even Grainne when she was big enough to be swung onto his shoulders. They would arrive back with red cheeks and tingling fingers and toes, glad of the cocoa and gingerbread their mother would have ready. When they were thawed out, Seamus would play dominoes with them, and

73

Snap with his set of playing cards, and end the day singing all the carols they could remember before it was time for bed. Lucy recalled how she loved the rounded tone of her father's voice.

But now, for her brothers and sister, Christmas Day had just become a day like any other. If there was a hen that had stopped laying they might eat that as a sort of treat, but there was no money spare for fancy food and she wondered what her brothers and sister would make of the vast array of food in the kitchen in Windthorpe Lodge, and the tantalising and spicy smells that lingered in the air and made her mouth water.

Cook knew she would be judged on her dinner, especially with visitors in the house, and she had pored over the menu for the Christmas meal with Clara, relieved when Lady Heatherington declared herself pleased with it. Later that day, Clodagh showed it to Lucy.

'So,' she said, 'after a full cooked breakfast at nine o'clock, they will be sitting down to Scottish salmon with lemon mayonnaise and beetroot dressing, followed by pheasant soup and warm bread rolls. Then they will be served goose, stuffed with apple, chestnut and sausage forcemeat, cooked in a red-wine-and-gooseberry sauce, roast potatoes and roast parsnips, Brussels sprouts, creamed baton carrots and lashings of gravy.'

'Golly,' said Lucy. 'And plum duff after all that.'

'Yeah, and served with brandy butter.'

'I'm surprised they will have any room,' Lucy said, and added in a low voice, 'and I can just imagine the temper Cook will be in, 'til it has all been served.'

'Oh, I'll say,' Clodagh said with feeling. 'We'll do well to keep our heads down. I tell you, we won't be doing right for doing wrong that day. And she told me that she's really glad that she is not responsible for any of the drinks, that Mr Carlisle will sort that out as usual, because there is mulled wine before the meal, champagne and red wine to serve with it, followed by coffee, and then the men have brandy and port. But that's for the nobs,' she finished with a laugh. 'I doubt you and I will be fed so well.'

'No,' Lucy agreed. 'Be nice to get a taste, though.'

'Yeah, though we're more likely to get the leavings,' Clodagh said. 'Cook said that if any of the goose is left she will make it into croquettes and serve it with mash for us the next day. That might be all of the goose we see.'

'What are croquettes?'

'I haven't a clue,' Clodagh admitted. 'But we will find out. For both of us it will be a voyage of discovery.'

The following day, Evie enthused about the beautiful Christmas tree Clive had decorated in the hall.

'Oh, I wish we could see it, too,' Lucy said; and Clara, who had been to see the Mistress about meals planned for the day, said, 'You can, Lucy. All of you can have a peep, but you must wait until the gong goes for the family's breakfast.'

Never had the time passed more slowly, but eventually the clock ticked round to nine o'clock and Mr Carlisle sounded the gong.

75

The servants waited a moment or two until Mr Carlisle judged that Lady Heatherington, Master Clive and the General, carried down by Rory, had cleared the main stairs, because he said the tree was not far from the foot of it. When Lucy eventually saw it she gave a gasp of surprise because never in her life could she remember seeing anything so wonderful.

It was set in a smallish pot of earth and nearly reached the ceiling. Its branches were filled with glass animals and big balls that sparkled and spun in the flickering lights, sending a kaleidoscope of colours dancing on the wall behind it. These were interspersed here and there with gold and silver ribbons tied in bows, striped candy canes, small gingerbread men, white sugar mice and sugar plums. But at the top of the tree was the best thing of all: the star, which had a shimmering radiance all of its own.

'You approve of my decorations then?' said a young man who, descending the stairs, had been brought to a halt by the rapt expression on Lucy's face.

Lucy turned and saw the handsomest man she had ever seen smiling down at her. Shafts of winter sun were spilling out of the window on the half-landing so that he looked as if there was a halo surrounding his blond hair, and when her eyes met his she saw that they were the most startling blue.

Clive descended another few stairs and saw that the girl was just a child. She was dressed as a scullery maid yet surely she wasn't of an age to work. She looked about ten.

She still hadn't spoken. Then Carlisle said, 'We are all astounded, Master Clive. You have done a truly splendid job.'

'Thank you, Mr Carlisle,' Clive said. 'High praise indeed.'

He smiled and it was as if someone had turned the light on behind his eyes, and Lucy felt it almost like a blow to the stomach. Clive's smile, though, was for them all.

'Now I must away for my breakfast,' he said. 'I will catch it from Mother as it is for being late,' and with a wave of his hand he was off to the dining room, wondering why he had been so affected by an undersized scullery maid.

In fact, so affected was he that after he had greeted both his parents and apologised for his tardiness, he said to his mother, 'I didn't realise that we were employing children now.'

Amelia frowned. 'What on earth do you mean, Clive?'

'The servants were out admiring the Christmas tree as I came down the stairs and one of the girls there can be no more than ten.'

'Oh, that's Lucy Cassidy,' Amelia said. 'She is small, I grant you, but she is fourteen.'

'Never.'

'She is, I assure you,' Amelia said. 'She brought along her birth and baptismal certificates, and we also had the word of Mrs O'Leary, who grew up with her mother and has known Cassidy since she was born.'

'Must be right then,' Clive said. 'But it is unbelievable.'

'Why are you so interested?' Charles asked.

'I'm not really,' Clive said. 'It's just that she looks like someone dressing up, as if for a fancy-dress party or something.'

'I'd say she does more than look the part if she is under Mrs Murphy's direction.'

Clive chuckled. 'I'd say so, too.'

'Well then, I suggest we stop worrying about maids, small or large, and attack the breakfast,' the General said.

Clive gave a brief nod. He knew as far as his father was concerned the matter was closed.

In the early afternoon on Christmas Eve, the servants all heard the crunch of car tyres on the gravel path as the visitors arrived. Clara, Mr Carlisle and Jerry were summoned to stand beside Lady Heatherington, Clive and Lord Heatherington, to greet them in the hall.

'What are they like?' Cook asked Mr Carlisle when he returned to the kitchen.

He shrugged. 'Just ordinary.'

'How like a man,' she said disparagingly. 'I just hope they're not a picky lot, that's all.'

'Nobody could be picky over any of the food you cook,' Mr Carlisle said loyally. 'They are much more likely to be impressed, I should think.'

Mr Carlisle was right. He and Jerry heard the enthusiastic comments as those around the table were served first the pea and ham soup, then the roast beef, roast potatoes, Yorkshire puddings and vegetables. The butler told the kitchen staff as he returned the dirty plates. Cook was pleased and relieved, and loaded up their trays with a feather-light lemon sponge, which was to be served with cream, and would be followed by a variety of cheeses, biscuits and coffee.

Lucy and Clodagh exchanged glances as the delicacies were carried out of the kitchen. Neither of them had been able to eat or drink anything as they would be going to midnight Mass, where they would take Communion, and Lucy's stomach was protesting audibly.

Her hunger was forgotten, however, when just an hour or so after the coffee had been served, and with everything done, Clive popped into the kitchen. Clodagh, Lucy and Evie sprang to their feet, and he lifted his hand. 'Sit where you are,' he said. Then, addressing Cook, he went on, 'I've just come to tell you what a marvel the Mattersons and Farrandykes thought your food was, Ada. And you should have heard me singing your phrases as well.'

'Well, thank you, Master Clive.'

'Oh, praise where praise is due,' Clive said. 'And I am also here to stir the pudding for tomorrow. Did you think I had forgotten?' As he turned to the watching girls he saw the undersized scullery maid again – Lucy Cassidy, that's what his mother said she was called – and he smiled at her as he said, 'I always have a stir of the pudding at Christmas and I make a wish, don't I, Ada?'

'Yes, Master Clive,' Cook said, as she fetched the bowl. 'But I didn't know whether you would bother this year, with you being seventeen years old and all.'

'Oh, yes, Christmas is all about tradition, isn't it?' Clive said. 'I bet the girls have had a go.'

His radiant smile flashed over them all and they

all nodded and then he leant forward and said, 'And what did you wish for, little Lucy Cassidy?'

Clara's eyebrows rose and her eyes met those of Cook, who gave an almost imperceptible shrug as if to say that Clive was a law unto himself.

Lucy blushed to the roots of her hair being addressed in such a manner by the son of the house. Since her interview with Lady Heatherington the day she had begun work she had never seen her again, nor even caught sight of the Master, but Clara had instructed her how to address any of the Family she might meet, and also warned her that none of the Family would address her in any way but by her surname. And now here was Master Clive using both her Christian name and her surname, and in quite a teasing manner.

However, since she thought the rudest thing in the world was not to answer a person who asked a question, she said, 'I am unable to tell you what I wished for, Master Clive, because it might not come true then.'

'Just a little whisper?'

Again there was that smile, but Lucy's shake of her head was definite enough. 'No, I'm sorry, Master Clive.'

Clive was amused by her answer and couldn't explain to himself why he was so drawn to the child, and she was a child, only fourteen, and yet her size made her seem even younger than that. 'It might not come true anyway,' he said. 'You know that, don't you?'

Lucy nodded. 'Oh, yes, Master Clive, I know that,' she said. 'But I must give it every chance.'

'That's important, is it?'

But before Lucy was able to answer this, Cook broke in, 'Master Clive, leave the girl alone. You are embarrassing her, can't you see?'

He could see and he gave a rueful smile. 'Apologies, Lucy Cassidy.'

There it was again – her full name.

Cook said, 'Are you going to give this pudding a stir or aren't you, now I have got it out especially?'

'Of course,' Clive said. 'That's one of the main reasons I came.'

'Really?' said Cook. 'I thought the main reason was to harass and tease my kitchen staff.'

'Oh, Ada, you are very harsh...'

Lucy listened to them sparring with each other with only half an ear because Clive's question about her wish had brought her family to the forefront of her mind and suddenly she so longed to be there with them all. A pang of home-sickness hit her so sharply she gave a slight gasp.

'What's the matter with you?'

Lucy realised they were all looking at her in a concerned way and it was Clara who had spoken. 'Nothing,' Lucy said. 'Just a sudden pain in my stomach.'

'Hunger, I expect,' Clara said.

'Hunger?' Clive asked.

'Well, the girls will have eaten nothing since their dinner as they will be taking Communion at midnight Mass.'

'Why can't they eat anything?'

'I don't know why, Master Clive. That's just the way it is,' Clara said. 'And I really think now that

81

you should return to your guests.'

'Are you dismissing me, Mrs O'Leary?'

'No, sir,' Clara countered, 'I am making a suggestion. I don't want Lady Heatherington to complain to me in the morning.'

'Nor I, especially on Christmas morning,' Clive said. 'I will see you all in the morning anyway, but I will say it regardless. Happy Christmas to all of you.'

'Happy Christmas, Master Clive.'

Clive, leaving, almost collided with Norah coming through the door at the same moment. Once in the kitchen, she collapsed into a chair. 'Golly,' she said, 'they're an untidy lot. I thought our ladyship bad enough but she doesn't hold a candle to these Mattersons and Farrandykes.'

Norah's job was to help the ladies dress for dinner and do their hair, and then, while they were at dinner, tidy up all the mess in the bedrooms, leave out their nightwear and, this time of year, put the pottery hot-water bottles in the beds to warm the sheets.

'Point is,' she said, 'they can't decide what to wear and so they pull one outfit after another out of the wardrobe, and all the accessories that go with them, and then just drop them on the floor.'

Lucy nodded sympathetically, along with the others, for she could just imagine the scene.

Norah went on, 'And do you know what Mrs Matterson said to me while I was doing her hair this evening?' Without waiting for a reply, she continued, 'She has her own personal maid, and I should imagine Mrs Farrandyke does, too, and when they knew they were coming here for

Christmas and all, she gave her maid leave so that she could have Christmas with her family. I ask you! I mean, wouldn't we all like that?'

Everyone agreed with Norah but no one said anything because at that moment Mr Carlisle, with Jerry, came through to the kitchen. Mr Carlisle disliked anyone criticising the Family in any way, and Lucy supposed he would view criticising guests to their home in the same way. She had actually heard him say that it was not seemly for lower orders to find fault with their betters. Lucy hadn't been at all sure that she had wanted to be known as 'lower orders'. It didn't sound a very nice thing to be, and what made the General and Lady Heatherington better than her? They might have more money and influence, but did that automatically mean that they were better people?

She had mentioned these concerns to Clara, but she said she wasn't to worry about it. Mr Carlisle had been with the family since he had been a boy and he was very old-fashioned in his viewpoint. Lucy supposed she was right, for Mr Carlisle was very old, his face was lined and his hair sparse, and she could never imagine him ever being a boy.

Cook was quite concerned about Lucy, Clodagh and Evie, who would be going out that raw night without even a hot drink inside them. When they returned from re-laying the table, she said, 'I have plenty of that pea and ham soup left over and some of the beef joint, and fresh bread and pickles, so make sure you make a meal for

83

yourselves when you come in.'

'Oh, thank you, Cook,' Lucy said. 'And we will all appreciate it, I'm sure.'

'Oh, I'll say,' Clodagh said. 'I'm as hungry as a hunter already.'

'So am I,' Lucy agreed. 'So just think how righteous we will feel when we are up at the rails.'

'Aye,' Cook said with a wry smile. 'And maybe you can say a prayer for the rest of the sinners while you about it. The Good Lord may listen to saints like yourselves.'

Evie gave a hoot of laughter. 'Hardly saints, Cook.' The girls knew that Cook had been brought up a Catholic, but she had lapsed mainly because of the Great War, which robbed the Heatheringtons of three sons. 'And they weren't the only ones, by any means,' Cook had told Clodagh and Lucy when they asked why she never went to Mass. 'That war was dreadful, thousands and thousands of young men killed, like the one I was sweet on myself. I want no truck with any God who allows that sort of thing to go on.'

But now she said to the girls, 'Don't think I'm laying this food out for you because I am going soft in my old age. It's just that I want plenty of work out of you tomorrow, and you'll need stoking up before bed. You'll hardly sleep well on an empty stomach.'

Lucy and Clodagh exchanged glances, but were wise enough not to say anything. Cook was very kind-hearted but she didn't always want to let that side of her show.

Lucy had never been to midnight Mass, and was

84

looking forward to it, though the frost was so thick it was like snow on the hedgerows and lanes, and biting winds buffeted the three girls. They shivered as they scurried as quickly as they could, their scarves wrapped around their mouths because the air was so cold that it burnt in their throats. The church was only slightly warmer, yet they were glad to reach it and be out of the wind, and they sighed with relief as they stepped into the porch.

'Golly, it's cold,' Evie said, unwrapping her scarf. 'Cold enough to freeze a penguin's chuff, as my father was fond of saying.'

'So what's a penguin's chuff when it's at home?' Clodagh asked.

'Not sure,' Evie admitted. 'But I can guess, can't you?'

'Yeah, I can, and it's probably not a thing to talk about in the porch of the church,' Clodagh said.

'Maybe not,' Evie said, totally unabashed. With a large grin, she went on, 'It's certainly not the sort of thing I would say to a priest.' As they made their way down the aisle, she whispered, 'Jerry said that it's only this cold because the skies are clear of cloud and in the morning, when it's properly light and the mist clears, it could be a nice day.'

'Oh, Jerry,' Lucy said contemptuously. 'What does he know about anything?'

'Not a lot, I grant you.'

'He knows a fair bit about skiving from work,' Clodagh said as they entered a pew and knelt down on the kneeling pads in front of them.

85

'Oh, yeah, he's a past master at that,' Lucy said.

No one said anything to this because they were suddenly aware of someone in the church eyeing their chatter with disapproval. Lucy bowed her head in prayer. Suddenly, the strains of the organ could be heard and the congregation got to their feet. The priest in his colourful vestments, and two young altar boys dressed in red with pure white surplices, came out of the vestry and Mass began. Lucy loved the Mass in Advent because of the expectation in the air and the age-old carols to sing instead of the dirgy songs the priest often chose. The Advent candles burning above the altar reminded people what it was all about.

The priest, no doubt feeling the cold himself, cut Mass short, and soon the three girls were hurrying through the dark again and were all mightily grateful to reach the kitchen when the welcome heat hit them as soon as they opened the door. They attacked the food Cook had left out with relish.

'That's lovely,' Clodagh cried. 'I'll be able to feel my hands and feet soon, no doubt.'

'Yes, I'm starting to feel a bit more human again, too,' said Evie. 'Oh, and Happy Christmas to you both.'

'Happy Christmas,' Lucy and Clodagh replied together. They raised cups of tea in a toast, and though Lucy regretted her Christmas wish was not to come true she felt blessed to have found such good friends in her new life.

FIVE

None of the girls wanted to leave her bed early the next morning, but on Christmas morning there was more to do than usual. Lucy, with a sigh, began to dress quickly, for the cold was so intense her teeth were chattering. The family and their guests were going to church that morning, but before that all the servants were summoned to the library. Clara, Mr Carlisle, Cook, Jerry and Norah seemed to be expecting this, but the girls looked at each other in surprise.

'It's when they give us their presents,' Clara whispered to Lucy.

Lucy's mouth dropped agape. 'Presents?' she echoed. 'They give us presents?'

'Don't look so surprised,' Clara said. 'It is Christmas Day.'

'I know,' Lucy said, 'but somehow, I never associated it with presents and certainly not from the Family. I mean, presents are not much a part of the celebrations at home.'

Clodagh's eyes were sad as she asked, 'Did you not ever hang stockings for Santa to fill?'

'When Daddy was alive and well enough to work we did,' Lucy said. Her eyes were bleak as she went on, 'He used to make everything more alive somehow. I used to think Christmas was magical and there was always something just lovely in my stocking that Santa had brought.'

87

'I knew your father well,' Clara said gently, 'because he and my own husband were great friends. I know how fine a man he was.'

'He was, yes,' Lucy maintained, 'though the younger ones can barely remember a time before he was sick and there was no money. Mammy used to try really hard to put a good meal on the table and, believe me, that was treat enough. I didn't look for presents as well. Here I get all that, anyway. I am warm and well fed and don't really have a need for anything else.'

Clara was very moved by Lucy's words. In the household, she was the bottom of the heap, she worked long hours and the work was hard, especially for someone her size, and yet she never moaned and usually had a smile on her face. Lucy was content as few people are and Clara was glad that in the little card she would give her later, when she might get her on her own, she had put in five shillings.

They walked past the magnificent Christmas tree in the hall and they were told to enter. Lucy had her first glimpse of Lord Heatherington and she suddenly felt immensely sorry for him. She imagined that once he had been a fine, upstanding man, before his injuries had robbed him of his health and stripped the flesh from his bones.

She was unaware how expressive her face was, or that Lord Heatherington was amused by the little maid's scrutiny – and she was a little maid. In fact, he thought, he had never seen such a small girl in his employ before and realised that she must be the scullery maid his son had referred to when he had asked Amelia how old she was.

Lucy, embarrassed that Lord Heatherington had seen her regarding him, averted her eyes and looked instead at Rory Green, who stood behind him. Then she glanced discreetly round to take in the others. Lady Heatherington was seated beside her husband, and a smiling Master Clive was on the other side. In front of them on the table were a selection of gifts, which Lady Heatherington and her son proceeded to dispense. Lucy bobbed a curtsy as Evie and Clodagh, who were in front of her, had, as she accepted the package Lady Heatherington gave her, and shook hands with Lord Heatherington. He said to each employee, 'I hope you have a very happy Christmas Day.'

Lucy was the only one who answered him. 'I hope you do, too, sir,' she said. 'I hope all of you have a good day.' She heard Mr Carlisle's hiss of annoyance and knew that she shouldn't have spoken, just accepted the greeting, but it had slipped out automatically.

They all returned to the kitchen to open their packages, and though the butler glared at Lucy, it wasn't the moment to upbraid her among all the bustle and excitement of present-opening.

Lucy had a set of six soft cotton hankies with yellow flowers all over them and trimmed with lace at the sides. She had never owned hankies and thought that ones like these were far too good just to wipe a person's nose. She also had two pairs of black woollen stockings, which she knew would keep her legs warm all winter. Clodagh and Evie had the same. Jerry had hankies and three pairs of warm socks, but Mr Carlisle was given sparkling gold cuff links as well as the hankies and socks. Cook was given a shawl with a pretty brooch to fasten it, and Clara had a pretty pearl necklace.

Lucy, while admiring the presents of the butler, Cook and Mrs O'Leary, was more than pleased with hers, and the morning seemed to fly by because there was so much to be done. The servants' dinner that day was stupendous – that was really the only word to describe it, Lucy thought.

Mr Carlisle agreed. 'Ada,' he said, 'you have excelled yourself.'

Lucy had never heard Mr Carlisle address Cook as anything other than 'Mrs Murphy' before, and her eyes widened, especially when she saw Cook's cheeks look more crimson that they did when she bent to withdraw something from the range oven.

She looked across to Clodagh, who winked in response, as Cook, almost simpering, said, 'It's very nice of you to say that, James.'

'I'm only saying what everyone around this table is thinking,' the butler said. 'Isn't that right?'

There was a murmur of agreement to this. Then the butler got to his feet, for he had to see if the male guests needed help getting dressed for dinner, and Jerry followed him. Norah had to do the same, for her Mistress and the female guests, and Lucy had to start on the mountain of washing up.

'What was up with old Carlisle at dinner?' Clodagh whispered as she passed Lucy.

'I don't know,' Lucy said. 'But I have heard him praise Cook before. He likes his food, does Mr Carlisle.'

'Yeah, but I have never heard him call Cook

90

"Ada" before. He's had a little bit of the Christmas spirit, if you ask me,' Clodagh grinned. 'I think he has been on the bottle.'

'No!' Lucy said, shocked.

'Well, he keeps a bottle of whisky in his pantry,' Clodagh said, knowledgeably. 'Jerry told me.'

Lucy couldn't quite believe it. The butler was so prim and proper. 'Huh,' she said, 'I would take anything Jerry said with a pinch of salt.'

However, both girls had forgotten to lower their voices sufficiently and Cook shouted across the kitchen in a caustic tone, 'I hate to break up the conversation or anything, but there is work to be done and I have no intention of doing it on my own.'

'Sorry, Cook,' Clodagh said, crossing to join her, and Lucy resumed washing the pots, deep in thought.

The staff were more or less free for the rest of the day because Lady Heatherington said after such a dinner a cold buffet would be all they would need to eat later.

'So, what shall we all do with our time off?' Clodagh asked.

'Well, it's not the weather for the walk, that's certain,' Norah said, crossing to the window. The early morning sun had long gone and, despite Jerry's predictions of a fine day, the rain was coming down in sheets.

'Well,' said Cook, sinking into her chair with a grateful sigh, 'I can think of nothing nicer than a snooze.'

'No, no, Ada,' Mr Carlisle said. 'We can't sleep

away Christmas Day.'

'Don't see why not,' Cook said truculently, just as Norah said, 'We used to play blind man's buff and charades on Christmas Day in Maxted Hall, didn't we? Jerry, you must remember?'

'Do you always have Christmas afternoon off then?' Lucy asked.

Cook nodded. 'Yes, but then it was usually only the family for Christmas: Lady Heatherington's parents and some elderly aunts. But the aunts died and then her ladyship's parents, too, just a year or so before the Master was injured. I always used to think it was a pity it wasn't the Master's mother who died, and I know that's wicked of me but she is one body's work.'

'She is,' agreed Norah. 'And so bad-tempered.'

'So where is she now?'

'She is in this sort of rest home,' Cook said. 'She wanted to come here with the family, but her ladyship put her foot down. She said that she had enough on her plate with his lordship so ill, and then when he was discharged from hospital and they said he needed peace and quiet she knew that he would get little of that with his mother about.'

'Between me, you and the gatepost that was one of the reasons she came so far away,' Norah said.

'I don't think we should be discussing Lord and Lady Heatherington in this manner,' Mr Carlisle said. 'And certainly not in front of the younger girls.'

'Oh, don't be so stuffy, James,' Cook said sharply. 'We are doing no harm, and it is as well

92

to warn them. They may well come across her yet, for we will not be in Ireland for ever. Anyway,' she said, turning to Lucy, 'that answers your question. Because the Master and Mistress have guests this Christmas, I didn't know whether we would be given the time off or not, but I made things that could be served cold just in case and isn't it a good job I did.'

'Yes,' Norah said. 'It means that we can play blind man's buff.'

'Oh, do it if you want to,' Cook said resignedly. 'I suppose we will get no peace else, but don't anyone try and blindfold me. I'm too old for such things but I will watch the rest of you.'

And so she did, and Mr Carlisle and Rory Green sat with her while Jerry, Norah, Clodagh, Evie and Lucy enjoyed themselves so much so that in the end even Clara and Mr Carlisle took a turn. Lucy watched the butler playing the fool with the others and wondered if Jerry was right after all and he had taken a drop of whisky, for he was not acting at all like the butler she had become accustomed to. She remembered describing him on her visit home and saying that everything had to be just so, and he sat and walked so straight it was like he had a poker up inside him. Minnie hadn't approved of the analogy but the children had been laughing so much she hadn't had the heart to correct her. Well, Mr Carlisle's poker had slipped somewhat that afternoon and Lucy stored everything up to tell them all on her next visit.

She felt a stab of shame as she realised that, despite her wish, she would rather be here in the servants' hall, warm, dry and well fed and having fun with friends, than home in that cheerless cold kitchen trying not to eat too much so that the others could eat more.

After a huge supper, the evening ended with songs from the music hall that the Irish girls didn't know, though they soon picked up the choruses, and then carols they all joined in with.

'Been a good day, though, hasn't it?' Evie said later as they got ready for bed.

'Oh, yes, the best,' Clodagh replied.

Lucy agreed as well because though she had enjoyed Christmas when her father had been alive and well, those had been childhood Christmases and she knew she was fast growing out of childhood. Her toes curled in anticipation as she wondered what the future held for her.

Once the visitors had gone home, Cook said they would more than likely see more of Clive because, she told the three girls, Clive had hung about the kitchen since he had been a young boy.

'Lady Heatherington didn't like him doing it, didn't think it suitable, and maybe it wasn't, but to tell you the truth I often felt sorry for him. He lacked company his own age and when he was sent away to school, though he might have been homesick at first, at least there were boys there his own age, and he did settle to it in the end.'

She was silent for a minute or two and then went on, 'I should imagine he didn't like the holidays that much because the nanny left when he went to school and so in the holidays there was no one to see to him or take him places. His father bought him a pony and, when he'd learnt to ride it, he used to ride out with the groom every day, but there were still a lot of hours to fill and what he did most times was hang about the house.'

'I can't imagine what it would be like to be all on my own, especially in a great big house like this,' Lucy said.

'Well, the house in England is bigger than this one,' Cook said. 'So when he would sneak into the kitchen I would turn a blind eye and often found him a wee job to do, and I would always find him something tasty to eat.

'Sometimes Lady Heatherington's friend Lady Sybil Ponsomby would call with Jessica, her spoilt daughter. Master Clive would find himself landed with her, and a fine madam she was. Wanted her own way in everything and Clive, who always hated unpleasantness, would give in to her. He brought her into the kitchen a time or two, but it was obvious, though she was only a girl, that she thought us all beneath her and I was relieved when Clive stopped bringing her.'

'Did Master Clive mind playing with her?' Lucy asked.

'Don't think he was that fussed, to be honest, but course he couldn't say anything,' Cook said. 'And the mothers were all for them getting on. But for all her mother is a good-enough-looking woman, by all accounts, the daughter, Jessica, has no beauty to speak off. Proper plain Jane, she is.'

'Never?' Clodagh said.

'Yes, she is,' Cook maintained with a definite

95

nod of the head. 'Of course I saw it myself when she was a child, but I thought she might have improved, but the housemaid used to serve tea to the Mistress when the Ponsombys came to call and she said she got no better. I could never understand it.'

'What a shame,' Lucy said. 'Still, I suppose that didn't bother Master Clive, and I suppose this girl Jessica was better company than no one at all.'

'Maybe,' Cook said, 'but there is no Jessica here now and Master Clive will be along before either of us are much older, you'll see.'

Cook was right. The following morning, Clive sidled in to lean against the cupboard. He ran his finger around the mixing bowl on the counter and pinched a couple of cakes from the cooling trays. Cook's lips pursed, but both Lucy and Clodagh knew that she wasn't really cross and there was no snap in her voice when she said, 'Master Clive, if you keep on, I'll cut your fingers off.'

'You know, Ada, you have been saying that as long as I can remember.' Clive, a twinkle in his eyes, suddenly leapt forward, grabbed Cook around her waist and planted a kiss on her cheek.

Cook was flustered. 'Oh, give over, do, Master Clive.'

'Ah,' Clive said, pulling Cook even closer. 'You know you love me really.'

Cook's face was flushed crimson to the roots of her hair. Lucy was astounded and so, she saw, was Clodagh.

'You should have seen her, Evie,' Lucy said when they reached the safety of their room very late that night. 'Bright red, she was. Golly, just imagine what she would do to me and Clodagh if we behaved half as bad.'

'Ah, yes,' said Clodagh. 'But he is the master's son, don't forget, and one that Cook has obviously got a soft spot for.'

'Oh, that's as plain as the nose on your face,' Evie said. 'Real favourite, he is, I'd say. And I tell you what, I wouldn't complain if he gave me a big kiss on the cheek.'

'Evie!'

'What? It's not likely to happen, is it?' Evie said. 'But he is devilishly handsome, don't you think?'

'I think he is the most beautiful man I have ever seen,' Lucy said simply.

Evie hooted with laughter. 'You don't call a man beautiful! Anyway you are far too young to be thinking of things like that.'

'Leave her alone,' Clodagh said. 'She's only expressing an opinion, and he is nice-looking and seems to have a soft spot for you as well, Lucy.'

'He hasn't,' Lucy protested. 'What do you mean?'

'Well, look how he was just before Christmas,' Clodagh said. 'Calling you by your full name and all.'

'Yeah,' Evie added. 'And he watches you all the time and smiles at you a lot.'

'He smiles at everyone,' Lucy said. 'He's just a smiley person.'

'No,' Evie said. 'He definitely has a soft spot for you.'

Lucy blushed and Clodagh said, 'Don't worry about it, Lucy. The gentry don't usually bother with the likes of us and our Master Clive will probably be just the same when he has grown up a bit. Just now you probably amuse him because you are so small for your age.'

The girls weren't the only ones to notice Clive's attention to Lucy, for he visited the kitchen at least once a day and he always had some word to say on a teasing note to Lucy in particular. She was well aware that Mr Carlisle didn't like special notice taken of a girl on the bottom rung of the ladder, but she didn't see what she could do to stop him. If she was honest she didn't want to stop him because he disturbed her in a way no man or boy had ever done before – not that she'd had that much experience in that department. But with Master Clive she only had to see him, or hear his voice, and she would start to tingle all over.

There were no festivities planned for New Year. Rory told them that though Lord Heatherington had enjoyed the visit of the Mattersons and the Farrandykes, he had been exhausted after their departure. In deference to that, the staff's own celebrations for the coming of 1936 were muted. As for Lucy, she was quite dispirited because the harsh winter weather that held the North of Ireland in such an iron grip meant that she was unable to go home in January when the rails were too coated with ice for the rail buses to run. She was especially disappointed because as well as her wages she had the five shillings that Clara had given to her on Christmas Day, and she had

98

thought at the time that she would use it to buy some little things for all of them in Letterkenny, but the weather had been too bad to allow her to go there either.

She was thinking about this one day in early January as she scrubbed the steps up to the front door when she was startled as the door suddenly opened and Clive stood there, illuminated in the threshold for a moment. He was dressed in riding gear and appeared annoyed to see her on her hands and knees scrubbing away.

He knew that she must have started before it was light because the black winter's night was only just turning into the gloom of a grey pearly winter dawn. It was also so cold that whispery breath escaped from his mouth as he said, 'Lucy why don't you go inside, now? They say it will snow later, which is why I want to get my ride in early, so all your work will be in vain, and what's more it's bitterly cold.'

'It's all right, sir,' Lucy said. 'I'm used to it.' She spoke the truth and just then she wasn't cold, for the proximity of Clive Heatherington had caused the heat to flow through her body in a very odd way.

Her words, though, seemed to irritate Clive. 'This is nonsense,' he said as he took her elbow to encourage her to her feet. 'Get inside, little Lucy. Whatever you say it is far too cold for you to be out like this. If anyone complains tell them to come to me.' Their eyes suddenly met and it was as if they locked together. Lucy was unable to tear her gaze away and then, without any warning, Clive bent his head and kissed her cheek.

She gasped and put her hand to the place he had kissed, which seemed to burn under her fingers as he bounded down the rest of the steps. She returned to the house in a sort of daze as she recalled his eyes so intense and deep blue that she'd felt as if she were drowning in them. She knew she would tell no one of the encounter. She wanted that memory all to herself.

When he came into the kitchen later that day, though, Lucy was at first very embarrassed, but Master Clive was just as normal so she was soon as relaxed as much as she ever was when he was around. Not that he was around much longer, because just a few days later he returned to school. Lucy knew it would be a duller kitchen without the possibility of Master Clive's visits.

Adding to the despondency of them all was the snow. It began in earnest the day that Clive left and fell so thickly that the Lodge was virtually cut off.

'I know we always have snow, but I can never remember it like this,' Clara said to Lucy one day when the snow reached halfway to the window-sills.

It was the evening before Lucy should have seen her family in Mountcharles, but no one had been able to leave the grounds. Though the gardener had made valiant attempts to clear the drives, as soon as he had, the unrelenting snow covered them again.

'I've never seen it this bad either,' Lucy said to Clara. 'But I had never been as far as Letterkenny before.'

Clara nodded. 'You're right, of course, and yet

I should have given it some thought, for we are quite a lot further north. Do you mind very much?'

Lucy did mind, but she reasoned it was no good saying that to Clara, for she could hardly do anything about it. 'Well, it's not just me, is it?' she said. 'Clodagh and Evie can't go home either.'

'It is good too to see that you are being so mature about this,' Clara replied. 'And I am glad to see that you get on so well with the other two girls. It is what you needed, friends of more or less your age.'

Even royalty, it seemed, was not immune to the rigours and dangers of the extreme cold, and the English King George died on 20 January. It was reported on the wireless and Rory told them all about it as they sat having their evening meal.

'So his son Edward will be the new king, then?' Clara said, wrinkling her nose in disapproval.

Rory shrugged. 'Seems so.'

Lucy had seen the expression on Clara's face. 'Don't you want this Edward to be king?' she asked, wondering why she or any other ordinary person should care who was on the throne, because it would hardly change their lives in any way.

'He likes the Germans too much,' Clara said.

'Yeah, and a murdering lot of buggers they are.'

'Mrs Murphy!' Mr Carlisle exclaimed outraged.

Cook gave a defiant toss of her head as she went on, 'You can say what you like and be as shocked as you like as well, but I'll say it again, the Germans are buggers and murdering buggers into the bargain. Look what they have done to this family. Three sons, they've lost, and if that isn't enough to make someone swear then I don't know what is.'

'That's not the point—' Mr Carlisle began primly.

But Cook cut him off: 'Oh, yes, it is exactly the bloody point, Mr Carlisle, and I don't want a king of this country to be friends with a nation that started a war that stripped England of thousands and thousands of fit young men.'

'She's right,' Norah said. 'Madame said something similar. And then there's that Wallis Simpson that Edward is always seen with.'

'Who's she?' Lucy asked.

'Some American heiress,' Norah said, 'and a divorcee, into the bargain.'

'Well, he will have to give her up if he is to take up the crown,' Clara said. 'We could hardly have a divorced American called Queen Wallis sharing it, can we now?'

The three young girls giggled, for it was just too ridiculous, but there was no time to talk further then because Cook had jobs for them all. The topic of the succession didn't go away, and as time passed it seemed the staff at Windthorpe Lodge were not the only ones to be concerned, especially as the new king continued his association with Wallis Simpson, who seemed to like the Germans even more than he did.

A month or so later there was news closer to home. Rory told them that the General had been more active since Christmas and had taken a few steps up and down his room. 'He wants to walk outdoors really,' Rory said. 'He is an outdoor sort of person. Course, I know he is really hankering to get back on a horse.'

'Oh,' Mr Carlisle said, his thin mouth pursed in disapproval. 'Do you think that wise?'

Rory gave a rueful grin. 'No one really thought he would make it at all at first, not realising what a fighter he is and, as he said to me, it was no good him hanging on to his life if that life was to be played out in his bedroom and his only means of getting about was being pushed in a wheel-chair. He says he wants to feel the grass under his feet and the wind in his hair,' Rory said.

'Well, he may get his wish,' Mr Carlisle said. 'There is definitely a thaw on the way.'

Mr Carlisle was right. The icicles that had hung from the windows had melted away and the frost no longer gilded the hedgerows and covered the lawns. Streams had begun to run freely again. The snow that had fallen had melted into soiled and slushy dark grey lumps and there was the sound of dripping water everywhere and a feeling of dampness in the air.

Rory nodded. 'I know,' he said. 'He wants to be really well when Master Clive comes home again in the summer, for they won't have all that long together because Master Clive starts his European tour in early July.'

Lucy, though knowing that when Mr Carlisle was at the table, the three younger girls were not to speak unless addressed directly, was surprised enough to burst out, 'European tour?'

Mr Carlisle glared at her, but before he could deliver one of his scathing remarks, Clara said, 'A lot of young men from this type of establishment do this kind of thing before they go off to university.'

'Oh,' Lucy cried. 'Wouldn't that be just wonderful, to see lots of other countries?'

'Whether it would or not, Cassidy, is no concern of yours,' Mr Carlisle snapped. 'Kindly attend to your breakfast.'

Lucy obediently bent her head over her food, but she wasn't too bothered about Mr Carlisle. She hadn't much to do with him really. She was always careful not to offend Cook or Clara, though, and Clodagh gave her a furtive kick under the table in sympathy. However, Lucy listened avidly to the adventures planned for Master Clive so that she could tell her family the next time she visited.

It was early March before she was able to go home and then, as the Cassidys sat down after Mass to a bacon and egg breakfast courtesy of Mrs Murphy, they listened to Lucy's tale.

'So where is he going?' Danny asked. 'I mean, what countries?'

'I'll hardly remember them all,' Lucy said, her brow furrowing as she tried to recall what Rory and Mr Carlisle had said. 'It will be France first – I do know that – and Spain, and they are due to go to Italy, too, but of course, the main country they will be heading for is Germany.'

'Why's that then?' Danny asked

'Because of the Olympic Games.'

'And what's that when it's all about?' Minnie asked.

Lucy gave a secret smile of satisfaction because she hadn't known a thing about it until Clara explained it.

'It's a special games where one country can compete against others in all sorts of sports and all the people who compete have got to be amateurs. That means they can't get paid for it,' she went on, knowing that 'amateur' was a word that they wouldn't be familiar with. 'And they pick three winners for each event, the first one gets a gold medal and the one who comes second has a silver one and there is a bronze for the athlete in third place. Lots of countries join in and it's held every four years. Each country sort of takes it in turns to put it on and this year it's Germany's turn.'

'Well, you seem to know all about it, at least,' Minnie said, 'though I doubt it will make any difference to our lives.'

'Nor mine,' Lucy admitted. 'But they all talk about it round the table and that, and you can't help listening. It all began because Rory was saying that the Master – you know, the General – wanted to be well enough to spend some time with Master Clive before he sets off on this trip.'

'Isn't he an invalid?'

'Well, he was when I got there first,' Lucy said. 'He spent a lot of time in his room and only came down for meals, and then Rory had to carry him down.'

'So is he getting better now?' Danny asked.

Lucy told her family that the General had confounded doctors by getting to his feet and started the long process of learning to walk again. 'Course, I don't know how much better he will get, but Rory said his ambition is to be able to ride horses again.' She shrugged and went on,

'He might never be able to ride again, for all his determination, but Rory said that he has made greater strides since the great freeze ended and he has been able to get outside in the fresh air.'

'Well, that would make anyone feel better, especially after being cooped up in a room for a long time,' Minnie said. 'Anyway, we have some news of our own. Tell Lucy about it, Dan.'

'I have got a job as well,' Danny said. 'Or at least I had a job through the winter.'

Lucy had sensed in the house a small ease of the extreme poverty that she had experienced before she left. It was such a slight shift that anyone else might not have noticed it, but it was there and she thought that it might have been her money or maybe Clara's gift portioned out that had made the difference and now it seemed that ease in the house was due to Danny's endeavours. She was irritated and couldn't really understand why.

'How can you have a job when you are still at school?' she demanded.

'It's weekends,' Danny said. 'I work for Farmer Haycock. I went and asked him if he had any jobs I could do.'

'So what do you do?'

'Well, he keeps lots of horses, as you know, and they weren't getting any exercise with the ground so hard and they had to be taken out into the yard, but first I had to use boiling water to melt the ice coating the yard and a really stiff brush 'cos there can't be the slightest bit of ice that the horses might slip on. Then I have to lead them out one by one and walk them round and round and then clean out their stalls. Farmer Haycock showed me how to make a bran mash for them and I must always make sure their drinking water is not iced over. Then I have to groom them, put the blankets back over them and clean all the tack. He says I am a natural with the horses, like Dad was with cows, and he gives me five bob a week.'

'Five shillings!' Lucy cried, thinking life was unfair when she worked much longer hours for not much more. 'Still,' she said, 'I get all my meals thrown in.'

'I do too,' Danny said. 'Haycock's wife gives me a big feed in the kitchen at dinnertime, with pudding and everything, and a few sandwiches to take home for my tea. And if we didn't eat all the pudding she lets me take that home as well for the others. Point is, though, that job might have come to an end now the ice has thawed. I mean, I went up yesterday and there was no ice in the yard and when I said you were coming home today Haycock said to have the day off. So I only got half a crown, and he might not want me at all next weekend. I will go up and see, though. Maybe there will be something else. He says he will employ me to get the harvest in later in the year and pay me a proper wage so that's something to look forward to.'

Lucy was thoroughly ashamed of her annoyance at Danny getting any sort of job. All he was trying to do was help their mother and his siblings. Her mother looked better than Lucy had seen her in years, and she knew that, though Minnie was still very poor, Lucy's own contribution, and the added extra from Danny, had removed the worry

107

from her mind that they might starve to death or be taken to the poorhouse. That alone had made her look better. The clothes from Clara had made a difference too. Lucy was quite surprised to see that with more food, less strenuous work and more money to dress nicely and look after herself better, her mother could look quite pretty.

SIX

After such a ferocious winter, the spring was a good one, and Easter, in the second week of April, was almost balmy. Lucy had hoped that Master Clive might be home for the holidays, but Clara told her that as the exams for his Higher School Certificate started not that long after Easter, he was staying with a schoolfriend in England where they were having extra revision lessons. 'And, I believe, seeing quite a lot of the Ponsombys, or probably, I should say, it is Jessica Ponsomby he is interested in visiting.'

A totally unreasonable and unexpected stab of jealousy shot through Lucy as she said, 'Cook told me about her. She says she's a spoilt madam.'

Clara's lips nipped together in annoyance. 'Cook has a slack mouth at times,' she said. 'And I don't know that she has seen that much of Miss Jessica to make such statements. Anyway, people change. The Ponsombys are old friends of the Heatheringtons. Norah told me that Lady Ponsomby had lost a son in the Great War, and when she learnt that Lady Amelia had lost sons as well, it was like a bond shared between them. Jessica is a year younger than Clive and their mothers have high hopes of them.'

'High hopes?'

'Yes,' Clara said. 'To marry. It really would be eminently sensible.' And she added, 'With her brother dead, Miss Jessica will inherit everything when her father dies, and she will also have a sizeable settlement when she is married. Sometimes the size of a dowry is better than a pretty face.'

Lucy was quite shocked. She had naïvely thought that you married someone you loved, who could easily not be that eminently sensible or very rich, but your choice at least. However, she was too miserable to say any of this. She knew that people like those she worked for often had different ways of doing things and this choosing someone who was eminently sensible to marry was just another indication of that.

As spring slid into a mild summer, Lord Heatherington got astride a horse again and Rory told them he had been like a dog with two tails. There was also no problem with Lucy going home every month, and, though she looked forward to it, she was always concerned by how much her siblings seemed to change each time and what little part she had in their lives now.

This was more or less confirmed when Liam made his first Holy Communion in late June.

'It isn't even that I can't be there,' she complained to Clodagh. 'I mean, I would like to be there, it is a special day, but I am more upset by the fact that he more or less expected that I wouldn't make it. He wasn't the tiniest bit upset, like it didn't matter to him one way or the other.'

'Did you want him to be upset?' Clodagh asked. 'Would it have made you feel better if he was breaking his heart crying over it because you couldn't be there, however upset he was?'

'I know,' Lucy said resignedly. 'And no, I suppose that I don't want him upset, of course I don't. It's just...'

'Lucy, it would be the same if you were married and lived a distance away.'

'I don't want to be married,' Lucy said. 'Do you?'

'Not likely,' Clodagh said. 'Well, not yet, anyway. Good job really, because where do we go to meet any men or boys?'

'We go to Mass.'

'Well, I've seen no likely looking chaps there, have you?'

'No,' Lucy said with a smile. 'But then I haven't been looking.'

'Haven't you?' Clodagh asked. 'You probably will in a year or two, but I wouldn't waste your time looking in Letterkenny. And then if you found a boy you fancied, you would have no time to see him.'

'Does that bother you?'

'No, at the moment it doesn't,' Clodagh said. 'But I'm definitely not going to stay in service for ever. For now, though, there is going to be a bit of excitement for us because Master Clive will be home next week.'

'Oh, yes,' Lucy said, 'I had almost forgotten that.' She blushed as she spoke because she knew exactly when Clive was expected home. The date seemed to be engraved on her heart.

Clodagh hadn't noticed Lucy's blushes, and she went on, 'I wonder what Master Clive will make of his father's progress. Neither the Master nor the Mistress has told him in letters or anything because Rory said the Master wanted it to be a total surprise.'

'It will be a surprise all right,' Lucy said. 'Or maybe shock is a better word, because didn't Rory say that the Master was trotting round on his horse the other day as if he'd never been out of the saddle?'

'He did,' Clodagh said. 'He did indeed.'

Clive was indeed shocked, but also delighted to see his father so well. The first thing they did was go for a ride together. Word of this soon reached the kitchen and everyone was pleased. Clara had seen them both ride out together and said that it filled her heart with joy to see Lord Heatherington almost returned to the man he had once been. Aware of the short time he would have alone with his parents before his travelling companions arrived, Clive rode with his father every day and was also an amusing companion at the dinner table in the evening.

When his three friends arrived the house became instantly more alive and vibrant, and the kitchen a far busier place. They all seemed to have voracious appetites, and after dinner on the first day they insisted on being introduced to the cook

111

who had produced the delicious food they had just enjoyed. They almost burst into the kitchen, and though Lucy thought they all seemed so nice, friendly and smiling, she was suddenly overcome by shyness. She retreated to the scullery and watched from the door.

She saw that Clive was his usual amusing self, putting his arm around Cook as he introduced her.

'This is the one responsible for all the culinary delights you have just enjoyed, and will, I promise you, continue to enjoy, for she is the best cook in the world and she answers to the name of Ada, Ada Murphy.'

A young man with a shock of black curls and dark eyes, whom Clive introduced as Colin Braithwaite, shook hands with Cook and said, 'Mrs Murphy, I have to say every mouthful I have eaten so far has been exquisite.'

Cook's face was as red as a ripe tomato. 'Oh, sir,' she cried, 'you're too … too…'

'He's not too anything,' said another young man, who was slight of build and had sandy hair and eyes a sort of hazel colour. 'Exquisite is exactly the right word.' He also took Cook's hand. 'My name is Phillip Banister and I am delighted to make your acquaintance, Mrs Murphy, and I know my friend Mathew will agree. Likes his grub, does Mathew Mainwaring.'

Mathew was as broad as Phillip was skinny. His dark brown eyes twinkled as he said to Cook, 'I'll say so, Mrs Murphy. In fact, I can't ever remember a time that I have eaten better.'

Cook recovered herself enough to say, 'You're

so kind, young sirs.'

'Not at all,' Colin said. 'Credit where credit's due and all that.'

'Hear, hear,' Mathew put in. 'Clive is always saying what a treasure you are.'

'And was I right, or was I right?' Clive laughed.

'You were right,' chorused his grinning friends.

'And you know what they say?' Clive continued, putting an arm around Ada's ample waist. 'Never trust a thin cook.'

'Master Clive,' Ada remonstrated, though Lucy knew that she wasn't cross at all but really enjoying every minute of it. Cook introduced the young men to Clodagh, Jerry and Mr Carlisle. Clive's eyes, meanwhile, were raking her kitchen and he suddenly walked quickly to the scullery. Lucy had dodged back when she realised Clive had caught sight of her and she was just about to plunge her hands into a sink full of hot water and pots when Clive drew her out into the kitchen by the hand. His attention sent a tingle up her arm and all through her body, bringing a tinge of crimson to her cheeks that, had she but known it, made her even more attractive.

'This,' Clive said, as he drew Lucy along behind him, 'is the scullery maid, Lucy Cassidy. And in case you think my parents are involved in child labour, for all Lucy's size, she assures us she is fourteen.'

Cook saw Lucy's flushed face and said, 'Shame on you, Master Clive. Lucy doesn't like the constant reference to her size, which she can do little about, as much as I don't like being referred to as fat.'

'Sorry,' Clive mumbled, though Lucy saw the spark of mischief was still there behind his eyes. 'No offence intended. And, Ada, if you were any slimmer, who would I put my arms around when I came home?'

'Master Clive,' Cook said, and there was a steely tone to her voice, 'I suggest you take your guests out of the kitchen before I feel the urge to wrap the rolling pin around your neck.'

'I think a tactical withdrawal is best,' Clive said, but he planted a kiss on Cook's cheek before turning to his friends. 'Let's leave these good people to have a well-earned rest after all their hard work, and return to my father before he has drunk all the port.'

The kitchen seemed a duller place when they had gone, and Lucy couldn't help feeling a pang of envy that Master Clive and his friends seemed to live in a different world from her.

The house was a much noisier place suddenly, with boots ringing on the stairs or sudden guffaws of laughter emanating from one or other of the young men. They never seemed to stay still a moment. As they all liked to ride, Lord Heatherington hired mounts for them. Lucy loved the regal stance of them as they led the horses down the drive, but to her there was no nicer sight than that of them all galloping over the hills.

'Those young men seem to enjoy everything,' Mr Carlisle said one day, bringing back empty plates. 'Though their manners are impeccable and they are respectful, there is more fun and laughter around the table at luncheon or dinner than I have

114

ever seen. They are a tonic to have in the house.'

Lucy and the rest of the kitchen staff saw a lot of Clive and his friends, for, despite the sumptuous and very satisfying meals that were offered to them three times a day, they were forever on the scrounge between times. Cook said she had never cooked so many cakes and biscuits and scones in her life before, and Clara added hefty slabs of fruit bread to her tasty tea-time pastries. Cook was convinced that the lads either had worms or hollow legs, but despite the extra work, everyone in the household appeared happier. The young men were always very appreciative as well as being full of fun and ready for a good laugh, often at themselves. With the kitchen staff, they took their lead from Clive and, as he singled out Lucy and Cook, they did the same. Though Lucy often blushed to the roots of her hair and sometimes protested, secretly she enjoyed the extra attention.

The time when the boys would leave for their European tour drew closer. They were so excited it was hard not to get caught up in it, though everyone knew that when they left they would be missed. In the relatively short time they had been at Windthorpe Lodge, they had made an impression on everyone.

'Even the Mistress liked them,' Norah said. 'Said to me that it was gratifying to see that Master Clive has such nice friends and it has eased her mind about him going abroad with them.'

Lord and Lady Heatherington were going with them as far as the port in Belfast. The morning they left in two taxis, all the staff came to wave them off. As they returned to the kitchen, Mr Carlisle declared, 'Well, that's that, and for many weeks. Now our lives can get back on an even keel.'

Lucy stared at him but didn't dare say a word. In bed that night, she said to Clodagh and Evie, 'Don't know about you but I think an even keel is a very dull and dreary place to be.' With heartfelt sighs the other two girls agreed.

They all looked forward to the postcards, which began to arrive not long after the boys reached France on 10 July. The first was a view of the French countryside with a message scrawled across it: *'Parts of Northern France are very flat. Can see now why a lot of the Great War was fought in trenches.'*

'He doesn't say much,' Clodagh said, 'but then I suppose he writes to his parents as well.'

'What we need is some sort of board to fasten them to,' Rory said. 'I'll have a look round and see if I can find anything that will do.'

He was as good as his word. By the time Clive's next card arrived, the board was in place and Mr Carlisle bought a map of Europe, which he pinned up beside the cards. The second card carried a picture of Lyons and Clive wrote that they had intended to travel to Spain next but were advised not to as there was trouble brewing there.

'I wonder what the trouble is in Spain?' Cook said, with a worried frown.

'I shouldn't let it bother you,' Mr Carlisle said. 'These Latin countries are very hot-headed and trouble is never that far away. Spain has had periods of unrest for years.'

116

The next postcard was from Lombardy, on the borders of Switzerland, and featured beautiful, snow-covered mountains that Mr Carlisle told them were called Alps. Lucy felt she would give her eyeteeth just to get a glimpse of those mountains.

However, by the time Clive and his friends sent the postcard from Prague, the trouble in Spain had erupted into civil war. He didn't mention it, but Mr Carlisle said English newspapers might be difficult to find.

The news about Spain got worse. Cook said some war in far-off Spain was nothing to do with them and they had to let the Spanish get over it in their own time and in their own way. She was just glad that Master Clive and his friends, now ensconced in Berlin, were miles away, according to Mr Carlisle's map. As they waited for the Olympic Games to start, they went out and about in the city and so the first postcards showed the Berlin Cathedral, a spectacular edifice, the elegant and embellished bridges over the River Spree, the wide thoroughfares, colonnaded and castellated buildings. When the Games began, however, although they still received postcards of the stadium itself and others of the tiered amphitheatre beside it, the messages had changed. Instead of explaining what the things were in this city that Clive originally thought so wonderful, they were cryptic sentences: *'Things aren't always what they seem'* or, *'I have never seen so many soldiers, and all with serious faces. I think we are entering worrying times.'*

No one knew what to make of what he seemed

117

to be trying to say. The Games drew to a close and the postcards ceased.

It was a surprise to everyone when, a few days later, Clive arrived back home. Gone was the carefree youth that had travelled out with such enthusiasm.

He asked to speak with both his parents immediately, and barely had they reached the sitting room before Charles said, 'What went wrong, son? You were supposed to stay in Europe until the university term was due to begin.'

'I know that, Father,' Clive answered, 'but things happened in Germany that have changed everything for me and my friends.'

'Well, I will say the tone of the last letters you wrote was quite worrying,' Amelia said. 'What do you mean when you say that things have changed for you?'

'Well, for a start I don't want go to university just now.'

'Why on earth not?'

'I feel there is something more important that I can and must do.' Clive looked from one to the other of his parents, but it was his father he addressed. 'Berlin is a beautiful city, the home to many wonderful buildings and sculptures, and some of their churches are magnificent. The German people are always considered cultured and erudite. Isn't that so?'

'Yes,' Charles said. 'That's what many believe.'

'Well, we all saw a different Germany,' Clive went on. 'There is a definite air of menace in the streets, and soldiers, many of them dressed like storm troopers, are everywhere.'

118

'Wasn't that just to keep order?' Amelia asked. 'You know, with so many people coming in to see the Games?'

'No, Mother,' Clive said. 'It wasn't just for that. It is for something much more sinister, which is to intimidate certain groups of people, mainly Jews. A lot of Jews have recently come to England from Germany and the tales they carried about what was happening to many of their country-men were so incredible we could scarcely believe them. We got hold of British papers on board the boat going out and read a lot of this kind of stuff, and I am ashamed to say I thought it couldn't be true or at best, a gross exaggeration. I think this is because we have a view of Germany, as I said before, as a nation of courteous and civilised people, lovers of fine art and music and opera, and fiercely proud of their country. But I know now these tales of what Hitler's troops are doing to the Jews are true and it appears that it's not only Jews he is targeting.'

'What do you mean?'

Clive didn't answer his mother straight away and when he did it was to speak of the Games. 'We were there for the opening ceremony and we tried to ignore the sense of unease we felt. It was as if the Germans were saying, "Look what we can do. See how efficient we are." Colin, who studied German, said the papers were full of the Master Race, those with blond hair, blue eyes and fair skin who will one day dominate the world.'

'Yes,' Charles said. 'It always struck me as odd that the man spouting all this rubbish that the German people seemed to fall for hook, line and sinker was himself a black-haired, brown-eyed Austrian. And not a big man, either.'

'That's what makes it all the more ridiculous,' Clive agreed. 'Anyway, when the bell began to toll to signify the start of the Games the crowd erupted in cheers. It was hard not to get caught up in the atmosphere of being there at the Olympic Games. Forty-nine countries were taking part and the unease returned a little at the raising of each country's flag. There was Germany's black swastika on a red background, fluttering in the breeze, looking so menacing. Then there was the parade of the athletes. Germany's team was led by this chap called Lutz Lang, who is the epitome of this "Master Race", with his blond hair, blue eyes, height and build.'

'I read about him,' Charles said. 'Wasn't he beaten by an American in the long jump?'

Clive nodded. 'By a black American, that's the point. He was an African-American. Altogether they had ten in the Olympic team and this one, Jesse Owens, broke eleven Olympic records. The long jump was close, really close, and it seemed like everyone in the whole stadium was holding their breath. From where we were sitting we could see the podium where Hitler was and he went puce with temper when it was obvious that Owens had won, though I have to say that Lutz Lang was the first to congratulate him. And then Hitler refused to put the medal around his neck.'

'Can he do that?' Amelia asked, intrigued.

Clive shrugged. 'I don't know whether he can or not, Mother. To my knowledge it has never been done before, but Hitler is a law unto himself. In

120

his twisted mind he thought Owens racially inferior and he even refused to shake hands with him. Afterwards he said that America should be ashamed to let Negroes win their medals for them, and that he would not be photographed shaking hands with one of them.'

'Goodness...'

'That is the type of man he is and it is what I meant when I said that Jews are not the only ones he has no time for. But many of them too are suffering. A couple of days after the Games began we met this Jewish man. When he first saw us he quickly moved away, but the following day he sought us out in the street and asked in really good English if we were from Britain. When we said we were, he drew us into the partial shelter of an alleyway where he said things were happening in Germany that had to be brought to the eyes of the world and yet he knew that he was risking his life even talking to us.

'He had been a university professor before the Nazis came to power in Germany and threw him out of his post and out of his house. His son opposed the government and their agents shot him dead, and now he and his wife live on the streets of Berlin, for it is death to any who offer them shelter. They live as fugitives, trying to dodge Nazi soldiers, who, he said, would kill them if they were caught.

'He claimed no Jew can hold any post of responsibility, work in any business or live in any house the Nazis deem unsuitable, and their children cannot attend school. They are thrown on to the streets and their houses given to Nazi supporters and their businesses are often destroyed. And there are a great many other things Jews cannot do and places Jews cannot go. We saw no signs to this effect, but our informant said Hitler ordered all the signs removed so those visitors from other countries would not know how bad it was.'

'If all that is true,' Amelia said, 'then it is truly dreadful.'

'It's true, Mother,' Clive said. 'I would stake my life on it. And Franco in Spain is another fascist, isn't he, Dad?'

Charles nodded. 'He is, and the news from Spain is not good. The rebels appear to be making for Madrid.'

'Yes, I read about that in one of the English papers on the boat we came back on,' Clive said.

'But what can we do?' Amelia said plaintively. 'Surely this is Spain's problem?'

Clive didn't answer his mother. Then he said, 'The day after we had spoken to this Jewish man we went looking for him again.'

Clive was silent for so long that Charles eventually asked, 'And did you find him?'

'Oh, yes,' said Clive. 'We found what was left of him.'

'What do you mean?'

'I mean, Mother, they had beaten him to a pulp,' Clive said, 'and dumped him in the street as if he was a pile of rubbish. He was almost unrecognisable as a human being. He looked like a bundle of rags.' Clive remembered the horror and revulsion he had felt when they had found the body, and, when it had dawned on the young men who it was and what had been done to him, they had all felt guilty. 'I think he was so badly beaten because he had been seen talking to us,' Clive said. 'Of course, it also acted as a deterrent to anyone else tempted to do the same thing. The man's death decided us, and we made arrangements to come home immediately.'

'But why?' Amelia cried.

Charles had heard the new steeliness in his son's voice, and suddenly knew what he was going to say.

'We could do nothing to save that wretched man, but we can listen to what he told us,' Clive said. 'Fascism is rising in Germany and will be in Spain, too, if Franco isn't stopped. We met some English fellows on the way home and they told us about some International Brigade being formed to help the elected government stay in power in Spain. Ordinary people are joining up because the British government is not prepared to step in. Do you know anything about it, Father?'

'A little,' Charles said. 'Apparently, there is a big contingent in Liverpool.'

'Yes,' Clive said. 'And from what I understand, these chaps intend leaving for Spain in early September, so there is little time to waste. Colin, Phillip and Mathew went straight home to talk to their parents, as I am talking to you, because we all intend to be part of that brigade.'

There was a gasp of dismay from Amelia. 'You cannot do this,' she cried. 'You will not. I will not risk another son. Charles, say something. You must stop him.'

Charles could see his wife's acute distress etched on her face. He remembered how he had watched

123

her die a little as each telegram announcing the death of one of her sons was delivered. It was having Clive, he believed, that had saved her sanity at the time. He knew it would be terribly hard for her to know that Clive, this precious and now only son, was prepared to risk his life, however good the cause. But he knew he could not deter his son from doing what he thought was right. It was what he would have done himself as a young man. He had wanted Clive to go into the army when he left school, for officer training, as he had done, but Clive had said from the first that the army life wasn't for him and he intended to study law.

Charles had been just the tiniest bit disappointed, but Clive was showing now that he was fully prepared to stand up for what he believed in. So, though his words were gentle, in deference to his wife's feelings, they were firm enough. 'I can't stop Clive doing this, my dear, if it's something that he feels he must do.'

'What has Spain to do with us?' Amelia demanded of her son.

'Well, it isn't Spain so much as who will lead it,' Clive said. 'If the government is defeated, Franco and his fascist supporters will be in charge, and the greatest ally to the rebels in Spain is Hitler and the Nazi Party. If Spain falls, Europe will have another unstable country.' He put his hand over Amelia's. 'I do understand, Mother, and I know you want to protect me, but if we fight now, we may avoid a worse conflict later on.'

'And what do you know about fighting?'

Clive shrugged. 'As much as the next man. And I suppose I will be trained.'

Tears spilt over Amelia's lashes and trickled down her cheeks. Clive felt a stab of guilt, for never in his life had he made his mother cry. He looked helplessly to his father, who put his arm around his wife and led her from the room.

SEVEN

The news of Clive's plans to fight in Spain filtered down to the kitchens. Lucy felt as if someone had squeezed her heart tight and she had a sick feeling in her stomach. Norah said the Mistress was nearly destroyed and Lucy knew exactly how she felt.

'Seems to me he was far more considerate to some old Jew that he met in Berlin than he is to his own parents,' Cook said grimly.

'It was because the man died after talking to them,' Norah said. 'Beaten to death, he was. That's what her ladyship said to me.'

'Ugh,' the three girls said together.

'It should have come as no surprise,' Mr Carlisle said. 'Hitler is a racist. You all read what happened at the Olympic Games with that black athlete.'

'Yes, but what's that got to do with Master Clive fighting in Spain?' Cook asked.

There was no answer to this.

Cook continued, 'I still maintain that Master Clive never gave a thought to his parents, and especially his mother, and I shall tell him so at

125

the first opportunity.'

Later that day, when Clive popped his head into the kitchen, Cook asked him straight out what he was playing at, proposing to fight in Spain. 'This isn't your war,' she said bluntly, 'so why are you sticking your neb in?'

'To stop the rise of fascism,' Clive said. 'Hitler is helping the rebels and they will overthrow the government if we are not careful. It could be worse for us if Franco wins and joins with Hitler and the Nazi Party.'

'You have thoroughly upset your mother.'

'I know,' Clive said. 'I was sorry about that, but this is something that I have to do.'

Two angry spots of colour appeared on Cook's face. 'Master Clive,' she snapped out, 'you have no idea how it feels to give birth to children you love better than you love yourself and then lose them one by one. You will have no idea of your mother's pain.'

Clive glared at Cook. 'Yes, and let me remind you, Ada, that every man jack who joins the Brigade – and there are many who feel as I do – will be someone's son. What would you have me do, stand back and watch?'

Before Cook had time to say anything else, he turned on his heel and left.

Mr Carlisle said, 'Mrs Murphy, I think it was beyond your authority to speak to young Master Clive like that.'

'Oh, do you?' said Cook. 'Well, let me tell you, I have known and loved that boy from the day that he was born, and this is the very last thing that I thought he would do. What was I supposed to say, "Congratulations"?'

'It may have been better to say nothing,' Mr Carlisle said stiffly. 'You abused your position and you got his answer, too, and though I am sorry for his parents, Master Clive has made a very brave decision. However, it's not our place to comment on the doings of our employers and I might say that you've set a very bad example to the younger servants.'

'Well, you stick to your view and I will stick to mine,' Cook said. 'I've said my piece, and I'm not sorry, for I think Master Clive is selfish to even consider this.'

The atmosphere remained tense all evening, and if Mr Carlisle and Cook spoke at all it was in icy tones.

The three girls discussed the argument when they went to bed that night.

'D'you think him selfish or brave, Lucy?' Clodagh asked.

'Oh, I don't know,' Lucy said. 'Brave, I suppose, but I still wish he wasn't going.'

'And me,' said Evie. 'But it is awful what happened to that Jewish man that spoke to them.'

'And then they felt guilty and they had to sort of avenge his death,' Lucy said.

'I think it's the sort of thing men do that we will never understand,' Clodagh said. 'Mammy said that in the Great War men were falling over themselves to enlist. Couldn't wait to get over there and get the Jerry on the run.'

'Daft way to go on, if you ask me,' Evie said.

'Ah, well...' Clodagh said, with a sigh. 'Anyway, I have no intention of discussing this any further.

127

I need my beauty sleep.'

'You're not kidding,' Evie said with an impish grin, and Clodagh lobbed a pillow at her, though they muffled their giggles in case they were overheard.

Lucy lay awake long after her friends. She knew that Clive would go because she had seen the resolve on his face, and part of her was proud that he was prepared to fight for something he saw as right, but a far greater part of her was worried for his safety. When sleep eventually claimed her, she was beset by horrific nightmares.

Clive left, then sent a letter to his parents saying that he had arrived safely and met up with his friends. There was nothing else, and as one week followed another with no further news, Mr Carlisle said he wasn't surprised.

'Master Clive will not be in any sort of regular army,' he said, 'so he probably will be unable to contact anyone here, and even if he did manage to get the odd letter home, it's highly unlikely that they would be any sort of address on it to enable his parents to write back.'

Lucy hadn't thought of that, and she felt even more sorry for Lord and Lady Heatherington. She herself already missed Clive with a pain she could barely understand and, anyway, could never confess to.

'They must be worried sick,' she said one night as she undressed for bed.

'Yes,' Evie said. 'You know, the Mistress asked Norah yesterday if she had ever heard the expression that the silence can be deafening and when

Norah said she hadn't the Mistress said that she'd not understood what it meant until now.'

'Ah,' Lucy said, 'it is sad, isn't it? And I think the only thing we can do is keep our heads down, and hope and pray that this business in Spain won't go on too long, and that Clive will be coming home again soon.'

Lord Heatherington wanted to find out as much as he could about the conflict in Spain, so he ordered more English papers and began to listen to the wireless news intently. In early October, he read the accounts of Oswald Mosley's attempt to lead his party, the British Union of Fascists, in a march through the East End of London, where a lot of Jews had their homes and businesses.

Lord Heatherington could hardly believe what he was reading. 'What is it, my dear?' Lady Hetherington asked, noticing his agitation. 'What's upset you so?'

'It's Mosley.'

'Oswald Mosley?' They had met the man many times when they had lived in England. 'What's he done?'

'His damned party – the British Union of Fascists or some such rubbish they're called – tried to march through the East End of London where a great many Jews live, apparently. Good God, Clive didn't have to go so far to fight fascists; we have them on our own doorstep.' He shook his head, bewildered. 'I didn't imagine for a moment that British people would get caught up in this racial hatred. To think, I have sat at the same table and had a drink with that man.'

129

'But what happened?' Lady Heatherington asked. 'You said, "tried to march". You mean they didn't succeed?'

'No, Mosley didn't succeed, for the simple reason that, according to the paper, three hundred thousand decent human beings turned up to oppose him.'

'Three hundred thousand?' Lady Heatherington could hardly believe it.

'There is unrest everywhere,' Lord Heatherington said.

About the same time as Mosley's aborted march through the Jewish areas of London, two hundred men began another march from Jarrow to London to highlight the unemployment crisis in the Northeast. The march caught the spirit of the nation, as the men walked through towns and cities often plagued with unemployment themselves, and the papers showed them striding out jauntily to the music of a mouth-organ band. They reached London on 31 October, just a month after they began, and the Prime Minister, Stanley Baldwin, not only refused to see them but told them they'd be arrested if they didn't make their way back home again.

Lord Heatherington listened to the account on the wireless. He knew Baldwin had refused to see the men because he was afraid of inciting unrest, but in his opinion he had made a grave mistake. Later that same evening, he said to Rory, as he helped him dress for dinner, 'I tell you, Britain is a terrible country at the moment.'

Rory was used to Lord Heatherington going on like this, using him as a sort of sounding board.

He usually didn't want any smart replies, and Rory would just answer, 'Yes, sir.'

'And the King still knocking around with that bloody American divorcee, Wallis Simpson,' Lord Heatherington went on. 'Quite apart from her being entirely unsuitable, the woman is far too friendly with the Krauts for my liking. I think we could have trouble in that quarter before long. Clive saw it too. That's why he wanted to fight and beat Franco, but God,' he added with a sigh, 'I miss him like a nagging tooth.'

When Lord Heathcrington had finished with the newspapers they went down to the kitchen, where Mr Carlisle would scan them before putting them with the kindling to help light the fires. That was when Lucy might squirrel them away. She had little leisure time to read but, like Lord Heatherington, she was anxious to learn as much as she could about Spain because Clive was involved. She would scan the news in any free time she got and so she learnt not only about Spain but also all about the trouble the King was in for his association with a woman by the unusual name of Wallis Simpson.

So when in December Rory told them that the King was abdicating in favour of his younger brother, George, Lucy wasn't as surprised as some of the other servants.

Cook gazed at him open-mouthed. 'You are kidding,' she said.

'I assure you I am not,' Rory said emphatically. 'He said that he couldn't perform his duties as King without the woman he loves by his side. He did a broadcast on the wireless yesterday evening and I heard the words myself.'

'Such a thing has never happened before, I think,' Clara said.

'No, it hasn't. The announcer said as much,' Rory agreed.

'Well,' said Cook, and the word spoke volumes. 'That's just poppycock. Duty comes before love, as far as royals are concerned, and that man has been trained to become King of England since the day he was born.'

'I agree with you,' Clara said. 'And yet in the end we might be better off with George.'

Lucy remembered that Clara hadn't liked the idea of Edward becoming the king when she'd heard of his father's death. 'How d'you work that out?' Mr Carlisle asked.

'Well, he isn't as flamboyant as his brother,' Clara said. 'With Britain in the state it's in, do we really want such a playboy at its helm? George is far more level-headed, and maybe, as we live through these turbulent times, those qualities are needed in the leader of the country.'

'You could be right, Mrs O'Leary,' Rory said. 'You are certainly spot-on as far as the state of the country goes. The General said the country is going to rack and ruin while he languishes here, and that there is nothing wrong with him now and he wants to go back to England.'

'What, now?'

'Well, December is not the time to cross the Irish Sea, if you have a choice about it, I'd say,' Rory said with a grin. 'But I bet by springtime we will be moving from here.'

132

The three girls looked at each other. That night in bed they fell to discussing the move.

'I'm for going with them if they're agreeable,' Clodagh said.

'Are you?' Lucy said. 'What about your parents?'

'What about them?' Clodagh said. 'This is my life, not theirs. They may kick up but I'm still going. I am determined about it. What about you, Evie?'

Evie shook her head. 'Not a chance,' she said. 'My parents are on about me staying on in Donegal every time I go home. Point is, my aunt is opening a grocery store and wants a girl to train up, and she asked my dad if she could consider me. I said no at the time but if the Heatheringtons decamp to England...' She gave a shrug. 'Let's just say, I'm pretty certain that I won't be coming.'

Lucy shook her head. 'Nor me,' she said. 'I couldn't leave my mother.'

'Oh, but–'

'How could I go off like that, Clodagh?' Lucy cried. 'Even now I think going home once a month is not enough.'

'Maybe not,' Clodagh said. 'I bet, though, your mother is grateful for the money you bring.'

'Course she is.'

'So how will it help her if you go back home? Evie might be all right but I doubt you'll find it easy to get employment.'

Clodagh was right and Lucy was well aware of it. If she were to return home, it would be to the poverty she had once endured. The few shillings

133

Danny earned would not help much, especially with another mouth to feed and no laden basket of goodies from the Lodge each month.

She bit her lip in consternation. 'I'm due home this Sunday,' she said, 'providing the rail buses are running, and I will talk it over with Mammy. You never know, it might not be happening for a good while yet.'

She saw her friends' eyes fasten on her, full of sympathy, and she knew they didn't believe that any more than she did. In the relatively short time she had been at the house she had realised that Lord Heatherington was a very determined man and that once he had decided something he wouldn't be changing his mind.

If she could forget about Master Clive in danger in some far-off land, Lucy could feel almost happy because she had been given a rise of sixpence a week in October. She didn't tell her mother because she was used to the money she got, and there was a little more now that Danny was at work with Farmer Haycock, and she desperately wanted to buy presents for all her family for Christmas.

So on the last half-day before her whole Sunday off she went into Letterkenny for some serious shopping and bought fur-lined slippers for her mother, a warm scarf and gloves for Danny, a skipping rope with proper wooden handles for Grainne, a football for Liam and a spinning top for Sam. As it was coming up to Christmas, Cook packed a festive hamper for her to take home so, together with the normal fare she usually sent of eggs, butter, cheese and tea, she added a big knuckle of pork with plenty of meat on it, a Christmas cake and pudding, and a tin of short-bread biscuits that Clara had made.

Lucy set off in high spirits that Sunday morning, 13 December, anxious to be home, thinking about the faces of her mother and brothers and Grainne. The food would be treat enough for them, but when they realised that she had presents for them to open on Christmas Day she knew they would be so excited. As the rail bus ate up the miles she began to tingle in anticipation.

Lucy was surprised that Danny was the only one to meet her, and even more surprised that he had a good thick jacket and long trousers on. 'Farmer Haycock's wife gave them to me,' Danny said as they made their way to the cottage. 'She said it was time that I was in long trousers and she has given me jumpers too, and good thick shirts.'

'But who are they from?'

'Her sister's son,' Danny said. 'Older and taller than me. Mammy unravelled a couple of the jumpers to knit up some things for the others.'

'I didn't know Mammy could knit.'

'Well, she can now. Said it made sense.'

'I suppose it does,' Lucy conceded. 'Where are the others?'

'They went to the half-six Mass with Mammy this morning,' Danny said.

That was a surprise for Lucy, but Danny forestalled any questions by catching up the bulging bag. 'Come on,' he said. 'We'll leave this in at the cottage and then we will have to get our skates on

135

or we'll be late.'

However, as they neared the cottage, Lucy's eyes opened wide with astonishment, for it had been newly whitewashed and there was a fresh coat of paint on the door. The cultivated garden looked better than it ever had done and so did the hens that were pecking at the grit in the cobbles in the yard. Once through the door the warmth hit Lucy and she noted the fire blazing in the hearth where normally a few embers eked out the turf. The children, who had been on the rag rug in front of it, ran towards her in welcome, and her mother, who had been turning something in a frying pan, looked round with a smile. But though she saw all this, her attention was rooted on a chair to the right side of the fire, the chair that her mother had put away in her bedroom the night her father had been taken to the sanatorium. 'No one will ever sit in that again,' she'd said at the time.

But the chair was back, and sitting in it as if he belonged there was a thickset man. Lucy glared at him. He had dark hair streaked with silver, a ruddy complexion, a large mouth and very dark eyes. In those eyes was a certain wariness, for as Minnie approached her daughter, her arms outstretched, Lucy pushed her aside. The man got up a little uncertainly and the atmosphere seemed suddenly charged as Lucy spoke and her words fell into the room like chips of ice.

'What are you doing sitting in my father's chair?' she demanded.

There was an audible gasp from the children and Minnie barked out, 'Lucy! That was a most

136

incredibly rude thing to say.'

'No, it wasn't,' Lucy protested. 'You said no one would ever sit on it again.'

'I'm real sorry,' the man said. 'I had no idea the chair belonged to your father. The settle will do me well enough.'

'Don't be silly, Declan,' Minnie said. 'Why sit on the uncomfortable settle when there is a perfectly acceptable chair to use?' Then she turned to her daughter, her eyes full of reproach. 'Lucy, apologise to Mr McCann this minute.'

'No,' Lucy said. 'I will not. You said no one would ever use Daddy's chair and you put it away, and I come home to find a stranger is sitting in it.'

'Declan McCann is no stranger to me,' Minnie said. 'Though there is no reason that you should know him because he has been in America some years.'

Declan, still standing before the fire, said, 'I went to America the day after your mother married, Lucy. I was a great friend of your father, Seamus, and also of Sean O'Leary, who married Clara.'

'So why have you come back now?' Lucy asked truculently.

'Lucy...' Minnie began, but the man, Declan, put up his hand. 'No, Minnie,' he said. 'She has a right to ask.'

'Did you know my father was dead?' Lucy asked bluntly.

'Not till I arrived here, no,' Declan said. 'I was not a regular correspondent since I left Ireland.'

Lucy was still suspicious. 'Why not?'

'There was little need,' Declan said, 'for I had few belonging to me here. My parents had both died and the family scattered. I had three sisters over in England and three brothers in New York.'

'Lucy, we'll be late,' Danny said.

At that moment, Lucy cared more about the man in her mother's house, trying to take her father's place, than she did about Mass. But it was a mortal sin to miss Mass and, if she didn't go, Danny probably wouldn't go without her, and that would be a sin on his soul too, and so she turned from the man, as Minnie said to her, 'Be away now, the two of you. We can talk later.'

Lucy inclined her head and followed her brother.

They were almost running on the road to the church when he said, 'What you got against Declan, Luce? It isn't like you.'

'Oh, I don't know.'

'Everything is easier now,' Danny said. 'You must see that. Boys need someone like him around. I mean, he promised to teach us all how to play baseball. Stuff like that is important – to the young ones especially.'

'I know all that, Danny,' Lucy said. 'But he is only here on holiday, isn't he? Has anyone asked him how long he is staying?'

'No.'

'Well, what happens if he's off soon?' Lucy asked. 'What will Mammy and the others do then? It's like he's shown them how good life can be and then snatches it away again. Where will that leave them, because it sounds to me that he is the sort that thinks, Out of sight, out of mind.'

'You don't know what he's like,' Danny protested angrily. 'You haven't given him a chance.'

138

Then more gently, he went on, 'I can see what you say, but I still think you have a downer on him. Honest, Lucy, if he is able to improve our lives, particularly for the younger ones and Mammy, then I'm backing him until I know different.'

Lucy was silent because she knew Danny had a point. Anyway, as they reached the church, many wanted to greet her and ask her how she was keeping, and how she liked her fine job, so she was polite to them all, even the ones who rather pointedly asked how her mother was.

Lucy and Danny didn't hang about after Mass, for they were both starving hungry, and, as they hurried along the road, Lucy said, 'So why has this Declan turned up all of a sudden?'

'Oh, he told us all about that,' Danny said. 'When his parents died he was only a child and so he was taken in by a neighbour till he was old enough to look after himself. Then his brothers sent him the money to join them in New York and in time they were able to set up their own building firm. Declan said it took years of saving, but none of them was married and so they were able to plough all their money into the business. Then twelve months ago his eldest brother died. Declan said it had shocked him because he had never had a day's illness. The brother had always intended to visit Ireland again and had always put it off, and Declan decided to come back in his stead, so that's what he did. Once he arrived in Mountcharles, he heard about Daddy and came to see how we were placed.'

Lucy was silent but, when she got into the cottage, she said to her mother, 'Why didn't you

139

write and tell me about this?'

'About what?' Minnie asked. 'Tell you an old friend that I hadn't seen for years had come to visit us? I didn't think that you would be the tiniest bit interested.'

'I would be well interested in the fact that he was sitting in my father's chair.'

'Lucy, it is just a chair,' Minnie said; and at Lucy's start added, 'You have to face it, child, because that's all it is. And you can't hold me to account for what I said when your father was taken away that time, because then I was hurting and coming to terms with the fact that my husband was dying. And, yes, it's true that at first I didn't want the empty chair sitting there reminding me of the hours he spent in it. Lately, I got to thinking that it was maybe a silly thing to have a good armchair hiding in the bedroom of no use to anyone, and you know that if your father had been here he would have laughed at my foolishness, wouldn't he?'

Lucy shrugged but she knew her mother was right.

'So Declan is going to sit in your father's old chair and let's have no more nonsense about it,' Minnie said. 'Now, come up to the table and I will give you and Danny a hearty breakfast – we have already eaten – and when you are warm, well fed and rested, I'm sure you will be in a better temper.'

Lucy begrudgingly did as her mother bade her because, what else could she do? Her mouth watered at the plate her mother put before her, for there were succulent rashers of bacon, fat juicy sausages, fried eggs with bright yellow yolks, fried bread and tomatoes. There was also soda bread and butter for them to help themselves to, and a cup of hot sweet tea to drink. Lucy could never remember having such a meal in her house before. The children talked to her as she ate, regaling her with the attributes and generosity of Declan McCann. He seemed rather embarrassed by the children's saying all this, but Lucy thought that was probably all an act.

The fire burnt brightly because of the coal he'd had delivered to the barn. 'Coal,' he declared, 'burns hotter than turf.'

'And we've all had new boots,' Sam said, sticking his feet out so Lucy would see.

'Oh, my! What fine boots!' Lucy said, for the child's benefit.

'They're grand, aren't they?' Liam said. 'And we have thick socks as well.'

'Yeah,' Grainne said. 'We always have warm, dry feet now.'

'And we have more food,' Sam said. 'As much as I can eat, even.'

And so it went on. Lucy couldn't seem to think of anything to say to steer the conversation away from Declan McCann. Minnie did ask if anything had been heard of Clive Heatherington, but nothing had, and Minnie could only express her sorrow at what his parents – most particularly his mother – were going through.

'Yes,' Lucy said. 'I think Christmas is going to be a muted affair for us all this year.'

'Not for us, though,' Sam said, ''cos we're going to cut some holly and pick up a real tree, aren't

141

we, Declan?'

'We sure are.'

'And we've already got dangly things to decorate it,' Liam put in.

'Yes, and, if you're ready, we can go and get that tree right now,' Declan said.

Squealing with excitement, the children put on the coats and hats and gloves their mother insisted on, while Lucy wondered that they had such things, and then Danny and Lucy watched them streaking across the yard.

Minnie closed the door with a smile and, as she crossed the room, Lucy pushed her plate away with a sigh of contentment. 'Mammy, that was a delicious meal,' she said. 'Thank you.'

'It's a pleasure to cook good wholesome food,' Minnie said.

Before she could tell her again that that too was all due to Declan's generosity, Lucy turned to her brother and asked, 'How will they get a Christmas tree home?'

'Declan has hired a car,' Danny said. 'It's the other side of the shed, that's why you didn't spot it. He calls it an old jalopy, but I think it just grand. He has taken us all out in it, even Mammy.'

'Why aren't you going to help carry the tree?'

'I can't, because Farmer Haycock has more work for me. He gave me a few hours off to meet you, and so we could go to Mass and have a meal together. He's been good to me and I don't want to take advantage.'

'No, I can see that.' Lucy was sorry that her brother was going and leaving her with her mother, who she was sure was going to tell her

142

more about the attributes of this man, Declan.

But Minnie didn't do that. They washed up together and then she unpacked the hamper, exclaiming in delight at each item, and was even more delighted with the presents Lucy had for them all and astounded that she had been able to afford them. Then Lucy told her about her rise.

'Well, my dear girl, you can keep all your money for yourself now,' Minnie said. 'Declan was very insistent about that.'

'And what about when he goes home?' Lucy said. 'What will you live on then?'

'We'll cross that bridge when we come to it,' Minnie said.

'Don't you mind taking money from him?'

'I did at first,' Minnie admitted. 'But he is a good kind man and told me that I was not to have a moment's guilt about anything, for he was wealthy and he was sure that Seamus would want him to see that we were all right, and that if the boot had been on the other foot he would have done the same thing. And he would, for your daddy was generous to a fault.'

Lucy nodded. She knew that was true.

Minnie went on, 'So now, what do you say to me making a big pot of tea, and we can open up the shortbread, and you can tell me about that fine job of yours?'

Lucy smiled at her mother and tried to dispel her bad humour, and they were still talking when Declan burst through the door – nearly hidden by the large fir tree he held in front of him – accompanied by laughing, excited children. A pot was soon found and the tree sunk into it. Then the children began to dress it and, though they urged Lucy to join in and help them, she refused, although she had to admit that it looked quite magnificent when it was done. The boys hung around Declan all day and even Grainne seemed to have a certain glow about her when he was around. As for her mother, Lucy had never seen her eyes so bright or heard her laugh so heartily in years, and she realised that she was happier than she had ever seen her in recent times. That thought hurt her and she realised that she was jealous of Declan and his influence on her family.

It was a very disappointed girl that returned to Windthorpe Lodge. She hadn't gone very far, however, when she realised that she had been so agitated she had forgotten to tell her mother of the Heatheringtons' plans to return to England.

EIGHT

Lucy seemed unable to shake off her melancholy. She sought out Clara straight away and asked if she could have a word. Clara took one look at Lucy's white face and her eyes laden with sadness and took her into her private quarters. She sat her down on the small settee, busied herself making tea from the kettle standing on the trivet over the crackling fire, and not until she had placed a cup and saucer on the table beside Lucy did she say, 'Now what's upsetting you?'

Lucy sighed. 'Oh, Mrs O'Leary, I don't know if

it's just me. I was thinking it all out all the way home on the rail bus. See, Mammy has met this man she knew from years back called Declan McCann...'

'Declan McCann!' Clara repeated. 'My goodness, is he back after all these years?'

'He said he knew you too.'

'Oh, he did,' Clara said. 'There was him and Seamus and Sean. Thick as thieves, they were. Minnie and I used to call them the Three Musketeers. Declan went to the States. People said it was to help heal his broken heart when your mother married Seamus, but then people often spout a lot of nonsense.'

'D'you think that was true?'

Clara knew full well it was, but sensed that Lucy didn't need to know that so she said, 'Oh, I don't know, Lucy. What I do know is that there was nothing to keep Declan in Ireland; he had no one belonging to him left.'

'I know,' Lucy said. 'But if he loved Mammy one time then he could have come back when he heard Daddy died.'

'Did you ask him?'

Lucy nodded. 'Sort of, and he said he didn't know that Daddy was dead until he got to Mountcharles.'

'And you don't believe him?'

'Oh, I don't know...' Lucy said uncertainly. 'And yet how would he know? He said he hadn't kept up writing much and so he was probably telling the truth?'

'And?'

'Well, he has made things much better for them

145

all: new boots and good food. Why should I mind that?'

'And do you mind?'

'Yes,' Lucy said. 'And I shouldn't. I went to work to try and make life easier so I should be glad for them, and it bothers me that I can't be.'

'Is it because it's Declan who is providing it?'

'I suppose,' Lucy admitted. 'But that's mad, isn't it? I mean, I shouldn't care who it is making life better for them, but it's like he's taking over. And what happens when he leaves, because it's unlikely he can stay in Ireland for ever. The kids hang around him all the time and Danny said that's a good thing, that he is some sort of father figure. That thought disturbs me a bit because surely it will be worse for them when he's not there any more, just as they've been given a glimpse of a different sort of life. And then, to cap it all, he was sitting in my father's chair, just as if he belonged there.'

Clara could see that Lucy was thoroughly outraged by this and so she said gently, 'Lucy, your father doesn't need his chair any more.'

'I know that, but that's not the point,' Lucy protested. 'When Daddy went to the sanatorium, Mammy put it away and said no one would ever sit in it again.'

'Lucy, that would be how she felt at that time, but you can't hold her to that for ever,' Clara said. 'She was in shock, and frightened and upset, and definitely not thinking straight.'

Clara's words were so like her mother's that Lucy was silenced.

'Let it go, pet,' Clara said gently. 'How does

146

your mother feel about Declan?'

Lucy shrugged. 'I suppose she likes him well enough.'

'You know she is only a young woman yet?'

'She isn't, Mrs O'Leary,' Lucy cried. 'She's well over thirty.'

Clara hid her smile as she said, 'She is thirty-five, the same age as myself, and I suppose you think that ancient, do you?'

'Not ancient,' Lucy conceded. 'But not young either.'

And certainly far too old to have another stab at happiness and even think of marrying again, Clara thought, but she didn't share that. It was better by far for her to see for herself how the land lay. So she said to Lucy, 'Where is Declan staying?'

'Well, I shouldn't think there are many places in Mountcharles,' Lucy said, 'so he is staying at a place called McMullen's on Bridge Street, Donegal Town, but he has hired a car so it is no distance away.'

'Well,' said Clara. 'Maybe when you have had time to think it through you will feel differently about seeing Declan in your house.'

Lucy certainly hoped so. On the journey home she had examined not only the way she had behaved but also the things she had thought. She knew it was some sort of rogue trait in her that caused her to begrudge the things her siblings had been given that made their lives more bearable. And wasn't it obvious that they were going to like and be grateful to their benefactor? It bothered her that, despite acknowledging this, a

147

little nub of resentment against Declan McCann had lodged in her consciousness.

The following Sunday, Clara took the earliest rail bus running so that she was standing outside McMullen's in Donegal quite early in the morning. Biddy McMullen looked at her with distaste when she asked if she could speak with Declan McCann.

She gave a sniff of disapproval as she said, 'I don't know that he is up yet. He never has breakfast on Sunday because of taking Communion.'

'Maybe you could see?' Clara suggested. 'Or maybe I could—'

'You will stay right where you are,' Biddy McMullen snapped. 'I don't have any of that sort of carry-on in my house.'

'What are you talking about?' Clara said. 'Declan McCann is a very old friend of mine and all I was suggesting doing was knocking his door.'

'That's my job,' Biddy said sharply as she began mounting the stairs. 'It is not seemly for women to knock at the bedroom doors of single men. What did you say your name was?'

'Clara O'Leary,' Clara said. 'And I know he'd like to see me.'

And he did. Declan took the stairs two at a time, and when he reached the hall where Clara still stood, he threw his arms around her.

'Clara O'Leary,' he said, 'it's good to see you.' Then he held her away from him and said, 'You haven't changed a bit.'

'Oh, you old flatterer,' Clara said with a laugh. She regarded Declan with approval. His eyes

148

were as dark as she remembered their being, and his mouth as wide. He was a big man but not a fat one, and his skin had a glow of health about it. Even the silver streaks in his black hair didn't age him at all. He looked what he was: a fit and prosperous man still in his prime. Clara knew that if he still held a candle for Minnie and told her, she would be mad to reject him.

'Does Minnie know you are here?' Declan asked.

'No, I wanted to see you before I spoke to her.'

'That sounds ominous.'

'No, not at all,' Clara said. Then, catching sight of the landlady standing just behind the door and listening to their every word, she said, 'Can we walk out somewhere?'

Declan nodded as he took his coat down from the peg in the hall, and led the way outside.

The door had barely closed when Clara said, 'Lucy came to see me after her last visit. Did Minnie tell you she is a scullery maid at a big house in Letterkenny where I am housekeeper?'

Declan nodded. 'She mentioned it. Well, let's say Lucy's visit was not an unqualified success.'

'I know, but the girl got a terrific shock,' Clara said. 'I promised to come and see for myself. Declan, do you still love Minnie?'

'As much as ever,' Declan said earnestly. 'Over the years I tried to forget about her, but it was impossible. No one matched up to her but I would have done nothing if Seamus had been here, as I thought he would be. I said hurtful things to Seamus when I left. I came to make my peace. I would never have wanted to cause either of them pain.'

149

'I know.'

'When I saw the state the whole family was in, regardless of how I felt about Minnie, I would have helped them for Seamus's sake,' Declan said. 'When I saw her so wan and downtrodden I was pierced to the soul.'

'What happens when you leave, as you must one day?'

'I have taken a year off,' Declan said. 'I hadn't intended that when I left. I thought of staying just a month or two, but when I saw how badly off Minnie was I knew she needed help.' He stood on the road and faced Clara. 'I will be straight with you. What I really want is to marry Minnie and take proper care of her and the children, and take her home to the States with me. But she has refused me before, so this time I want to go real slow and be more patient. My brothers understand this because they knew how cut up I was after losing Minnie to Seamus all those years ago.'

They began walking, for it was too cold for standing.

'If despite everything she does refuse to marry you a second time, what will you do?' Clara asked.

'Go back to the States and settle some money to be sent to her every month,' Declan said. 'I don't want her reduced to such destitution again, nor the children, because they have really got under my skin.'

'That will settle Lucy's mind,' Clara said. 'Because she was worried about that.'

They turned back to the lodgings so that Declan

150

could collect his car.

'I don't intend to rush Minnie,' he said. 'I know she dearly loved Seamus and I wouldn't disrespect his name by speaking before she is ready but, if she accepts me, I will be the happiest man in the world and love her till the breath leaves my body.'

Clara felt tears prick her eyes at the sincerity in Declan's words and truly hoped that Minnie would take this second crack at happiness, and that after a gentle, undemanding courtship, Minnie would agree to marry such a kind and generous-hearted man. Unfortunately, Clara had forgotten about the Catholic Church, which seemed to worry ceaselessly about the moral fibre of its flock.

Minnie couldn't believe her eyes when she saw her good friend Clara climb out of Declan's car. She flew down the steps as the children launched themselves on Declan. As Clara hugged Minnie, she was glad that she had lost the skeletal thinness she once had.

'Oh, Clara,' she cried. 'It is so good to see you.'

'And I you,' Clara said. 'In fact, it is good to see all of you.'

The children looked healthier, and were warmly clad too, and the whole place looked much sprucer. They caused more than a little consternation when they walked to church, and Clara noticed the malevolent looks some of the women shot them and felt the first stirrings of alarm. Neither Minnie nor Declan seemed to notice anything, and so Clara resolved to say nothing,

151

half hoping that she had imagined the animosity.

After Mass they were glad to reach the cottage, for the day was raw, and, as soon as she did so, Clara felt assailed by the heat from the blazing fire. The low-slung grey clouds had darkened the sky and there was little light coming through the small window, but the Tilley lamps had been lit, one on the mantelpiece and one on the table already set for breakfast, and she knew that lighting the lamps in the daytime would once have been a luxury that Minnie would not have allowed herself. Now they lent a cheerful glow to the room and made it feel cosy and snug.

There were things Lucy had not told Clara when she'd spoken about her visit home: about how her family were preparing for Christmas. The room was festooned with streamers and the hearth was decorated with garlands of plaited holly with a Nativity scene on the mantel shelf. A fairly large and bushy Christmas tree stood by the window. It was threaded with tinsel and sparkly glass baubles that glittered and shimmered in the light from the fire and the lamps, the heat causing them to spin a little. The tree was further adorned with candles that, Minnie told her, they lit every evening, and a beautiful angel was fastened to the top.

The effect was lovely and very seasonal. Clara opened her mouth to say this but Minnie forestalled her.

'Grand, isn't it?' she said as she began layering rashers of bacon in the pan and Declan helped Clara off with her coat. 'Tell you the truth,' Minnie went on, 'I don't know who was the more

152

excited, Declan or the children.'

Declan had a broad smile on his face as he said, 'Ah, but you must allow me my moments of silliness. I am a bachelor and so I have never celebrated Christmas with a family before and seen delight on the faces of children.'

The delicious smell of frying bacon was in the air and Grainne cut slice after slice of soda bread and fetched a tub of yellow butter from the press, and the boys brought chairs and soon they were all sitting down to a big feed.

As they ate, they talked together and the years fell away as they reminisced. Clara couldn't remember when she had enjoyed a day so much. Minnie and Declan were easier together than many married couples she knew, Clara observed, and yet she wasn't sure if Minnie loved Declan enough to marry him, or was just grateful for his kindness.

Christmas in Windthorpe Lodge was quite a miserable affair. The meals sent out from the kitchen were just as good as they had been the previous year, but Lord and Lady Heatherington were so anxious about Clive that their worry seemed to permeate everywhere. A few meagre decorations were put up by Evie and Norah, but the tree that Jerry decorated was a poor specimen, for Jerry hadn't Clive's flair. Lucy saw it for the first time on her way to the library to collect her Christmas box on Christmas morning and thought the one at home in the cottage in Mountcharles looked much finer.

In the little cottage in Mountcharles, none of the gaiety was forced, for the children were beside themselves with excitement. Declan stayed the night on Christmas Eve, cramped up in the opened-out settle, because he wanted to see the children's faces when they found the stockings he had encouraged them to hang up were now filled to overflowing. In each one there was an orange and an apple, a bag of sweets, a chocolate bar and a thrupenny bit. And then in Danny's was a penknife with lots of gadgets, which Declan had seen him hankering after in Donegal, and a baseball bat sticking out of the top. Grainne had a paint box and a small sketchbook sticking out of hers. Liam had a whip and top and a big bag of marbles that Declan promised to teach him to play, and Sam had a selection of small toy cars and a wooden garage laid out on the floor.

For Minnie, Declan had a big parcel, and when she opened it she was rendered speechless with pleasure, for it was a thick black winter coat with a fur collar, and folded inside was a fur hat to match and black sheepskin mittens. 'Oh, Declan, thank you so much,' Minnie said when she was able to speak. Tears prickled her eyes at his kindness. She didn't let them fall, however. Christmas was not the time for tears.

They had to hurry for Mass, and as they went in together, many heads were turned to look at them and more than a few women viewed Minnie disapprovingly, especially as she was wearing such an obviously new and very fine coat. Minnie paid no heed to any of them and slipped out of Mass before Father McGinty could ask awkward questions, and home to a good big breakfast and to open the presents from Lucy.

After that, Minnie began to prepare the dinner, helped by Grainne, while Declan had a kickabout with the boys using the football Lucy had given Liam. The day continued to be wonderful. None of them could recall a better Christmas Day, and it filled Minnie's heart with joy to see such happy faces.

Two days after Boxing Day, Clara received a letter from Minnie. With a smile, she took it to her room, settled herself comfortably with a small glass of sherry and prepared to read of the wonderful Christmas her friend had enjoyed.

Initially, Minnie did just that, starting at Christmas Eve, when Declan helped her fill the children's stockings. She went on to explain that it had got so late and, anyway, Declan wanted to see the children's faces when they saw the presents, that they opened out the settle and he spent the night there. Clara smiled when she read that, for she knew that Declan was far too big a man to be truly comfortable on a settle, which was usually where the children would sleep. She had no inkling, though, of how this might be misconstrued. Minnie spoke of the children's delight at their presents the following morning and her own at the coat and accessories that Declan had bought for her, which she had worn to Mass. The first stirrings of concern came when Minnie wrote:

I saw some of the women looking at me malevolently

but I thought them jealous. I never thought it anything more sinister.

However, it was hideously far more menacing than that, and Clara felt the blood run like ice in her veins as she read on.

Then early on Boxing Day the priest and a hefty nun appeared at the door to remove the children to protect them for what they claimed were my immoral ways.

Clara gave a gasp. God Almighty! She knew the power the clergy had, and was well aware that they really could remove Minnie's children. She'd heard of it before, and on the flimsiest evidence of any wrongdoing by their mothers, and, once taken away, usually those mothers never saw them again. It was obvious Minnie knew this too, for she continued:

Declan had forgotten the hold the priests and the Catholic Church have on this country, but I should have thought, for it is how their minds work. They said I had a man who was unrelated to me here at all hours of the day and even staying through the night. The only one that knew Declan stayed Christmas Eve night would be Biddy McMullen, and I bet she had gone hotfoot along to tell the priest. I tried to tell them that the reason Declan had stayed the night on Christmas Eve, but they wouldn't listen. They said I had shown scant regard to the Catholic Church and even Jesus Christ himself by flaunting around in a fancy coat and hat I could never have afforded to buy myself to attend Mass on the holiest day of the year,

156

and even go to the rails for Communion, and all without a hint of shame. And when I said the coat was a present, they intimated that it was for services rendered. I was, they said, 'judged and found wanting, and so not fit to have the care of impressionable young people'.

Tears ran down Clara's cheek as she read of her friend's despair at the thought that she might lose her children. She felt her heartache keenly.

Oh, God, Clara, if they had taken my children, I wouldn't have wanted to go on. Danny, who had been up at Haycock's farm, was on his way home and, thank God, Declan arrived when he did because they had all the others in the car though they fought like wildcats. The priest had locked the boys in the back and I could hear them screaming and kicking the back of the car, and the nun manhandled Grainne, and she was kicking out at her legs and sobbing in fear while the priest prevented me from getting near them.

I was beside myself by then, screeching at them both and scared rigid, but Declan was just so angry, I thought he was going to kill the priest. He shook him like a rat and said if he ever came here again, his cloth wouldn't save him. I knew, though, the threat was an empty one because the next time the priest would come – and there would be a next time, for they never give up – they would probably bring the guards, and neither Declan nor I could do a thing about it then.

Even when the priest and nun had left, I was a nervous wreck. The vitriolic and unjust abuse thrown at me by both nun and priest had hurt me more than

157

blows would have done, and I felt bruised and battered and absolutely drained. The children had been badly frightened and were all in a state, even Danny, who felt a bit responsible that he hadn't been there to try and protect us.

We talked it over and over but really what Declan said was true. The only way for him to be able to keep us all safe was for us to marry. I was shocked, for Seamus is hardly cold, and then I never let myself feel anything for Declan but friendship, because I knew one day he would be going back to the States. Added to this, he had never given me any indication he felt for me in any way other than as an old friend. But then, Clara, you could have knocked me down with a feather because he said he loved me as much as he ever had.

Clara smiled grimly because it had been obvious how Declan felt about Minnie, but she imagined the shock he had felt, arriving in Mountcharles to find his good friend dead and the girl he loved not that long widowed. It wouldn't have been right at all to talk about his feelings but the events of Boxing Day had changed everything. She returned to the letter.

And he said that I shouldn't worry about my feelings for him too much, for deep liking for someone often comes before loving and he was prepared to take a chance on that. Marrying him, though, would mean that I would have to leave behind all that is familiar to me. I must say I felt suddenly saddened, when I realised this because I had been born and bred in Mountcharles and had never thought I would have to leave it. I thought of friends and neighbours I'd known for years and how kind and supportive many had been when Seamus was sick. I thought of the people who helped me when I cultivated the garden, telling me what seedlings to buy and how to tend them. I remembered the kindness of the man who gave me a present of the chickens, and the shop who used to let me barter my produce for essential items I couldn't grow and Farmer Haycock who had kept Seamus on long after he was of any use to him and now found work for Danny. And then I remembered that it would be some of those same neighbours who carried tales to the priest. Without Declan, the clergy would have taken my children from me and I knew then I would never feel safe in Ireland again and I doubt the children would either. It was far better for us all to start a new life with such a caring, considerate person as Declan McCann, and so we are to be married. Will you please try and explain this to Lucy, though I am writing to her as well? She might feel bad about it because Seamus has not been dead that long, but it really is the only way.

Clara sighed as she got to her feet. She fully understood the dilemma that Minnie had found herself in and really she had taken the only course of action she could. She never mentioned the word 'love' and maybe she didn't truly love Declan but would marry him to keep her and her children safe. Well, Clara reasoned, many had married a man for poorer reasons than that, and at least Declan was a decent man who would treat them all right, and love could always grow. She wished, though, Minnie hadn't got to go to America, for it was one hell of a long way away and she would probably never see her again once she left.

Still, this was no time to think of herself and she decided that she would bring Lucy into her rooms to talk to her in case she got upset.

Lucy did get upset when Clara told her of the letter she had received that morning, and she was also very angry. She jumped from the armchair Clara had directed her to, far too agitated to sit, and exclaimed, 'What's she doing marrying that man? And why are you telling me all this? Shouldn't it be Mammy?'

'She is writing you a letter,' Clara said. 'You'll likely get it tomorrow.'

'And you were asked to soften me up, were you?' Lucy said disparagingly. 'Well, that's not going to happen when my father's hardly cold. And he is buried here. Who is going to tend his grave with my mother in America?'

'You know the type of man your father was, Lucy,' Clara said. 'Would he rather your mother suffer in poverty and deprivation, and your brothers and sister as well, or else torn from your mother altogether just so that she can tend a grave that is nothing more than buried bones?'

Lucy gasped and Clara sat her back in the chair before sitting down beside her. 'I'm sorry if that upset you,' she said. 'It wasn't my intention. But I think you have to come to terms with the fact that after all this time that is probably all that is in your father's coffin. The essence of him has gone but it is in you and all your siblings, and memories of him will stay alive in your heart. That's far more important than flowers on a grave.'

'The younger ones won't remember him. How

would they?'

'I doubt Declan will let them forget your father,' Clara said. 'He will be able to tell them tales of him as a boy, of them growing up together.'

'That's all very well,' Lucy said truculently, 'but it is far too soon. My father died in March 1935 and I came here just before Christmas that year and now we have had another Christmas. My mother hasn't waited even two years.'

'The speed of the wedding was forced on them both,' Clara said. 'I told you about the priest and nun visiting and what they threatened to do. And your mother didn't go looking for anyone to take your father's place, remember.'

'Doesn't Mammy mind going all the way to America?'

'I suppose it is the lesser of two evils,' Clara said. 'I think she is far more frightened of the clergy, or at least the power they wield, than she is of starting again on a new continent entirely. If the priest and nun had had their way and succeeded in removing your siblings from the cottage it's highly unlikely you or your mother would ever see or hear of them again. How d'you think your mammy would ever have been able to cope then?'

Lucy doubted that she would be able to cope at all. 'It's just ... that man ... I just can't take to him,' she said eventually.

Clara reached for her hand and gave it a little squeeze. 'He isn't the devil incarnate, Lucy, really he isn't.'

Lucy gave a sniff and nodded.

'And he truly loves your mother and he makes her happy ... makes them all happy.'

'I know that too,' Lucy said brokenly.

'Then don't spoil it for her, Lucy,' Clara said. 'Put her happiness before your own because up until now she had been dealt a very bad hand in life.'

Unbidden in Lucy's mind, pictures flashed of her mother toiling in the garden or in the house, the clothes hanging on her sparse frame, her careworn face drawn with fatigue and extreme and constant hunger. Then she contrasted this with the last time she had seen her, with the light back in her eyes and a spring in her step. Her figure was fuller and so was her face, and she was happy and humming to herself. Lucy knew, however she felt, that she could not be the one to turn that light off.

'You're right,' she said to Clara. 'Mammy has suffered enough and I will not spoil it for her, but I will not go to America with them.'

'Lucy, if you stay behind, won't you miss them most dreadfully?'

Lucy shrugged. 'I missed them when I came here and I got over it,' she said. 'Anyway, Rory has been saying recently that the Master has a hankering to return to England in the spring and I want to go as well. I didn't think I could be- cause of leaving Mammy – leaving them all – but now that doesn't matter.'

'There you are then,' said Clara. 'Don't I always say that every cloud has a silver lining?'

NINE

Lucy couldn't understand why everyone in Windthorpe Lodge was interested in her mother getting married. She also worried that people might think it was too soon for Minnie to consider marrying again. There was no way she wanted to relate the whole incident with the priest and Clara was of like mind.

'There is no need to go into any of that,' she said. 'All we say is that Declan has to return to the States, and after losing Minnie once before he has no intention of leaving her behind.'

'Good,' Lucy said. 'To be honest I would be really embarrassed telling everyone what happened, and anyway, non-Catholics would probably not understand the iron grip the Church has over its parishioners and might imagine Mammy had been misbehaving in some way. I couldn't bear them to think badly of her.'

The explanation for the hasty marriage that Clara suggested was accepted by everyone and, as far as Clodagh was concerned, that made it even more moving.

'Oh, it's so romantic,' she said, as they got ready for bed that night. 'I mean, this Declan chap carried a candle for your mother all these years. I just can't understand, though, why you don't want to go to America with them.'

'I just don't,' Lucy said. 'I want to make my

163

own way in the world and go to England with the Heatheringtons. I thought you wanted that too.'

'Um, I don't know,' Clodagh said. 'I think if I was offered the chance to go to America, I'd grab it with both hands. Tell you something as well,' she went on, 'I might not stay in service long either when I go with the Heatheringtons to England, not if there is anything more lucrative going. I want more free time, don't you?'

Lucy shrugged. 'I suppose.'

'No suppose about it,' Clodagh said. 'I mean, you don't aim to be a nun, do you?'

Lucy giggled. 'Hardly.'

'It's no laughing matter,' Clodagh said. 'If we are never let out to places where we can meet chaps, we might as well be in a convent. Course I'm not going to breathe a word of this to my parents, but there is bound to be more and different kinds of work in Birmingham. More than here, in any case.'

'Not according to Mr Carlisle,' Lucy said. 'Seems England has a massive slump, the same as Ireland.'

'Maybe,' Clodagh conceded. 'But I think I would like to see that for myself.'

A few days after this, Clara told Lucy that Lady Heatherington wanted to see her. She was astounded because she had not spoken to Lady Heatherington since that first day when she had started at Windthorpe Lodge.

'Am I in trouble about something?' she asked Clara, anxiously, as they passed through the green baize door and into the passageway leading to the

164

main house.

'You are not in any trouble, of any kind,' Clara said with a smile. 'So you can take that frown off your face. She just said she would like to talk to you about your mother's impending marriage.'

Lucy sighed in relief and padded behind Clara without another word.

Lady Heatherington was in the library, and though she smiled, Lucy saw the sadness that lurked behind her eyes. 'Mrs O'Leary tells me that your mother is marrying a good man, known to you,' she said.

'Not known to me, my lady, but known to my mother for many years,' Lucy said. 'He was a friend of my father's and they grew up together. But he was in America and didn't know of my father's death until he came back to Ireland a couple of months ago. He knows Mrs O' Leary too because he was also a friend of her late husband.'

'And your mother is going back to America with him after the wedding — so we are going to lose you?'

'Oh, no, my lady, I'm not going with them.'

'Not going?'

'No, my lady,' Lucy said firmly. 'I have never had any desire to go to America. England, however, I have always wanted to see, and Mrs O'Leary said that you are thinking of returning to your old home soon and I would like to go with you, if at all possible.'

'Oh, it will be possible all right,' Lady Heatherington said. 'Cook has sung your praises very often. We will return in the springtime, and I would be quite happy to take you with us. Max-ted Hall is bigger than here and we do a lot of entertaining. More staff will have to be engaged and Cook, Mrs O'Leary and Mr Carlisle will be glad to have some staff already trained.'

'Yes, my lady.'

'But you are sure about this decision not to go to America? You'll not change your mind?'

'No, my lady,' said Lucy decisively. 'I will not change my mind.'

Minnie was another one who couldn't under-stand why Lucy was refusing such a wonderful opportunity, yet she was certain she would be able to win her round. So was Clara. She didn't want Lucy to leave – she had become very fond of her – but she was worried that she was wasting her young life in service, when a better more fruitful one might lie across the Atlantic Ocean. She knew she would have encouraged her own daughter to go to America, even if it meant she would never see her again.

Lucy was adamant in her refusal, though. 'I never want to be beholden to Declan. I want to make my own way.'

Clara saw Lucy's determined face, heard the steel in her voice, and knew that Lucy had made her decision. Minnie, though, refused to accept the excuses Lucy made about not going because Lucy could hardly give her mother the reason she had told Clara. The two younger boys were also very tearful that Lucy wasn't going to live in America with them, and Danny and Grainne lent weight to their mother's arguments.

Grainne said it was like some great adventure that she never thought would happen to her and she couldn't understand the point of view of anyone who thought differently.

'It's a new world, the Land of Opportunity,' Danny said, as he went for a walk with Lucy to try to change her mind. 'Why can't you see that?'

'Maybe I don't want a new world,' Lucy said. 'I like the one I am in just fine, and, as for opportunities, I prefer to make my own and not have someone hand them to me on a plate.'

'It isn't like that and you know it,' Danny protested. 'Lucy, you're cutting off your nose to spite your face.'

'Maybe,' Lucy said. 'But it is my life and I can decide what I want to do with it.'

Minnie was surprised that not even Danny had been able to talk Lucy round and, she realised, to have the man she was beginning to love and also to give the younger children a much better life, she would have to face the prospect of losing her eldest daughter. It would break her heart but she had to accept it.

'The door isn't shut,' Declan said. 'If she should change her mind sometime in the future then we will send for her, but for now if the girl so desperately wants to stay here then that is what she must do.'

Meanwhile, the plans for the wedding went ahead. Minnie wanted a no-fuss wedding and told Declan that she would buy nice outfits for them all from Magee in Donegal Town. 'It will be treat enough,' Minnie assured Declan, 'because I have never bought anything in that shop and it would be far more practical than buying special wedding clothes.'

Declan wouldn't hear of it. 'My darling girl,' he said, taking hold of Minnie's hands. 'I have waited seventeen years to marry the girl of my dreams and we have to do the job properly.'

To please him, Minnie agreed, and a dress-maker was called. Grainne told Lucy this, for Declan had also insisted on Lucy and Grainne being bridesmaids, and Lady Heatherington was very accommodating about allowing Lucy time off for fittings and so on.

'So what are the dresses like?' Clodagh asked her one evening on her return from a dress fitting, just a few days before the wedding.

'They're midnight-blue velvet, trimmed with ivory-coloured lace,' Lucy said, 'with the softest little waistcoats to wear over them, in the same ivory colour as the lace, and knitted in Angora wool so they're fluffy and warm. Declan got them from a mail-order shop in New York and he bought Grainne and me beautiful cream-coloured boots in the softest leather, silk stockings for us and Mammy, and a fringed silver cashmere shawl for Mammy to wear over her dress.'

'And what's her dress like?' asked Evie.

'Oh, there's hardly words to describe it,' Lucy said. 'It's ivory satin with a multitude of petti-coats that fall in soft folds. There is lace at the neck and the hems of the petticoats, and at the cuffs of the long sleeves, and seed pearls cover the bodice. The top petticoat is lace and caught up here and fastened with little blue rosebuds, and it rustles when she moves. The veil is set on a band covered with the same rosebuds and, now that her hair is thicker than it was, it curls a bit and the veil sort of encircles her curls.'

'Ah, it sounds lovely.'

'It is,' Lucy said. Her mother had tried on the whole outfit before she left that afternoon and it almost took Lucy's breath away. She hoped Declan recognised what a lucky man he was, and she suddenly realised how much she loved her mother and how much she would miss her when she sailed for America. But, she reminded herself, it had been her choice to stay behind. 'And you should see my brothers,' she continued to Clodagh. 'They all have suits, even Sam, and polished leather boots. Danny's is different from the younger boys' as he is going to walk Mammy down the aisle, so his is like Declan's: a grey pinstripe, and his silk tie matches the handkerchief in his top pocket. He has a good tiepin and cuff links as well. I have never seen any of them so smart before.'

'No expense spared, then?'

'No,' Lucy said. 'Declan said he is a wealthy man and for years he has had no one to spend his money on.'

'I suppose he has a point,' Clodagh said.

'Yes,' Evie agreed. 'After waiting so many years for your mother, he'll want everything absolutely right.'

Lucy was given the entire weekend off for the wedding and allowed to leave on Friday evening so that she would be at home on Saturday morning to help her mother dress.

169

Cook had made the wedding cake, which had two tiers, and, as she packed it carefully in the basket, she said, 'Tell your mammy to keep the top tier for the christening.'

Lucy gave a start, shocked to the core. She hadn't thought that her mother might have another child, a half-brother or -sister she'd never know. But then, she told herself as she made for the rail bus, her mother and Declan would hardly get up to any shenanigans at their ages.

On the morning of the wedding, Lucy stayed to help her mother dress, while Grainne went to help Mrs O'Leary lay out the food for the reception in the village tavern in the main street of Mountcharles. Then they got ready themselves.

'There is so much I want to say to you,' Minnie said, when she and Lucy were alone. 'And we have so little time. You are on the verge of womanhood and I always imagined I would be there by your side.'

'I thought so, too, Mammy,' Lucy said. 'I will miss you so very, very much.'

'And I you, my darling child,' Minnie cried. 'Oh, won't you now, even at this late stage, change your mind and come with us?'

Part of Lucy wanted to, and she almost said she would, but then she remembered that by agreeing she was beholden to Declan and therefore under his jurisdiction, and she couldn't bear that, especially if he started behaving like a father, ordering her about, perhaps, or arranging her life. She shook her head slowly and saw the tears glistening in her mother's eyes. 'I'm sorry, Mammy.'

Minnie sighed. 'Just promise me one thing,' she

said, and without waiting for a reply went on, 'Declan said the door is never shut and if ever you change your mind and you want to come over, he will send the tickets. You only have to write and say so. Will you promise to think about that if ever you change your mind?'

'I will, Mammy,' Lucy promised. It was the least she could do.

Since the altercation with the priest, they had not attended Sacred Heart church in Mountcharles but Clar Chapel, the other side of Donegal, on the way to Barnes Gap. Most people could not make that journey unless they had transport of their own so the reception was going to be held in Mountcharles. Farmer Haycock was drafted in to escort the wedding party. Declan took the boys, and Clara, so she could keep a weather eye on the younger ones, while Farmer Haycock, after delivering his own family, returned for Minnie and her bridesmaids.

When they arrived at the chapel, Danny was waiting for his mother in the porch. Lucy rearranged Minnie's dress in the few moments before the organ began the Wedding March. Then, Danny and their mother were walking in perfect step down the aisle, with Lucy and Grainne following behind.

Lucy saw Declan at the rails with his best man, Farmer Haycock, who had been a good friend to them all, and, as Minnie drew nearer, Declan turned. The look of absolute and total love in his eyes caused a large lump to form in Lucy's throat, which threatened to choke her. She knew whatever she felt about Declan, he loved her mother to

171

distraction. She might be homesick for Ireland at first, but with such love surrounding her she would have a happy life, the life she deserved.

After the Nuptial Mass, they went to the reception in Mountcharles, where the company was a select one. Some people resented the Cassidys' good fortune and others thought Minnie no better than she should be, and there had been some scathing looks and comments made in Mountcharles about her and her 'swanky American'. None of those people were invited to celebrate with Minnie and Declan on their special day. It was a great occasion all round, and the cake was praised by one and all, though Lucy was careful not to pass on Cook's comments about the top tier.

Everyone lined up outside to say goodbye to the family, and, as Minnie was bidding farewell to people she had known all her life, it was very emotional. It was particularly poignant saying goodbye to Clara, her friend from childhood, for she knew the barrier that would soon separate them was virtually insurmountable, and she kissed her, knowing that the chance of seeing her ever again was remote.

Then there was her daughter, looking at her with anguished eyes. As if by tacit agreement the crowd fell back. Lucy was suddenly filled with panic. Declan had arranged for a small bus to take them to Derry, where they would board the ocean liner SS *Caledonia,* and a sudden pang seemed to pierce her very soul as she realised that between her and the people she loved most in all the world was the gigantic Atlantic Ocean.

Spasms of regret were flowing through her and were so painful as she hugged her tearful mother that she almost said she had changed her mind, that she would go with them to America after all.

The Heatheringtons would understand. Clara could explain that in the end she couldn't bear for her family to be so far away, that it had proved too painful. It didn't help that Sam and Liam were clinging to her legs, both sobbing, and she could hardly see the tears falling down Grainne's cheeks nor the brightness of Danny's eyes because her own vision was blurred. Declan watched the upsetting scene, regretting that he had to tear his beloved Minnie away from her daughter. He dearly wished she would consider coming with them. But Minnie said she had talked to her and she was still adamant that she was staying behind, and he knew anything he said now was not going to help the situation.

Meanwhile, they had to make their way to the hotel in Derry, where they would stay the night before setting sail the following morning, and to further prolong their goodbyes would not help anyone, so he said, 'We really need to be getting on our way now, folks.' And so saying, he peeled Sam and Liam from Lucy and placed them gently on the bus, and Lucy saw their mournful faces pressed to the windows as she put her arms around Grainne and Danny.

Then there was just her mother, whom she embraced again. 'Remember what I said this morning, my darling girl,' Minnie said. 'It would make my joy complete if you were to come with us.'

Lucy was quite unable to speak and Clara

173

moved to be by her side as her mother moved sorrowfully away. Declan held out his hand and, for her mother's sake, she took hold of it, for she would do nothing to spoil her mother's special day. As Declan shook it, he reiterated what her mother had said, 'Your mother is right, Lucy, you will always have a home with us. If things don't work out, or for any other reason, if you want to come to the States, you just write and say so and I will send you a ticket and be glad to do so.'

'Thank you,' Lucy said, for she could hardly say anything else. As the family got aboard the bus and it roared into life, Clara's arm went around Lucy's shoulder, as if fearing she might run after it, as indeed she might have done. Everyone was waving, and those on the bus waved back but, when the little bus was just a dot in the distance, Lucy buried her head against Clara and cried her eyes out. But even through her distress she knew that for her the die was cast.

Lucy felt very despondent as the days passed and she thought it was lucky she had little free time to brood because by February they had started to pack up the house. The Heatheringtons would be leaving in early March and Lucy was at it all the time. At least it ensured that she was thankful to seek her bed and was asleep as soon as her head touched the pillow.

'Time is a great healer,' Clara said to Cook. 'And hard work. It certainly saved me going off my rocker altogether.'

'Well, I can find her plenty of work if you think that will help.'

'I think a change of scene might help her more just at the moment,' Clara said. 'The Mistress told me that she wants me to go ahead with the girls to get the house ready for them next week.'

'Evie won't be going.'

'I know, but I will have to engage more staff anyway, and nurses too, because the older Lady Heatherington will be joining us at the house. Lady Heatherington says she has become so frail that at least two nurses will be needed to deal with her.'

'Poor nurses, whoever they are. That's all I can say,' Cook said. 'But how am I to manage here without any staff?'

'Lady Heatherington told me that when we leave they intend staying at a hotel for a few days while we get the house to rights and get staff engaged, and they will sort out accommodation for you too.'

Cook nodded. 'Well, it might do Lucy some good, going somewhere completely different. It's maybe just the thing for her, and I hope it is because I miss her ready smile.'

Both Lucy and Clodagh were stunned when they were told that the departure to England was so imminent.

'I thought it would be a little later than this, when the spring had really taken hold,' Clodagh said.

'It was supposed to be,' Clara said, 'but the elder Lady Heatherington has become quite ill and the home hasn't the staff to deal with her, so Lord Heatherington is arranging to have her transferred to a suite of rooms in Maxted Hall. That is something else that has to be organised.'

Lucy was glad to be going and didn't care how soon it was. Only a few days later, she said a tearful farewell to Evie, who was returning to Donegal to work in her aunt's grocery store, and set her sights on Birmingham, England.

They began their travels early the following morning, when it was still as black as night, and, though the frost crunched under their boots and it was icy cold, Lucy felt a little thrill of excitement as the rail-bus station's lights came into view. Clodagh was excited too, but she couldn't really understand why because, as she had said to Lucy the previous night, as they undressed for bed, their lives were not going to change in any way, at least at first, because they would be doing exactly the same as they had at Windthorpe Lodge.

'I know that,' Lucy said, 'but I want to be in another place, away from the memories of Ireland. Anyway, travelling anywhere when you have never been that far from home before is a sort of adventure in itself.'

Clodagh agreed until she saw the huge steam train they had to change on to at Strabane station.

'This is the train that will take us halfway across Ireland, to the port at Dún Laoghaire, where we will catch the ferry to England,' Clara said.

Lucy thought the panting, puffing train, which lay like some strange untamed beast, was one of the scariest things she had seen, and she could see that Clodagh felt the same. Both girls were more than a little nervous travelling in it. This was especially so after they passed the throbbing engine at the front, which Clara said pulled the train, and saw the man in overalls feeding shovelful after shovelful of coal into a roaring furnace, which spat red and orange flames into the air. Sour smoke emanated from the brass funnel with a shrill, unearthly shriek that gave both girls such a fright they nearly jumped out of their skins.

Clara hid a smile, remembering how frightened she had been the first time she had heard that noise. 'Don't worry, that screech is just the funnel letting some air out. Let's get on board quickly before the train goes without us. It would never do to miss the ferry.'

The train was jam-packed with people but, even so, their journey south was uneventful. To fill the empty hours, Clodagh and Lucy asked about the area they would soon be at work in.

'We will be living in a place called Streetly,' Clara said, 'and the nearest town to us is Sutton Coldfield. It is only a small market town, but it has a cinema.'

'Ooh,' Clodagh said. 'I would just love to see a film, wouldn't you, Lucy?'

'I suppose,' she said. 'I've never thought of it much.'

'I'm sure you would love it, Lucy,' Clara said. 'There are cinemas peppered all over Birmingham, but they say that dancing is all the rage now.'

'Dancing?'

Clara smiled. 'Yes, the quickstep, the foxtrot and the waltz – dances like that. I read in the papers there are dancing classes everywhere. It seems to be the most amazing fun and there are

177

certainly plenty at it.'

Lucy's eyes met Clodagh's and they both wondered if they were ever going to be able to sample this tremendous fun or would have to be content just to hear about it, but there was nothing to be gained by going down that road yet.

So instead, Lucy said to Clara, 'Is anyone living in the house?'

'No,' Clara said, 'but Bert Mason and his wife, Hilda, live in the lodge at the entrance to the drive. They will be keeping the house aired, lighting fires and such, and Hilda at least will probably be there to welcome us. Mr Carlisle will have sent them a telegram by now. She is a very good cook, Hilda, though I would never mention this to Ada Murphy in a week of Sundays. I have no death wish.'

Lucy and Clodagh grinned.

'Anyway,' Clara went on, 'Hilda prides herself on a good table, so she will probably have something ready to eat when we do arrive.' She looked at the two girls and said, 'We're nearing the docks now and the wind is high, which might mean a turbulent crossing for us. I hope you two are good sailors. Seasickness can be wretched.'

'Are there many sick?'

'Oh, a fair few if the weather is rough enough.'

'Well, we'll soon find out if we are or not,' Lucy said. 'Thank God, the crossing only takes three and a half hours.'

Just a few minutes later the train steamed into Dún Laoghaire, and Clara led the way to the ferry looming majestically before them. The day

178

had begun while they travelled on the train, and Lucy and Clodagh now looked about them with interest, quite awed at the sight of the ferry. However, there was no time to stop and stare, for the train passengers were moving towards the ship in droves and they were carried along with them.

Once on board they put their cases down, with a sigh of relief, leant over the rail and looked down on the teeming noisy dockside. Sailors seemed to be everywhere, calling out to one another as they loaded the ferry with cargo and with more and more people. Then there were those travellers who were bidding farewell to loved ones and friends on the dockside. Some wept, others laughed and joked, some hugged and kissed, and others formally shook hands before mounting the gangplank.

The ship was listing slightly in the scummy grey water lapping the sides of it. The girls watched as the gangplanks disappeared. Then the ship's hooter gave a screech similar to that of the trains, setting the wheeling seagulls squealing as black smoke belched into the air. A few moments later, Lucy felt the engines begin to throb. Her shining eyes met those of Clodagh and Clara. She was barely able to believe that soon she would leave Ireland far behind, and she felt exhilaration spread all through her body.

As the ship began to move, people on the dockside waved and shouted. Lucy, taken up with the moment, waved too, as the ship pointed towards the two piers it had to negotiate between before it would be out in the open sea.

Beyond the piers the sea became more tempestuous as the waves rose and fell and everyone was tossed from one side to the other. The girls watched the ship plough its way through the broiling water, sometimes riding the crest of a turbulent wave or carried on a roller, only to crash down into the water again with a cascade of foam. As the sea became rougher and the ship gathered speed, more and more people deserted the salons to be sick over the side.

Eventually, though, they were driven inside by the icy-cold rain lashing into them, but the smell was almost overpowering, for the salons stank of people crowded together, damp clothes and a whiff of vomit from those who hadn't made it outside in time. Cigarette smoke hung in the air like a blue fug and over all this was the pervading smell of Guinness. It gagged in Lucy's throat, but the rain-soaked deck was not inviting either.

'Come on,' Clara said. 'We'll go to the canteen. It has to be better than this.'

'I'm all for that,' Clodagh said. 'I could murder a cup of hot tea anyway.'

They reeled and stumbled from side to side as they tried to make their way to the canteen, but when they got there it was warm and welcoming with a wholesome smell of cooking food in the air. Lucy saw with surprise that there were pink curtains at the portholes.

Porridge, toast and jam and a pot of tea was one and six and, as Clara had been given travelling expenses, she decided to treat all three of them. Lucy had to admire the waitresses crossing the heaving floor to serve them, and the diners had to hold tight to plates, bowls and cups, to prevent them sliding off the table. It had been a long time since Clara and the girls had eaten the sandwiches Cook had packed. They did justice to the meal and felt a lot better after it. They were tired already, yet they knew after the ferry docked there was another hefty train ride before they reached Birmingham.

Lucy had got so used to fighting to keep her balance, it felt strange to be on solid ground again when she left the ferry. The rain was still coming down in sheets and she, Clara and Clodagh hurried quickly into the station where the train was waiting for them,

Lucy settled herself back on the seat and closed her tired eyes, and the next thing she knew she was being roused from her sleep by Clara as they pulled into New Street Station. They gathered their things together and stepped out on to the busy, noisy platform. Full darkness had fallen while Lucy had slept but the station was lit by dim lamps, and in the swathes of light she could see the throngs of people around her. Trains were clattering in from other platforms, stopping with squeals of brakes and hisses of steam, while porters, their trolleys piled high, weaved between the people, cautioning them to, 'Mind your backs, please.'

Nearby a newspaper vendor was obviously ply-ing his trade, but Lucy could not decipher a word, just as she couldn't understand the loud, but indistinct, disembodied voice telling people which platform to go to and which train to catch.

'What's he saying?' Clodagh asked.

'No idea,' said Clara. 'Never have been able to work it out. Never mind, we've arrived where we should have done and now all we have to do is find a taxi.'

'A taxi!' squealed Lucy, almost in disbelief. In her experience, only rich people rode in taxis. Her eyes met the equally astonished ones of Clodagh and the girls were glad to follow Clara, who seemed to know just what to do. She wasn't even fazed when they walked out of the station after her and were met by a volume of traffic such as they had never seen before. Cars, vans, lorries, horse-drawn carts – all vied for space, their headlights gleaming on the wet streets, and another clanking swaying monster ran along rails set into the road. Clara ignored it all, as if it were commonplace and went straight to the taxi rank.

'Pity it's too dark for you to see Birmingham city centre,' she said. 'It's well worth a visit.'

Lucy couldn't see Clodagh's face in the dimness of the taxi, but she didn't need to. She knew Clodagh would feel very much as she did. They were being driven through the first city Lucy had ever been in, and she thought it very frustrating to be able to see nothing but indistinct grey shapes, with, now and again, a tantalising glimpse of a store or an office block caught in the pool of light from a streetlamp.

It seemed darker still as they left the city centre behind and drove along the endless lanes. The rain continued to fall and Lucy was almost lulled to sleep again by the hypnotic sound of the swishing wipers.

She was just closing her eyes when suddenly

Clara said, 'Oh, Bert's waiting for us.' Lucy saw a figure dressed head to foot in oilskins to the side of the road ahead of them, waving a lamp, causing the raindrops caught in the beam to look as though they were doing a dance.

The taxi driver slowed down and stopped, and the man in the oilskins stuck his head through the window and said to Clara in the broadest Brummie accent Lucy had ever heard, 'Hello, Mrs O'Leary. Good to see you back.'

'Thank you, Bert,' Clara said. 'Nice to be back. Hilda not about?'

'She's up at the house, likely, with the kettle on,' Bert said. 'She has a pan of stew ready for you and all the fires lit, rooms aired and the beds made up and warmed.'

'Oh, she is an angel,' Clara said fervently.

Bert chuckled. 'Can be the very devil too sometimes, as I know to my cost.' Then he turned to the taxi driver and said, 'I've opened the gate so you can drive straight up to the house.'

'Right-oh,' said the driver, and he turned the taxi through some wrought-iron gates. Lucy heard the tyres scrunch and guessed they were going down a gravel drive. The house was caught in the beam of headlights and Lucy saw it was enormous. It had imposing steps leading up to a balcony stretching along its length and many beautiful windows. She looked forward to seeing it properly in the daylight. The man drove his taxi to the back because he knew his passengers were not the owners of such a property and so wouldn't enter through the front door.

Clara got out and paid the fare, while the two

girls scrabbled after her. Then she led them to a door in the centre of the building as the taxi pulled away.

'This is the way to the kitchen, which is where our supper will be,' she said, and she opened the door and waved them through. 'Come in, and welcome to Maxted Hall.'

TEN

The girls looked about with interest as Clara led Lucy and Clodagh to a sort of dimly lit lobby, where they could take off their damp outer things and deposit their bags before following her into the kitchen. Warmth enveloped them, most of which Lucy, blinking a little in the light, saw came from the enormous range, twice the size of the one in Ireland. A delicious smell set her stomach rumbling as she realised how hungry she was.

The kitchen too was much bigger than the one in Windthorpe Lodge. Either side of the range were floor-to-ceiling cupboards, and on the far wall were shelves stacked with gleaming copper pans. A scrubbed table was set on the shiny quarry tiles in the middle of the room. Hilda, had obviously laid the table for them. She was a buxom, homely looking woman with a mass of frizzy grey hair and an apron tied around her waist. The smile on her round open face lit up her blue eyes, and she fussed over them like a mother hen, with a voice as broad Brummie as her husband's.

She was so pleased to see Clara back, and very welcoming to Lucy and Clodagh, and was delighted by the news Clara gave her about Lord Heatherington's recovery.

'Best thing I have heard in ages,' she said. 'The place has been dead without the family. Now I'm sure in no time it will be back to normal. I am longing to see Master Clive too.'

Hilda didn't know that Clive had given up his place at university to fight in the Spanish Civil War and that no one had heard from him since he'd left.'

'His parents must be distraught,' she said, when Clara told her.

'They are, of course,' Clara said. 'According to Rory, Lord Heatherington intends to go to Liverpool once he is in England, which is where Clive sailed from, and see if he can find any information on where he might be.'

Hilda sighed and her eyes darkened with sadness. She opened her mouth as if she were about to say something more, but then saw Lucy's hungry eyes fastened on hers and said instead, 'Tch, tch. Here's me standing talking when I'm sure you think your throats are cut.' She lifted the pan off the range and began ladling stew into deep bowls, which she placed on the table. 'And Bert will be waiting for his bite of supper too, so I will leave you to it,' she said, as they all eagerly sat down around the table.

When she had gone, Clara smiled at the girls, and said, 'Hilda has a very strong maternal in-

185

stinct and no one to lavish it on but Bert now her children have left home.'

'Ah, I think she's nice,' Lucy said. 'And this stew is delicious. But as you advised, I'll never say that to Cook.'

'Nor will I,' Clodagh said, her eyes twinkling. 'I agree with you, Lucy, but I like my head firmly fastened.'

The two girls laughed together and, when Clara joined in, Lucy realised how free and easy they had become while travelling together. Clara obviously felt it too because she suddenly said, 'I've been thinking that this "Mrs O'Leary" is a bit nonsensical in this day and age, and though standards have to be maintained in the house, certainly when we are alone, I can be referred to as "Clara".'

'Oh, I'd like that,' Lucy said. 'It's more friendly, somehow.'

'Yes, it is,' Clara agreed. 'But both of you remember that there will be no change in the kitchens with other staff around.' And a smile played round her mouth as she added, 'If only to stop Mr Carlisle having a fit of apoplexy. Can't blame him totally,' she went on. 'It's all he has ever known and, while the world outside might change, he wants things done as they always have been done.'

'Life isn't like that, though, is it?' Lucy said.

'No,' Clara said, 'nor should it be. We have to adapt to the changes and Mr Carlisle might find that out for himself.'

Lucy thought so too, but she didn't say so because she was suddenly overcome with weariness.

She dragged herself to her feet and began to collect up the plates and bowls.

Clara put her hand on her arm. 'Leave them for tonight,' she said. 'You both look dead on your feet. And mind,' she cautioned, pointing her finger in a dictatorial way, 'that is something else Mr Carlisle is to be unaware of. Goodness me, the man would not be able to sleep in his bed if he knew that we had left dirty pots in the sink.'

Despite their weariness the two girls grinned at one another. Clara urged, 'You go on up. You will be in the attics like you were at the house in Ireland. But, as Bert said, the rooms will have been aired for you and the beds warmed.'

And they found Clara was right. Pottery hot-water bottles were upended in two of the beds and the bedding tucked in, keeping them that way so that there were little pools of warmth for the girls to sink into. They lost no time in shedding their clothes, pulling nightwear out of their cases they'd retrieved from the lobby and climbing in between the crisp sheets and soft blankets. Lucy had assumed that she and Clodagh would talk about it way into the night, but the first thing she remembered was waking up to the pearly dawn of a late February morning.

At breakfast the next morning, Clara told them that she would be interviewing all day, and, as there was little for them to do, they might as well take themselves into Sutton Coldfield for a look around. 'Take the opportunity to do this before the family return,' she advised, 'for once they do, you'll be hard at it. If the day was a better one, I

187

would advise Sutton Park, for it is well worth a visit, but it will be better still when the spring really sets in. Anyway, get yourselves ready and we'll be off.'

'Are you coming with us?'

'As far as Sutton,' Clara said. 'The interviews are being held at the Royal Hotel, so it makes sense to go in together and I can show you the ropes on the buses and so on.'

The girls were quite happy with that. Lucy was a little unnerved by the thought of using the buses.

When they arrived they went their separate ways. The girls wandered about, looking around the shops, and Lucy admitted to Clodagh that she was a little disappointed.

'I mean, it's pretty enough and all that,' she said, 'and looks really nice with all the trees at the sides of the road, but it's no bigger than Letter-kenny and I haven't seen the cinema that Clara spoke of either.'

'I'd like to do more than see it,' Clodagh said. 'I'd like to go inside and see a film.'

Lucy's heart leapt. 'Oh, Lord,' she breathed, 'that would be just so exciting.'

'Then we'll have to find it before we can do anything. Let's ask someone.'

They did ask and found the cinema was not near the nucleus of shops but quite a way up a long straight road. It was a huge tall building to the side of an extremely elegant curved frontage with CINEMA written on the top of it in big letters in case there should be some doubt. Lucy felt her body tingle with excitement as she went up

188

the curved steps and peered through the mottled glass to the magical world beyond. It had posters on the walls, depicting films that they were showing now, and those to come, and Lucy's eyes were drawn to one in particular: *Captain January,* starring the little girl star Shirley Temple. She gave a sigh.

'Penny for them,' Clodagh said, coming to join her.

'Don't know if they're worth a penny,' Lucy said, 'but I would just love to see that film.'

Her mother, in one of her many letters, told her that she had seen it in New York. She hadn't answered that letter, in fact she didn't answer any letters they sent her any more, because of the photograph included in one of them of her family all standing outside a fine house that Declan was buying for them.

Lucy had studied the picture for a long time. She saw the proprietary arm Declan had draped over her mother's shoulder and she realised that they were a family, already complete, and in that picture, in their lives, there was no space for Lucy. It seemed suddenly as if a deep chasm had opened up between her and the mother she had once adored.

'Well, let's ask Clara if we can come here tomorrow afternoon after Mass.'

Lucy considered it. Maybe seeing the same film as her mother might make her feel a little closer to her, especially if she felt she could write to her about it. 'All right,' she said. 'We had best make our way back now.'

'There's a bus stop across the road,' said Clodagh. 'Let's see if any of the buses go to Streetly.'

Clara was in the house when the girls returned. She looked exhausted and admitted she was glad of the meal that Hilda had cooked. The girls too had a good appetite and no one said anything for a time as they were too intent on eating. Hilda said it warmed her heart to see that. 'Best thing you can bring to a table is a good healthy appetite. A full stomach puts a different complexion on things altogether. Now have you all got room for a piece of nice apple pie and custard?'

They did, and it was while they ate the apple pie that Clara told them about the people she had seen that day. 'I have seen a vast change in the attitudes of the young people,' she said. 'In fact, I doubt that I would have got anyone at all if there hadn't been such a massive slump throughout the country. Anyway, Lucy, I talked things over with the Mistress before I left and she felt it right that your job changes as I suggested.'

'Oh?'

'Yes,' Clara said. 'I have engaged a new scullery maid, and you will be a tweeny, which means you will sometimes help Cook and Clodagh and sometimes the housemaid, and you are each to have a wage rise: ten shillings for you, Lucy, and, Clodagh, you will have twelve and six.'

Both girls gasped. It was good money, and to Lucy it seemed riches because she could have it all. Her family no longer needed money from her and hadn't accepted anything since December so she had saved her money, not being used to spending it on herself.

'So now, tell me what you have been doing with yourselves today?' Clara asked. The girls told her about all the things they had seen in Sutton Coldfield and the shops they had gone into.

'And did you find the cinema?'

Lucy nodded eagerly. 'Yes, it's called the Odeon and it's wonderful. *Captain January* is showing, with Shirley Temple, and I really would like to see that.'

'Why that particular film?' Clodagh asked.

'Because my mother went to see it in New York and wrote and told me all about it,' Lucy said.

'Oh...'

Clara could see that Clodagh hadn't grasped the significance of that, and she hid a smile as she said, 'I have never seen the cinema myself because it was only just being built as we moved to Letterkenny. So what d'you say to us taking a dander up there tomorrow afternoon?'

'Ooh, yes,' Lucy cried, and Clodagh nodded avidly. Though she hadn't a clue why what film Lucy's mother saw in New York had any relevance to what Lucy saw in Sutton Coldfield, if it meant they got to see a film of any sort then she was ready for it.

'You are a clot, Lucy,' she said fondly.

Clara laughed at both of them before asking Lucy, 'Will you write and tell your mother about the film?'

Lucy hung her head and mumbled, 'Yes, I probably will.'

'You haven't written for ages, have you?' Clara said gently.

Lucy's head shot up. 'How do you know that?'

'Because I write to your mother as I always have,' Clara said. 'And she told me. She would love a letter from you. She says they have all written to you but you have not replied.'

Lucy flushed. She didn't know how to explain to Clara how detached those letters made her feel. The first one, written not long after they arrived in New York, had mentioned that they had all started school, even Danny, and they said the schools were huge – nothing like the small low building in Mountcharles – and the American school teachers far less strict than those in Ireland.

But the most exciting and entertaining thing that happened not long after they had arrived in New York was that snow had fallen and lots of it. Declan had bought them a big sledge and taken them to a place called Pilgrim Hill in Central Park to use it. They said lots of other people were doing the same thing and afterwards, back home, they had built the biggest snowmen ever. They had sent a photograph of them grouped around the snowmen. Lucy had noted how warmly they were dressed, in thick snowsuits and hats, gloves and scarves and big boots. She knew the cold would not have touched them and remembered when it had snowed in Donegal, their clothes were generally too threadbare for them to be able to play out in the cold for long. Her mother's first letter said how much she was missing Lucy, and told of the vibrant city full of people of all colours and creeds. She said the very tall buildings were dubbed skyscrapers, and little wonder, and she described the huge and lavishly stocked shops.

The next letters told her about the cinema, and the boys wrote about the ball games they'd seen. In contrast, Minnie's letter spoke again of how Lucy was missed and she told her how beautiful parts of New York were, which she would love her to see.

'Why haven't you written, Lucy?' Clara asked, jerking her back to the present.

Lucy shook her head. 'I didn't think they'd want to hear. Why would they when they're having such a fine time in New York?'

'Lucy, how can you say such things?' Clara cried. 'You are part of the family. Do you think because they don't see you that you don't matter? They will never forget you, and your mother, I know, will always feel the loss of you.'

Lucy was suddenly filled with shame, and she wondered if not writing to her family was her way of punishing them for leaving her behind. If that was so it was unfair of her because she had chosen to remain. They were just making every effort to settle down in their new life. How inconsiderate and self-centered she was.

'I will write to Mammy,' she promised Clara. 'I will write to them all.'

The following afternoon, as they made for the bus, Clara remembered her brothers taking her on her first visit to a cinema many years ago in an effort to take her mind off the terrible double tragedy she had suffered. Though she had desperately wanted to go, she had fought against it, feeling it was disloyal to the memory of her husband and daughter to go out anywhere, but they had been so insistent that in the end she had

193

agreed. She had thought the cinema a magical place, though she had felt terribly guilty laughing at the antics of Charlie Chaplin when she thought she would never laugh again. She had not been to the cinema in years and she intended to remedy that now and build a life for herself beyond work.

The bus they took stopped just outside the cinema, and Clodagh and Lucy alighted from it in a state of great excitement. A very important-looking man stood on the steps. He was dressed in a dark blue coat, which reached his knees, with epaulettes decorated with gold piping on his shoulders and a row of medals pinned to his chest. The coat was fastened with shiny brass buttons and a belt with a brass buckle, and he also had a shiny peaked military-style cap. Clara said he was a commissionaire.

Suddenly the commissionaire threw open the doors and the crowds surged forward into the foyer. Lucy gazed around her, open-mouthed because she felt as if she was bathed in golden light from the sparkling chandeliers hanging from the ceiling, lighting up the posters of a film called *Swing Time*, starring Fred Astaire and Ginger Rogers, which looked such immense fun. Beneath her feet was a gleaming patterned floor, while in front of her were wide stairs, the deep carpet fastened with shiny brass stair rods, the walls to the side decorated with elaborately patterned wallpaper.

When, minutes later, she walked up the stairs behind Clara and Clodagh, she felt her feet sink into that deep red carpet. She was so excited that she was standing in a cinema and that very soon she would be watching moving pictures.

The auditorium took her breath away completely, and she gave a gasp as Clara opened the double doors. It was so vast and filled with dark red velvet seats in front of a thick velvet curtain. A lady in a blue uniform with silver embroidery on the front and shoulders of a silver-buttoned jacket, took the tickets Clara had just bought and ripped them in half. Then Clara led the way down the steps to the seat number they had been allocated. Lucy shuffled her way along the row and thought the seats very high and uncomfortable until Clara showed her that they folded down.

'They're flip-up seats,' she said. 'Then if people want to get past you for some reason, you can stand up and the seats flip up behind you and there's more room for them to get through, see?'

Clodagh had done the same thing as Lucy and she quickly folded hers down too.

Lucy asked Clara, 'And who's the lady who ripped your ticket up?'

'She's an usherette. Did you notice the silver torch on her belt? If people come in when the film has started, and the whole place is in darkness, then she has to use her torch.'

'It goes darker than this, then?'

'Oh, yes, much darker.'

'Ooh, Clara,' Lucy said, hugging herself with delight. 'I can hardly wait.'

'You won't have to. Look.'

The thick curtain began to rise to reveal thinner curtains underneath and, when these were gathered to each side, Lucy's dancing eyes met

195

those of Clodagh, who she saw was feeling the same way. Then the lights began to dim, a whirring sound began behind them, and Lucy saw the beam of light directed on to the screen.

She loved everything about her first trip to the cinema. Even the trailers for what was coming next, and the B film, and the cockerel heralding Pathé News. She was very surprised when the lights came on again after that and usherettes appeared down each aisle, carrying trays around their necks.

'What sort of ice cream do you want?' Clara asked them.

The two girls stared at her, stunned, and had no idea what to ask for, so Clara bought three choc ices and Lucy thought it was by far and away the loveliest thing she had ever eaten.

The film itself, *Captain January,* captivated both girls. All the way home they talked about Shirley Temple, known as 'America's sweetheart', and how well she could sing and dance and act. In her head, Lucy began composing the letter she would write to her mother, so glad that they had watched the same film, though they were thousands of miles apart.

Lucy knew she needed some new clothes, for the ones she had had become a wee bit shabby and, also, were way too short and tight now. However, despite the little nest egg she had saved up, she'd been astounded by the prices of clothes in the shops in Sutton Coldfield. As they sat around the table, eating the evening meal after the visit to the cinema, she voiced her concerns.

'Well, the Bull Ring in the city centre is the place for bargains,' Clara said. 'You'd get far more for your money there. Tell you what, as long as the rain isn't teeming from the heavens the three of us will take a trip to Birmingham and the Bull Ring tomorrow.'

Luckily, the next day was dry, though incredibly cold, and they set off in a buoyant mood and caught the bus all the way to the city centre. Lucy, on her rare visits to Letterkenny, thought it busy enough but when she alighted from the bus she was amazed at the scurrying crowds filling the pavements and the constant rumble of the numerous vehicles on the roads.

Most alarming of all were the large swaying and clattering monsters that ran along rails in the roads that Clara told them were called trams. 'Glad there are none of those our way,' Lucy said. 'I can manage rail buses and ordinary buses, and even trains, but I wouldn't go in one of these for a pension. It doesn't seem safe to me.'

Clodagh nodded in agreement. 'And what's that stink? It's caught right at the back of my throat.'

'That's the petrol fumes mainly,' Clara said. 'It's a city smell. You'll get used to it. Like you'll be hopping on and off trams without thinking about it before long.'

Lucy shook her head determinedly. 'I don't think so.'

'One day,' Clara said with a smile, 'I might remind you of this conversation. But are we going to stand and discuss the trams or do you want to look around the shops before we make for the Bull Ring?'

197

'The shops, definitely,' the girls said in unison.

They were enchanted by the shops and stores that Clara led them into. There was one strange one called Lewis's, which seemed to be in two shops either side of a small cobbled street. 'That's a department store and sells everything,' Clara said. 'It joins up on the third floor and is all one shop, and there are seven floors altogether. But come on because there are lots more to see.'

They admired the highly decorated shop windows. Many shops were on more than one floor, with moving stairs between, much more entertaining to use than lifts, Lucy thought. Some of the women's clothes for sale were draped on models set around the stores and were so beautiful that Lucy and Clodagh were often rendered speechless. Lucy thought she would be a little apprehensive to work in such salubrious surroundings, handling the most delicate and gorgeous fabrics, but most of the assistants were very elegant and appeared self-assured, and punched in the prices of customers' purchases with great aplomb on massive silver cash registers.

But the shops both girls preferred had no tills or cash registers at all. There the bill for the articles purchased was written out by the assistant and put with the money into a canister. This was carried on wires crisscrossing the shop until it reached the cashier, who would sit in a high glass-sided office. She would issue a receipt and this, together with any change, would be put into the canister and the process reversed. Lucy and Clodagh found it really enthralling, and their excitement made Clara smile.

They had spent longer than Clara had thought they would, for everything was so new to the country girls, but she had recognized that and not wanted to rush them too much.

'Come on,' she said at last. 'What do you say to a bowl of soup and a roll before we hit the Bull Ring? My treat?'

'It would be terrific,' Lucy said. 'I didn't realise how hungry I was, but are you sure?'

'Course I am. Lyons Corner House, which does very good soup, is just here, a stone's throw away from the Bull Ring.'

The delicious soup and warmed crispy roll put new heart into them, and after it they followed Clara down an incline with shops of every description grouped along it, even a pet shop with a parrot tethered outside, squawking to everyone as they passed.

'I've never seen a parrot before,' Clodagh said. 'Does he really talk?'

'He repeats what you say to him, when he wants to,' Clara said, 'but you can't have a meaningful conversation with him.'

Lucy barely heard Clara's words because they were by then at the bottom of the incline and on the cobbled streets of the Bull Ring. She looked around with amazement and she sniffed the air, fragrant from all the blooms of the flower sellers grouped around a statue. 'That's Nelson,' Clara said as they approached. 'He was a famous admiral.'

All around, hawkers plied their wares, crying out what they had to sell or bartering with the customers. There was a special smell too, from

199

barrows selling fish, vegetables, fruit, meat and cheese, mixed with those selling curtain material, bedding, antiques and junk, and there were cheap crockery and pans in baskets on the ground. One strident voice rose above the clamour: that of an old lady selling carrier bags and telling everyone about it, 'Carriers, handy carriers!' Clara said that no one could remember a time when she wasn't there. 'And she always stands in that same place,' she went on. 'In front of Woolworths – that's nicknamed the tanner shop because nothing there costs more than sixpence.'

'Sixpence, is that true?'

'Oh, it's true all right,' Clara said, 'so if you ever have the odd tanner then you can go in there and buy something.'

'Look, the hawkers' barrows sweep all the way down to that church at the bottom,' Clodagh said.

'It's nice, isn't it?' Lucy said, 'ringed by trees like that?'

'Well, the church is called St Martin in the Fields,' Clara said. 'No fields now anywhere near, but there must have been when the church was built. I want to take you to the Rag Market, so we have to go down by the church. Watch out for trams and dray horses!'

Inside the Rag Market was a different world. Normally, Lucy would have little idea of the price of clothes because she had never had the money to buy anything, but she had noted the prices in Sutton, and in some very expensive shops and stores in Birmingham today, where the price tags had staggered her. The Rag Market was completely different, and though some of the clothes were not new, they were all of good quality and cheap. Lucy was able to buy herself two winter dresses, a cardigan and a jumper and skirt, which all fitted her a treat, as well as much-needed underclothes, including a couple of brassieres, which Clara declared were quite the latest thing.

Clodagh had treated herself to a new dress and cardigan too, and before they undressed for bed later that night they tried on the new clothes. Lucy felt again the glow of happiness she had had when Clara had bought her the new garments to start at Windthorpe Lodge, but it was enhanced by the fact that these were bought with money she had earned herself and she was astounded the difference the brassieres made to her shape and how comfortably they cupped her budding breasts.

Lucy's enthusiasm for a few new clothes touched Clara, and she knew that she was the sort of daughter to be proud of. Keeping a weather eye on her, as she had promised Minnie she would, had eased the ache in her own heart a little. But she knew that now there was work to do to make the house ready for the family. On Tuesday morning, she said, 'Now, we've had a few days off but we must get this house into shape. Lucy and Clodagh, you can start cleaning the bedrooms, please, because I have got to conduct some more interviews.'

It was as they were removing the dust sheets, which Clara told them had to be packed up for the laundry, that Clodagh said, 'You know what I said about leaving service at the first opportunity?'

Lucy nodded.

'Well, I think I would be stupid to leave at the moment. I mean, even from the bus, we saw the gangs of men hanging about the streets. And in the Bull Ring we saw the ragged, barefoot children and the women with babies tied up in shawls, and the veterans from the last war reduced to begging or trying to sell things from trays. So old Carlisle was right. But if I am staying I want a different working pattern from the one we had in Letterkenny and I am going to insist on it. You should too if you have the gumption to stand up for yourself.'

'There is nothing wrong with my gumption, Clodagh Murray, I will have you know!' Lucy exclaimed.

'All right, keep your hair on,' Clodagh said. 'Trouble with you is you are too anxious to please; don't like upsetting people.'

'Yes, but–'

'Look, Lucy,' Clodagh said, 'the gentry won't change things for the likes of us, because as long as their lives are comfortable that is all they are concerned about. But I came to work "in service", not "in slavery", and while I have no objection to doing a decent day's work I want a bit of a life of my own as well. Are you with me or not?'

'Yeah, I'm with you.'

'Right,' Clodagh said. 'I think the first thing to do is talk it over with Clara. She makes most of the decisions anyway, seems to me.'

Clodagh was not the type of girl to wait when

she had something to say and so once Clara arrived home and they sat to eat the lunch Hilda had made, she waited only until the woman left before telling Clara of her concerns about the time they were allowed off once the family were back and they were working to capacity again.

Clara was tired, it had been a long morning, but at the end of it she had engaged a night nurse and a day nurse for the older Mrs Heatherington, and they had come with a load of demands too. As nurses they could pick and choose their employment and so Clara had had to agree to what she thought were vastly inflated salaries, and working conditions and regular time off that they wanted written into their contracts.

She knew that world was changing and young people didn't appear to see any pride in being 'in service', but rather the reverse, and all the kitchen staff and housemaids had to be given more freedom, and that included Lucy and Clodagh.

'We can't decide anything definite without Cook and Mr Carlisle being aware of it,' Clara said. 'And of course you also need Lady Heatherington's approval, but your time off and hours of service will certainly have to be looked at and altered.'

'We have never been allowed to go out in the evening,' Clodagh said. 'That means that we will never be able to attend any of the dances you said were all the rage, or even learn to dance in the first place. And neither of us has ever been to a cinema till before Sunday.'

'You have a valid point,' Clara said. 'And I promise that I will attend to it as soon as possible.'

ELEVEN

The following day, Clara told them that the rooms assigned to the old lady were the old nurseries. 'Lord Heatherington thinks these will be the most suitable because two further rooms, which were originally for the nanny and nursemaids' use, lead off from the main room, and it has its own bathroom. Of course,' she added with a wry smile, 'it is also well away from the main body of the house. His lordship wants any trace of them ever being used as a nursery to be completely eradicated. The first thing we must do is give the rooms a thorough clean.'

The girls hadn't been into the nursery, and they stood at the threshold of the room and stared. The walls were incredibly grubby, with cobwebs trailing everywhere, the paintwork smeared, and a layer of grime lined the tops of the skirting boards. The bare floorboards had a film of dust covering them and were stained in places, and tattered curtains fluttered at barred windows that were too filthy to see through.

Lucy and Clodagh looked at each other with dismay. 'Oh, come on,' Clara urged. 'This won't get the baby a new bonnet.'

Lucy grinned at her and they all set to work with a will, their hair wrapped turban-style in scarves. Even Hilda came to help when she knew what they were about, and by the end of the day they all felt shattered but they were pleased with what they had achieved.

'Now,' Clara said, 'it's ready for the decorators to come in, and then the new carpets and bedroom furniture will be arriving. Lady Heatherington has chosen the things from a catalogue and I must phone through the measurements of the rooms and the windows so that carpets and curtains can be fitted.'

While the refurbishment of the old nurseries was taking place, Clodagh and Lucy had plenty to do in the kitchen, especially when two crates of everyday crockery and other kitchen equipment arrived. It had all to be unpacked, washed and put away. Then every room in the house had to be thoroughly cleaned.

Ada, Mr Carlisle and Jerry were catching the ferry on Friday evening and would arrive in the early hours of the morning, while Lord and Lady Heatherington, together with Norah and Rory, would spend the night in a hotel at the docks and sail on Saturday morning. 'That way, when they arrive here in the early evening, everything will be in place and the same as it was before they left,' Clara said drily. 'So they will not be inconvenienced in any way.'

'Not inconvenienced in any way,' Clodagh mimicked. 'What a selfish way to live while we scurry around making sure that everything really does happen like that.'

'What else would you do?' Clara asked. 'What job would you do if you could choose?'

'I hadn't thought that far ahead,' Clodagh said.

'And at the moment, with Birmingham seemingly so depressed, it might be hard to get any other kind of job. But doesn't all this bowing and scraping get to you?'

Clara was silent for a moment. Then she said, 'When I first came to work at the Heatherington's, I was like a lost soul. Working hard saved my sanity, I believe, and this house became a sort of haven for me. It also meant I could stand on my own two feet, so in a way I am grateful to Lord and Lady Heatherington. But you, Clodagh, are only expressing the mood of today. Unemployment, and the extreme poverty some endure because of it, is causing great unrest, especially when they see the lifestyles of the wealthy, which haven't changed one jot.'

'What d'you think will happen?' Lucy asked.

'I have no crystal ball,' Clara said, 'but I very much think that this lavish sort of lifestyle is on the way out. I have no idea what will replace it, and what the wealthy will do without their bevy of servants.'

But if change was in the air, it hadn't yet filtered through to the Heatheringtons. By the Friday evening before their arrival the nursery was transformed. Lucy and Clodagh had had a peep in that morning, for the carpets had been laid only the night before. The walls were covered with pink and pale blue flowers, and the thick carpets were the same shade of blue. The nursery bars had been removed from the windows, which were also painted blue to match the doors, and now pretty flowered curtains fluttered there. The

206

nurses' rooms were similar, and even the adjoining bathroom had been decorated. No trace of the original use of the rooms remained.

'It's so pretty,' Lucy said. 'If the nurses don't like this, they are hard to please.'

'Well, they are, aren't they?' Clodagh said. 'You heard Clara say they want their rooms cleaned and their meals brought up to them. Cook will be raging about that, you'll see. I mean, as if we haven't enough to do.'

'Yeah, and talking of new arrivals,' Lucy said, 'the new scullery maid and housemaid are coming this afternoon, so we best get our jobs done so we can show them what's what.'

They went down to the kitchen and were soon hard at it. Clara was pleased with them both. After dinner the two other kitchen staff arrived. Lucy was put in charge of Emily, who was to be the new scullery maid. She had a sallow complexion, a slack mouth, quite insipid grey eyes, and lank brown hair, which Lucy told her she would have to tie back from her face and hide under a cap because, 'It's more hygienic, and Cook is a stickler about that, I can tell you.'

'My dad said that people like these would take the coat off your back and I have got to question everything.'

'Good job your dad's not here,' Lucy said sharply. 'He wouldn't last five minutes, and neither will you with that attitude. Is your father a communist?'

'No, but he is a shop steward,' Emily said. 'And he told me not to take bullshit from anyone.'

Lucy gave a gasp. 'You use language like that

207

here and you risk having your mouth washed out with carbolic soap,' she said firmly.

'That ain't a bad swear.'

'Bad enough for here,' Lucy said, 'believe me. Anyway, what did your dad want you to do? Had you anything else lined up?'

'No,' Emily admitted. 'That's why my mom said I had to take this job.'

'I'd say your mother was right,' Lucy said grimly. 'And if you want to stay here keep your head down, do your best and don't go looking for trouble, for it will find you quick enough.'

Clodagh was having the same trouble with Hazel, who was supposed to be taking over housemaid's duties. She was a pale-faced girl with dark eyes, a sulky-looking mouth and head of nearly black curls. She seemed not the slightest bit interested in the work she was expected to do. Clodagh felt like shaking her for her indifference and the shrug that was often her only answer when she asked her something, but remembering how nervous she had been when she first started at the house in Letterkenny she gave her the benefit of the doubt.

'Have you got that now?' she asked, giving her a rundown again of the duties expected of her.

'I'll say,' Hazel said. 'Should do, shouldn't I, 'cos you've gone over it enough bleeding times.'

'If they hear you swear like that you'll be in trouble.'

'Think I care?' Hazel said. 'Soon as there's a vacancy in the factory where my sister works she's going to speak for me and I shall be out of here like a shot. They ain't half so prissy there.'

'Well, you aren't there yet,' Clodagh snapped. 'You are here and it's best you remember that.'

'If you ask me there is far too much work for one person here.'

'I already explained that if you are too hard-pressed then Lucy will help you,' Clodagh said. 'And if we need her in the kitchen then she helps us out, so you don't have to worry on that score. There is not that much work anyway when Lord and Lady Heatherington are the only ones here.'

'I heard tell there was an old woman as well.'

'There will be, yes,' Clodagh said. 'She is Lord Heatherington's mother and she has been in a home. But her health has deteriorated and the home can no longer cope, so he is having her back here. But there are nurses engaged to see to her, so she will be no bother to you.'

The nurses, Lydia Pringle and Martha Towns-end, also called that evening to inspect their rooms and reiterated what they had already said to Clara: that they expected their rooms to be cleaned by one of the maids and their meals brought up to them.

'Lord, I just don't know what Cook and Mr Carlisle are going to say,' Clara admitted to Lucy and Clodagh. 'But I'm afraid that we will have to agree, for now at least.'

'We'll soon know how they feel,' Lucy said. 'They are home tomorrow.'

'Yes, but do you see what it means, Lucy?' Clara said. 'I don't think Hazel will be half the maid that Evie was. But even if she was she can't clean two extra rooms and carry meals up- and downstairs as well. You will be drafted in on a daily basis, I think, and little help to Cook.'

Lucy made a face because she wasn't that keen on either nurse. However, she knew that she could do little to change the situation.

When Lucy woke the next morning the house was silent. She shook Emily awake roughly, knowing that the kitchen had to be clean and tidy before Cook saw it, and she told Emily she should thank her lucky stars that after her late arrival the previous night the Cook was taking an unaccustomed lie in.

'There's far too much to do,' Emily complained.

'No, there isn't,' Lucy snapped. 'I'll help you today, but don't expect this all the time. And for goodness' sake give the steps at the front of the house a good going over today because it is the first thing Lady Heatherington will notice.'

Grumbling, and with a glare at Lucy that she failed to see, Emily made her way to the front of the house with her bucket and cleaning utensils, and, with a sigh, Lucy set to work putting the kitchen to rights. She had a feeling it was going to be a very long day.

Despite that, it was nice to see Cook again, and even the starchy Mr Carlisle. Luckily, because of the hard work Lucy had put in as she helped the inept and lazy Emily, the state of the kitchen pleased Cook and she surveyed the room with pleasure.

'I'm that glad to be back,' she declared. 'There is nothing like your own kitchen. Now, Clodagh, it's time to get our aprons on and cook up a feast for Lord and Lady Heatherington's return.'

Jerry was as cheeky as ever and, predictably, began flirting with Hazel. Unlike Lucy and Clodagh, the girl seemed flattered by his attention, but Cook noticed and barked at her, 'You haven't time for daydreaming, my girl. Those rooms will not clean themselves, so get to it.' With a sullen look at them all, Hazel flounced out of the kitchen and Cook gave a heartfelt sigh.

Lord and Lady Heatherington arrived that evening and declared themselves delighted with the changes made to the old nursery. All the bedroom furniture was in place by then, but Lady Heatherington dispatched Jerry to the attic on the other side of the house, which was used for storage, to fetch down rugs, pretty bedspreads, cushions and bedroom chairs, to make the place look more homely.

True to her promise, Clara broached the subject of the girls' free time right away. Lady Heatherington wasn't really in agreement with them having more time off because she didn't really see servants as people with lives of their own, and Mr Carlisle was sniffy about it too. Cook, on the other hand, knew how hard both girls worked and said they were young and needed a bit of fun now and then. And then Clara found a surprising ally in Lord Heatherington, who agreed with Cook. And so both Lucy and Clodagh were told that their Monday afternoon off could be extended to eight thirty so they could attend the dance classes held in Erdington from half-past six till half-past seven. On Thursday it was even better, for they could stay out until eleven so that they could visit a cinema, or even a dance once they had become competent, and they still would have a full day off once a month. They were delighted with their new-found freedom.

None of the staff was looking forward to the nurses moving in, but their arrival was delayed because the old lady took a turn for the worse and Lord Heatherington travelled to the home to see her. Though she rallied, the doctor didn't advise moving her for two to three weeks, so everyone at Maxted Hall had a little respite before the arrival of the nurses for which they were most grateful.

The following week, Rory told them the Master had bought a car, a Rolls-Royce. That caused a stir. Norah said it would please the Mistress no end and that she had been on to him for ages.

'He said he saw no point when he was in the army,' Rory said. 'And then he had the accident, of course, and now he wants me as chauffeur. He's getting me a uniform and everything.'

'I didn't know you could drive,' Mr Carlisle said.

'Well, I picked up a few tips in the army,' Rory said. 'And I have driven trucks a time or two. There's not that much to it – not that I've ever handled a beauty like this, of course. Anyway, we pick it up tomorrow and then we are going to Liverpool soon to seek news of Master Clive.'

'Hope he finds something out,' Clara said. 'It must be awful not knowing anything.'

There was a murmur of agreement.

Then Mr Carlisle said, 'You are a military man, Rory, so what d'you think the outcome of this war will be?'

Rory was silent for a moment or two and then said, 'I don't think the Republicans will have a chance if the International Brigade is pulled out, and that would be a damned shame. Beg your pardon, ladies, but that's how I feel.'

'But they're not likely to pull them out, are they?' Clara asked.

'Ah, but that's it, you see,' Rory said. 'According to the General, way back in September, Britain agreed among a number of countries not to send any troops to Spain and so they are pulling out the International Brigade because it breaches that agreement.'

'In September?' Lucy echoed. 'Well, why isn't Clive home now?'

Rory was silent and Lucy looked at him fearfully. 'You mean he could be dead, don't you?'

'Yes, he could be dead or injured,' Rory admitted. 'But it needn't be that.'

'What else could it be?'

'Any manner of things,' Rory said. ''Cos they are not the regular army, maybe they haven't been able to get word to them that the war is over for them. Maybe none of them has come home yet. But whatever the news is, bad or good, it is always better to know.'

Oh, yes, Lucy agreed with that, but felt an ache in her heart at the thought that Clive might be dead or dreadfully mutilated.

'Who is this Clive anyway?' Emily suddenly said.

Lucy turned to face her but she felt tears

213

welling up in her eyes and knew if she tried to speak she would cry and that would never do, and so she mumbled something about cleaning some pots in the scullery and got up from the table, leaving the others to explain who Clive was.

'But you haven't got to do that now,' Ada said. 'You've barely touched your dinner and I have jam roly-poly for afters.'

'Not hungry,' mumbled Lucy, and Cook was left reflecting on the variability of young people, for Lucy usually had a really good appetite.

In the relative privacy of the scullery, Lucy didn't even try to prevent the tears gushing from her eyes and trickling down her cheeks for she had seldom felt such misery in the whole of her life.

A week later, Lord Heatherington and Rory went to fetch the car, and though Lucy thought it one of the finest she had ever seen, and that Rory looked resplendent in his new chauffeur's uniform, she knew that having a car would not affect her life in any shape or form.

What did affect her, though, was the arrival of the nurses to prepare for the elder Lady Heatherington, who was expected the following day. Almost at once the nurses had put everyone's back up by their supercilious and arrogant manner.

'Huh,' Cook said wearily the first night, as she and Clara sat before the range, each with a cup of cocoa before seeking her bed. 'I'm beginning to wonder who is the gentry in this place. Fetching and carrying and cleaning the rooms of people who are just employees, same as you and me, just ain't right.'

'Right or not, it has to be done that way,' Clara said. 'I did tell the Master and he said that the nurses will have trials enough looking after his mother, and he can't cope with the thought of them leaving because they think they haven't been treated right, so we must give them what they want.'

'Well,' Cook said, 'if that's how the Master wants it then that's how it must be, though it goes totally against the grain, and I don't think pandering to them is the way to go on. But when did our opinion ever count for anything?' She shrugged and went on, 'And it will be just one more job for Lucy to do, for that Hazel often has a face on her that would sour cream, and her manner is not so good either. She could probably upset them without even trying. I am worn out, to tell you the truth, for I have to be on at them all the time and even then I know that Lucy does the lion's share of the work in the house and Clodagh often has to finish Emily's jobs in the kitchen because she is so slow.' She gave a grim smile and went on, 'Tell you what, Clara, I would hate to see the other girls you interviewed if these two you did employ were the best of them.'

Clara coloured slightly because she did feel almost responsible for the girls' ineptitude and their aggrieved demeanour as they went about their tasks. 'Do you think it would help if I was to have a word?'

Ada shook her head. 'I don't know that it would help, Clara, to tell you the truth. I have had plenty of words, for all the notice they take. Let's hope they shape up in time. Lucy doesn't complain much anyway, though I know that she resents taking trays to the nurses. She said to me that she's glad that they seldom come into the kitchen because if there had been a prize for haughtiness they would both have won it hands down.'

'She has a point. But once the old lady is here she'll be up and down with trays anyway because Lord Heatherington told me his mother is virtually bedridden now.'

'Yes,' Cook said with a sigh. 'Comes to us all, I know, but I doubt she will cope with frailty very well. Ah, well, she will be here tomorrow and we will see this for ourselves.'

There was no failing to notice when the elder Lady Heatherington was brought home by ambulance after lunch the next day because she roared at the ambulance men who carried her in. Lord Heatherington, who had gone to meet the ambulance, was surprised and shocked to see that his mother looked no better than she had when he went to see her at the home, when she had been at death's door. But the matron at the home had phoned and said her health had improved and she was now fit to be moved. In his opinion, she looked far from fit, and once his mother was settled in her room he arranged for his own doctor to come and look her over.

Before the doctor arrived, Lucy took a tray up to the old lady and was quite shocked. No amount of cosmetics could hide the pallor of her face or mask her rheumy eyes where the whites had a definite yellowish tinge. Behind those eyes, Lucy read fear and helplessness, and she told them all this in the kitchen.

'I know she used to be some sort of harridan,' she said in the end, 'but now she is one very sick woman.'

'I think you're right,' Rory said. 'Fair upset the Master, seeing her in that state.'

Lucy wasn't surprised. She was going up the back stairs to collect trays from the rooms later that evening when the doctor came out with Lord Heatherington. Knowing that none of the upper classes liked to sec servants actually working, she lingered on the stairs just out of sight.

Dr Gilbert was younger than she had thought he'd be, and though he sported a small beard, she thought he had probably grown that on purpose to make himself look older. He was the doctor Lord Heatherington had seen after the military hospital had done what they could, and it was he who recommended they sojourn to the country so that he could fully recover both physically and mentally. It had been absolutely the right thing to do and so Lord Heatherington had full trust in the man. That evening they were barely through the door before his lordship faced the doctor and said, 'Well, what did you think of her?'

'Charles, she is a very old lady,' the doctor said gently. 'Her heartbeat is extremely weak and so is her pulse.'

'Are you telling me my mother is dying?'

'Ah, we are all moving to that end,' the doctor said as they began walking across the landing to the main staircase. Lucy moved closer as the doctor went on, 'Her organs are getting ready to close down because they are tired. She has no obvious illness, just old age, though from things she told me I would imagine that her liver is barely functioning any more. She says she has no pain, but if that changes, send for me. My guess is one day she will die in her sleep and, believe me, there are worse ways for a person to end their life.'

Lucy thought that probably Lord Heatherington didn't expect such a diagnosis because he seemed flustered.

'Yes, of course. Yes, it is, I know. I had no idea she was as bad as this. The home should have informed me things were getting critical.'

'Even if they had, you could have done nothing, Charles,' the doctor said. 'And of course she has had the upheaval of moving in here today. I imagine that she has little energy, and anything like this will probably exhaust her and make her appear worse than she is.'

They had reached the bottom of the stairs so, to Lucy, Lord Heatherington's voice was a little fainter as he asked, 'Can you give us some idea of how long she has got?'

Lucy strained further for the doctor's reply. 'It's impossible to tell because, as I say, she is suffering from nothing but old age,' he said. 'All the nurses can do is keep her comfortable. At the moment there is no actual nursing needed and she could go on like this for weeks, or months, but I shouldn't think it will be longer than, let's say, six months. If she is here for Christmas, I will be surprised.'

Lucy told them in the kitchen the following morning at breakfast. And those who had known her before found it hard to come to terms with the fact that the vitriolic old woman who could, and often did, cut a person to ribbons with her tongue had turned into a frail old lady soon to meet her maker.

'Mind you,' Lucy said, 'you would never think she was at death's door the way she shrieks and roars at the nurses.'

'It is not for you to comment on your betters, Cassidy,' Mr Carlisle said.

But Cook cut in, 'Huh, I wouldn't count that one any better than I am myself, and I would say Lucy has a perfect right to say what she likes about her.'

'I grant you she is not an easy woman,' Mr Carlisle said.

'Not easy!' Cook cried. 'There are a fair few words to describe the elder Lady Heatherington and "not easy" would be at the bottom of the list.'

'What's on the top?' Hazel asked with an impish grin, and Cook snapped out, 'Never you mind, young lady.'

Rory grinned at Hazel and said, 'Anyway, the illness of the General's mother has decided him because, as he said to me, the old lady will get worse, not better, so we are off to Liverpool next week. As a matter of fact, she insisted he go because she didn't know beforehand what Clive had done, you see.'

'Well, there was little point in telling her,' Clara said. 'I mean, it wasn't as if she could have done anything about it.'

'No,' Rory said. 'The General said that he didn't want her fretting when he was not here. Anyway, by all accounts, she was real upset when he told her and she said he must go as soon as he can and try and find out all he can about Master Clive.'

'She always had a soft spot for Clive, I remember,' Clara said. 'When she couldn't seem to bear anyone else she always had time for Clive.'

'Ah, yes,' Cook said. 'The old besom thought the sun shone out of Clive's backside.'

'Cook!' Mr Carlisle cried, outraged.

Cook glanced from his face to those of the girls – their hands over their mouths in a vain attempt to stifle their giggles – and said to him, 'You know, you could get work as a tailor's dummy, you are that stuffy, and I'm sure the girls will hear worse than that before they are much older.'

TWELVE

Lord Heatherington left on a blustery late March day. That same afternoon, Lucy had just returned from the nursery floor when Mr Carlisle, who had answered a knock at the front door, said to Clara, 'Lady Ponsomby and her daughter, Miss Jessica Ponsomby, would like to call on Madam. Will you see if it is convenient?'

The door had barely closed behind her when Cook remarked, 'Oh, she'll see her, all right.

They have been friends for years and I think she missed her company when she was living in Ireland. Surprised she's left it so long to call.'

'Mrs O'Leary said that they wanted Master Clive to marry this Jessica Ponsomby,' Lucy said, though even saying the words caused an uncomfortable lurch in her stomach.

Clodagh was amazed. 'Aren't people these days free to choose their own partners?'

'Not in these big houses,' Cook maintained. 'Marriages are often arranged for convenience. Ain't that right, Mr Carlisle?'

'That is absolutely correct, Mrs Murphy. It is sensible to keep the well-to-do families together to protect the bloodline.'

Bloodline, Lucy thought disparagingly. What about loving someone, especially if you are going to spend the rest of your life with them? She knew better than to voice these thoughts, though, as Mr Carlisle went on, 'Marriage between Miss Jessica Ponsomby and Master Clive would, I'm sure, be eminently suitable. But of course no one knows where Master Clive is at the moment.' Or whether he has even survived. Mr Carlisle didn't say that because he didn't need to; the unspoken words hung in the air.

Clara came back just a few minutes later and said to Lucy, 'Lady Heatherington will want tea in an hour or so for her and her guests.'

'Isn't that Clodagh's job?'

'No,' Clara said. 'It used to be, but it's yours now. Come on. We'll have to get you fitted out with a black dress and frilly apron and cap.'

Lucy followed Clara up the first set of back

221

stairs and said, 'Can't Hazel do it?'

'People want a happy, smiling face bringing in the tea.'

'I'd be too nervous to smile,' Lucy said. 'Honestly I would.'

'You'll be fine,' Clara said, stripping off her kitchen uniform. 'Good job we haven't the problems we had when you first started here, when everything drowned you because you were so small.' She surveyed her up and down as she added, 'You have grown a lot since then, and in all the right places. Oh, now don't be blushing because I am speaking the truth.'

Lucy couldn't help the blushes because she thought Clara was making fun of her. She had never taken much notice of her appearance and was unaware that she had blossomed, that her burnished hair shone with health, like her tawny-coloured eyes. Even her nose was a neat shape and in proportion to the rest of her face, and set above a very determined chin. Dressed in the black dress and lacy apron, with the lace cap secured with Kirbigrips, she looked very fetching as she knocked on the shiny cream door of the sitting room an hour or so later and tried to ignore the trembling in her legs and the dryness in the roof of her mouth.

When she was bid enter she went in, pushing the laden tea trolley with a little difficulty because the wheels sank into the patterned carpet. She had never been into the sitting room before and she took a swift look round. Her first impression was that it was very pleasant and quite spacious, the light coming from the floor-to-ceiling windows incorporating a glass door that led out to the balcony. The windows had cream curtains draped at the tops and down each side. Standard lamps stood on either side. Two rattan baskets stood against one wall and a dark wood chest against the other, while the small tables were dotted about holding arrangements of flowers. The fireplace and mantelshelf were of white marble, with a large gold-framed mirror above. A brass fender encircled the hearth, a brass coal scuttle stood beside it, and a small fire burnt in the grate.

But Lucy noticed something else and that was the film of dust over the tops of the rattan baskets, chest and the mantelshelf. The hearth and fender were unpolished and the carpets and the rugs were decidedly grubby. Her lips pursed in annoyance.

Lady Heatherington smiled at her and said, 'Put it on the small table, Cassidy,' indicating the one between the ornate and patterned chair she was sitting on and the matching settee where the other woman and her daughter sat.

The girl had her head slightly bowed, but Lucy noticed Mrs Ponsomby was so heavily made up that traces of powder were visible in the lines of her face. There were also bags under her dark eyes and her hair was pulled up tightly to fit under her large-brimmed hat.

'I'll pour, if you hand round the other cakes and pastries,' Lady Heatherington said. She eyed the trolley, before adding, 'I advise you to try the sponge, Diana and Jessica, for my cook has a feather-light hand.'

Jessica raised her head and her eyes met Lucy's, who suddenly felt immensely sorry for the girl. Cook was right: for all her wealth, she was as plain as a pikestaff. She had a completely dull face, lifeless eyes, a nose with little shape to it, a slack mouth and drab mousy hair, and made an altogether very unbecoming picture.

Lucy bent her head quickly and began to cut the cake into segments, as Lady Ponsomby said, 'But, Amelia, you must be distraught not hearing from Clive for all this time.'

'It has been very hard for both of us,' Lady Heatherington said. 'Charles left for Liverpool this morning to see if they have any news.'

'Why Liverpool?'

'It's where they set out from,' Lady Heatherington said. 'It's where he joined the brigade or unit or whatever it was they called themselves. They might not know much, if anything at all, but it's better than sitting here doing nothing.'

'Oh, I do agree,' Lady Ponsomby said. 'Anything is better than that.'

She accepted a plate from Lucy, with a piece of cake on it, without a word of thanks, and then she took a bite and urged the girl beside her, 'Try the cake, my dear. It is divine.'

Lucy put a segment on a china plate. 'Your cake, miss,' she said, holding it out.

The women had begun to talk about the number of unemployed making a nuisance of themselves hanging around the streets and so only Lucy saw the glitter of malice that burnt in Jessica's eyes. Suddenly she brought her hand down on Lucy's arm with such force the plate spun from her hand

and fell against the fender so that it was smashed to smithereens and bits of sponge cake littered the carpet and the hearth.

For a second, Lucy didn't know what to do. Neither of the two women had seen what had happened before the plate had been knocked from her hand, and she could hardly accuse the daughter of a favourite friend of her employer of causing the mess. Jessica knew this too and she cast her a look almost of triumph as, in her shrill, piercing voice, she screamed at Lucy, 'Well, don't just stand there, stupid girl. Clear it up!'

Lucy was stunned by the injustice of it and her eyes sought those of Lady Heatherington. She saw that her employer was annoyed that a young guest in her house had the temerity to berate one of her servants.

Yet, Lady Heatherington reasoned, Cassidy had been inordinately clumsy and she had no wish to risk a quarrel with her friend. So her voice was clipped and cold as she said to Lucy, 'How could you have been so careless? Go and get something to clean it up at once, and before you do, apologise to Miss Jessica.'

Having no other option, Lucy did apologise, though the words nearly stuck in her throat, especially when she saw the supercilious smile playing around Jessica's mouth. Her smile widened still more as Lucy cleaned away the mess. She was filled with resentment that she could say nothing, and was glad of the sympathy of those in the kitchen who didn't doubt a word she said when she related the incident later.

'Heard she could be a nasty piece of work,'

Cook said. 'My sister's neighbour had a daughter took a job at the Ponsombys', but she didn't stay. She said no one does for long and that young miss is worst of the lot. Talks to the servants like they're dirt, so I believe.'

'Going by the way she spoke to me, I would say they are absolutely right,' Lucy said. 'But you know what got me? Lady Heatherington turned on me as well.'

'Did you expect her to support you rather than a guest in the house?'

'No, I suppose not.'

'And you did drop the plate and smash it,' Clara said. 'You say she didn't see what that young Ponsomby did.'

'No, I don't think so,' Lucy said.

'Look, we are the lowest of the low as far as they are concerned,' Cook said. 'And when the chips are down they will always support their own. It's unchangeable so it's something you have to get used to. But has that Miss Jessica improved any? I mean, she was at the back of the queue when the good looks were given out.'

Lucy smiled. 'No improvement, I'd say. She is really plain.'

'Oh, well, that explains why she acted like that.'

'Does it?'

'She's jealous of your prettiness, Lucy.' At the disbelieving look on Lucy's face, she said, 'You don't know your own worth, child.'

'How on earth can Master Clive like a person like that?' Lucy asked.

'Oh, she wouldn't behave like that in front of him,' Clara said. 'I've met her sort before. She would never show that side of her nature to him. You can count on that.'

'She can't keep it hidden for ever, though,' Clodagh said. 'And I pity the man she does marry, whoever he is.'

'He'll have to have a broad back, right enough,' Cook said with a chuckle. 'As for looks, well, they fade and money doesn't. As an only child she is set for a big inheritance when she marries, and another when the old folk die. You can always put the light off in the bedroom.'

'Mrs Murphy!' Mr Carlisle said, clearly shocked, but Lucy and Clodagh had turned away and had their hands over their mouths so Mr Carlisle wouldn't see their hilarity. After all, Lucy thought, what odds was Jessica Ponsomby's ill humour to her? She would likely have little to do with the girl, and if she had to wait on her again she would watch her like a hawk and try to keep out of her reach.

Lucy didn't forget the state the sitting room had been in, though she wasn't one to tell tales. The next morning, coming down from taking the breakfast things up, she decided to find Hazel and put her right on a few things about earning her living. She knew she would be in one of the downstairs rooms, but she wasn't in the dining room or the library. She wasn't in the sitting room either, but she had been in there. The carpet sweeper had been brought in and so had a duster and the polish, though there was no evidence that they had been used. The ashes had not been touched either, there was no coal in the scuttles and the door leading through to the garden was slightly ajar.

If the door had not been slightly open, Lucy might well have assumed that Hazel had returned to the kitchen for something. But, as it was, she wandered over to the door. It was the giggle that alerted her. She knew who it was, though Hazel had not giggled much in the kitchen unless Jerry was there. With apprehension running all through her she stepped on to the balcony, walked to the end of it and round the side of the house.

She found them in the slight alcove of the door to the coal cellar. Neither of them noticed her because they were locked in a passionate embrace and both had their eyes closed. Lucy noticed one of Jerry's hands was running over the curve of Hazel's bottom and pulling her tighter against him.

'How long has this been going on?'

At Lucy's words the two jerked apart. Hazel's face was aflame, though she faced Lucy squarely, but Jerry was wearing his usual nonchalant expression. Lucy had no authority over Jerry, but she still said, 'Get yourself away. Mr Carlisle will hear of this,' and she had the satisfaction of seeing him blanch.

'And you, my girl, are coming with me,' she said to Hazel, gripping her arm tighter so her nails dug into Hazel's skin. Avoiding the servants' hall and the kitchen, she yanked her up the back stairs to the attic where she plonked her on one of the beds and, taking hold of her shoulders, she shook her so hard her head snapped backwards and forwards. 'You stupid, stupid little fool,' she said. 'Did you let him touch you, and you know exactly what I mean?'

In the face of such fury, Hazel was helpless and she looked at Lucy with eyes brimming with unshed tears. 'Well, we kissed and that,' Hazel admitted in a voice little above a whisper. 'You saw us kiss.'

'Yes, and I saw what his hand was doing while you were kissing him,' Lucy said. 'Have you done more than kiss?'

Hazel hung her head and Lucy snapped, 'Well, have you?

Hazel nodded. 'A bit more.'

'You haven't let him—'

'No. I ain't,' Hazel said, and added with spirit, 'But it don't matter if I did 'cos Jerry is going to marry me, he is, and take me away from here.'

'Dear God!' Lucy cried. 'Haven't you even the sense you were born with? Jerry won't marry you and he's in no position to take you anywhere. He says that so that you'll let him do things you know are wrong.'

Hazel was openly sobbing, but through her tears she maintained, 'We weren't doing any harm.' And then at the look on Lucy's face her voice faltered. 'It ... it was only like a bit of fun.'

'Fun!' exclaimed Lucy. 'There is no fun to be had in having a baby out of wedlock, I can tell you that for nothing. By rights I should go for Mrs O'Leary now and she would in all likelihood dismiss you at once and without a reference. You seem to set great store on your father – well, what would he feel about you if you were dismissed for immorality?'

Hazel knew her father would take a very dim

view of her turning up out of the blue, and he would know what she had been dismissed for when he realized that she had been given no reference. Her father's temper was legendary, and though it had never been directed at her she imagined it might well be if he thought she had been engaged in any sort of hanky-panky, especially the sort that might fill her belly, so she said, 'Please, don't do that. I ain't a bad girl, really, I ain't, but Jerry made me feel so special. No one has ever done that before.'

'And did he tell you how beautiful you are and how attracted he'd been as soon as he had cast eyes upon you?'

Hazel nodded. 'Yes. But how did you know?'

Lucy didn't answer, but instead she went on, 'Did he say he had never seen hair so luxuriant or eyes so enticing?'

Hazel nodded miserably. She remembered too how he had stroked her hair and kissed her lips, which he described as sweet, and said he thought her the most wonderful girl in all the world.

'Jerry Kilroy has flirted with all of us, or should I say tried to flirt, because none of us has taken that much notice of him,' Lucy said. 'Now, I expect you to act the same way.'

Hazel nodded. Her tears had dried and she just felt daft because she knew that, given the chance, he would have acted in a similar way to any number of girls. 'What you said has made me feel right daft,' she said. 'Please give me another chance because I am really sorry.'

'I'm prepared to keep it between ourselves if you're being honest with me,' Lucy said. 'But I'll be watching you from now on. You put a foot wrong and I will spill the beans.'

Hazel shook her head. 'You needn't worry. I'll not give Jerry Kilroy the time of day after this. And you will never regret giving me another chance, for I swear I will never let you down again.'

'Then as long as you don't we will say no more about it,' Lucy said.

Hazel realised the lucky escape she had had and what she owed Lucy, and she sighed with the relief and said, 'Thanks, Lucy.'

To keep her promise to Hazel Lucy said nothing to Mr Carlisle about Jerry's entanglement with Hazel, but he didn't know she wasn't going to tell him and so he was very subdued as they sat down to dinner later. Hazel was quiet too because she knew what a fool she had been and how close she had come to losing her job after only a few weeks. She knew now her card had been marked and she and Jerry would be watched closely by everyone. But Lucy didn't need to worry about Hazel's behaviour now because she had learnt her lesson.

Old Lady Heatherington had thought that Lord Heatherington only had to go to Liverpool and he would find out all he needed to know about his son and without any significant delay. He had promised he would telephone the minute he heard anything, but two days had passed with no news of any sort.

Lucy didn't need to tell them of the strained atmosphere in the old lady's bedroom, for even in the kitchen they could hear her strident voice.

'She is so selfish,' Norah said. 'She is just concerned with herself and doesn't even try to think how Lady Heatherington may be feeling after all this time with no news. She's terribly worried and dreadfully sad.'

'Lord Heatherington's mother doesn't seem to get sad,' Lucy said. 'She just gets angry.'

And she did get angry, so angry that the following day she threw a pepper pot at Nurse Townsend and cut her above the eye, and without hesitation both nurses packed their bags and left. They wouldn't listen to any placating words nor pleas from Clara or even Lady Heatherington. They said they had suffered abuse hurled at them since the very first day they'd begun work and now with one of them attacked they couldn't wait to see the back of the place. Lucy had never had a great liking for the nurses because she considered them snooty and arrogant, yet she thought no one should have to put up with having things thrown at them, or even being screamed at, the way they had been.

Yet everyone knew the old lady, bad as she was, could not just be neglected and Clara felt somewhat responsible. After all, she had hired the nurses in the first place. 'I'll go and see old Lady Heatherington and have a word,' she offered, lifting up her lunch tray as she spoke.

'Watch yourself then,' Cook cautioned. Clara approached the old lady's bedroom door cautiously and grasped the handle. However, she wasn't even through it when a paperweight narrowly missed her head and smashed into the door. 'Stop that, Lady Heatherington!' she said sternly.

'Get out!' bellowed the old woman, and, when

she picked up a second paperweight, Clara beat a hasty retreat.

Clara returned to the kitchen and told them what had happened.

Lucy was filled with rage. 'She thinks that she can do just what she likes and get away with it,' she said, 'and she has to learn that she can't. Mrs O'Leary, she could have killed you.'

Clara grimaced. 'Could have done me some damage all right,' she said. 'Gave me quite a turn when I saw it come flying for me, and it hit the door with such force that there is a sizeable dent in it.'

'Yes,' Cook said. 'She may be at death's door but she can still do a body a mischief.'

'Yes, but what's to be done?' Clara said. 'The nurses are gone, Lord Heatherington is away and Lady Heatherington won't have anything to do with her.'

'Wouldn't help if she did,' Cook said sagely. 'The elder Lady Heatherington can't stand the younger one. It would only inflame the situation if she got involved.'

'I'll take the tray up,' Lucy said suddenly.

'No, Lucy.'

'She has to be seen to by someone,' Lucy pointed out.

'Yes, but...'

'I know what she is capable of, Mrs O'Leary,' Lucy said. 'I have seen her more often than any of you, and someone has to do this.'

She took the tray from Cook as she spoke and made her way firmly up the back stairs, anger still coursing through her as she thought what might have happened to Clara. So, she didn't open the door slowly, she burst through it instead with the tray held in front of her and glared at the woman in the bed, whose fingers had closed around another paperweight.

'If you throw that at me, madam, you will get it right back again,' she hissed.

To say the old lady was astounded would be putting it mildly. 'You impudent young pup.'

'Maybe I am, madam,' Lucy said, approaching the bed. 'But as you appear to have driven off the nurses, you and I might have more to do with each other and so it is best that we get a few things straight. One is that I do not like being shouted at and I absolutely will not tolerate being slapped, pinched or having things thrown at me, and it is right that we understand this from the outset.'

Lucy was sure that she saw the ghost of a smile tug at old Lady Heatherington's mouth, but then it was gone in an instant and she lowered the paperweight as she said, 'So I've frightened off the nurses, have I?'

'You have done more than frighten them,' Lucy said. 'You have injured Nurse Townsend, and she might need stitches for the cut the pepper pot made.'

'Serves her right.'

'No, it doesn't,' Lucy countered. 'Whatever she did, that was no way to behave. You could have killed her and you could have done the same to Clara – Mrs O'Leary – who was only trying to help you.'

The old lady sank back on to the pillows and her eyes appeared as hard as steel as she said, 'Don't I

234

frighten you, too?'

'I don't frighten easily, madam,' Lucy said. 'And I think we understand each other now.' She hauled the old lady into a more upright position and put the tray on a little table that went over her knees.

'I often don't have much appetite,' she said peevishly.

She didn't need to tell Lucy that because however tasty the meal, there was always a fair bit sent back to the kitchen. But feeling sorry for the old lady was, Lucy was sure, no way to handle it. 'Well, you wouldn't get that hungry, would you, because you're not using much energy,' she said. 'Now, I belong to the school that believes a little of what you fancy does you good and so you eat what you want and leave the rest.'

The old lady definitely did smile this time, the skin stretched across her face as she said, 'I have seen you collecting trays, but what's your name?'

'Lucy Cassidy, my lady.'

'From Ireland?'

'Yes, my lady.'

'Papist, I suppose.'

'Yes, my lady.'

'Never could abide Papists.'

'Can't help that, my lady,' Lucy said firmly. 'And I may as well tell you here and now that I will not change my religion to please you or anyone else.'

The old lady gave a very unaccustomed chuckle. 'Well, Lucy Cassidy, you certainly know your own mind,' she said. 'And it just might be that you and I could get on very well.'

'Yes, my lady,' Lucy said. 'You could be right there.'

Lady Heatherington had taken to Lucy, and it was just as well because no one else wanted to take on the job of caring for the old lady, so Lucy was spending most of her time in her bedroom. Her time off was severely curtailed and so was Clodagh's because she had extra work to do. Lucy felt bad about that because they had been given extra time off and had enrolled in the dance classes, and now it had been snatched away.

Lucy's life seemed to be turned on its head and she wasn't that pleased. She missed the company of the others, for she ate with the older Lady Heatherington at her insistence. She missed the long chats she used to have with Clodagh at night in their attic room because Clara said the old lady might need something in the night so Lucy slept in the room the night nurse had occupied. In fact, the only thing she was pleased about was that Clodagh was appointed to serve tea to Lady Ponsomby and her dreadful daughter. Clodagh found her as unpleasant as Lucy had, and she told Lucy so as she was loading the tray for afternoon tea that she was sharing with the old lady. 'Glad it wasn't just me she took against,' Lucy said.

'No, I think it's the whole flipping world,' Clodagh said. 'And her daughter is plain, but she would look a whole lot better if she was just to smile. Everyone looks better then, but she has that horrible pout fixed on her face and she never says please or thank you. Mind you, her mother doesn't either. Glad I don't work in their house, 'cos I don't think I would have lasted long.'

'No one does,' Lucy said. 'Cook said they can't keep staff. And talking of that, I'd better get this upstairs quick or Madam will go for me.'

'Does she go for you?'

'Not so often now,' Lucy said. 'She doesn't mean half of what she says anyway, and mostly it's like water off a duck's back to me. She did scratch me badly the other day, though, and screamed abuse at me, and I just walked out. She yelled blue murder but I didn't go back till she stopped.'

Clodagh nodded. 'We heard her. Clara was all for going up but Cook advised her not to.'

'I'm glad she didn't interfere,' Lucy said. 'I went into old Lady Heatherington later, when she'd stopped yelling and I really let her have it.'

'What did she say?'

'Said she'd have me dismissed and I told her to go ahead, that she'd be doing me a favour. I said that I would get a good reference from Lord Heatherington and from Cook, and would soon get another job, and this time I would take care that it didn't involve looking after a bad-tempered old lady who thinks it's her right to bawl and slap people who are trying to help her.'

Clodagh's mouth dropped open. 'You didn't?'

'Oh, yes, I did,' Lucy said with a wry smile. 'I surprised myself, but the old lady was staggered because I don't think that anyone has ever spoken to her like that before.'

'No, I'd say not.'

'Well, maybe it should have been done because she has been much better behaved since, and though I do understand how frustrated she must get, I told her it was unacceptable to lash out at people and scream at them the way she does at times.' She gave a slight chuckle as she went on, 'I told her to let me know when she felt like screaming and we could do it together.'

'Oh, I'd like to see that,' Clodagh said with a laugh. 'And has she?'

Lucy shook her head. 'No, not yet. Time does drag for her, though. I do understand that and I had her bed moved across to the window so at least she can look out, and I brought some flowers from the garden to brighten up her bedroom. That pleased her. She said I was like a breath of fresh air.'

'You are,' Clodagh said. 'In fact, you're even better than that. You're a flipping marvel, that's what they are all saying in the kitchen.'

'Shut up,' Lucy said, lifting the tray, her face flushed crimson. 'You're embarrassing me, and old Lady Heatherington will want to know what's what if I go in with a red face.'

'I'm only saying the truth,' Clodagh said. 'But you're right. If you go in to her with your face the colour of a beetroot she will think you are up to no good.'

'Ha! Maybe I would be if ever I had the chance,' Lucy said grimly, and Clodagh's laughter followed her up the stairs.

THIRTEEN

Lord Heatherington returned two evenings later and the news he brought was good, though Lady Heatherington noticed that his eyes were red and his face was grey with fatigue. She passed him a glass of brandy while he told her of the search for news of their son.

'It seemed that everywhere, we were hitting a brick wall, and we were ready to give up and come home when Rory suggested trying the hospitals.'

'He is injured!' Amelia exclaimed, leaping to her feet. 'Clive is injured?'

'No, no,' Lord Heatherington said. Sitting beside her again, he took hold of her hand as he said gently, 'Clive is fine. I met a man in one of the hospitals who not only knew Clive, but had spoken to him just two days before. Then the man himself was injured and shipped out.'

'Did he say how Clive was? Is he well?'

'He said that he is as well as anyone is when they are fighting a war,' Lord Heatherington said with a sigh. 'But, my dear, he is alive and that's all that matters. He also said that the International Brigade are being rounded up and will be sent home shortly, so soon our son will be home where he belongs.'

'Oh, thank God!' Lady Heatherington said fervently. She saw the tears of joy welling in her husband's tired eyes and she regretted having to mar the moment, but Charles had to know what his mother had done.

As she told him, he listened open-mouthed, and then he dropped his head in his hands and asked, 'What are we to do with her?'

'We'll have to engage more nurses, that's all,' Lady Heatherington said. 'Mrs O'Leary has already put an ad in the *Birmingham Mail*.'

'But who will see to her meantime?'

'The girl who has taken over so far, I'd say,' Amelia said. 'It's Cassidy, the between maid.'

'Cassidy...' Lord Heatherington said, wrinkling his brow as he tried to remember. 'Oh, yes, isn't she that wee strip of a thing?'

'That's right.'

'Surely she will never manage my mother?'

'Mrs O'Leary assures me she can,' Lady Heatherington said. 'In fact, Mrs O'Leary says she seems to be the only person that can cope with your mother at the moment. And it will only be for a week or two.'

Lord Heatherington got to his feet. 'I must see this for myself. Rory will have told the other staff the news about Clive by now and my mother will not be best pleased if she thinks she is the last to be told, and anyway she has some serious explaining to do.'

For all his resolute words, though, Lord Heatherington paused outside the bedroom door, for he knew only too well just how difficult his mother could be. But on the threshold he stood and stared and wondered what was so different about the room from when he had last seen it. The bed was by the window, he noticed, and yet it wasn't that alone. The whole room seemed lighter somehow, and the air was fragrant from the two vases of spring flowers placed on the dressing table.

His mother looked much better too, he thought, and she was laughing at something Cassidy had just said to her. The girl herself looked calm and professional in the white coat she had covering her uniform.

However, his mother had lost none of her spirit and her bright eyes regarded him coldly as she said, 'You took your time. I saw you drive in and you know how anxious I was about news of Clive.'

'Were you, Mother?' Lord Heatherington said. 'Well, it might surprise you to know that his mother was most anxious too, and she was the one I had to tell any news to first, but you can stop worrying now for the news is good. Clive is alive and as well as can be expected.'

Lucy let out the breath she hadn't even been aware she was holding, in a gasp of blessed relief, as Lord Heatherington told them how he had found out about Clive. He watched astounded as his mother dabbed at her eyes with a pure white hanky, for he had never seen his mother cry before. However, he had other matters to discuss with her that couldn't wait, however upset she was, and he brought up straight away the attack she had made on Nurse Townsend, which had resulted in both nurses leaving.

'Serves the damned woman right,' old Lady Heatherington snarled. 'Foisted them damned nurses on me. I had no say in it, and they treated me with a total lack of respect and talked to me as if I was six. And,' she added threateningly, 'if you engage people like that again they will be treated in a like manner.'

'Mother, you cannot get away with insulting and hurting people,' Lord Heatherington said. 'And certainly not people in my employ.'

'Then don't engage nincompoops,' old Lady Heatherington spat out. 'I want to have the final say in anyone else you propose to care for me.'

Lord Heatherington threw his hands in the air helplessly and, with a deep sigh, said, 'As you wish, Mother.'

'Good,' old Lady Heatherington said. 'Now, Charles, do not harass me further. I would like young Lucy to fetch my dinner now. I'm sure you have matters to attend to and I should not wish to detain you.'

'In other words, you're dismissing me?' Charles said.

Old Lady Heatherington nodded. 'Yes, that's right.'

There was really nothing else he could say, and he stepped out of the room, followed by Lucy. 'How do you stand it?' he said to her as they stood on the landing.

'Oh, she's not so bad,' Lucy said. 'And when people are helping you, especially in sensitive areas, then it helps if you like the person doing it, I should think.' And then, before she could stop herself, she went on, 'You probably can imagine how she feels, being reliant on other people, as you had a taste of that yourself.'

Immediately, she clapped her hand over her mouth, but Lord Heatherington seemed amused rather than annoyed. 'Do you usually speak your mind like that?'

'No, sir,' Lucy said, and added, 'Servants are not supposed to have opinions, or at least if they have them not express them. Sorry, sir, for speaking out of turn.'

Lord Heatherington actually gave a low chuckle before saying, 'And you're right when you say I hated asking for help to do things I used to do myself without a thought. Fancy you noticing that.'

'Oh, servants notice a lot about the families they work for,' Lucy said. 'But most keep their mouths shut and I shouldn't have opened mine.'

'I'm glad you did because it has made me think,' Lord Heatherington said. 'I mean, everyone gets old and it is just something that happens. I never gave a thought to how it must feel to be getting stiffer and more infirm with each passing year, espccially for my mother. When she was young she was so very beautiful and, people tell me, a wonderful dancer.' He looked at Lucy directly. 'How did you tame my mother?'

Lucy flushed and stammered, 'I'd ... I'd rather not say, sir. You may not approve and I value my job.'

'You'll not lose your job, whatever you have done or said, I promise,' Lord Heatherington said.

Lucy, thinking old Lady Heatherington might take it upon herself to tell her son anyway, said, 'She lifted a paperweight into her hand. She had already thrown one at Mrs O'Leary and I told her if she threw it at me then I would throw it straight back.'

Lord Heatherington's eyes widened in amazement and he gave a bellow of laughter. His eyes still twinkling, he said, 'I bet that took her by surprise.'

'It did,' Lucy said. 'But I was angry because I had just seen the cut on Nurse Townsend's forehead and then she threw a paperweight and she only just missed Mrs O'Leary, and I saw red, I'm afraid, sir. I wouldn't have done it, though, sir. I wouldn't really have thrown something at an old lady.'

'But she didn't know that,' Lord Heatherington said. 'And don't you ever tell her. We will keep this whole conversation to ourselves.'

The whole atmosphere in the kitchen lightened with the news about Clive being alive and well, and, even better, that the International Brigade was finally being disbanded.

'Won't it be grand to have Master Clive home again?' Cook said. 'I must look up his favourite dishes. He'll likely need building up after all he's been through, and in foreign parts too, and you, Clara, will have to make those choux buns he is so fond of.'

'Don't worry, I will,' Clara said. 'And take joy in it, just as soon as he is back with us again.'

However, there was no further news, though Lady Ponsomby and her daughter, Jessica, seemed to be seldom away from the house, anxious for news of 'Dear Clive'.

Late April was so warm and sunny that Lucy could open the bedroom window sometimes and so give old Mrs Heatherington some fresh air, and she tried to interest her in the gardens she could see below.

She was hard to distract, however, because, since Lord Heatherington had come back from Liverpool, she had expected Clive to turn up at the house any day. It was hard for Lucy to calm her when she felt as anxious herself and, fond as she was of the old lady, it wasn't as if she could see light at the end of the tunnel because there had been four nurses arrive for the old woman's inspection and she had rejected them all out of hand.

Lord Heatherington too was a troubled man. He was worried about his son, and his wife, who had gone into a decline as the days passed and there was no communication from Clive, and he had no idea what to do about his mother.

'What about asking the doctor?' Lady Heatherington asked one day. 'He might know of nurses seeking employment that your mother could take to?'

Lord Heatherington's face brightened. 'What a good idea, my dear,' he said. 'He is calling in to see Mother today anyway and I'll have a word then.'

So Lord Heatherington was waiting for the doctor as he descended the stairs, and explained to him the difficulty he was having in employing nurses that his mother approved of.

'What about the wee lass in there with her now?'

'Oh, she's just a housemaid filling in until we could get qualified people. She has no nursing skills.'

'Well, your mother doesn't really need nursing, and the two get on well together from what I could see,' the doctor said. 'You could look further and fare worse. I could pop in every week and if you need me in between times I'm at the end of the telephone. Would the girl take on the care of the old lady on a permanent basis?'

'I don't know,' Charles said. 'We've never discussed it.'

'Put it to her and see what she says.'

Lord Heatherington sought Lucy out as soon as the doctor left. He found her taking trays back to the kitchen. 'Can I have a word, Lucy?'

'Certainly, sir,' Lucy said, wondering if the doctor had given him bad news.

'I have a proposition to put to you,' Lord Heatherington said.

Lucy nodded, but she was totally unprepared for him asking her if she would consider working for his mother on a permanent basis and that they would engage someone else to do her old job.

Lucy hesitated, not entirely sure she wanted to be at the beck and call of old Lady Heatherington all day every day, for all she was becoming fond of her. 'But I have no nursing skills,' she said at last.

'The doctor said she doesn't need nursing, just basic care,' Lord Heatherington said. 'He recommended I ask you, actually.'

'Did he? Golly.'

246

'Yes, and I will be straight with you. My mother hasn't got long and I don't want to upset her by installing nurses that she might not take to if she only has months left. If you took this job on the doctor will come every week – and more often, if necessary – and it would please my mother because you are one of the few people she has taken a liking to.'

Lucy knew if she refused this she would always feel guilty.

Lord Heatherington went on, 'And you will, of course, get more money for the extra responsibility. I thought maybe a pound a week to start.'

Lucy started. A pound a week was a sizeable wage, though she thought she would probably earn every penny, but she had also to look to the future and so she asked, 'And what about after, sir? When it is all over, what will happen to me?'

'I will never forget what you agreed to do,' Lord Heatherington said earnestly. 'And a good position will be found for you. I promise you that. Will you think it over?'

Lucy, however, had thought it over, weighed the pros and the cons, and thought really there was only one road she could take. It wasn't just the lure of more money, though a pound a week was not to be sneezed at. She looked into Lord Heatherington's slightly anxious eyes and smiled. 'It's all right,' she said. 'I have thought it over and I will tend your mother, if that's what you want and she is agreeable.'

The day after Lucy agreed to look after old Lady Heatherington she had taken the trays down after the evening meal, leaving her charge to doze. As she entered the kitchen, Rory was telling them all news of a German bombing raid on a Basque town called Guernica that day, which had come through on Lord Heatherington's wireless.

'Apparently it was only a small place,' he said, 'but lots of refugees running away from the fighting had arrived there. Added to that it was market day so the town was full, and they pounded it for four hours. Hundreds were killed, the reporter said, and those who attempted to escape were strafed on the road by machine-gun fire.'

It was chilling listening to this, but the following day the morning papers showed the devastation. Aghast, staff gathered in the kitchen to look at the grainy newsprint photographs: the town in ruins and the dead lying in the streets, often in pools of blood or with missing limbs or grotesque body parts mixed with the ruins of buildings that had collapsed around them. And in the roads leading out of the town were the bodies of the old, women with children, and even swaddled babies. None was spared. They were all killed along with their pet dogs and cats, or donkeys or small ponies still shackled to carts.

'It's barbaric,' Clara said. 'There is no other word for something so vicious and savage.'

'Take it from me, one who was a soldier for many years, this is Germany's way of showing us what it is capable of,' Rory said.

'What are you actually saying, Rory?' Mr Carlisle asked.

'I'm saying that in my opinion we could easily have one heap of trouble with Germany,' Rory

248

said. 'We beat them before and it might be up to us to teach them another lesson with another war.'

Cook gasped and opened her eyes wide because she could remember the Great War and had often told the girls tales about the way of life then and how bad things were; the numbers of young men and boys who never came back at all or came home maimed. 'Surely,' she said, 'no one will want that carnage again.'

'I think it just might come to that,' Rory said, and his words hung in the air because no one could think of a thing to say.

A pall of anxiety seemed to hang over the whole house with the news of the bombing of Guernica, though Lucy kept the disconcerting news from old Lady Heatherington. And, thought Lucy, where was Clive in this? It was all right the man Lord Heatherington spoke to in Liverpool saying he saw Clive alive and as well as could be expected, but that had been ages ago, and now there was this bombing raid. She didn't imagine the International Brigade having any defence against bombs hurtling through the air.

Everyone seemed to accept now that the rebels would win the fight, for they were firmly allied with Germany and Spain. Lucy could have wept for the young men who had given up their lives in vain, and one of those could be Clive. Even if he was not killed or badly injured by the rebels he may have been captured, and she knew that men who could gun down the old and weak and women and children would show little mercy against these adversaries who had come to fight independent of their own country's policy.

Later she was to think that that year she spent with old Lady Heatherington was as if time had been suspended. Each passing day with no news, the certainty that Clive was dead and that she would never see him again seemed to hammer inside her. She felt as if she had a hole where her heart had once been and a cloak of misery surrounded her.

She eventually lost her ready smile and cheerful outlook and Cook remarked grimly that that was not to be wondered at. Closeted as she was with the old lady day after day; it would put years on anyone.

That was only partly true. The worst part about grieving for Clive was that there was no one to confess her feelings to, no one to share her intense pain. She could never tell how even the mention of his name, or the memory of that one light kiss on the cheek, made her feel. She was certain that she had loved Clive, but she could never admit to that.

They all missed Clive in various ways and so as if by tacit agreement his name was seldom mentioned. As Cook said, it helped no one; it was like poking at a bad tooth. On the other hand, old Lady Heatherington talked about him constantly at first, and each time Lucy felt as though she had been stabbed with a steel blade. She didn't even have the ease that tears might have brought to her intense heartache, not even at night lest the old lady heard.

Lord Heatherington was at a loss to know how

to deal with his mother's gloom. He came to see her most days and tried to get her interested in the Coronation of the new King, George VI, which had been on 10 May.

'Can't understand it,' he said to Lucy. 'Mother has always been an ardent royalist and I offered to have the wireless set up in here so that she could hear the proceedings, but she wouldn't hear of it. She wasn't even interested in the pictures in the papers I brought up.'

'No, sir.'

'I know what's eating her,' Lord Heatherington went on. 'Does she think everyone in the house doesn't feel the loss of Clive, my wife and myself most of all? But life must go on, though it's devilishly hard at times. Clive would have wanted us to do that.'

'Maybe when you know your life is drawing to a close it puts a different complexion on things, sir.'

'Maybe,' Lord Heatherington said, and touched Lucy gently on the shoulder. 'You are a good girl, Lucy, and so very understanding with my mother.'

Lucy felt quite guilty when he said that because in truth she had been more concerned with her own misery than anyone else's. Some days she woke up after a night peppered with distressing dreams feeling totally wretched, but after Lord Heatherington's words, she decided that moping around and dwelling on things was helping no one, least of all herself. As Clara had once said, she wasn't the first person to lose someone they loved and she wouldn't be the last. Old Lady Heatherington, whom everyone said had had little time for many people, had always loved Clive, and Lucy decided she owed it to him to make his grandmother's last months on earth as pleasant as she could.

With this resolution in her head, she rose the following morning with a smile on her face. 'What's up with you?' Old Lady Heatherington growled.

The smile stayed in place. 'Nothing. What do you mean?'

'Well, you have been a right misery guts of late. Now it's like you have lost a sixpence and found a pound, as my old nanny used to say.'

Lucy was surprised the old lady had noticed her mood because she was remarkably self-absorbed. 'Maybe I have,' she answered. 'That's for me to know and you to find out. Now, do you want a hand getting to the bathroom or would you like a cup of tea first?'

Not aware of Lucy's decision, Cook had been worried enough about the change in Lucy's attitude to mention it to Clara, who had of course noticed herself, and had a good idea what could help her. A girl called Phoebe had already been engaged to do Lucy's job and so that morning, as soon as the family had eaten breakfast, she asked if she might speak to them. She suggested to Lord and Lady Heatherington that Lucy and Clodagh have the time off agreed to before the incident with Nurse Townsend, which had effectively bound Lucy to old Lady Heatherington's room.

Lord Heatherington felt guilty that he hadn't stipulated anything about time off when he had

252

offered Lucy the job and he knew it should have been discussed at the time. It was obvious that she couldn't do this round the clock with no respite at all, especially as she was still such a young girl. Lady Heatherington too knew the difficulties of hiring nurses that the old lady would tolerate. Her husband had said his mother was slowly dying and until she was laid in the earth he didn't want Lucy Cassidy upset in any way. 'Give her anything she wants, Charles,' she advised. 'More money, time off, whatever it is. She is the only one able to manage your mother.'

'I agree,' Lord Heatherington said. 'So, who will see to her when Lucy is not there?'

'She doesn't mind me for short amounts of time,' Clara said. 'I do it now on Sunday when Lucy goes to early Mass but she is usually home again before old Lady Heatherington wakes up. And if she was out in the evening, your mother is usually sleeping then too, for she tires easily, so it shouldn't be a very onerous task.'

'So you and I will do it between us,' Lord Heatherington said emphatically.

Clara's mouth dropped agape. 'You, sir?'

'Yes. Me, sir,' Lord Heatherington said with a smile. 'She is my mother and I should take some responsibility for her. I'll put it to her.'

'If I were you, sir, I would leave that to Lucy,' Clara advised. 'She definitely has a way with her.'

Clara knew the old lady had to be handled delicately, so she waited until Lucy came down to collect the tray at dinner time, when she told her what was proposed. To say Lucy was excited would be an understatement. She grasped Clod-

253

agh around the waist and galloped her around the kitchen. And far from being vexed, Cook laughed along with the two girls while Hazel remarked that time off should have been established at the start and it just proved what her dad said: that this lot wouldn't give you the skin off their rice pudding.

But Lucy gave no mind to Hazel. She just went up the stairs as fast as she could, aware of the tray of dinner that she carried, and then she curbed her impatience until old Lady Heatherington had eaten her fill, which didn't take long with the small appetite she had now. Then Lucy removed the tray, sat on the bed and told her about the hours off she was going to have when either Mrs O'Leary or Lord Heatherington would stay with her. She glared at Lucy and, with her flash of her old imperiousness, she snapped, 'No, you shall not, for I will not allow it.'

Lucy gave a short laugh. 'You don't get a say in it, I'm afraid. It has all been decided. And don't sulk,' she added, as old Lady Heatherington pulled a face. 'And if you're going to start yelling, forget it, because I will just walk off and leave you till you feel better.'

'I don't know why I put up with you,' the old lady grumbled.

'Nor me,' Lucy said, not looking a bit abashed. 'You'd better tell your son and he will get nice nurses to look after you and I will move on elsewhere.'

The old lady was silent and Lucy felt sorry for her, for she knew her age and frailty rendered her vulnerable and powerless, and these are hard things to come to terms with. So she said, 'You are being silly about this and very unfair. It isn't unreasonable for me to want to go out some-times. Didn't you at my age?'

'Don't know. What age are you?'

'Fifteen,' Lucy said. 'Sixteen in October.'

'I was in the schoolroom then and allowed no-where without a chaperone,' old Lady Heather-ington said. 'Nor could I put up my hair or dine with my parents until I was sixteen. How would you like that?'

'Not much,' Lucy said. 'But that was the way it was for you. And at least you didn't have to earn your living at fourteen, like we all have to.'

'No, we didn't.'

'So don't you think I deserve time off?'

The old lady didn't answer that, but what she did say was, 'Where will you go?'

'The cinema.'

'Oh,' said the old lady. 'I have never been to a cinema.'

'I hadn't until I came here,' Lucy said. 'They didn't have cinemas in the little place I came from.'

'There were no cinemas when I was growing up,' old Lady Heatherington said. 'By the time they did come in I was married with a son of my own and they were considered rather vulgar.'

'Oh, they're much better now,' Lucy said, 'and not silent any more like Clara – Mrs O'Leary – said they were in the beginning. Look,' she said suddenly. 'I will tell you everything about it the next day and paint the picture of the cinema so that you will be able to visualise it. If you can't go there, I will bring it to you.'

And when she looked up at the old lady to see what she thought of this, she was startled to see tears in her eyes.

FOURTEEN

Lucy and Clodagh valued their free time, knowing that in service it could all be changed at the whim of their employer and so they haunted the cinema, able to forget everything for a while as they lusted after Errol Flynn, Clark Gable and Cary Grant. Or they could be stunned by the sweetness of Shirley Temple or the beauty of Dorothy Lamour, and they were frankly amazed by the attributes of Jean Harlow, but then they could laugh themselves silly at the antics of Laurel and Hardy. But while Lucy told old Lady Heatherington about the films she saw, as she had promised to do, she said not a word about Pathé News, for the world seemed a turbulent and frightening place and the old lady didn't need to know that.

Old Lady Heatherington was very interested in the cartoon films Lucy described, for they stirred up memories of the lantern shows she had seen in her youth. 'Of course they were childish pastimes,' she said. 'When I was more grown up I was taken to the theatre, to see an opera or ballet, or occasionally a play.'

Lucy encouraged her to talk about the old

times, seeing the animation in her eyes as she relived the days that were gone for ever, when she was fit and active and her life was full. Lady Heatherington was surprised and pleased, for no one had shown much interest in her ramblings before.

The summer was a good one and so the girls didn't confine their outings to the cinema, but spent many fine days in Sutton Park, wandering through the meadows and woods and locating the seven lakes and the meandering streams that fed into them. Old Lady Heatherington told Lucy of the times her governess would take her there. However she said she always had good clothes on and so the walk was a sedate one. She couldn't climb the trees, plodge in the streams or walk through the woods, kicking clouds of leaves in the air as she had seen other children do and Lucy began to think there were disadvantages to being rich.

The leaves turned from orange and yellow to brown, and were blown from the trees in the winds of autumn. Old Lady Heatherington seemed set to defy the doctor's predictions on the time she had left. In fact, Lucy was becoming very fond of the old lady. She was too weak now to do much roaring and had come to some sort of acceptance of this, but she told Lucy she didn't intend to go till she heard what had happened to Clive one way or another. Lucy told Clodagh this as they made their way to the pictures one night.

'But we might never know,' Clodagh said.

Lucy sighed. 'I know, and she is so incredibly skinny. She seems to be willing herself to live on and on. Every day I give her a blanket bath like I told you has to be done to try and prevent bed sores, but she is so light it's like lifting a bag of bones. Her skin, which I put cream on afterwards, is almost translucent and I have to be so gentle.'

'What do you talk to her about?'

'The things we do, mainly – you know, the films we see and our walks in Sutton Park – but she does a lot of the talking too. She tells me of the elaborate dinners she used to go to, the kind of function neither of us is likely to see. And she said we must go back to the dancing class, that every young lady should learn to dance. Lord Heatherington once said that he remembered his mother as very beautiful and hearing people say what a superb dancer she was.'

'Isn't it boring, hearing all that old stuff?'

'No, I like it,' Lucy said. 'It's like having snap shots of her life in Victorian times. And it gives me something else to write to Mammy and the others about. It was difficult to write about anything really upbeat when I was closeted in with old Lady Heatherington day after day. They seem to be having such a grand time in the US of A that I don't want to have them fretting over me.'

'Well, why don't we start dancing again?' Clodagh suggested. 'Then that will be something else to write and tell them, though I doubt anyone would call us superb.'

'Oh, I don't know,' Lucy said. 'We had so few lessons before we had to stop that we are almost an untapped source. We might be able to trip the light fantastic with the best of them when we have had a few lessons.'

'Oh, yes, we might indeed,' said Clodagh with a sardonic grin.

As the weather became colder, Lord Heatherington was amazed at his mother's indomitable spirit. He would sometimes stop outside the door and hear the voices of Lucy and his mother rising and falling as they talked easily together. He found himself envying their apparent closeness and wondered how it was that a young girl he would have said had nothing in common with his mother could entertain her so well when he was sometimes scrabbling around for things to tell her.

The doctor also sang Lucy's praises as he accepted a drink from Lord Heatherington after he had examined old Lady Heatherington in mid-October. He said she seemed to have natural compassion and an affinity with the old lady that was usually not found in one so young. 'She is so bright too,' he went on. 'You tell her a thing or demonstrate something and she has it first time. And she is gentle and has soft hands. Your mother has lost so much weight, for Lucy said sometimes she eats less than a bird, and her joints are so swollen that it would be easy inadvertently to hurt her, but your mother maintains that Lucy never does that. She takes her time, she said to me.'

He shook his head and went on, 'You have a gem in that young girl, and she looks after your mother so well that she could easily go on way after Christmas. I must say this to you, Charles, that girl is wasted in service and would make a first-rate nurse.'

The following week was Lucy's sixteenth birthday. She received cards from all the family, and her mother had also sent her a beautiful watch, and there were two twenty-dollar bills inside the card, signed, 'From Mammy and Declan'.

'It almost makes me not want to accept the money if it's from him as well,' Lucy said to Clodagh as she made up old Lady Heatherington's breakfast tray.

'Are you completely bonkers?' Clodagh asked. 'Your mammy and this Declan are married whether you like him or not, and so they are going to do things together like write cards because that's what marriage is all about. That money will be from your mother as well as Declan. But I'll tell you this much: if someone, anyone, was to send me so much money then I would write straight back and say thank you very much. But if you really can't bring yourself to take it then please send any donations my way and book yourself into the loony bin.'

'All right, all right, you win,' Lucy said. 'But for now I have to get this tray upstairs. I don't want the old lady shouting at me, today of all days.'

But old Lady Heatherington had no desire to shout at Lucy; quite the reverse, in fact. She called her over to the bed as soon as she entered the room. 'Put the tray down somewhere. I'll see to it in a minute because I have no appetite today anyway, and I have something for you.' She withdrew from the jewellery box beside her bed a magnificent sapphire pendant on a shimmering golden chain. 'Happy Birthday, Lucy.'

'Oh, no, my lady,' Lucy protested. 'I cannot possibly accept that. It is far too valuable.'

'It is also mine and I can give it to whoever I want to give it to,' old Lady Heatherington said. 'But you are right to be cautious because after I am gone there are those who might say that you stole that from me, or that you inveigled it from me when the balance of my mind was disturbed.'

'Madam,' said Lucy with a short laugh, 'no one would dare say that about you.'

'Believe me, Lucy,' the old lady said, 'people will say anything when there is money involved. I want no nastiness to occur to you so tomorrow I will ask Charles to contact my solicitor and draw things up legally, and then there can be no argument.'

'Are you sure, my lady?'

'Absolutely. I have always been very fond of that pendant, and you were right when you said it was valuable, so guard it well.'

'Oh, madam, I would be afraid to wear it,' Lucy said. 'Isn't there someone else that you can give it to?'

'Undoubtedly there is,' old Lady Heatherington said, 'But I want you to have it and no other. It will remind you of me when I am gone.'

'My lady,' Lucy said firmly, 'I need no pendant to remember you, for with or without that I will never forget you. But thank you so much for such a wonderful gift.'

As Lucy had passed another birthday she'd had a rise, and because of the responsible job that she was coping with so remarkably well, Lord

Heatherington gave her another five shillings a week. Though Lucy thanked Lord Heatherington profusely she had never had so much money in her life before and she felt uncomfortable.

'You haven't got to spend it just because you have it,' Clara advised her when Lucy turned to her in a panic. 'If I were you I would open a Post Office account and put any spare cash in that. Put your dollars in there too, and they will convert them to pounds so you can spend them if you need to.'

'I can't ever imagine needing so much money.'

'Maybe not,' Clara said, 'but you will soon have to spend some on yourself because you are still growing and the clothes you bought last year no longer fit so well.'

Lucy nodded. 'I could do with a winter coat at least because the one I have leaves a lot of leg exposed.'

It was almost Christmas and still Lucy had not got round to buying herself a new coat. Then huge parcels arrived from America. They tantalised Lucy and eventually she opened them in her room on Christmas Eve, just before meeting Clodagh to go to midnight Mass. She opened the first one from her mother and Declan and withdrew a beautiful coat. It was deep golden in colour, padded and slightly shiny, and it also had a snug-fitting hood with fur around the edge. It was quite the finest coat she had even worn. She put it on straight away and admired herself in the mirror before scanning the letter her mother had put in with the parcel: *Thought of you when we saw this. They are all the rage in America, and whatever the weather you will be warm and snug in this.'*

More eagerly now, Lucy tore open the other parcels. Grainne and Danny had bought her sheepskin mittens, the same colour as her coat, and Liam and Sam a fluffy cream scarf. She was still in the coat, the other things scattered on the bed, mixed up with brown paper and string coated with sealing wax, and she thought of her mother, brothers and sister in far-off America choosing all the lovely things for her. She put her hand over her face and cried so much that the tears ran down between her fingers.

Eventually, she pulled herself together and went in to check on the old lady before going down to the kitchen, when Clara would take her place until she returned from Mass. She tiptoed across the room where only low lights burned. As she had expected, old Lady Heatherington was fast asleep. Lucy gently tucked the blanket in more securely and had turned round to tiptoe out again when Lady Heatherington, with her eyes still shut, said suddenly, 'You were crying.'

Her voice was slurred with tiredness so all Lucy said was, 'Hush. You must sleep or you will be too tired to enjoy tomorrow.'

Old Lady Heatherington opened her eyes and fastened them on Lucy as she said, 'I will soon have all the time in the world to rest, so tell me why you were crying?'

'Because...' Lucy began and stopped. 'They were happy tears,' she said. She heard the old lady sigh as she went on, 'I will tell you all about

263

it in the morning.'

A brief smile tugged at the corners of old Lady Heatherington's mouth and her eyes were fluttering shut again as she said, 'Happy tears are good. You are made for happiness and joy,' and more tears stung Lucy's eyes as she stole from the room.

Despite the words the old lady exchanged with Lucy, she had been too sleepy to notice what she was wearing, but that wasn't so in the kitchen, where there were cries of delight.

'I couldn't wait until tomorrow,' Lucy explained.

'Good job you didn't,' Clodagh said as they scurried down the road. 'It's now you need it because the night is bitterly cold. Anyway, when we come back it will be after twelve and Christmas Day.'

'Oh, yes, I never thought of that.'

'You are lucky, though,' Clodagh went on as they were hurrying down the road clasped together for warmth. 'That's the nicest coat I have ever seen. I bet they have some terrific clothes in America.'

'I'd say so,' Lucy said. 'If what they send me are anything to go by. But as well as the things, it's lovely to think of them going out and choosing clothes for me. Having me in mind.'

'I'd say that you are often in their minds, and your mother at least will be missing you loads,' Clodagh said. 'Mine tells me so in every letter she writes.'

'Yeah, and mine.'

'There you are then,' Clodagh said. 'Didn't you believe it or what?'

Lucy gave a shrug. 'I thought it was maybe just words.'

'Yeah, but words they mean,' Clodagh said, giving Lucy's arm a tighter squeeze. 'You know you are a right crackpot at times.'

Danny had sent a packet of photographs with his letter and Lucy showed some to old Lady Heatherington and pointed out who was who.

'What a fine family you have,' the old lady said approvingly. 'I would have loved brothers and sisters, and then I went on to have only the one son myself. When he goes there will be no one else to take over because there is no point my waiting any more. I know my lovely Clive is dead and soon I will be with him.'

'Don't upset yourself, my lady,' Lucy said, her own voice choked with emotion.

'I'm not really upset, my dear,' the old lady said, patting Lucy's hand consolingly. 'The tears are just a product of age and tiredness, and I am tired and ready to go. I have had a good long life so that is nothing to get upset over. But your life is just beginning, so tell me what you are doing here in service with such a fine family in New York, for they obviously think the world of you and your father looks a successful man.'

'He's not my father, only my stepfather.'

'Ah, is that it?' old Lady Heatherington said. 'Would you like to tell me about it, my dear?' In all her years she had never expressed the slightest interest in the lives of the servants she had in her household, but she was suddenly very interested in the life of the young girl who tended her so well.

Lucy pulled no punches, nor did she exaggerate, and the old lady learnt of the happiness of her early life and her love for her father, who had so obviously loved her in return. She felt envious, for she had hardly known either of her parents. However, the happiness in the Cassidy home didn't last. The family was reduced to penury due to the illness and death of Lucy's beloved father, which forced Lucy to seek employment outside the home as soon as she was old enough. Then Lucy told her about the arrival of Declan, and although she didn't speak of her initial antagonism or resentment, it was written all over her face. She didn't speak either of the speed of the wedding being forced upon them by the Church, because few non-Catholics would understand that. She just said that Declan had had to return to work and had to get married first so that he could take Mammy and the children back with him. She was honest and told old Lady Heatherington that she had been urged to go too.

'And you chose not to. Why?'

'I suppose I didn't want Declan telling me what to do,' Lucy said. 'I had been away from home some time and although I am answerable to people here, it wasn't the same as home. I am more independent and I like that. I want to stand on my own two feet.'

'Doing what?' the old lady asked. 'In service all your life?'

'Not likely,' Lucy said, and then seeing the shocked expression on the old lady's face, she said, 'Sorry, my lady. I mean no, and at one time I wouldn't have said I knew what I wanted to do,

266

but caring for you and the urging of the doctor has led me to think that I would like to work in a hospital.'

'A nurse?'

Lucy shook her head. 'I don't think I will make it as far as being a nurse. There's exams to take.'

'What of it?' the old lady snapped. 'You're a bright girl.'

'There is no real evidence of that,' Lucy said. 'As I said, I left school at fourteen. But even if I could pass exams there are things to buy, like uniform and books, and then nurses get paid very little while they train. The doctor said most get some help from parents.'

'What about your stepfather?'

Lucy's head shot up and she said very definitely, 'I would never take anything from him.'

Old Lady Heatherington threw up her hands. 'So what are you to do, young Lucy?'

'Oh, don't worry about it,' Lucy said. 'Something will turn up, and meanwhile I will stay here as long as I am needed.'

FIFTEEN

It was after the turn of the New Year that old Lady Heatherington started to go downhill fast. Lucy had seen a change in her on Christmas Day, for after the sumptuous dinner, which she had been unable to eat much of, she asked to see all the staff. She had never done such a thing

267

before and she asked particularly to see Cook and Mrs O'Leary, whom she thanked for looking after her so well. Lucy could see how astonished they both were because old Lady Heatherington was not renowned for her good manners. She even apologised to Cook for being unable to eat much of the delicious food sent up to her room and Cook had been touched by that.

'That's all right, my lady,' she said. 'Everyone's appetite is different, but as long as you enjoyed what you did eat, that's the important thing.'

'How could I not?' old Lady Heatherington said. 'You are such a marvellous cook. And your pastries are delicious too, Mrs O'Leary.'

'Thank you, my lady.'

The other staff were clustered around the door, and the old lady signalled for them to come in. The girls filed into the room one by one, bobbing a curtsy to the old lady propped up in the bed. Jerry and Mr Carlisle followed, Lord Heatherington brought up the rear and even Lady Heatherington had been prevailed upon to attend. With them all assembled, champagne was poured for everyone and Lord Heatherington proposed the toast to his mother.

Even in her bed, Lucy thought she looked very regal, and she let her eyes rest on each one of them as she sipped the champagne. Lucy had the sudden feeling that she was saying goodbye and this was how she wanted to be remembered. However, when everyone left at last she was exhausted and she slept most of the afternoon and evening away, and so deeply that Lucy was able to join in some of the festivities in the servants' hall.

Lord Heatherington saw his mother slipping further and further away in the following days and he knew that he would miss her when she was gone. That surprised him because he had begun to realise that he hadn't really known her. Brought up like other boys of his class, he had been reared by a nanny and a succession of nursemaids. Sometimes his nanny took him downstairs to see his parents, who had been remote figures. He had hated it and he imagined so did they, because they knew nothing of their son and he was always happier when his nanny took him back to the nursery. He was away at school from the age of seven and his schoolfriends became his family. Later the army took up that role when he had joined as an officer cadet at the age of sixteen.

He had cared for his mother because it had been his duty to do so, and not because he had any affection for her, and the affection had developed only because a slip of a servant girl had somehow turned his mother from an embittered and hostile old lady into a human being. He regretted the lost years, when he might have been able to get closer to his mother if he had tried harder. Not, of course, that he would admit any of this, but he knew that he owed Lucy Cassidy a big debt.

Lady Heatherington couldn't understand why her husband was in the least upset about the imminent death of that objectionable old woman, mother or not. She had only agreed to go into her room on Christmas Day because it would have been remarked on if she hadn't, and she resented the fact that the old woman had just sat there as if she was the Queen of Sheba and had summoned all her subjects to her side.

And her husband went over the top as usual. Champagne for servants, I mean, really... And she could say nothing about it. She could see though that the old woman was on her last legs and she wouldn't be sorry to see the back of her. At least with her gone no one else could use the title Lady Heatherington. That would be hers and hers alone.

The kitchen staff were more forgiving.

'You could have knocked me down with a feather when her ladyship spoke to me so pleasant, like, and actually thanked me for the food. I never expected that,' Cook said. 'Did you put her up to it, Lucy?'

'No,' Lucy said. 'I honestly didn't know what she was going to do. Anyway, she would hardly listen to me.'

'She does listen,' Clara said. 'She must do because you have worked miracles with that old lady.'

'I haven't really,' Lucy said. 'Under all that bluster and anger, the old harridan I met was just an old lady. Now she's just tired and ready to go.'

'Well,' said Cook, 'I don't think she will have a long wait.'

Lucy didn't think so either, but it seemed as if old Lady Heatherington was in no hurry. The year turned 1938, and January came in with snow and ice and intense cold. Old Lady Heatherington slept most of the time, but then suppurating sores broke out on her torso despite the oils that Lucy applied after her blanket baths.

'It isn't your fault,' Dr Gilbert said. 'It's because the skin is so thin.'

He left ointment for Lucy to apply to the sores and, because Old Lady Heatherington complained of pain for the first time, he left painkillers. He advised Lucy to crush them up in milk to make them easier to take. Lucy took all this in her stride, but there was a smell to the room now. It was the smell from the sores, but overriding it was the smell of death and decay.

Old Lady Heatherington lost her tenuous hold on life at the very end of January and Lucy was pleased that at last her suffering was at an end. Lord Heatherington had just left the room after visiting his mother, though she had been asleep and so he hadn't been able to speak to her. Lucy had taken his place by the bed and enfolded the old lady's bony, heavily veined hand in hers when she heard the death rattle in her throat. She tried to get up from the chair, intending to call Lord Heatherington back, but she felt her hand caught in a vicelike grip. Then she was released, old Lady Heatherington's hand fell back on the counterpane, the room was suddenly very still and quiet, and Lucy knew that she was gone.

She couldn't go to the funeral service as she was a Catholic, and neither could Clara and Clodagh, but a week later they stood together on a miserably cold day with clouds the colour of gunmetal and so low and dense that they turned the afternoon to evening, and they watched the coffin being lowered into the grave. Lord and Lady Heatherington stepped forward and each threw a clod of earth on top of it. Thud! Thud!

It was done, and there would be hordes back to the house for the buffet that Cook had been working on for two days.

'Who are all these people anyway?' Lucy asked as they started up the road towards home.

Clara shrugged. 'Friends, some of them, I suppose. I mean, Lord and Lady Heatherington are pretty influential anyway, and you always have friends if you have a title.'

'I'll tell you two who will be up at the house,' Clodagh said. 'I saw them in the crowd at the grave, and that's that flipping Jessica Ponsomby and her mother.'

'You haven't said much about them lately.'

'That's because they haven't come, or at least not half so often, and sometimes the mother has come on her own. Compared to her odious daughter she isn't that bad, as long as you accept that she is stuck up, toffee-nosed and has no manners at all.'

'I wonder why they have cooled off.'

'Because of Master Clive, I'd say,' Clara said. 'That's who Jessica wanted, and seemingly that's what their mothers wanted too. Now that it seems apparent that Master Clive is not going to come back, she maybe has to cast her net wider.'

'Well, I feel sorry for anyone she catches in it,' Lucy remarked.

Before anyone could make any sort of reply to this, there was the peep of a horn and Dr Gilbert's car drew up beside them. 'Can I give you young ladies a lift?' he said, and they all accepted with pleasure, though their talk about the Heatheringtons and their guests had to stop.

The following day, Lucy was stunned to be summoned to the library. 'But why?' she asked Clara. Clara, Cook and even Mr Carlisle had just returned from there, where they had been given small gratuities from old Lady Heatherington's will.

Clara shook her head. 'They didn't say why, but I shouldn't keep them waiting.'

'No,' Lucy said, and she stopped only to tuck her hair more firmly under her cap and change her stained apron for a spotless white one before hurrying along the corridor.

Lord and Lady Heatherington sat on dining chairs facing the table, behind which sat the family solicitor, Mr Theodore Braithwaite, with a sheaf of papers in front of him. Lucy had seen him before because he had attended the old lady at the time she had been given the pendant. He looked up as she entered and smiled as he indicated a vacant chair to the side of him. Feeling Lady Heatherington's eyes boring into her, Lucy crossed the room and sat on the chair gingerly. She saw Lady Heatherington glare at her, and even Lord Heatherington had a slight frown on his face.

'This is the last will and testament of Miranda Elizabeth Heatherington,' the solicitor said, riffling the papers. 'It is a new will drawn up by me in October and witnessed by my clerk as the elder Lady Heatherington wanted. It supersedes all other wills, and she was definitely of sound mind at the time.'

'Oh, do get on with it,' snapped Lady Heatherington.

The solicitor pursed his lips. 'Very well,' he said stiffly. 'The first bequest was a blue sapphire pendant that she has already given as a gift to the person nursing her at the time, a Lucy Cassidy.'

There was a low hiss from Lady Heatherington and she snapped at Lucy, 'You conniving little guttersnipe. How did you inveigle her into giving you that?'

'Amelia!' Lord Heatherington said, clearly shocked, while the solicitor said, 'Calm yourself, dear lady.'

Lucy, however, was not going to be spoken to like that by anyone, and she turned to face Lady Heatherington. 'I am no guttersnipe, my lady,' she said, 'and you have no right to say that about me. I inveigled the elder Lady Heatherington into nothing. She gave it to me for my sixteenth birthday and insisted on putting it in the will in case anyone claimed I had stolen it.'

'That is exactly what she told me,' the solicitor said.

'And I didn't want to accept it either,' Lucy said. 'It is so very beautiful and I said that there was probably someone in the family she should give it to.'

'There was, you wretched child!' Lady Heatherington ground out. 'Me. It was mine by right. You must have talked her into it.'

Lucy shook her head. 'No, my lady, I did not.'

'Well, you must give it to me now,' Lady Heatherington demanded. 'It is unthinkable that you should have such a valuable pendant.'

Lucy's head went a little higher so that she was staring Lady Heatherington full in the face. 'The elder Lady Heatherington didn't seem to feel that it was unthinkable for me to have such a pendant, and it would be disrespectful of her memory, surely, if I was to just give it away.'

'Charles, do something!' Lady Heatherington demanded.

'My dear,' Lord Heatherington said, 'I know that you have always admired that pendant, but it belonged to my mother and she could give it to whoever she wanted. I'm afraid that is the end of it.'

'I'm afraid it's not quite all,' the solicitor said.

'Oh, do let's hear it all then,' Lady Heatherington said witheringly.

Ignoring that, the solicitor went on, 'There is another bequest for Lucy Cassidy and it is for two hundred and fifty pounds so that she can train as a nurse if she wishes to do so.'

There was a gasp from all those assembled, and the solicitor hid a smile. He had always liked the elder Lady Heatherington and when she had him draw up the will she would have no one in the house witness it, which was why she had asked him to bring his clerk along. 'This will is full of surprises,' she had said, 'and will set the cat among the pigeons right and proper.'

Lucy was looking at the solicitor as if she couldn't believe her ears.

'Two hundred and fifty pounds to a servant!' Lady Heatherington spat out. 'How ridiculous.'

Lucy herself was completely dumbfounded and yet moved to tears over the old lady's generosity. But then she caught sight of Lady Heatherington's eyes glittering in anger and she knew she had made a very bad enemy.

The news flew around the kitchen and reactions were mixed. Some were plainly jealous of Lucy's good fortune. Hazel, knowing what she owed Lucy, said nothing, but even Clodagh said she was a right jammy devil, and she had said it with envy in her eyes. Others muttered about her and she overheard Phoebe saying that she must have sucked up to the old lady to be left so much money.

'Never see me do that,' Emily said. 'I ain't sucking up to anyone, and least of all the nobs. My dad says there'll be a revolution if things don't change soon.'

'And you'll be out the front holding a banner,' interrupted Cook. 'But you work here for now, so don't bite the hand that feeds you. Principles don't fill empty bellies, and don't you forget it. Now get away to do the job you are paid to do and give us some peace.'

Phoebe had gone with a look of resentment towards Lucy, but Lucy didn't care about Phoebe. She was concerned about the opinions of the others, however, and on her next half-day she bought Clara and Cook a large box of chocolates each, and treated Clodagh to a night at the pictures and a fish-and-chip supper after it. The rest of the money, though, she put away in the Post Office, in the account she had opened on Clara's advice. That money was her passport out of her life in service, and the idea that she might actually be a real nurse one day began to grow in her mind.

However, she didn't know how to go about it and she didn't see the doctor, whom she might have asked, on a regular basis any more. She hesitated to ask Lord Heatherington, who seemed strangely distracted, and Clara said that they had money worries. Remembering her life after her father died, Lucy thought this was all relative. In fact, Lord Heatherington had a further dilemma other than the financial pressures in the days following the reading of the will because his wife had told him she could not tolerate Lucy Cassidy working for them any longer.

She was still annoyed about the pendant, but even more upset by the state of their finances and the way Lucy had spoken to her, and had quite forgotten the care Lucy had taken of her mother-in-law. Lord Heatherington had not forgotten, nor had he forgotten the promise he had made to Lucy that after his mother had died there would be always be a position for her in his household.

One evening in late February, worn out by his wife's nagging, he called in to his club, hoping a couple of whiskys might hold his troubles at bay for a while, and was delighted to find Dr Gilbert in there.

'My God, man,' Gilbert said. 'You look as if you have the weight of the world on your shoulders.' Lord Heatherington confided in him about Lucy.

Dr Gilbert had also been thinking about Lucy and he said, 'Could you manage without Lucy if she were to find a position somewhere else?'

Lord Heatherington nodded. 'My wife tells me the household would manage very well, that we have no need of her at all. But I promised her...

277

Anyway, where would she go? She is tainted by that bloody money my mother gave her. I mean, what was she thinking of? And my wife is not helping there because I know for a fact, though I can prove nothing, that she is keeping the rumours going that Lucy somehow bamboozled my mother into leaving her that pendant and a large bequest.'

'Your mother wouldn't be easily bamboozled.'

'It wouldn't matter,' Lord Heatherington said. 'Many don't know my mother, and whatever glowing reference I would give Lucy, and whatever she says, the doubt will remain, especially with Amelia behaving as she is. I tell you, Gilbert, I fear Lucy Cassidy would not get further employment if she were to leave us, and yet she cannot stay.'

'Then let me make a suggestion,' Dr Gilbert said. 'From what you tell me and from what Lucy herself has said, she doesn't want a life in service, where once I said she was wasted, and I stick by that. She wants to nurse and your mother has made that possible, though there is still the little matter of the nurse's exams to pass.'

'Yes, but my wife—'

'Let me finish,' Dr Gilbert said. 'Trainee nurses do not start until they are eighteen or at least nearly that age. How about if Lucy leaves your employ and works as a volunteer in one of the hospitals for now? It will help her to be taken on by one of the teaching hospitals later, and keep her out of your wife's hair. I have connections in the Cottage Hospital in Sutton Coldfield and I know willing volunteers are always welcome. How about if I find her a job there? She could live in with my mother, and that would do me a favour because she's lonely since I moved to live over the surgery. If you pay her about half a crown a week pocket money she will be happy enough, I dare say. And don't look like that,' he snapped as he saw Lord Heatherington's eyes widen. 'You owe her that and more. She took on the care of an irascible old woman that no one else seemed able to handle. She solved a massive problem for you and saved you a fortune in professional nursing fees. Now she needs your help to carve a future for herself.'

Lord Heatherington felt ashamed, for he knew Lucy had looked after his mother better than any had done before, and he had got to know his mother better because of her. He would not mention it to Amelia, but he nodded to the doctor. 'You are right. I owe Lucy a great deal.'

'Yes,' said the doctor. 'But one thing I have discovered about Lucy is that she's very proud, and if she thought you were in effect paying for this she would probably have no truck with it, however much she wanted to. Put it to her and say that there is a bursary for this type of pre-nursing course and I can pull a few strings to make sure she gets one. Leave the details to me and meanwhile I will teach her what she needs to know to pass the nursing exams.'

'By Jove, Dr Gilbert,' Lord Heatherington said, 'you have thought it out well. I think she will jump at that.'

'She will,' Dr Gilbert said. 'She is a very sensible girl.'

Lucy was a sensible girl, and she was well aware what Lady Heatherington thought about her. So when Lord Heatherington sought Lucy out the following morning and told her what Dr Gilbert had proposed, she couldn't have been more pleased. She expressed surprise initially, for she hadn't been aware of any bursary such as he mentioned. But then, she told herself, how would she have known? And she thought it extremely generous of Dr Gilbert's mother to allow her to stay in her house, and two shillings and sixpence perfectly adequate when she was being trained. But she did ask, 'Will I have to give the money to Mrs Gilbert for my lodgings?'

'No,' Lord Heatherington said. 'Dr Gilbert is arranging that payment for you, and that money will be just for your expenses, I believe. All he is waiting for is your answer.'

There was only one answer she could give. She knew she would miss Clara, Cook, and Clodagh in particular, but she knew they too had recognised that her position at Maxted Hall was becoming untenable.

'I would love to do this, Lord Heatherington,' she said, and the light shone in her excited eyes. 'Thank you for thinking of me.'

SIXTEEN

So began one of the happiest periods in Lucy's life. Dr Gilbert came to fetch her a few days later. All the staff came out to wave her goodbye and she felt a rush of affection for all of them. As the car turned at the end of the drive and the house was out of sight she settled back into her seat with a sigh. She had butterflies in her stomach because she was so nervous, but the doctor seemed aware of this and as he drove her told her all about the cottage hospital. To Lucy it was like some sort of dream that she was actually going to work in a hospital in any capacity, but that he thought that she might actually train to be a nurse... Well, that was something she thought would never happen.

'Mum lives in Maney Hill, not that far from Sutton Coldfield,' Dr Gilbert said as he turned the car into the Parade and past all the shops. 'And not that far from the cinema either,' he continued. 'Just before the cinema we will pass right by the hospital and I will point it out to you.'

Lucy had a glimpse of the red-brick building with SUTTON COLDFIELD COTTAGE HOSPITAL written on a plaque above the arched front door. Seconds later they were passing the cinema, and then Dr Gilbert was driving down a wide tree-lined road.

'Does your mother mind my going to live with

281

her?' Lucy asked.

'Not a bit of it,' Dr Gilbert said, drawing to a stop outside a very elegant house. 'She'll love it. Now, come on, let's go and introduce you and you will see that for yourself.'

Mrs Gilbert was waiting at the door to meet them, a surprisingly small woman with brown hair and twinkling brown eyes, plump pink cheeks and a smile of welcome on her face.

'Good evening, Mrs Gilbert,' Lucy said with her arm outstretched.

'Good evening, my dear,' Mrs Gilbert said, shaking her hand warmly as she ushered her inside. 'And you are very, very welcome. But we mustn't stand on ceremony so you must call me Gwen. And now,' she said, 'I'm sure you would like to see your room.' And then, turning to Dr Gilbert, she said, 'Will you bring the case?'

'Of course,' Dr Gilbert said. 'Follow me, Lucy. I know the room Mother has chosen for you.'

'Oh,' said Lucy in delight moments later, for the room was lovely and cosy-looking, with pretty flowered curtains drawn across the windows, shutting out the night, and the light on the table beside the bed was turned on, lending a pink glow to the room. The pale blue carpet covered the whole floor and was the same shade as the candle-wick bedspread, and there was a wooden dressing table and wardrobe for her things. It was just about the prettiest bedroom that she had ever seen.

'Oh, it is so kind of you to put me up like this,' Lucy said later as she returned downstairs.

'Not at all, my dear,' Gwen Gilbert said. 'Don't

know who's doing who a favour, to be honest, but since Chris moved into the flat above the surgery, I haven't known what to do with myself. It will be nice to have the company. Now, I'll put the kettle on and we'll have a cuppa and you can tell me all about yourself.'

Dr Gilbert gave a rueful smile as his mother made for the kitchen. 'I'm warning you, she'll talk the hind leg off a donkey.'

'She's nice.'

'I didn't say she wasn't nice,' Dr Gilbert said, 'but she will want to know your life history.'

'That's all right,' Lucy said. 'I have nothing to hide. And,' she added, 'I don't think that I have thanked you enough for everything you've done for me.'

'Just you make a first-rate nurse,' Dr Gilbert said. 'That's all the thanks I need.'

Lucy was to find that Dr Gilbert was right, his mother did want to know all about her, but she thought that was only fair enough as she was living in her house. So she told her everything about her family, culminating in her mother meeting Declan after many years.

'He had never married,' Lucy said. 'Clara said he had always loved my mother and when she married my father he went to America. He didn't know my father had died until he arrived in Mountcharles because as he had no one belonging to him in Ireland he had no one to write to him with news.'

'And he found he still loved your mother?'

'Mmm. I suppose so.'

Gwen thought that was one of the most romantic things she had ever heard. 'And what did you think of the man?' she asked Lucy. 'Not much, I expect.'

'How did you guess?'

Gwen laughed. 'It wasn't hard, my dear. You have a very expressive face.'

'Yeah, well...' Lucy said. 'If they'd stayed in Ireland even for a bit so I could get to know him better it wouldn't have been so bad, but the Catholic Church wouldn't let them do that.' And she went on to explain what had happened and Gwen listened open-mouthed. 'Can they really do that?' she asked. 'Take your children away?'

'Oh, yes, they can do it all right,' Lucy said almost fiercely. 'And Mammy was doing nothing wrong, you know what I mean.'

'Yes, I know, my dear.'

'She'd have been destroyed if they had taken the children away.'

'As any women would be,' Gwen said. 'So isn't it wonderful that she found happiness again?'

'Yes, I suppose.'

'She is happy?'

'Oh, yes,' Lucy said. 'She seems very happy, and the children love Declan.'

'Must be a good man then,' Gwen said. 'Children sense these things.'

Lucy said nothing, but that night in bed she did a lot of thinking. Nearly everything she had said to Gwen about Declan had been good and positive, so what was her problem with him? There wasn't one, she suddenly realised. It was all in her mind. At that, her resentment against Declan

McCann seemed to float away.

The following morning, Lucy was very nervous starting at the hospital and couldn't really do justice to the bacon and egg breakfast Gwen had cooked for her. She did her best, but her stomach was churning in quite an alarming way and so Gwen, obviously worried that she would die of starvation, pushed a packet of sandwiches in her hand as she was leaving.

'Provisions for the troops?' Dr Gilbert asked as she leapt into the car.

She grinned at him. 'Yeah, something like that. I couldn't eat all my breakfast, you see. My stomach was doing somersaults.'

Dr Gilbert laughed. 'Oh, my mother will make sure you don't starve, at least,' he said. 'But there's no need to be nervous. I'm going to leave you in the capable hands of Nurse Patterson and she will see you right.'

Nurse Patterson had very red cheeks, the brightest green eyes Lucy had ever seen and a head of black curls so that her nurse's cap had to be secured with a great many Kirbigrips.

She shook hands with Lucy vigorously. 'Awfully glad to see you,' she said. 'An extra pair of hands is always useful in this place.'

Lucy was to find that she was right. In time she fitted in perfectly and was very popular because she didn't seem to mind what she did.

Her life was very full because she still went to the dancing classes and cinema with Clodagh, and they always met on Clodagh's full Sunday off. Some evenings, Dr Gilbert would put Lucy through her paces, teaching her the things she would need for her nursing exams, and on others she would sit and talk to Gwen, or they'd listen to the wireless. Lucy loved the wireless, though she thought there was a downside to it, for as well as the plays, music and comedy shows, it brought world affairs straight into the living room, in a far more compelling way than the same things written in the newspaper. So she heard about Hitler's troops invading Austria when she had been at the hospital a couple of weeks.

'The point is, Austria didn't seem to mind,' one of the nurses said. 'Old Adolf calling it the Anschluss, whatever the hell that is.'

'Maybe they don't mind because Hitler is Austrian, isn't he?'

'Is he?' another asked. 'Well, I couldn't care less really. I just think that if Austria isn't making a fuss, then we should keep out of it.'

There was a murmur of agreement to this. Lucy also agreed wholeheartedly. Hadn't they lost enough young men in Spain without going looking for trouble in other countries as well?

By the time that Lucy had been with the hospital six months no one knew what they had done without her. She had a calm personality and a low voice, pleasing on the ear, with a delightful lilt, and she was marvellous at soothing agitated or nervous patients. She had learnt how to take a person's temperature, thoroughly clean wounds and dress them effectively, administer medication and prepare needles for injections, and as she was not the slightest bit squeamish she had

286

no hesitation holding people still when splints had to be applied or injections given. She would also gently wash the frail and elderly, or help with their meals if it was awkward for them, or she would just sit and talk, knowing just what tone to adopt. And when the patients were all dealt with, she would always be found scalding bedpans, scrubbing rubber sheets with disinfectant, or making up spare beds.

All in all, she was a treasure, and that is what Nurse Patterson told Dr Gilbert. 'I tell you, I bless the day you brought her here,' she said. 'And I will miss her when she goes for training, but you are right, she is a natural nurse. How is her book learning going?'

'Not bad,' Dr Gilbert said. 'Not bad at all. But then I think you apply yourself better if you really want to do something.'

'Oh, I agree with that,' Nurse Patterson said. 'No one could say that I was really brainy, but I passed my nursing exams all right.'

'There you are then. Let's hope that Lucy does too.'

That evening, Lucy hurried home after she finished at the hospital, shivering a little for the day was bleak, the sky gunmetal grey, misty rain in the air and the winds sweeping down the streets in icy gusts. Gwen had the house beautifully warm, though, and she said to Lucy, as she was taking off her coat in the hall, 'What a dreadful day, my dear. Makes me think we might be in for a harsh winter if it is this cold and dismal when it is only just September. Anyway, I thought we would eat in the kitchen as it will be cosier. Come through when you are ready.'

As usual the casserole was delicious. While they ate, Lucy told Gwen of her day at the hospital and Gwen filled her in with day-to-day gossip she had gleaned when she was shopping. She was never able to discuss such things with Chris, who would often chide her gently for listening to gossip and rumour, which he claimed often led to people jumping to the wrong conclusions. Lucy, Gwen had decided almost as soon as she had arrived, was a far more comfortable person to talk to. So they lingered over their stew, and the apple crumble and custard afterwards, and were relaxing with a cup of tea when there was a terrific banging on the door.

Lucy was totally surprised on opening it to see Clodagh, her eyes alive with excitement. Lucy pulled her into the house. 'What's wrong?' she asked.

'You must come back to the Hall,' Clodagh said. 'Master Clive is home.'

Lucy's mouth dropped agape and she suddenly felt very light-headed. 'Master Clive,' she repeated, not quite believing she had heard right.

'Yes,' Clodagh said. 'You must come.'

'You mean, he's alive?' Lucy said almost breathlessly, aware that the ache in her heart that had lodged there from when she accepted that she would never see Clive again had eased a little.

'Oh, yes, he's alive all right,' Clodagh said. 'And asking for you.'

Lucy was stunned. 'Me?' she repeated. 'Why's he asking for me?'

Clodagh shrugged. 'I don't know. But what I do

288

know is that he's not right. He went mad when he knew you had left. He was raving. The Master told Rory to bring me to fetch you. He's waiting in the car outside.'

Lucy's heart was thumping wildly as she cried incredulously, 'Master Clive is alive! Oh, God, I can hardly believe it.'

'Clive?' Gwen said, coming into the hall, hearing the commotion. 'Isn't that the name of Charles Heatherington's son, who they thought had been killed in Spain?'

'Yes,' Lucy said. 'Isn't that wonderful news? Alive after all this time.'

'It is indeed.'

'And he's asking for Lucy.'

'Why?'

'No one seems to know,' Lucy said.

'You will come?' Clodagh insisted.

'Of course,' Lucy said, 'if you think that it is that important.' She turned to Gwen. 'I won't try and get back tonight. Please, could you get word to the hospital in the morning?'

'Don't worry about these things,' Gwen told her. 'Everything will be done. You just get your-self away, for the Heatheringtons must be beside themselves.'

'Oh, they are,' Clodagh said. 'Lady Heathering-ton hasn't stopped crying and the Master looks sort of stunned.'

'Well, you can't wonder at that, can you?' Gwen said, as Lucy fastened her coat and pulled on her boots. Her mind was teeming with questions and as she climbed after Clodagh into the car, which Rory had parked right outside the house, she

289

remarked, 'I bet Lady Heatherington wasn't best pleased that you were asked to fetch me.'

'I think the only thought in her head at the moment is that her son is not dead,' Rory said. 'She's still coming to terms with Clive's reappearance because it was such a shock for them both.'

'Yeah, we had no notice,' Clodagh said. 'There wasn't a letter or telegram or anything. He just arrived.'

'And this was tonight?'

'Yeah,' Clodagh said. 'Lord and Lady Heatherington were just finishing their dinner and we were having a few minutes' rest with a cup of tea in the kitchen when there was this banging on the door. As usual, Mr Carlisle went, and then he came back and told us there were two men in the hall dressed in some strange sort of uniform carrying Master Clive on a stretcher. According to Mr Carlisle, these chaps are sort of committed to getting the injured back to where they came from. They said he should have been in hospital, but Master Clive refused to go and insisted on coming home. Apparently, when the men driving the makeshift ambulance saw the size of the place, they said he would probably get better care at home.

'Mr Carlisle took charge and sent Hazel and Phoebe to get the bed turned down in Master Clive's old room, and Jerry to light the fire, and even advised Cook to have hot water at the ready. Then he went himself to break the news to Lord and Lady Heatherington.'

'I was in my room,' Rory said, 'but I came out sharpish when I heard the howls.'

290

'Ugh, yeah,' Clodagh said. 'Bloodcurdling, they were.'

'But why was he howling?'

In the dimness of the car, Lucy felt rather than saw Clodagh's shrug. 'No one knows. Hazel and Phoebe said the howls began after his parents went in and spoke to him.'

'God, I have heard those sort of noises from animals caught in a trap,' Rory said. 'Whatever that chap has gone through he is in some torment. I have seen some young soldiers and some not so young acting in a similar way and I always find it distressing to see, and if I feel that way you can only imagine what his parents are going through – and after thinking him dead all this time too. Anyway, the General told me to take Clodagh to ask you to come and see him.'

'I don't mind coming,' Lucy said, 'but I can't see what good I can do.'

'Well, we might know what it's about soon enough,' Rory said, 'because we're here now.' He drove expertly through the gates and down the gravel path, and Lucy, with a wry smile, noted that even now when she was brought by invitation and as a matter of urgency, she still entered through the kitchen. It was nice, though, to see the staff. They all greeted her warmly, especially Clara, who she had missed and who hugged her tight, delighted to see her looking so well.

'The young Master is in a bad way,' Cook said as Clara released Lucy.

'So I believe.'

'Well, if anyone can fix him, you can.'

'Don't expect me to work any magic on Master

291

Clive,' Lucy warned. 'I am here only because he asked to see me, so now I'd better go up.'

Rory went with her and as soon as the baize door shut behind them and they moved into the corridor, Lucy heard the shuddering sobs and her eyes met Rory's.

'I'll go and tell them you're here,' he said, and she nodded. She watched him bound up the stairs while she went more slowly, almost hesitantly.

By the time she reached the landing there was no sign of Rory. Lord Heatherington had Clive's bedroom door open and she had never seen his face so grey, nor his eyes so saddened. 'Lucy,' he said with a sigh of relief. 'Thank God you've come.' The noise in the room was incredible, for Clive was in the throes of the worst paroxysm of weeping that Lucy had ever seen. She felt her heart contract in pity for the suffering young man she had loved secretly for years.

Lady Heatherington was in the room but away from the bed and her face was awash with tears. Lucy remembered Clodagh's words. Her ladyship looked up as Lucy entered the room and over her face flooded resentment and intense dislike.

Lucy wasn't that surprised, but she wasn't here for Lady Heatherington, but for her son. Lord Heatherington at any rate looked pleased and very relieved to see her.

'Clive won't let either of us near him,' he said.

Lucy nodded, for she had guessed as much, and again pity welled up in her, for Clive's every breath seemed tortured. The sound of his sobs seemed to reverberate off the walls and she thought he was probably deaf and blind to anything but the acute distress that had overwhelmed him.

'See to your wife, sir,' Lucy said. 'Let me try.'

Lord Heatherington gave a brief nod. He walked across to his wife and patted her shoulder comfortingly as Lucy approached the bed. Avoiding Clive's flailing arms, she put her own arms around him firmly and lifted him from the bed slightly.

'Hush, Master Clive,' she said gently. 'Hush now.' And she rocked him gently as she remembered rocking her wee brothers, saying the same words over and over: 'Hush now ... hush now...'

When she had first lifted Clive, he had been limp, but gradually Lucy felt his body stiffen and then his arms rose and touched her, tentatively at first and then more confidently until his arms encircled her waist. His sobs eased, and then ceased altogether as he leant against her and sighed, 'Little Lucy.'

Lucy was embarrassed at Clive's obvious show of affection in front of his parents, particularly his mother. But there was nothing to do about it because even as she held him she could feel the tension running through him and so would do nothing to break the moment. It seemed that she sat holding him for hours and all the time his parents were absolutely quiet.

Eventually, Clive's breathing grew easier. Lucy's arms began to ache, and when the ache became unbearable she gently unclasped his arms and laid him gently down on the bed.

'He's asleep,' she said. 'I think we should leave

him now and let him get his sleep out.' She led the way from the room and faced Lord and Lady Heatherington on the landing. 'Tomorrow, I really think you should have the doctor look at Master Clive.'

'I wanted him called tonight,' Lady Heatherington snapped, 'but I was overruled. Lord Heatherington sent for you instead.'

'He asked for Lucy, said he has had his fill of doctors,' Lord Heatherington said. 'I told you this. He was in a state and I thought it best to do as he asked.'

'He was probably too exhausted tonight, anyway,' Lucy said. 'I'm sure that when he has had a decent night's sleep he will agree to see the doctor.'

'Will you stay and help convince him?' Lord Heatherington said, and he saw Lady Heatherington's lips purse in annoyance.

'I can tonight,' Lucy said. 'I didn't think I would try to get back tonight and I would like to see Master Clive before I leave tomorrow.'

'But where will you sleep?' Lady Heatherington asked.

Lucy hid her smile. 'With Clodagh,' she said. 'We'll bunk in together for one night. It's all right, Lady Heatherington. I'll not clutter up one of your guest rooms.'

'Oh, it's not that.'

But it was that and they both knew it. Lord Heatherington watched the interchange with wry amusement. Lucy was different, more self-assured since she had left them. 'The work at the hospital suits you,' he said.

'Oh, I love it,' Lucy replied. 'With every passing day I am more sure that that is what I want to do.' She gave a chuckle then and said, 'I think Dr Gilbert has the worst of it, trying to tutor me for my nurse's exams, though, because trying to get things into my thick skull near defeats him at times.'

'I think that's nonsense,' Lord Heatherington said.

However, Lucy wasn't watching him but his wife, and she guessed that she hadn't been privy to the arrangements her husband had made with Dr Gilbert. It was obvious that she thought it totally inappropriate because Lucy saw her lips purse and thin disapproving lines appear either side of her pinched nose.

'Dr Gilbert tutors you?' she repeated.

'Yes,' Lucy said, deliberately not addressing Lady Heatherington as 'my lady'. 'It's handy, you see, with me lodging with his mother, Gwen.'

Lucy wasn't sure Lady Heatherington wasn't going to have a fit of apoplexy as she repeated, 'You call the doctor's mother by her Christian name? Don't you think that that is most appallingly rude?'

'No,' Lucy said cheerfully. 'No, she prefers it. She told me so herself.'

'Well, I never,' said Lady Heatherington in amazement.

'Lady Heatherington is still in the Dark Ages,' Lucy said to Clodagh as the two of them cuddled up in Clodagh's bed later. It was lovely being back with Clodagh, for nice though her bedroom was in Maney Hill, she was lonely sometimes.

'She is,' Clodagh agreed. 'And,' she went on, lowering her voice to little above a whisper so the others wouldn't hear, 'if you took what Hazel and Emily say as gospel, their days are numbered.'

'Yeah, if we have a revolution,' Lucy said. 'Hope we don't. Very uncomfortable things, revolutions.'

'I'll say,' Clodagh said. 'And wars are not so great either.'

'No,' said Lucy. 'But we had this fellow in the hospital the other day telling us of this car factory near to where he lives that has built another factory beside it just making military vehicles. So what does any peaceful country want with all those military vehicles?'

'Mmm, certainly makes you think.'

'I'll say. Anyway, Dr Gilbert said that even if half the stories of what Hitler is doing to the Jews are true then he doesn't know whether we can just sit back and do nothing. I mean, in a way that's why Master Clive went to fight. That Jew told him how bad things were for Jews then, and Dr Gilbert says that events have escalated since. No sane person would want a war, and yet I hate to think of dreadful things happening to innocent people and us just turning the other way.'

'Do you think Master Clive is ever going to be right again, Lucy?'

'Oh, I hope so,' Lucy said. 'I think he probably will be, but that will depend on what the doctor says tomorrow.'

When Lucy woke up the next morning it was eight

o'clock and the other girls had already left. She slipped out of bed and dressed hurriedly, intending to see Clive before Lady Heatherington rose. It wouldn't really matter if he was asleep: she wouldn't wake him, for sleep was what he needed.

However, she had a pleasant surprise. Clive was not only awake but looking very much better than he had the previous night, and his eyes were no longer red-rimmed and glazed over with tiredness. His face, though, was still pasty white except for the blue-black bruises on both cheeks.

Lucy saw his eyes widen with pleasure when she came into the room, and, as she sat in the chair by the bed, she said, 'Oh, I am glad to see you looking so much better. Have you been awake long?'

'A fair while,' Clive said. 'My father has just left. He couldn't sleep much, he said, and we have had quite a chat.' And then he looked at her ruefully under his amazingly long eyelashes as he said, 'He told me that I made one unholy show of myself last night.'

'I wouldn't describe it that way,' Lucy said. 'But I am intrigued as to why you asked to see me.'

'Because I thought about you a lot in Spain,' Clive replied. 'You were sort of like a symbol of everything we were fighting for. I used to think of this place. It was something permanent and solid, where one season follows another and nothing ever happens, and I wanted to come back to that and wipe away the last three years and go back to the way it was before, and you were part of that.'

'Only a very small part, Master Clive,' Lucy protested. 'I was a scullery maid. In a house like this, that's about as low as you can get.'

'Not in my book it isn't,' Clive said. 'You were so small and thin the first time I saw you. You were vulnerable and I felt in Spain that we were fighting for those sort of people. If I lost sight of that I would conjure up that memory of you.'

'But I didn't stay small and vulnerable,' Lucy protested. 'I wasn't caught in a time bubble. I grew up. I'm nearly seventeen now and a different person from the child I once was.'

'Oh, I know that well enough,' Clive said with a grin, and he went on with the smile that made her whole body tingle, 'I was in no state to notice anything much last night but when you walked into my room just a few minutes ago, you were like a picture of loveliness.'

Lucy felt the heat of embarrassment rising up through her body.

'You're blushing!'

'Can you wonder at it?' she said angrily. 'Master Clive, you have no right to say such things.'

'Even if they are true?'

'Whether they are or not makes no difference,' Lucy said firmly. 'You have no right to embarrass people that way.'

'When, then, do I tell a girl how incredibly beautiful she is?' Clive said. 'Like I do now, for instance?'

'Do give over, Master Clive,' Lucy pleaded. 'Be serious for a minute. You were very distressed last night, and when the doctor comes it might be better if you told him honestly how you feel. It might be better to talk to someone about your experiences.'

'My experiences! Huh,' Clive said ironically, and then he was silent for so long that Lucy wondered if she had offended him in some way.

'Master Clive?' she said tentatively.

He looked her full in the face and said almost harshly, 'Do you want to know what happened to me? Do you want to listen to my experiences?'

Lucy wasn't sure if she did. Clive was in a very strange mood, but he gave her no time to state any reservations she might have. 'Right from the start it was a very bloody war,' Clive said. 'I didn't think it could get much worse, but then they bombed Guernica. Our company arrived just after that raid and I looked at the buildings bombed, the small town flattened, with bodies and parts of bodies sticking out of the rubble and the streets lined with the dead and the dying, and the gutters running with blood. But worse in a way was the sight of the people who had fled the town in a bid to escape – the old, young children, women, even babies, all machine-gunned and all dead. There were pet dogs and cats, even a bird in a cage, and small ponies and donkeys, and some of them weren't quite dead. They screamed in pain and looked at us with pleading, helpless eyes and so we put them out of their misery.' He looked at Lucy and said, 'I wasn't the only one who wished we could do the same for those in the town who weren't quite dead. They lay with their guts hanging out, or their limbs blown off, or their faces just not there any more. We all knew that they faced a painful, lingering death. It was the most evil thing I have ever seen.'

Lucy recalled the conversation she had had

with Clodagh the previous night. In any war situation innocent people suffer and there was no getting round that, and if Britain decided on conflict because of Germany's treatment of the Jews there would be more bloodshed.

Suddenly, Clive grasped Lucy's hand. 'You know what tortures me?' he said. He didn't wait for an answer but went on, 'That it was all in vain. That's what's so hard to bear, especially after my friends were killed in a bomb blast.'

'All of them?'

'All of them. Colin, Phillip and Mathew were blown up along with others.'

Lucy felt a momentary pang for the young men she hardly knew, who had seemed to ooze life and vitality. She was so sorry that their lives had been snuffed out before they had really begun and she recognised how much worse that would be for Clive, who had known the boys for years, lived with them at school, probably been as close to them as family.

She swallowed her own feelings, for Clive's eyes were filled with anguish as he said, 'They came to bury them in makeshift graves, and I was nearly buried along with them till they saw me move.'

Lucy was silent.

Clive went on, 'Sometimes it's hard to be a survivor, the one left, and I wondered for ages why I wasn't killed too.'

'I'm glad you weren't,' Lucy said. 'And maybe there isn't an answer. It's just like people say, if your number's up...'

'Maybe,' Clive said. 'Did you mind me telling you all that?'

'No, Master Clive,' she said truthfully. 'No one can change what happened, and I'm sure it does no good to bottle things up.'

'And that's another thing – this "Master" business,' Clive said. 'If there is one thing fighting in the Spanish War taught me it was that I was no better than anyone else. I stood shoulder to shoulder with the type of people I had never encountered before. There were a few rich chaps there, but many were poor and some had been very badly educated and yet we were closer than brothers, facing the same danger and would look out for each other. There were dozens of times when we relied on each other and I'll tell you, Lucy, there are better men left behind on Spanish fields than I will ever be. I'm not talking about just the three friends that I went out with either. So let's drop this "Master Clive" business?'

'Your mother won't like it, Clive,' Lucy said. 'Not that I will see much of you, I don't suppose.'

'What do you mean, not see that much of me?' Clive demanded. 'I thought that you'd come back to nurse me.'

'Don't be silly, Clive,' Lucy said. 'That wouldn't be at all suitable and, anyway, I have a job. I work in the Cottage Hospital.'

'Yeah, voluntarily, Father said, and he told me that you nursed my grandmother.'

'Let me tell you, Clive Heatherington, that just because I am not being paid for a job doesn't mean that I can up and leave it on a whim,' Lucy said. 'I have more integrity than that. And my nursing your grandmother has nothing to do with anything. I sort of fell into it because no one

301

else wanted to do it.'

'My father told me that too,' Clive said. 'And he said that far from being the battle-axe that most people thought she was, she became a different woman with you and you got on well together.'

'By the time I got to know her she was old and frail, and her battles were mostly behind her and, yes, we did get on well together.'

'Well, *we* get on well together.'

'Clive, I hardly know you.'

'You didn't know my grandmother either when you started nursing her,' Clive countered. 'If you agree to look after me you'll get to know me.'

'Clive, talk sense,' Lucy said, exasperated. 'Your grandmother was a woman.'

'Was she?' Clive said sarcastically. 'Do you know, I never noticed that.'

'Your mother would never agree to my nursing you, even if I wanted to,' Lucy said, and added, 'which incidentally, I don't.'

'Because I'm a man, you mean?' Clive said. 'So when you are a proper nurse, are you just going to treat women? Is that what you do now at the Cottage Hospital?'

'No, it isn't,' Lucy said. 'You know that's a different thing altogether, and anyway this isn't just because you're a man. It just wouldn't be right, and added to that your mother dislikes me intensely.'

'Nonsense.'

'She does, Clive,' Lucy insisted. 'It was all because of the terms of your grandmother's will.' She told Clive about the legacy left to her and the sapphire pendant she was given for her birthday, and he gave a low whistle when she had finished.

'I don't think your mother and father had half as much as they thought they would either,' Lucy said. 'Obviously, the rest of the will and the amounts left to them were discussed in private, but these sorts of things get out, and, anyway, servants pick up an awful lot because sometimes employers forget we have ears, and then your mother wasn't quiet either about showing her displeasure.'

'Oh, I bet she wasn't,' Clive said wryly. 'It would have been a blow, because I know my parents were relying on some money from my grandmother to do some basic repairs to this place. But we are talking big money here. What my grandmother gave you is chicken feed compared to the money needed to keep this place afloat, even if you add in the sapphire pendant. Anyway, none of it was your fault, so I am not going to give up this idea of you using your nursing skills on me. I'm sure I would recover much quicker if you were the one mopping my fevered brow.'

'Then you'll have to recover slowly,' Lucy said with spirit. 'I am really pleased that you survived that war, which many didn't, and I'm sure that you will be as good as new in no time, especially if you have the doctor visit and you do as he advises. But get it into your head that I will have no hand in it. That, I should imagine, will be Rory's job.'

She got to her feet, as Clive said, 'Is that your final word?'

'Yes it is.'

'Kiss before you go?'

'That, Master Clive, would be entirely inappropriate,' she said, as she shook him by the hand, 'Goodbye, Clive.'

Clive watched Lucy walk from the room and knew that she had taken a piece of his heart with her. One day he would make her believe that.

Lucy fought the urge to do what she wanted to do, and that was to gather Clive in her arms, kiss him till they were both breathless and nurse him until he was better.

SEVENTEEN

After a little time spent with the kitchen staff, who were anxious to learn how she had fared since she had left, Lucy headed for home, knowing that Gwen would want to know what had happened. As they drank tea, Lucy told her all that had transpired and Gwen was full of sympathy for both Clive and his parents.

'But he's alive,' she said. 'That's the main thing.'

'Yes,' Lucy said, 'you'd think so. And his mother seemed upset – you know, really upset – and yet what appeared to scandalise her more was the fact that I call you by your Christian name. I mean, how important is that kind of thing?'

'None at all, I'd say,' Gwen said with a rueful smile. 'There's a whole lot more to worry about than what to call someone and she must have little to occupy her if it matters so much. But there, I suppose that it isn't entirely her fault. It's

304

the way she has been brought up.'

'I know. It makes them all stiff and starchy,' Lucy said. 'The old lady, you know, the elder Lady Heatherington, used to tell me bits about when she was growing up, and to be honest it didn't seem like a whole lot of fun. They always had plenty to eat and lovely clothes to wear and more money than they needed, but didn't seem to enjoy themselves as much as we do, who have very little compared to them.'

'I agree,' Gwen said.

'The point is,' Lucy said, getting to her feet as she spoke, 'the world is changing. If the work situation generally was to ease, people like the Heatheringtons would find it very difficult to get staff.'

'They would indeed,' Gwen said. 'Generally, people don't want service work today.'

'And Clara always said she didn't know how they would manage without their bevy of servants,' Lucy said. 'So it will be interesting to see how that affects them.'

'Very interesting indeed,' said Gwen.

Over the next few weeks, Lucy found it hard to think that though Clive was living only a short bus ride away she couldn't see him. There was no earthly reason for her to go to Maxted Hall any more. She was glad he was alive and would be well again – of course she was – but she had accepted his death, grieved for him, even though he would never have been hers, and had begun to look forward once more. Now her feelings were in a state of flux.

She pumped Clodagh mercilessly for news of Clive as they got on the bus to go to their dance class.

One Monday evening in early November, she said, 'He thought I would go back and nurse him, you know, that night you came for me. I mean, he doesn't listen because I told him I already had a job and, anyway, even if I was willing, which I wasn't, could you see his mother agreeing to it?'

'No,' said Clodagh, giving Lucy a rueful grin. 'She wouldn't exactly roll out the red carpet, would she? And she wouldn't let you get your paws on her darling son. But you know this lot: they're so used to getting their own way that it's like second nature to them.

'Time does hang heavy on his hands, though, and his mother's answer to that was to ask Jessica to call more often. That will cheer him up, I don't think. I mean, the look on that girl's face would sour cream, and even when she's not scowling she looks like the back end of a bus.'

Lucy laughed. 'Oh, Clodagh, she's not that bad.'

'All right,' Clodagh conceded, 'but never in the wildest stretch of the imagination could you call Jessica Ponsomby pretty.'

'No, I suppose not.'

'And if that Ponsomby girl came more often she may as well bring her bed in, because she's seldom away from the place as it is. The day she moved in, I would move out.'

Then Clodagh looked at Lucy through narrowed eyes and said, 'You are always talking about

306

Clive. You sweet on him or what?'

'Shush,' hissed Lucy urgently, looking round the bus furtively to see if she knew anyone that might have heard what Clodagh said. But the blush had given her away and, as they sat down, Clodagh said, 'Poor Lucy.' She grasped her hand and gave it a little squeeze as she said more quietly, 'You do know it's a lost cause, don't you?'

'Of course I do,' Lucy said forlornly. 'I'm not a fool altogether.'

'I know,' Clodagh said. 'But it's supposed to be truly ghastly when you love someone you can't have. Haven't experienced it myself, but it's what all the women's magazines go on about. Un-requited love, they call it, and it will always be like that if you fall in love with one of the gentry because people like the Heatheringtons do not marry the likes of us.'

'I told you I know that. But how does he react to Jessica?'

Clodagh shrugged. 'Oh, all right, you know?'

'No, I don't know,' Lucy said sharply. 'That's why I'm asking. Are they lovey-dovey or what? Come on, Clodagh, you know what I'm saying.'

'Yeah, I know exactly what you're saying,' Clodagh said. 'But whatever they do it's not going to affect you at all. I mean, will it help if I say that Master Clive obviously shows that he can't stand the sight of Jessica Ponsomby? He doesn't do that, basically because he is too polite and he has known her for years. Despite that, though, he isn't all over her like a rash and treats her more or less as a friend, I would say, though I don't know how they are when they are by themselves. She is, I

307

think, a lot keener than he is.'

The mental picture of Clive with his arms around Jessica that flashed into Lucy's head hurt her more than she would have thought possible and she barely heard Clodagh's next words.

'Mind you–' she gave Lucy a dig in the ribs – 'you wouldn't know that girl was the same person that we both know because she is all sweetness and light in front of Clive. She's even pleasant to us, and I get a please and thank you most of the time.'

'Never!'

'Yes,' Clodagh said with a definite nod of her head. 'And then last week I really think I saw her smile.'

'Now that I can't believe,' Lucy said in mock horror. 'It must have been a touch of wind she had.' The two girls fell against one another in gales of laughter.

Lucy tried hard to return to the happiness and satisfaction she had had in her life before she'd heard that Clive had returned home. He hadn't been a feature of her life then, just as he wasn't now. Nothing had changed except her attitude. It even affected her work at the hospital and most of the nurses saw that she was distracted over something.

'Bound to be something to do with a man,' Nurse Patterson said. 'It usually is.'

'Yes,' conceded another nurse. 'But I hope whatever it is resolves itself soon because I am missing Lucy's smile.'

However, just a week after Clodagh had chal-

lenged her about how she felt about Clive Heatherington, at the end of September, Lucy's smile
was very much in evidence as she saw the man
himself hobbling into the Cottage Hospital.

'What are you doing here?'

Clive had a grin as wide as Lucy's as he replied,
'Well, you know the old adage about Mohammed: that if he won't go to the mountain then the
mountain has to go to Mohammed.'

'Don't be an idiot,' Lucy said. 'What are you
really here for?'

'Physio and exercises to strengthen the leg
because I have lost a lot of the muscle tone,' Clive
said. 'Shouldn't take above half an hour, Dr Gilbert said. I'm surprised he didn't mention it to
you.'

Lucy knew why he hadn't because she studi-
ously avoided talking about anything to do with
the Heatheringtons, though at times she had
longed to know how Clive was doing. But she
knew that had she given in to temptation and
asked, he would probably have told her nothing
because Gwen had told her that he never discussed his patients.

Now she gave a shrug. 'Why should he?'

Clive knew why, because he badgered the doctor
about Lucy every time he saw him, but Dr Gilbert
answered in only the vaguest terms. He didn't
understand Clive's preoccupation with the girl,
and he certainly wanted no part in fostering any
sort of relationship between two people so widely
apart in upbringing and class that nothing could
ever come of it but heartbreak. The fact that Lucy
never spoke of the family convinced him that any

feelings Clive imagined he had for Lucy were not reciprocated and so he did nothing to encourage him.

'Just thought he might have mentioned it, that's all.'

'Clive, Dr Gilbert doesn't live in the same house as me,' Lucy said. 'He has a flat above the surgery and when he does come round it is to see his mother, not me, and the only time I see a great deal of him, apart from at the hospital, when we are usually busy with patients, is when he is tutoring me for my nurse's exams, and the syllabus is what we discuss. Now, do you know the way to the Physiotherapy Department?'

'Never mind that,' Clive said impatiently. 'Will you meet me when I have finished?'

'What for?' Lucy asked, suddenly aware that her mouth had suddenly gone very dry. 'Anyway, I'm a working girl.'

'You must have a lunch hour?' Clive said as he put a hand on Lucy's arm.

Immediately a tingling sensation ran all through her body. She raised her head and her alarmed eyes met those of his and she knew he had felt the same sensation.

'Please,' Clive pleaded.

Lucy knew further resistance was futile, but the day was cold and wet and she reasoned that Clive might not be able to walk any distance, so she said, 'Meet me in the visitors' room at the back of the hospital at half-past twelve. There should be no one in it at that time of day.'

Indeed, there was no one in it. They didn't touch

in any way but sat on the hard, uncomfortable chairs set aside for visitors and talked about Clive's injured right leg.

'I am really anxious for it to be fully functional once more because if I gain full movement of that and my foot, Rory will teach me to drive.'

'Isn't that rather short-sighted of him?' Lucy said. 'Isn't he doing himself out of a job?'

'Yes, but it's a job he no longer wants.'

'Oh?'

'He says there's going to be a war. Sure as eggs is eggs, was the way he put it. Before Father's accident, he was going to be a professional soldier and he initially signed on for seven years when he was eighteen in 1928. Then just as his seven years were coming to an end and he could leave, my father had the accident. Rory had been his batman then for three years and instead of signing on for a further term, which was what he had intended to do, he elected to look after my father. He told me straight that it was a pleasure to do it because my father is a great man. But he feels bad to be acting as nursemaid to me and driving a fancy car around when he can see war clouds gathering and he feels he could be of more use in the army.'

'And what if he's wrong and there is no war?'

'Well, he'll still be in the army, won't he, and that's where he wants to be.' Then Clive burst out, 'God damn it, Lucy, I didn't come here to talk about Rory Green but to try and understand what is happening to us, for I know you feel as I do.'

'Hush,' Lucy cautioned. 'Don't speak of such things.'

'Of course I must.'

'No,' said Lucy determinedly. 'It is ridiculous to feel this way. We barely know each other.'

'These things happen.'

Lucy shook her head. 'Not in real life they don't. That's only what you read in books and see in films. This is like a form of madness that will pass.'

'No, it won't.'

'It must,' Lucy said. 'There is a deep chasm between us that can never be bridged.'

'I don't care about any bloody chasms,' Clive said. 'I told you how I felt about this bloody class system after the Spanish Civil War.'

'You did tell me, Clive,' Lucy said, 'but usually society does not view things in the same way as you do.'

'Lucy!' Clive cried and tried to grab her hand, but she was up from the chair and out of his grasp in an instant.

It took an immense effort on her part to stand there and say words that wounded her very soul. 'One day, Clive, you will thank me when I say that there is no future for us.' And with that, before she broke down in heartbreaking tears, Lucy took to her heels and sped down the corridor.

She was glad she was kept so busy all afternoon, but the nurses she worked with were more worried than ever by her demeanour.

'She was pleased enough when that young Clive Heatherington came in,' remarked one nurse.

'Who wouldn't be?' said another. 'He's very dishy, very dishy indeed.'

'You are sex mad, you,' said Nurse Patterson

disparagingly. 'And I'm not talking of anything like that, but when she saw him walk through the door it was as if someone had turned a light on in her head.'

'Well, we always said her problems were probably man-related,' the first nurse said. 'Maybe he's the man.'

'Hope it isn't him,' Nurse Patterson said. 'In my opinion, men like that are only after one thing with girls like us.'

'Most men are like that,' the first nurse put in. 'It's not confined to the gentry.'

There was a murmur of agreement and then the second nurse said, 'Maybe they had a row or something.'

'They hadn't time.'

'Ah, but they had, you see,' said the second nurse. 'I went down to the laundry with a pile of soiled linen and I had to pass the visitors' room, as you know. I heard voices coming from inside. They weren't raised or anything, so I hung about to see who it was and after a few minutes Lucy came out in tears and then Clive Heatherington. But he just stood at the door a moment or two before moving away as if he was thinking. To be honest I thought he looked sort of lost.'

'Lucy looked more than just lost when I worked with her after lunch,' said the first nurse.

'Hope she isn't in trouble of any sort.'

'Not Lucy,' said Nurse Patterson confidently. 'She isn't that kind of girl, and anyway she wouldn't be that stupid.'

'Don't know that common sense has much to do with anything when you imagine you're in love with someone,' another nurse remarked.

Even Nurse Patterson then began to have her doubts because she knew that her colleague was only too right: common sense and love did not usually go hand in hand. She sincerely hoped that Lucy wasn't in that kind of trouble, because it would ruin the high hopes the girl had for her future, and she knew that she would feel somewhat responsible as well.

Unaware she was the subject of such speculation, Lucy worked on at the hospital. Though she did everything as well as she always had, she did it in a mechanical sort of way, as if the essence of her had gone, and she seemed unable to concentrate on the work she was doing with Dr Gilbert. He didn't understand her apparent disinterest, though he really thought she looked unwell, but when he asked her – or Gwen, who was even more concerned – she always maintained she was fine.

Lucy valiantly tried to lift her mood when she saw Clodagh. She didn't want her talking about her misery back at the Hall, for it would worry Clara and she would hate Clive to get wind of how unhappy she was. She wasn't entirely successful and often seemed to have two left feet at the dancing lessons, but Clodagh thought that was how a person was when they loved a person they couldn't have. Anyway, Lucy was much better, she reflected, at the cinema, where she could lose herself for an hour or two.

Lucy often contemplated in bed how it was that making the right decision about something – and she knew it was the right decision – could make her feel so wretched. It sometimes seemed that everyone else was living their lives and she was standing outside looking in. This was even more apparent when her birthday came round and she realised she had been almost unaware of it. Numerous parcels arrived from America of lovely clothes and perfume, the nurses gave her gifts of toiletries, Clodagh bought her a big box of chocolates and Gwen gave her a beautiful fluffy dressing gown, but though she thanked everyone she couldn't work up any enthusiasm for any of it.

November was a terrible month weather-wise. One day the rain was coming down in sheets as Lucy finished work. The nurse on the front desk advised her to stay for a while and see if it eased off a little as her coat was not waterproof and she had no hat. However, Lucy thought the torrential rain from the leaden grey skies suited her mood and she plunged out into the dusky evening.

She arrived home sodden, and Gwen fussed round her like a mother hen and wouldn't let her eat until she had stripped off, put on dry things and taken a towel to her hair.

She had been worried about her young lodger for some time and that night, as they sat before the fire with an after-dinner cup of tea, Gwen said, 'Can't you tell me what's eating you, my dear? Something is obviously making you feel so unhappy.'

'It's nothing,' Lucy began. 'Well, almost nothing, and no one can help me. I just feel pretty miserable at the moment.'

That was patently obvious. Gwen said, 'What we want is some jolly music to cheer ourselves up,' and she turned the dial on the wireless until music from the big bands filled the air.

Unfortunately, after just a few minutes, the programme was interrupted with a news bulletin. The solemn voice of the newscaster told them that, that night, storm troopers had attacked Jews in towns and cities all over Germany. They were thrown out of their houses and businesses into the streets, their property looted and burnt. Any who protested were shot, and even those who ran to the synagogues to take refuge were not safe. The synagogues were set alight, and observers said the sky was blood red with buildings burning.

Gwen and Lucy just stared at one another for a moment, hardly able to credit what they had just heard. Lucy crossed to the window and watched the rain hammer down. She thought of the German Jews, helpless against such brutality, and she wanted to weep for them. She knew that never did any good, but she understood Dr Gilbert when he said that the world couldn't stand by indefinitely and watch Hitler's treatment of the Jews.

The following day on the news the scale of the tragedy unfolded further. The Germans were calling it *Kristallnacht* – Night of Broken Glass – because it was said that in the houses, shops and businesses owned by the Jews so much glass was broken there wasn't enough in the whole of Germany to replace it. Countless Jews had been killed, many others seriously injured, and thirty thousand of them had disappeared. The broadcaster said many families had just committed suicide.

'And who in God's name could blame them?' Gwen said. Lucy just shook her head in bewilderment.

That night in bed, with the atrocities that had happened in Germany running round and round in her head, she realised that she had been indulging in self-pity. Not to declare her love for Clive had cost her dear, but it had been her decision, and though it had hurt her and was still hurting her a great deal, if it could not be compared to the truly awful things happening in Germany.

So maybe it was better to live for today, to take opportunities when they were offered, for no one knew what the future held. However, that was a difficult concept for Lucy to get to grips with. Her nature had never been to throw caution to the winds, but she acknowledged that a nation who could commit such atrocities on their own people who had done them no harm would not spare the citizens of a country it had conquered.

The image of Clive flashed through her mind, and she sighed because she knew, despite what was happening in the world, the vast differences between their lives still remained. That alone would hold them apart.

Clive was just as unhappy and confused as Lucy. Until that first morning at the hospital, he had heard about her only at odd times. Usually, this was from Clara, who tended him in Rory's absence, and she would maybe recount something Clodagh said Lucy had done or said, or something she wrote to her about. Clive had a great deal of time on his hands and he stored those snippets and wove them into his memories of Lucy, who, with every passing day, he was falling in love with.

Because he loved her with growing intensity, he thought she was bound to feel the same. Certainly, she had felt something between them when they touched, but then instead of going slowly, when he might have overcome her concern about their vastly different backgrounds, he had jumped in with two feet. What a fool he was!

Rory had been tidying Clive's room while he waited for his return. For some time now he had thought Clive didn't seem to appreciate what his parents had gone through when he was missing all that time and he decided to tell him.

So when Clive, already despondent, arrived home, he found Rory still in his room, and when Rory described how anxious and desperately worried his parents had been during his time in Spain, he listened in silence.

Rory went on to tell him of Lord Heatherington's journey to Liverpool to see if anyone had news of him, and of finding the injured soldier who was able to assure him that Clive was alive, which gave him and Clive's mother great ease. 'But,' Rory went on, 'not long after that the Spanish town of Guernica was bombed and eventually we all thought you had perished. Master Clive, you have no idea the distress you caused them.'

Clive felt guilt steal over him. They would have known he was facing danger daily and yet he hadn't been able to write and tell them how he was and he could see how unbearably hard that would have been for any parent. He had seen for himself how old his parents had become in his absence and he had thought it just part of the ageing process, even though he had been away only three years, and his parents seemed to have aged ten. The thought that his actions might have had some bearing on their health was a hard pill to swallow.

He vowed that he would make it up to them, and so he was patient with his mother when she talked of Jessica being a perfect match for him, and he even took tea with them and smiled tolerantly at the mothers' matchmaking plans. He would exchange knowing looks and conspiratorial winks with Jessica, certain she wasn't involved in these plans. They had been friends from childhood and he still thought of her as a friend. There had never been any romantic entanglement because Clive didn't feel that way about her. He knew where his heart lay, though he doubted that he would ever be able to convince Lucy of that.

The news of the pogroms against the Jews throughout Germany had made him feel very low. It brought back into his mind the Jew who had been beaten to death in Berlin at the time of the Olympic Games for talking to them, the one who had shaped his life for the next three years. And all that fighting and all those deaths had achieved nothing, and the Germans were continuing in their savage and merciless ways.

Lucy had been wrestling with feelings alien to her since she had listened to the details of the Night of Broken Glass on the wireless, and that was an impatience to live life to the full while she was still able to do it. She had deliberately not seen Clive since she had run from him, having found out the times of his physio and arranged to be elsewhere in the hospital. But just a week after the pogroms, his appointment was changed and she ran into him as he walked down the corridor.

'Lucy!' he said almost tentatively. 'I'm glad I have seen you. I want to apologise.'

'Apologise?'

'Yes, for the way I behaved the first time I came for physio. No wonder you ran away.'

Lucy swallowed deeply and said, 'I'm sorry too.'

'What for?'

Live life to the full, said a little voice inside her head. But while Lucy wanted to do that, there was nothing to be gained by running after an impossible dream, to think of any sort of future with Clive Heatherington, but she didn't have to deny him totally.

'Lucy,' he urged gently, and Lucy swung to face him. The look in his eyes caused her stomach to give a quite unsettling lurch as she said, 'Well, I told you that we have no future together and I stand by that, but since I heard about the pogroms in Germany, the Night of Broken Glass, I have felt a little differently. I realised then that war really is almost inevitable now and that changes everything.'

'Does it?'

'Well, yes,' Lucy said. 'If war comes, none of us might have much of a future. I mean, if we fight Germany and they win, what chance will we have?'

'None,' Clive said. 'So, what do you want to do, Lucy?'

'Take every opportunity while it is still ours to take, I suppose,' Lucy said. 'And that means I suppose we could be friends, if that's what you want.'

That wasn't what Clive wanted at all, but he knew better than to tell Lucy what he did want because he sensed that friendship was as far as she was willing to go, and that was a lot better than nothing at all.

'All right then,' he said. 'If that is how you want it. As a friend, would you like to go to the cinema with me tomorrow evening?'

Lucy thought for a minute and then said, 'Yes, I would like that, but what about Jessica Ponsomby?'

'What about her?'

'You can't just dismiss her like that, Clive. Clodagh said–'

'I don't care what Clodagh said, or my mother or hers,' Clive said. 'She is a friend, nothing more and nothing less.'

'They intend for you to marry her,' Lucy said.

'Oh, I think Jessica knows the score,' Clive said. 'As for our mothers, they can scheme all they like, but I will marry only for love.'

The words spoken with such conviction and the look shining in Clive's eyes seemed to melt a large chunk of Lucy's heart. Clive badly wanted to crush Lucy to him and cover her with kisses, but he restrained himself with extreme difficulty.

'Till tomorrow then,' he said, and gave her a chaste kiss on the cheek, as one friend to another.

EIGHTEEN

Clive was incredibly nervous the following night. Growing up in a boys' school, he had known few girls apart from Jessica, and he had never ever thought of asking her out. There had been plenty of girls in Spain, of course, raven-haired beauties, many of them with flashing black eyes, but no one could get anywhere near them for they were too closely chaperoned.

There were other women around the outskirts of the camp and many men used to take advantage of the favours they offered. Clive might have done the same thing but he and his friends were warned off by a man who had fought in the Great War. He said he knew of men, comrades, many of them, who had been infected by similar women and when he told them what might happen to them after a brief tumble they decided not to bother.

So Clive returned to England as inexperienced as he was when he left. He was totally bemused as to how to treat a girl who wanted to be a friend rather than a girlfriend. Should he take her chocolates, for instance, or would she view that as suspicious behaviour from a friend? There was no one he could ask, for he hadn't told anyone about his meetings with Lucy, knowing they would have been frowned on. His mother would probably have been upset, and he had always hated upsetting her, even more so after Rory's talk. In the end he took no chocolates and thought he would compromise by buying Lucy an ice cream in the interval.

Lucy had never been on a date in her life before either, but she had read a lot about what happens, and listened to the talk amongst the nurses. Apparently, in the darkness of the cinema all manner of danger lurked. 'Arms like a bloody octopus,' one nurse had said only the other day. 'In the end I told him that if he didn't behave decently then he could sit someplace else because I wanted to watch the film.'

'I know,' said another in sympathy. 'They buy you a box of chocolates and think it gives them licence to do all sorts.'

Lucy loved chocolate but didn't get to eat it much so her mouth watered at the thought of a whole box of it. 'Do they always buy you chocolates?' she asked.

The girls nodded. 'Mostly, especially at the beginning when they are trying to impress, like.'

'Yes, and when you start going out with lads you watch out for the ones who come with a really big box,' Nurse Patterson warned.

'Yeah, the bigger the box the more some expect you to do for it.'

'Goodness,' said Lucy.

'Oh, yes,' said another nurse. 'You have to be one step ahead of the boys. It's nice when they hold your hand, as long as that is all they do, or it's nice when they wrap their arm over your shoulder, except if they are using it to have a quick feel of your breast.'

Lucy was totally shocked. 'Surely they wouldn't do that.'

Nurse Patterson laughed. 'Some do,' she said. 'But not all men are like that. Now,' she admonished the other nurses, 'let's stop telling Lucy any more things that might happen in the cinema or it will put her off men altogether.'

Later, when they were working together, she said, 'Have you been out with a boy yet, Lucy?' She was relieved when Lucy shook her head, because whatever ailed Lucy she couldn't be 'in trouble' if she hadn't actually been out with a boy.

Nurse Patterson was surprised that admirers weren't beating a path to Lucy's door because she was so beautiful, and so she said, 'All the nurses were doing was trying to put you wise so that you don't let the boys take liberties.'

Lucy sighed and said, 'I wish there was some sort of guide book. How do I know what liberties are?'

'Well,' Nurse Patterson said, 'I think a good rule of thumb is that if you feel uncomfortable doing something then it is probably a liberty.'

Lucy thought of that when she was getting ready to meet Clive that night. She had told no one about her date, and when Gwen assumed she was going to the cinema with Clodagh, she didn't correct her. She had told Clive not to collect her from the house but that she would meet him outside the cinema.

He was waiting for her, and the first thing Lucy noticed was that he had no box of chocolates with him, either big or small. She was terribly disappointed but could hardly say anything about it, and didn't know then if he would try anything in the cinema or not, or if he was naturally mean-spirited. Clive noticed Lucy's slight restraint and, not totally understanding the reason for it, told himself that he had to conduct himself with the utmost decorum so that she would know he wished her no harm. So, though he longed to take her arm, and Lucy expected him to, he didn't and they walked side by side into the cinema.

The main film was *Pygmalion*, which was written by a man called George Bernard Shaw, Clive told her as they took their seats. Lucy found she was terribly affected sitting so close to Clive in the dusky cinema. She felt sure that he would be able to hear her heart thumping, or feel the trembling of her limbs, but if he did he made no sign.

Before the silence became uncomfortable, she said, 'What's it about?'

'Oh, from what I understand it's about how a professor has a bet that he can take a young flower seller from the street and turn her into a lady.'

'Oh,' Lucy said in amusement. 'Don't you see a similarity with us there? A titled gentleman takes up with a scullery maid.'

'You're not a scullery maid.'

'I was, though, and not that long ago,' Lucy said. 'And you see, it is such an uncommon occurrence they make films about it.'

Clive was laughing as he said good-naturedly, 'I'll see how he does it. I might pick up some tips. Now pipe down because the lights are dimming.'

Later, Lucy was to think that that was one of the nicest evenings she had spent, although, the human mind being what it is, in many ways she was disappointed, despite the choc ice Clive had bought her. All evening her body was on high alert in case Clive should take liberties, feeling sure that sooner or later he would feel for her hand in the dark, or she would feel his hand snaking around her neck, and she felt her breasts tingling as if in anticipation. Or maybe Clive would try to kiss her or else indulge in some of the embarrassing fumbling taking place in seats not that far away. She knew that she would have to rebuff any advances like those, but the fact that she didn't have to disconcerted her in a way she could barely understand.

Clive insisted on walking Lucy home, tucking her hand through his, and, though she enjoyed the closeness, they talked only of the film. She expected a kiss as he left her at the gate, but he just thanked her for a lovely evening, said they must do it again soon, and left.

Lucy was glad that Gwen had gone to bed and she hadn't had to answer any awkward questions. She retired to bed herself to go over the events of the evening in her head. In the end she decided that she had behaved like a total idiot, so afraid what Clive might do that it had put a slight damper on the whole evening, and if he didn't want to see her again then she had only herself to blame.

The nurses were the only ones aware of the relationship between Clive and Lucy, and when Lucy asked them to keep it quiet for now because his mother might not approve, they readily agreed. More than a few of them, who were dating only sons, had had to cope with jealousy from their mothers. They were just glad that Lucy's happy-go-lucky nature and ready smile had returned.

And so the relationship blossomed as Christmas grew closer, and Lucy could never remember feeling so happy. Neither of them was sure when the relationship stopped being that of friends and became one of lovers, but they did not care. Lucy only knew by early December that she loved Clive Heatherington with all her heart and soul.

Clive's last appointment at the hospital was just before Christmas and for that, now his leg was healed, he drove his father's car. He was taking Lucy to see *Snow White and the Seven Dwarfs*, the cartoon by Walt Disney, which was showing at the Odeon in New Street in Birmingham city centre.

'I will have only partial use of the car,' he told Lucy, opening the car door for her. 'Sometimes I will have to take the old man about because Rory is leaving us in the New Year.'

'Well, that was always on the cards, wasn't it?'

'Oh, yes,' Clive said. 'It was no surprise. In a way, and despite all that happened to him, I think my father is quite envious.'

'Well, he was a career soldier, too, wasn't he?' Lucy said. 'I suppose he thinks that in the event of a war he should be there doing his bit.'

'Even career soldiers have to hang up their boots eventually,' Clive said. 'Point is, he doesn't accept that he is getting older.'

'Neither did his mother,' Lucy said with a wry smile. 'I think it's harder for some people than others. Your father probably feels a bit useless. And what are you going to do with yourself now that your leg is better?'

'Oh, I don't know,' Clive said. 'I feel a bit at sixes and sevens, to be honest. I mean, I never took up my place at university and Father would like me to go on with that, but I would rather get a job, I think. Anyway, the decision might be taken out of my hands.'

'What do you mean?'

'What do you think?' Clive said. 'If we have all-out war with Germany there will be call-up and, as you so rightly say, I am as fit as anyone else.'

Lucy knew Clive was right: he would be called up and once again in the firing line, when they had only just patched him up from the last lot.

'Cheer up, Lucy,' Clive said. 'We can do nothing to change what is going to happen, so we must make the most of every day. At least this time I will be able to write, and you can write back and send me warm socks and bull's-eyes and cigarettes.'

Lucy looked at him in amazement. 'Why cigarettes, when you don't smoke?'

'Because lots of others do,' Clive said. 'There was an old soldier with us in the Spanish lot, and he said cigarettes were used to trade with in the last war, and he didn't see that they would be any less important now. He said you could get all sorts if you had enough fags, and that in the Forces they are more important than money.'

'Oh, right,' Lucy said with a wry smile. 'I'll

order a shipload then, shall I?'

'I should,' Clive agreed sombrely. 'It's always as well to be prepared.'

The day before Christmas Eve, Clive was waiting for Lucy outside the hospital. Knowing that they wouldn't be seeing one another again until the festivities were over, he took her for a drive before taking her home. The night was black and the headlights lit up the road in front of them, shining because it had rained all day. Lucy gave a sigh.

'What are you thinking about?' Clive asked.

'Nothing really,' Lucy said. 'It's just... I mean, if we're not doing anything wrong and not hurting anyone else, why do we have to hide away all the time?'

Clive stopped the car by the edge of the road and took Lucy into his arms. 'It won't be for ever, my darling.'

'You know, I'm beginning to doubt that.'

'Look, Lucy, I will try to sneak out the day after Boxing Day. Our visitors should be heading back by then.'

'But that's just what I am complaining about,' Lucy said. *'Sneak out.* Why should you have to sneak out? I do so hate this hole-in-the-corner affair we seem to be conducting.'

'I know you hate it, my darling, and so do I,' Clive said. 'But my mother–'

'She will have to know sometime,' Lucy pointed out. 'Look, I know your mother doesn't like me and probably never will, and will not approve of me either, and that too is unlikely to

329

change, but she may as well be told about us and let her shout and scream all she likes. Eventually, she will have to get over it.'

'Huh, you think so?'

'Clive, she'd have to. People do. I mean, there's far more for her to worry about than her son not marrying the girl of her choosing, and that's what it really all boils down to.'

'You're right, of course,' Clive said. 'And in a way I am doing her a disservice by letting her carry on with this fantasy about Jessica and me.'

'Yeah, you are.'

'I will tell her about us,' Clive promised. 'All this will be sorted out in the New Year.'

'All right,' Lucy said resignedly.

'And I'll be here as soon as I can after Christmas,' Clive said.

Lucy didn't speak. In the dimness of the car she couldn't see his eyes but she heard the emotion in his voice. 'Lucy, I love you more than life itself. You do believe that, don't you?'

'Yes, of course I do,' Lucy said.

'You're crying,' Clive said, and he bent and kissed the tears from her eyes.

She gave a gasp of pleasure before saying, 'I can't help it. I love you more than I thought it was possible to love anyone, and I will miss you so much.'

'I will miss you too, Lucy,' Clive said. 'Every minute that I will be away from you I will miss you.'

Her lips met his and the kiss they shared stirred emotions in Lucy. She longed for Clive to do more than kiss her and wouldn't have cared a jot that he might be taking liberties. Clive was affected too, and could feel the emotion running through Lucy, and he pulled back while he was still able to. He could not take what Lucy was willing to offer, not yet. He had to tell his mother and stand the flack he'd get before he and Lucy could embark on a proper courtship, and perhaps not even then if war was going to tear them apart.

'Come on,' he said, starting the engine up again. 'I'll get you home. You are shivering with cold.'

'It's not cold that I'm shivering with,' Lucy said.

'Hush,' said Clive. 'I love you too much to want to do anything to hurt you, but I am only a flesh-and-blood person, like anyone else.'

'I know,' Lucy said. 'I'm sorry.'

'You don't have to be bloody sorry,' Clive said. 'And it isn't you I'm cross with but myself.'

'Don't be cross with anyone,' Lucy said. 'It's Christmas. Peace to all men and that.'

'You're right,' Clive said, and Lucy knew by his voice he was smiling.

When he drew up outside Lucy's gate he said, 'I have a little something for you.' He ferreted around in the glove compartment, pulled out a small box and placed it in Lucy's hand. 'Happy Christmas, my darling, wonderful Lucy,' he said, and he planted another kiss on her partially open lips. 'Not to be opened until Christmas Day,' he cautioned, as Lucy got out.

But she'd barely waited until Clive had pulled out of the road before she shot in the house and was tearing the wrapping paper off as she mounted the stairs. Inside the wrapping was a

331

ring box, and Lucy opened it to find a golden band with a sapphire stone the exact match to the one in the pendant. It was so utterly beautiful she felt tears dribbling down her cheeks as she slipped it on her finger and turned her hand this way and that so it sparkled in the light. She put the ring into the leather box old Lady Heatherington had given her to house the pendant, knowing that was another thing that had to be kept secret until her relationship with Clive was out in the open.

Provided no one was inconsiderate enough to become ill on Christmas Day, Dr Gilbert was spending the day with his mother and Lucy, he told her as they decorated the house together the week before Christmas. He also said he would like her to call him Chris.

'Where else would I be on Christmas Day but here, where I can be fussed over and fed delicious food that I haven't cooked,' he said to Lucy. 'It would be a poor Christmas for me sitting on my own in an undecorated flat eating a cheese sandwich.'

Catching his mood, Lucy said, 'There's nothing wrong with a cheese sandwich, and you should know that, Dr Gilbert, but it's all you deserve if you are too lazy to learn to cook. As for not bothering to put up decorations, I think that's a shame because it sort of sets the scene somehow, as if Christmas really isn't that far away.'

She surveyed the room, festooned with garlands, paper lanterns and streamers, with satisfaction. Chris Gilbert watched Lucy, and instantly berated himself for it. He was ten years older than she was, and she was at the start of her life. He had nothing to offer her, even if she had shown him the slightest encouragement, which she hadn't.

She suddenly spun around and clapped her hands like a child, saying, 'Doesn't it look lovely?' Her beautiful face was all aglow and he felt as if he'd had a sudden kick from a mule in the pit of his stomach.

He willed his voice to be steady as he answered, 'Indeed it does. You and I have done a good job.'

On Christmas Eve, the telephone shrilled out. Gwen, who answered it, told Lucy it was for her: someone from Maxted Hall. Lucy had never received a phone call before, or even had the receiver in her hand, so she approached it with great trepidation. The only person she could think would ring her up was Clive, and though she longed to hear his voice she thought it a very risky thing to do. But maybe at least she could thank him for the ring.

She was flabbergasted to hear Clodagh on the other end, asking if she could come to see her for Christmas Day and if possible stay over till Boxing Day.

'But how will you do that?' Lucy answered, perplexed.

'I'll tell you tomorrow,' Clodagh promised. 'Just ask the doctor's mother if I can stay there, will you? We can share a bed if necessary; we've done it before.'

Gwen had no objection to one of Lucy's friends, staying over Christmas. She had spoken so often about Clodagh that Gwen felt as if she knew her,

333

and then, of course, Clodagh had been the girl who came to tell Lucy about Clive Heatherington. So Gwen told Lucy her friend would be most welcome and she would ask Chris to bring in another single bed from the spare room. It would be no bother at all.

Despite going to midnight Mass, Lucy was up bright and early on Christmas morning. When Rory dropped Clodagh at the gate, she ran out to greet her, and Clodagh put down the bag she had brought, to hug Lucy, both girls delighted to be together again. Then Lucy dragged her inside to meet Gwen, who welcomed Clodagh warmly and soon had them sitting around the kitchen table drinking tea and eating mince pies.

'All right, Clodagh,' Lucy said. 'I am delighted you are here, but how have you been allowed to stay?'

'Well, they could hardly have refused,' Clodagh said. 'Great changes are afoot in that place and if they had said no I would have come anyway.'

Lucy's mouth dropped agape and Clodagh went on, 'I'm leaving in the New Year and working in a factory in Aston, making bullet cases. Hazel is doing the same and I am lodging with her parents.' And then she grasped hold of Lucy's hands and urged, 'Why don't you come in with us? It will be a gas if we are all together, and we will be earning two pounds a week.'

'No,' Lucy said. 'Good luck to the pair of you, and I don't blame you at all, but one thing this time at the Cottage Hospital has taught me is that nursing is what I want to do, and if there is a war, nurses will be needed.'

'They will without doubt,' Dr Gilbert said. 'Aeroplanes will feature highly, and that means everyone will be in the front line.'

'Like Guernica?' Clodagh said.

'Yes, exactly like that,' Dr Gilbert said.

His answer sent a chill running all through Lucy because she remembered Clive explaining to her exactly what that had been like, and she desperately hoped that the doctor was wrong.

However, before anyone was able to say anything, the telephone rang and Dr Gilbert was called out to a person with stomach pains, which he said was probably overindulgence, and Gwen seemed to remember that it was Christmas Day.

'There is to be no more talk of war today,' she said. 'No past wars or those to come, because today is a day when there is peace wished for all mankind and we should respect that, and if we all pull together we will produce a sumptuous meal worthy of such an occasion.'

As it was cooking they exchanged presents. Clodagh had a selection of cards from people at the Hall for Lucy, and a lovely letter and beautiful leather gloves from Clara. She even had a short note from Cook, wishing her all the best, and a Christmas cake with her compliments, which Gwen said was kind of her. She wasn't the only kind one, though, Lucy thought. To show her appreciation, Lucy had drawn on her savings to buy Gwen a pair of fur-lined sheepskin slippers because she said her feet often felt like blocks of ice standing on the cold slabs of the kitchen. She also had a box of cigars for the doctor. Lucy, in turn, was flabbergasted when Gwen presented her

335

with two pairs of warm winceyette pyjamas.

'You already do so much for me,' she said. 'You really shouldn't have bought presents as well.'

'I enjoyed it,' Gwen said. 'And as for you owing me, I value your company and will miss you when you move into the nurses' home.'

'Only if I pass my exams.'

'Oh, you'll pass all right,' Gwen said. 'Chris said you have a good head on your shoulders and you are keen, and he is seldom wrong.'

Lucy wished that Gwen hadn't said that because she would feel even more stupid now if she failed. But she didn't say anything, as she began to clear away the debris and lay the table for Christmas dinner, because she knew Gwen was just trying to be reassuring.

Having soothed the patient who had just eaten and drunk far too lavishly for his innards to cope with, Dr Gilbert was back in time for the dinner. They all did justice to the food, which was delicious, pulled crackers, shared the silly jokes and donned the even sillier hats. Then, when they were almost too full to move, Dr Gilbert suggested a hike around the recreation grounds, which was just the other side of East View Road. Though the girls groaned they agreed reluctantly because they knew it would do them good.

The day was bleak and raw, and they returned with cheeks aglow and throbbing fingers and toes, and relished the hot chocolate and mince pies that Gwen had ready for them.

'I like your doctor,' Clodagh said that night as they prepared for bed.

'So do I,' Lucy agreed. 'But he is hardly mine.'

336

'You know what I mean.'

'Yeah, and I haven't seen him on such good form,' Lucy said.

'And he's a lot younger than he looks, isn't he?'

'Mmm,' Lucy said. 'It's the beard, I think. Gwen told me that he chose to grow one when he came out of medical school because no one thought he looked old enough to be a real doctor. I thought as much the first time I saw him, which was when Lord Heatherington asked him to call and see his mother when she first moved into the Hall.'

'Oh, yes,' Clodagh said. 'Lot of water under the bridge since then.'

'Just a bit,' Lucy agreed. 'I was surprised he didn't know about you and Hazel leaving.'

'He hasn't been to the house lately, because there hasn't been any need,' Clodagh said. 'Anyway, we didn't give them the month's notice that we should have given them. Once upon a time, you couldn't do that because you needed a reference to get another job, but when Hazel's sister, Mavis, tipped her the wink that there were jobs going at her place, we both went down to see the boss and he don't care about anything apart from whether we are prepared to learn how to make bullet cases. Then, as soon as I'd sorted my lodgings out, we went and told them and so we'll work till New Year and then we're off.'

'How will the Heatheringtons manage?'

Clodagh shrugged. 'Search me. It isn't our problem, is it?'

'No, but...'

'And it's set to get worse,' Clodagh said. 'Phoebe

337

said she isn't prepared to be left with everything to do and Emily's the same. You can't blame them. They'll be off first chance they get, I reckon, and if this war actually starts, then Jerry will be called up.'

'Of course,' Lucy said with a grin. 'The army would come as a shock to him.'

'Yeah, he will have to work for once.'

The two girls laughed together and then Lucy said, 'If you have just told the Master and Mistress then that would explain why Clive knew nothing.'

'Master Clive knows nothing because he's never there,' Clodagh said. 'Lady Heatherington is always giving out about it.' And then Clodagh's eyes narrowed as she said, 'Hang on a minute. How did you know that Master Clive knew nothing, anyway?'

Lucy shrugged. 'You may as well know. It will all be public knowledge soon enough. A lot of the time when Clive wasn't home he would have been with me.'

'Tell me you are joking?'

'I assure you I'm not.'

'Lucy, what's the matter with you?' Clodagh cried. 'You know what these people are like. They use you and then toss you aside when they are done. They've been doing it for generations.'

'They only use you if you allow yourself to be used,' Lucy said angrily. 'Don't you think I have a mind of my own?'

'Yes, but–'

'Anyway, Clive's not like that.'

'All men are like that, given half the chance.'

Lucy remembered with a little embarrassment the kiss in the car, and what a kiss like that might lead to, and the strange yearning it had sent through her whole body, and she was silent. Clodagh seized on that, and the slight flush to her cheeks, to say, 'See, you are having second thoughts.'

'No, I am not,' Lucy cried. 'And neither is Clive.' She pulled the leather box from her bedside cabinet and opened it. Clodagh had seen the pendant before, but she was held spellbound by the sparkling ring. 'He gave me that for Christmas.'

Clodagh chose her words with care. 'It is a beautiful ring, Lucy. But it is just a present. It's him trifling with your feelings I care more about.'

'We're in love, Clodagh,' Lucy said. 'Both of us.'

'I knew you were sweet on him.'

'Yes, but he feels the same way.'

'Why didn't you tell me?'

'Because I knew you'd do this,' Lucy said. 'I fought against loving Clive at first. I told him it would never work, and I didn't think it would either because we were like chalk and cheese. I was so unhappy. Tried to buck myself up when I met you. Then I suddenly thought, what the hell, we could be dead tomorrow, or next month or year. If war comes, what future can any of us guarantee? Well, I suddenly decided that I was going to grab a little happiness while I still could. And you know what, Clodagh, I'm damned glad I did.'

Clodagh didn't say anything more. She could

see that Lucy's mind was made up. She hoped she wasn't just tilting at windmills because in her experience men like Clive Heatherington did not marry girls like Lucy Cassidy. Only time would tell, but she was filled with a terrible sense of foreboding.

NINETEEN

Lucy saw Clive the day after Boxing Day, when she was able to thank him for the ring, and then she wouldn't see him again until after the New Year because he was visiting the homes of his friends who had been killed. He told her this as they walked home that night.

'I have written to them all,' he said, 'but it isn't the same as a visit. They need to know the type of soldier their son was, and the brave way in which he died, and try to make sense of the fact that I, who stood beside them all, am alive when their sons are not.'

Lucy saw at once that this was something that Clive had to do. 'You'll probably find it very distressing.'

'Quite possibly,' he said, 'though not half as distressing as it will be for them, I should say, and at least I will be able to talk about them, and with someone who loved them as much as I did. Odd, I suppose, to say I loved them,' he mused, 'but we had been together since the age of eight, taught in the same classes, played in the same playground

340

and housed in the same dormitories. They were like my brothers and sometimes even now I can't believe they are gone. If I try to talk about them to either of my parents they shut me up very quickly.' Clive ran his hands through his hair in a manner Lucy had learnt he did when he was agitated. 'I suppose they think I'll start weeping and wailing again but I think I am over that now, and not talking about them makes it feel like they never existed.'

'You can talk to me, if you like,' Lucy said.

'You wouldn't mind?'

'How could I possibly mind?' she said. 'When Daddy died, for a while I held my hurt and pain inside me tight, afraid almost to let go of it. It was Mammy who said we should talk about him, and, yes, we did cry, but it did us all good because it was like he was still with us in a way. So when Mammy met Declan it was like she was replacing him, but of course you can never do that.' She smiled. 'The first time I saw Declan, I was home for my Sunday off and he was there in my house sitting in my father's chair. I was so angry because the day my father was taken to the sanatorium, my mother put the chair in her bedroom. Daddy used to sit in it, before the fire, for hours, the sicker he got, and Mammy said she couldn't bear the thought of anyone else sitting in it. But time passed and Declan came to the house, and she took out the chair for him to sit on. I was totally irrational.'

'Is that why you didn't go with them to America?'

'I don't know,' Lucy said. 'But if I'm honest then

341

it probably had something to do with it. All I'm saying is that I understand grief and how it makes you feel inside, and I don't mind you talking about your friends or anything else that upsets you. I don't mind either if you cry, but seeing your friends' parents might bring you a measure of peace.'

'You are one very special lady, Lucy,' Clive said. 'There is no one quite like you.'

'Glad to hear it,' Lucy replied with spirit.

However, when Clive returned in January, Lucy saw by his haunted eyes that the experience had upset him greatly.

'It stripped everything away,' he said. 'This façade that I wear for fear of upsetting people so they think that I am all right and that I am over the obscene things I witnessed. That is what my parents want to believe. Feelings are never discussed. It's not a topic of polite conversation around the dining table. It is only with you, my lovely Lucy, that I can be natural, that I can confess that the manner of my friends' deaths almost consumes me at times. When I saw the anguish of their parents, I felt, and still feel, guilty that I didn't grieve for them enough and now there is an ache in my heart and a big hole in my life, and it is only being with you that makes these things bearable.'

Lucy held Clive tenderly and said, 'Listen, Clive, when a person dies, particularly when that person is a loved one, it's natural to feel guilty. There is always something you wished you'd said or done, and because death is so very final what was unsaid will be left unsaid and what was undone will be left undone. You have to deal with that and go on knowing that if the person had been alive that's what they would have wanted you to do.'

'You see, you are so good for me,' Clive said. 'You are prepared to talk about things that matter and things that make sense. You see, the very opulence of my home offends me. Half of the house is closed up now because Clara has been unable to find staff to fill the places of those who have left, and my mother is constantly bemoaning the fact. But she still has Norah to look after her and in a very small household we have a housekeeper, a cook, a couple of girls, a footman and a butler, who, now Rory has left, has assumed what he has always considered to be his natural role of caring for my father and, if I am honest, me too when I allow it. We do not need all these people bowing and scraping and kowtowing to us as they do jobs that we could very well do on our own.'

'Yes, but what would these people do if they didn't work there?' Lucy asked. 'I know now jobs are more plentiful for everyone, but for years they weren't, and homelessness and starvation are not routes I would like to travel. Yet often that was the alternative to work in service. Clara, for instance, thinks of your place as her saviour, that it prevented her going over the top altogether.'

'Why?'

'Don't you know what happened to her?' Lucy asked in surprise. 'Don't you know anything about the lives of the people you employ?'

'No,' Clive said. 'Not as a general rule. But in

343

this case, and in my defence, she arrived when I was just a child and I went away to school not long afterwards. So now I am curious. Tell me about Clara.'

So Lucy told him of the double tragedy in Clara's life, her flight to Birmingham to try to ease the painful memories, and her need to find a place to live and a job of work. 'She always said Maxted Hall fitted the bill,' Lucy said. 'And the hard work kept her busy and gave her less time to think and brood.'

'Do you think that's what I am doing – brooding?'

'Maybe a little.'

'The point is, I feel I am living an artificial life,' Clive said. 'I say only the things people want to hear and I smile at people I might easily despise and make inane meaningless small talk with people who bore the pants off me.'

Lucy laughed. 'Oh, what a Mr Grump you are.'

'It's true, though,' Clive said, though he was laughing too. 'I went to Father's club on his insistence and there are loads of old duffers there like that.'

'There are people like that everywhere,' Lucy said. 'It isn't a prerogative of the upper classes. You have to just get on with them. You must have met people that annoyed you when you were fighting in Spain?'

'I suppose I did,' Clive conceded. 'But it didn't seem to matter so much, I suppose, because I felt I was doing something useful even though it turned out so badly afterwards.'

'That wasn't your fault,' Lucy said. 'You hit the

nail on the head when you said you felt that you were doing something useful. You must find something to fill your days now.'

'I know,' Clive said. 'When I cannot see you, I ride one of my father's hunters till we are both worn out, walk for miles or drive around aimlessly. It's making my mother wild.'

'I bet,' Lucy said, and she sighed. Given Clive's nervous and remorseful state, and the strained relationship between him and his mother, now was not an ideal time for him to tell her about their feelings for one another. Yet she hated hiding away from people all the time and knew that if Clive didn't tell her soon she would find out some other way.

January gave way to February and, by halfway through the month, Lady Heatherington was worried enough about Clive to appeal to her husband.

'Charles, I do wish you would speak to Clive.'

'What would you like me to speak to him about, my dear?'

'You know what about, Charles,' Lady Heatherington said. 'Don't be so provoking. Haven't I enough trouble coping with such few staff without you being so deliberately obtuse? The boy is never here.'

'Well, what is there here for him?' Charles said rather testily. 'Remember, the years that should have been carefree were spent fighting in Spain.'

'And whose fault was that?'

'It doesn't help to apportion blame,' Lord Heatherington said. 'But during that same conflict, he

345

lost his three best friends. That takes some getting over, I can tell you, and I speak from experience.'

'Well, it makes life pretty dashed awkward when Lady Ponsomby comes with Jessica. Twice they have been this week and both times there was no sign of Clive. It's too bad. Diana and I always planned that we would announce their betrothal at Clive's twenty-first birthday bash at the end of April. We thought him lost to us all but when he returned we decided that it should go ahead as planned.'

Lord Heatherington was astounded. 'This is the first I have heard of such a plan.'

'That could be because you don't listen.'

'Poppycock! I have never been consulted.'

'Please, don't shout, Charles,' Lady Heatherington admonished. 'You are not on the parade ground now.'

Charles forgot himself enough to exclaim, 'God dammit, woman, you are enough to make anyone shout. Now tell me what you are on about?'

'Charles, we have planned this since they were children.'

'Amelia, you can't plan other people's lives.'

'They are not other people, they are our children,' Lady Heatherington said. 'And they are young still, and wouldn't have a clue what they need to be looking for in a life partner. It is far better to be guided by parents. They have more experience in such matters.'

'Have either of you thought to consult the two people concerned?' Lord Heatherington said. 'If you haven't, then I suggest you do so without delay, and certainly before you go any further with

346

this ridiculous notion. You may well find they have definite views on running their own lives, and that includes making their own mistakes. Clive is nowhere near ready to settle down yet. He maybe needs to sow a few wild oats.'

Lady Heatherington always thought that such a coarse, lewd expression, and Lord Heatherington saw the look of disgust on her face. 'He's a man, Amelia, in case it had escaped your notice,' he cried. 'And he has the same needs as other men, so I want to hear no more about this nonsense. Do you understand?'

Lady Heatherington looked at her husband nonplussed. He was almost invariably kind and gentle with her, but now it seemed that she had vexed him in some way, and for the life of her she couldn't understand what she had done. Lord Heatherington looked at his wife's bewildered face and strode from the room with a cry of exasperation.

A few days later, Lord Heatherington received a letter from the War Office.

'What is it, my dear?' Lady Heatherington asked.

'Mmm, not sure.' Lord Heatherington scanned the letter again. 'It's very vague, but the upshot is they have asked if I will report to the Council House in Birmingham at my convenience and talk to a man called Stanley Dalkey.'

'Who's he?'

'No idea.'

'Will you go?'

'Of course, and no time like the present. Clive around?'

347

'Why ask me?' Lady Heatherington said. 'But I doubt it. He has probably had an early breakfast and gone out. That's his usual pattern.'

'No matter, I will call a taxi,' Lord Heatherington said, and in a few minutes he had left the house, intrigued as to what the War Office wanted with him.

He returned that afternoon in great excitement. 'I can't tell you much about what they want me to do,' he said, 'but one of my roles will be to help protect Birmingham in the event of air raids.'

'What air raids?'

'If we go to war.'

'Bit premature, don't you think?' Lady Heatherington said. 'It's like wishing it on us.'

'We have to be prepared,' Lord Heatherington said. 'Anyway, I have to go away for training. Don't ask where or for how long, for I don't know the answer to either, and if I did I probably wouldn't be allowed to tell you.'

Lord Heatherington left the next morning, in delighted satisfaction. He had been so sure that in the war that they seemed to be hurtling towards, men like him would be sidelined. To have a function, however minor, gave him a new lease of life and he couldn't wait to get started.

Lord Heatherington had been gone two days and Lady Heatherington was alone in the house when Lady Ponsomby called to see her. She wasn't expected, though that wasn't unusual, but she saw immediately that she was really agitated about something.

'What is it, my dear Diana?' she cried, crossing the room swiftly to hold her friend's trembling hands in her own. 'Shall I call for tea?'

Lady Ponsomby shook her head. 'I want no tea. All I want to know is if Clive is playing fast and loose with my daughter's affections?'

'Of course not,' Lady Heatherington said. 'What do you mean?'

'I mean that I have been here a number of times and he has been noticeable by his absence, and then my maid saw him yesterday bold as brass.'

'Bold as brass?' Lady Heatherington repeated.

'Yes, bold as brass, and coming out of the cinema holding hands with some girl.'

Lady Heatherington gave a gasp. Her husband's comments about wild oats sprung to mind. 'Are you sure?'

Lady Ponsomby nodded emphatically. 'My maid would swear to it,' she said. 'She said she nearly spoke to him until she saw the girl wrapped around him, and him lapping it up, and thought they wouldn't take kindly to her interrupting them. She came straight to me, so Jessica is unaware of it so far. I don't think your son is playing fair by my daughter and I want to know what you are going to do about it.'

'I will speak to him, of course.'

'Well, all I can say to that is that your words had better be effective,' Lady Ponsomby said. 'My daughter has set her heart on marrying your son and Jessica usually gets what she wants. And I don't think you can afford for him to refuse her.'

Lady Heatherington was well aware she

couldn't, but she knew her problem would be convincing Clive of that and she hoped the dalliance he'd been spotted enjoying with another girl was just that – a dalliance that hadn't gone too far.

Lady Ponsomby left, disapproval bristling in every line of her body as the chauffeur helped her into her Bentley. Lady Heatherington went back into the house and gave instructions that Master Clive was to see her as soon as he came in, no matter what time it was.

For once, he was early because Lucy had gone to the pictures with Clodagh. Clive hadn't been pleased with this at first. He wanted to spend every minute with her that she wasn't working because he had nothing to occupy him and no old friends that he could look up. So when he complained about this again, not long after he had returned from seeing the parents of his friends who had died, she was irritated. 'What's the matter with you? What on earth is wrong with me seeing my friends?'

'Well, I don't see why you want to see your friends when I am here,' he'd said, belligerently.

Lucy had rounded on him. 'Oh, don't you, Mr High and Mighty Clive Heatherington? By God, you have got an inflated opinion of yourself. So if you take yourself off to God knows where, and for as long as it takes, which you did recently, I can see my friends. But then I must drop them like hot potatoes the minute you are back. You know, I think soon I wouldn't have any friends left.'

It was his selfish side coming to the fore again. Clive had recognised it, and he had apologised.

Now he just nodded when she told him she was seeing friends. That night he had even felt sorry for his mother, eating dinner all alone, and decided to keep her company, only for old Carlisle to tell him his mother wanted to see him as he helped him off with his coat.

Clive took one look at his mother's grim expression, went to the sideboard and poured himself a stiff brandy before facing her. 'You wanted to see me, Mother?'

Clive watched his mother wetting her lips and knew that she was very nervous. Her voice wavered slightly as she said, 'I wanted to ask you something.'

'Ask away then,' Clive said.

What she asked him surprised him initially. 'Did you go to the cinema yesterday?'

'Yes, I did.'

'Did you take anyone with you?'

Clive knew he had been seen with Lucy. He should have told his mother about his seeing Lucy long ago. Lucy was right: a hole-and-corner relationship was no relationship at all. However, he also thought his mother had no right to quiz him this way and so he answered, 'Yes, yes, I did. I have no wish to be rude but I fail to see how that is anything to do with you.'

'It has everything to do with me,' Lady Heatherington said. Tears prickled her eyes as she went on, 'You are promised to Jessica Ponsomby.'

Clive looked at her as if he couldn't believe his ears and then he tossed the brandy back in one swallow and growled out, 'No, I am bloody well not.'

'You are,' Lady Heatherington insisted. 'You must be because you are our only son.'

'I know that,' Clive said. 'How has that got anything to do with anything?'

'Because we need the money,' Lady Heatherington said. 'If any of your brothers had survived and married money then you would have more freedom to marry who you choose. As it is, everything rests on your shoulders.'

'Mother, we don't live in the Middle Ages,' Clive protested. 'You can't tell me who to marry. Anyway, what would have happened if I hadn't returned from Spain?'

Lady Heatherington sighed. 'Then, though it would have broken your father's heart, we would have had to sell everything. The house has been in his family for generations. Then there is the car you are making so much use of, and his beloved hunters. Everything would have to be sold and the servants would have to find new positions, and when all the debts were paid we'd see if there was enough to enable us to buy somewhere to live. You have the means to stop that happening.'

'Is it really as bad as that?'

'Oh, yes, Clive, it's as bad as that,' Lady Heatherington said. 'You grew up as a pampered and privileged only son. Nothing was denied you, and you went to a first-class school and were set to go to a top university. When you wanted to travel through Europe, no obstacle was put in your way and we financed it, though by then we were living on an army pension.'

'Why wasn't I told this?'

'You were eighteen,' Lady Heatherington said.

'What could you have done? Anyway, I wasn't fully aware myself then. I had never bothered myself about finances before, and even then your father seemed to think that when your grandmother died her money and the sale of her house would solve all our problems. But financial matters were not as important to us at that time because we were both so worried about you. Then your grandmother died. She had always seen to her own finances with the family solicitor because, as you know, she was fiercely independent. None of us was aware that your grandfather had been a profligate gambler and womaniser who had left your grandmother little but a pile of debt, and even a mortgage on the house. The solicitor said she was too proud to tell us any of this, aware of how ill your father had been, but when her meagre savings were exhausted the solicitor sold the house. By the time he had settled the outstanding mortgage and the interest accrued there was little left.'

Clive suddenly felt the ground beneath his feet, which he had thought so solid and secure, become as unstable and as slippery as sand.

'So,' Lady Heatherington said, 'you have a choice. You can either marry your floozie, whoever she is, and watch your father and me descend into penury, or step up to the mark and marry Jessica. You owe us something, Clive, and it isn't as though you don't know Jessica.'

'I know her as a friend,' Clive said, almost staggering from the news. 'I never thought I would marry her. How do you know she will be agreeable to all this?'

'Because, according to her mother, it is all she's ever wanted.'

That was a further piece of news that shook Clive and he poured himself another stiff brandy. But there was a matter he had to clear with his mother. 'And just to make things clear,' he said, 'the girl I took to the pictures last night is no floozie. Her name is Lucy Cassidy and she used to work in your kitchens as a scullery maid and then looked after Grandmother.'

Lady Heatherington's lips were drawn back almost in a snarl as she snapped, 'I know who she is – the type of girl who would coerce an old lady into giving her an exquisite and very expensive pendant.'

'It is lovely, I grant you; she's shown it to me,' Clive said. 'But I understood it was in Grandmother's will that she have it.'

'Yes, that she tricked her into writing.'

Clive gave a grim laugh. 'I doubt it very much,' he said. 'Lucy is not at all that type of girl, and even if she was, from my memories of Grandmother she was not the sort of person to be tricked or coerced into doing anything she didn't want to do.' And he let this sink in before he added, 'I actually bought her a ring to match the pendant.' He heard his mother's sharp intake of breath and then went on, 'It wasn't an engagement ring, but that was going to come afterwards because Lucy and I love each other.'

'Love!' Lady Heatherington said disparagingly. 'What do you know of love at your age?'

'Enough to know I love Lucy and want to be with her for always.'

354

'Well, that door is closed to you, isn't it?' Lady Heatherington said, and, with a sudden pang of loss, Clive realised his mother was right. How could he turn his back on his parents, and would he know a minute's happiness if he did? Or would it eventually taint the love he shared with Lucy? Dear God, he felt as if his heart was breaking.

Lady Heatherington said, 'And I will tell you the worst thing.'

'Can it get worse than this?'

'For me it can.'

'What?'

'Look, no one else is to know this lest it get back to your father. He has his head in the sand where our finances are concerned, but he might be very angry at what I felt I had to do.'

'Which was?'

Lady Heatherington sighed. 'I took a loan from Lady Ponsomby.'

'Oh, Mother!'

'It's all right saying that, Clive, but I had no choice,' Lady Heatherington said. 'Traders were pressing for payment, and then a stone was dislodged from the West Wing and crashed on to the courtyard in the back. I told your father the insurance would deal with it, but in fact that was just one other thing I couldn't pay. The builder I engaged said major restructuring work had to be done or the whole lot could come down and kill someone. There was no one else I could think of to borrow from but Diana. But she insisted she have the family tiara as surety.'

'Well, how did she know we had anything like that?' Clive asked testily.

'Well,' Lady Heatherington began, rather shame-facedly, 'I was boasting one day and showed it to her.'

'Damned stupid thing to do,' Clive burst out, and that he had sworn in front of his mother showed the level of his agitation. He wasn't surprised his mother was proud of the diamond-encrusted tiara, which legend said was a gift to the Heatherington family from Queen Elizabeth for something or other. That it should ever go out of their keeping was unthinkable, and she had shown it to a so-called friend that she now owed money to! He felt rage building up inside him, but it was rage at life and at his own helplessness to see any way out of this dilemma.

Lady Heatherington looked at her son's contorted face and went on, 'If you hadn't come back I would have had a good copy made and hoped your father did not look too hard at it.'

Clive knew that that tiara was one of his father's most treasured possessions and the loss of it would hurt him grievously.

'What if I marry Jessica?' he said, as if the words were pulled out of him.

'The debt is cancelled and the tiara is returned.'

Mr Carlisle came in then to announce that dinner was being served in the dining room, but they paid him no heed.

'Will you do it?' Lady Heatherington pleaded with her son.

Suddenly Clive felt as if the lifeblood were being drawn from him. He gave an anguished cry and, shaking his head wildly, he made for the front door, yanking it open with such force it juddered on its hinges. With her hand to her mouth, Lady Heatherington watched her son tearing out into the night, running like a man possessed.

TWENTY

Clive woke up with a thumping headache and such a dry mouth he could barely swallow. He wasn't that surprised because he'd drunk far more than was usual the night before, and then he hadn't slept well but had tossed and turned. But whichever way he looked at it he could see no alternative but to marry Jessica. If it was just he who was going to suffer he could face it, but what he could barely cope with was the deep hurt that he was going to inflict on his darling Lucy.

He was still blisteringly angry, that life had promised so much and now it was to be snatched away from him, and he groaned aloud. Dear God, how would he tell Lucy this? He was filled with shame that he would have to let her down, and mentally he recoiled from the pain of betrayal he would see in her eyes.

But there was no other option. The consequences would be too great if he did not do as his mother wanted, so there was nothing to be gained by keeping Lucy in ignorance a moment longer than necessary. Ignoring the headache and the nausea when he sat up, he heaved himself from the bed and began to dress hurriedly.

'Where are you going?' Lady Heatherington

357

asked as Clive opened the front door.

He could barely look at her as he spat out, 'To tell Lucy. I owe her that, at least.'

'But she will be at work,' Lady Heatherington said.

'Then I'll ask if she can leave work because this is too important to wait. God, I hate to think of it, because today I will break her heart.'

'Huh, you won't break that one's heart,' Lady Heatherington said. 'Lucy Cassidy has a heart of stone and she's in for the main chance. Do you think she would have looked at you twice if you weren't in line to be the next Lord Heatherington?'

'You know nothing about Lucy,' Clive roared at his mother. 'Do you hear me, you know nothing. You stop those scandalous lies and speak of her with respect or I will stop this sham of a marriage, and hang the consequences.'

Clive had never before hurled such abuse at his mother, but she knew it was the influence of that slut Lucy Cassidy trying to turn her son against her. The sooner he was away from her, the better.

'Well, go and see her, if you must,' she said, 'but Jessica and her mother will be arriving mid-morning.'

'No!' Clive cried. 'Almighty Christ, I can't see them today.'

'You *will* see them today. It is you they are coming to see,' Lady Heatherington snapped. 'I did try telling you last night, but you were in no fit state to hear or understand anything.'

'Can you wonder at that?' Clive said. 'I needed plenty to drink to come to terms with what you said yesterday evening.'

'And you will get yourself tidied up before you see Jessica,' Lady Heatherington said. 'You will find her standards are a lot higher than those of Lucy Cassidy.'

Clive didn't even attempt a reply, though the look he threw his mother should have laid her senseless on the floor.

However, once on the road, what he was going to say went round and round in his head. The image of Lucy's face floated before him as pangs of guilt flickered in the pit of his stomach and his heart ached. Eventually, he stopped the car, put his head on the steering wheel, and wept.

Lucy had never seen Clive look the way he did when he came into the hospital a little later. She took in the fact he hadn't shaved, his face was slightly swollen, and his hair stood on end, but it was his red-rimmed bleak eyes with blue smudges beneath them that caused her to run to him in concern.

'Clive, what is it?'

'I need to talk to you now,' Clive said. 'Can you get off?'

Lucy was flustered. Clive had never asked that before, but then she had never seen him in such a state. 'I don't know,' she said. 'I–'

Clive's hand shot out and grabbed Lucy's. 'Please, I wouldn't ask if it weren't important.'

'Go with him,' Nurse Patterson said. 'He has news that obviously won't keep.'

Clive sighed with relief as, with a fearful look at him, Lucy went to get her coat. Then, without another word, she got in the car, which Clive had parked just outside. 'Where are we going?' she asked, as he started the engine.

'It doesn't matter,' Clive said. 'Nothing much matters now.'

'Please, Clive,' Lucy cried. 'I can't bear this. Please, stop the car and tell me what's wrong.'

Clive pulled the car to a halt by the edge of the recreation ground where Lucy, Clodagh and Chris had walked on Christmas Day, and Lucy looked at Clive's face, so filled with foreboding.

'I have never ever met anyone like you, Lucy, and I would lay down my life for you gladly. Oh, Jesus Christ, this is breaking my heart, as it might well break yours. I cannot marry you.'

'You can't mean this?' Lucy cried in a voice filled with anguish. 'Why are you saying this? It cannot be true. I thought you loved me as I love you.'

'I do, I do!' declared Clive, punching the steering wheel with his fist to emphasise it. 'Oh, God, do you think I like saying these things to you? I must marry another, though I will never love anyone else the way I love you.'

Lucy looked at him with desolate eyes and wondered if he thought that made any difference. Shards of pain such as she had never felt before attacked her body while tears gushed from her eyes and she felt her heart shatter into a million pieces.

Clive told Lucy about everything, just as his mother had told him, except the bit about the tiara. Sometimes he was too overcome to go on and sometimes he cried too, but Lucy understood he was trying to say that he was poor and had to marry Jessica Ponsomby to enable his parents to live as they always had.

When he was finished, she just looked at him ironically, though her anguished eyes showed her acute distress. She understood about poverty. God, she had experienced it for enough years. It was having constant hunger in your belly and inadequate heat in the house, and inadequate clothes on your back, and those clothes just someone else's cast-offs given to you by St Vincent de Paul, and going barefoot if there were no boots in the bundle. That was poor. Not keeping up a big house full of servants with horses in the stables and a fine car in the garage.

No, Clive had tired of her, just as Clodagh said he would. She was all right to have fun with, but not marry, and she wasn't surprised that he was going to marry Jessica Ponsomby, for wasn't that planned since they were children? And, by God, they deserved each other.

'Say something, for God's sake,' Clive said.

Lucy looked at him coldly. Then she suddenly leapt out of the car and began to run through the grass towards the recreation ground. 'Lucy!' Clive cried, but she didn't stop. She had taken him unawares and by the time he had struggled out of the car and took after her she was nowhere to be seen, for she had crossed the stream and was hiding in the woods.

He searched this way and that because he wanted to know that she was all right, and he tried calling, but that drew no response either. In the end he had to return home, to make himself respectable to meet his intended wife, for if he was going to sacrifice himself for his parents' sake then he had better do the job properly.

Lucy stayed where she was till she heard the car being driven away. Then she came out of hiding. She understood why an injured animal crawls into a hole and licks its wounds, because that was exactly what she wanted to do. So she made for home, hoping Gwen was out shopping or something.

However, Gwen wasn't out, and she took in Lucy's distressed state immediately. 'My dear child, what is it?' she cried, putting her arms around her.

The sympathy in Gwen's response caused the tears to flow again from Lucy's eyes but, through the tears, she tried to explain. 'Oh, Gwen, it's Clive. He's ... oh, God, I don't know what I'm going to do... I didn't think anything could hurt like this...'

And then she felt a black mist envelop her and she slipped from Gwen's arms and fell to the floor in a dead faint.

When Lucy's eyes fluttered open again she was in her own bed, with Chris Gilbert by her side. 'What happened?' she asked, and then the memories came crashing back.

Chris watched the shadows wash over her face, but first he answered her original question. 'You fainted,' he said. 'You gave Mum quite a turn and she sent for me. Fortunately, I was only at the Cottage Hospital. Mum said you seemed upset about something and mentioned the name Clive.

362

I presume you meant Clive Heatherington. Has anything happened to him?'

Lucy gave a bitter laugh. 'Not him,' she said. 'Nothing will happen to him, or those like him, who ride roughshod over others without a thought.'

Tears trickled from her big beautiful eyes and ran down her cheeks, and Chris fought the urge to gather her up in his arms and kiss them away, and go on to kiss her face and her eyes and her throat and her lovely inviting mouth. Oh, God – he almost groaned out loud and pulled himself up sharply. He was a doctor, for God's sake, and it was the doctor in him who said to Lucy, 'Would you like to talk about it, my dear?'

How Lucy longed to unburden herself to some-one who wouldn't judge her and tell her she was stupid, for she knew that well enough herself. And a doctor was like a priest in a way, and would not breathe a word of what she told him if she asked him not to. So she told him everything, the words tumbling out of her mouth once she began. And so he heard of a young naïve girl, dazzled by the charm of the son of the house.

Chris had known of Clive's fixation on Lucy, for he had told him of it, but he didn't encourage his interest, feeling quite sure it would come to nothing. And in fact Lucy hadn't seen Clive again until they met at the Cottage Hospital, which he had arranged and for which he felt somewhat responsible because from then they had begun a friendship that had blossomed into love, at least on Lucy's part.

'And did he give you any reason for ending the

relationship?' Chris asked gently.

'Oh, yes,' Lucy said. 'He gave me some cock-and-bull story of how he had to marry Jessica Ponsomby because her family had money and without it his would be poor. I ask you. They don't know the meaning of the word poor.'

Chris had more understanding of the Heatheringtons' plight, for the general consensus at the club was that Lord Heatherington, who was a decent enough old stick, had drawn the short straw, mainly due to his lusty, profligate father, who had continued to gamble when he had lost all before him. He had gone through all his wife's money as well as his own, and it was said he had even sold some of her jewellery, though he wined and dined his women lavishly and often showered them with presents. Now they said it was his son – who had known nothing about his father's lifestyle, as he had been in the army for years – who had to cope with the fallout from this.

Yes, the doctor thought he might well have needed his son to marry money, so why did that son make a play for Lucy and upset her so? He would like to give him a piece of his mind and might yet, but there was another thing he had to know. History was peppered with stories of the lord of the manor taking advantages of servant girls, and, as Lucy had fainted, he had to know if there was a chance she might be pregnant.

'Did you have a physical relationship with Clive?' he probed gently.

'What d'you mean?' Lucy asked.

'Did you do more than kiss?'

Now Lucy knew what the doctor was asking

364

and she shot up in the bed. 'Not in the way you mean,' she said indignantly.

'Lucy's not that sort of girl,' Gwen said, coming into the room at that instant. She sat on the bed, put her arms around Lucy's shaking shoulders and glared at her son. 'I'm surprised you even thought to ask.'

'It's my job, Mother.'

'Well, you have done your job and got your answer,' Gwen said. 'So let's have no more questions of that nature. You go round to the hospital now and tell them that Lucy will not be in for a week.'

'But, Gwen–'

'No, Lucy, I insist,' Gwen said. 'You are absolutely exhausted – a man on a galloping horse could see that – and I want you well rested before you go back there.'

Chris wondered if that was the real reason. His mother might well have listened to Lucy's tale on the stairs and thought keeping her away from the hospital was the easiest way to make sure Clive didn't try to contact her and upset her all over again. If so, it was a good plan because the last thing Lucy needed now was to see Clive Heatherington. So he said, 'I think Mother is quite right. You're looking quite run-down and a little rest will do you good. In a day or two we will do some work for your exams too. They're only three weeks away and you have been rather distracted of late. Of course, I understand why now.'

Lucy coloured slightly because she knew Chris was right. 'I'm sorry,' she said. 'I will try harder.'

'Not yet, you won't,' said Gwen decidedly.

'Now you stay just where you are and I will bring you a spot of lunch.'

It was such a novel experience for anyone to look after Lucy she didn't say another word about it.

Lord Heatherington arrived home after his initial briefing to find the house in turmoil because of the more-than-lavish wedding being planned for his son.

'And who is he marrying?' he asked his wife testily.

Lady Heatherington laughed lightly. 'Really, Charles,' she said. 'Who do you think it is? Jessica Ponsomby, of course, and on his twenty-first birthday as well.'

'So your planning came to fruition in my absence?' Lord Heatherington said. 'I thought I told you–'

'Charles, it was his own decision,' Lady Heatherington said, thinking the white lie justified. 'As you pointed out to me, he is a grown man and therefore can make up his own mind.'

'Huh, must have made it up pretty damned quick, that's all I can say, because as far as I could see the only thoughts about those two getting together were in your head. Anyway, I thought you said that he was getting betrothed on his birthday? He is a bit young for marriage, I would have said.'

Lady Heatherington *had* said betrothal, and would have been happier with that, but Lady Ponsomby wanted nothing less than a wedding because that was what 'dear Jessica' wanted.

However, she couldn't let Charles know that, so she said, 'Oh, yes, it was going to be a betrothal, but with the world in the state it's in we thought a wedding was best.'

Lord Heatherington knew what a state the world was in better that most, and he had a vision of the future that he thought very grim. But he couldn't share that. 'Not even with your nearest and dearest,' he had been warned, and so now he went in search of his son.

He had expected to find him in the stable because he had heard the sound of hoofs on the cobbles while he had been talking to his wife. However, only Bert was in the stables, rubbing down the horse that Clive usually rode, which was lathered with sweat.

He straightened up when he saw Lord Heatherington, and said, 'Yon Master Clive is in some sort of tear, sir. No need to take it out on the horses, though. Begging your pardon, sir, but I had to say it.'

'Yes, yes,' Lord Heatherington said. 'I will go and have a word.'

Clive wasn't in his room and Lord Heatherington found him in the sitting room, lolled back on the settee with a large glass of brandy in his hand. 'Bit early for that, isn't it?'

Clive shrugged but didn't speak, and his father said, 'I expected to see you rubbing down the horse you had ridden so hard.'

Clive coloured. 'I know, I know. Bert's already had a go at me. And he wouldn't let me see to the horse. Said the state I was in I would hardly do the job properly.'

'And what state are you in?'

'A bloody awful one, if you want to know the truth,' Clive said. He raised his head and Lord Heatherington was shocked at the desolation in his eyes. 'The future doesn't look good from where I'm sitting.'

'I guessed as much,' Lord Heatherington said. 'Why did you do it, son? Why did you agree to marry Jessica Ponsomby? Just to please your mother?'

'It wasn't just to please Mother,' Clive burst out hotly. 'It was to save her, and you as well. God, Mother said you buried your head in the sand and she was right because you must be aware of the dire straits you're in and how close you've come to losing everything.'

Lord Heatherington hung his head in shame. 'I didn't want to think about it.'

'Good job somebody did then,' Clive said. 'Basically, you are in hock to the Ponsombys and my marriage to Jessica means you get to keep your house, your car and your comfortable way of life, and I think it is one bloody high price to pay.'

Lucy was so angry with Clive. She thought he had made a fool of her, and she regarded herself as little better than Hazel, whom she had castigated for beginning a relationship with Jerry. When Lucy had opened Hazel's eyes to the truth, Hazel had said that she felt a fool for believing Jerry's lies, and now, Lucy realized she was the fool for believing Clive's. The anger helped her cope with the loss of him, at least in the day. Her nights, however, were punctuated with sorrowful dreams in which Clive was getting further and further away, and her pillow was often damp in the morning.

It also helped that Clodagh, whom she told at their dancing class, didn't say or even intimate that she had prophesied it would end that way. There was to be no 'I told you so' from Clodagh, and her sympathy and support were all for Lucy, who was, she said, far too good for one of the Heatheringtons, however handsome. Though that sympathy often made Lucy tearful, that didn't embarrass Clodagh in the least, and she said that they were good tears, which she needed to shed.

Lucy's fellow nurses at the Cottage Hospital were shocked by Clive's behaviour. 'When someone plays you for a fool like that you can feel really stupid,' Nurse Patterson said to Lucy, 'but there is no need because we were all taken in.'

'I'll say,' another nurse said. 'Real charmer. Fancied him myself.'

'Didn't we all?' said another. 'I knew we didn't stand a chance, with Lucy, though, and he did seem smitten. Just shows you. I never for one moment would have guessed he would turn out to be such a bad egg.'

All this was good for Lucy's confidence, which had taken a massive knock as she struggled with the grief, which, despite everything, threatened to overwhelm her at times.

'It is bound to hurt for a little while yet,' Gwen said when Lucy told her how she felt one day. 'You put all your heart into loving that chap and you can't just turn that love off like a tap. Eventually, it will slow to a dribble, and then stop, and the only way I know to help that along is to keep busy.'

'Clara said that too.'

'Did you tell your mother?'

Lucy shook her head. 'There was nothing to tell. I had never mentioned Clive because it would only have worried her.'

'What if you were going to be married?'

'Well, I couldn't have, could I, not until I'd finished my nurse's training? We never thought that far ahead, but Chris was right when he said that people like the Heatheringtons don't like waiting for things. Clive wouldn't have wanted to hang about for four years and I would have had to give up my course or lose him anyway.'

'What would you have chosen?'

'I would stay in nurse-training now without a doubt,' Lucy said. 'But when I was so in love with Clive, I couldn't think straight. I don't know what I'd have done. But I do know if I'd given up the course I might well have resented him for making me make that choice.'

'So he may have been doing you a favour?'

Lucy gave a rueful grin and said, 'Yeah, and I might get to see it that way in time.'

She kept her promise to the doctor too, and worked harder with him and concentrated more, pushing thoughts of Clive Heatherington and the future they may have once shared to the furthest recesses of her mind. Her nursing was more important to her than ever and she was determined to pass these exams.

Through the winter, Lucy had been wrapped in a bubble of happiness and unaware of the unrest in the world. By the first week in March, the Spanish government forces had surrendered to the dictator, Franco, and his fascist followers. Then Czechoslovakia surrendered its independence to Hitler the day Lucy took her nursing exams. Though the news was bad, and it was being shouted out by the newspaper vendor on the council steps where the exams were being held, Lucy was more concerned with the exam she had just sat and whether she had done enough to pass.

Chris was coming around that night to see how she had got on, and she had managed to retrieve her paper for him to see. Chris was glad that she had done that and he scrutinised it carefully, glad to see that many of the things he had taught her had come up.

'How did you find it?' he asked, handing it back to Lucy as Gwen shouted out that dinner was ready.

'Not bad,' Lucy said as they moved into the dining room. 'I've never had an exam like that and to be honest, I wasn't too worried. I mean, I answered everything.'

'I never doubted you would,' Gwen said as they took their places at the table. 'You're a very bright girl.'

'Oh, I think the quality of the teacher had something to do with it.'

'I can only give you the information, Lucy,' Chris said. 'It is your brain that has to assimilate the facts. But let's not dissect it now, for it's done and over, the first leg of your quest to be a nurse.'

As Lucy continued to work at the hospital and waited for her exam results there was no denying that the country was gearing up for war. In April, the Territorial Army overseas was recalled, and the rumour was that there was to be a call-up of young men aged twenty and twenty-one. Lord Heatherington knew it was no rumour because he had been told about this weeks before and, old soldier though he was, his one thought was to save his son, whom he thought had been through enough in Spain.

It was a week before the wedding when he broached the subject. 'I could pull strings to keep you out of the active side of it, at least.'

'And why would you do that?'

'Because you are my son, dammit.'

'Isn't every man who joins up someone's son?'

'Clive, I've lost three sons to war already.'

'Don't lay their deaths at my door,' Clive snapped. 'All my life I have grown up in their shadow, had to do even things I wasn't keen on because I was the only one left. Even this marriage business. Mother said if one of my brothers had married into money then I could probably have married whoever I wanted.'

'And have you anyone in mind who you would rather marry?'

'You bet I have,' Clive said. 'Lucy Cassidy.'

Lord Heatherington's mouth dropped open. 'Clive, your mother would never have stood for that.'

'Father, I'm not a little boy any more, and, if I'd had free choice, she would have to stand it

372

because that's who I would have married.'

'She's a comely little thing, I grant you.'

'She's beautiful,' Clive said. 'We met when I was having physio at the Cottage Hospital and we started going out. She probably hates my guts now, but I love her and I know I will do so till the day I die.'

'I'm sorry, son.'

'Me too. But it changes nothing,' Clive said. Then he sighed and went on, 'I will have to get a grip of myself, though, because it isn't fair to Jessica.'

'Well, is it fair to leave her so soon after the wedding, as you'll have to if you answer this call-up?' Lord Heatherington said. 'Are you sure you don't want me to try and wangle it for you?'

'I'm positive.'

'Didn't you do enough in Spain?'

'Obviously not, for we lost. If we go to war with Germany, losing is not an option.'

Despite Clive's determination to get a grip on himself though, Chris, who had been invited to the wedding, confided to his mother that he had never seen a more reluctant or miserable bridegroom. He didn't mention the wedding to Lucy or say that the couple had no time for a honeymoon because, less than a week later, at the beginning of May, Clive had to report to Thorpe Street Barracks.

TWENTY-ONE

On Friday 7 July, Lucy received notification that she had passed her nursing exams with flying colours, and Gwen was full of praise. Chris had already told her that there were only two teaching hospitals in Birmingham that took on student nurses, and one was Queen's. The other, the one that Lucy was assigned to, was the General in Steelhouse Lane. 'Oh, yes,' Gwen said. 'That used to be a workhouse but lots of them were turned into hospitals. I suppose they had to use the buildings for something.'

'There's a map showing me how to get there.'

'You'll hardly need that,' Gwen said. 'It's a direct route.'

'There's the hospital,' Lucy said, tracing it with her finger. 'And over the road, look, is a police station.'

'That's why it's called Steelhouse Lane,' Gwen said, and added with a smile, 'There for locking up unruly nurses, no doubt.'

'Bound to be,' Lucy said with an answering grin. 'There is a list of things to buy too, so I'll go and see Clodagh tonight and see if she'll come to Birmingham with me tomorrow. But I must send a telegram to my family in New York. They will be waiting for news.'

'Yes,' Gwen said. 'In your mother's last letter, you said she was asking you when the results

374

would be out. It's obvious that she would be a little anxious.'

'Yes,' Lucy said, and went on, with a wry smile, 'Mammy hasn't a nasty bone in her body and will congratulate me with the best of them, but if she was truly honest she might have preferred me to fail.'

'Why would she want that?'

'Because she was hoping that if I hadn't made it into nursing, I might have gone over to them and trained for something else. She said as much in her last few letters. Sort of, "If it doesn't work out you can come here."'

'Would you have done that?'

Lucy shrugged. 'I don't know,' she said. 'I nearly went before, when Clive finished with me. I felt so stupid because I thought he really loved me and was honest and believed in the future we were mapping out together. I even asked him about Jessica Ponsomby, and he assured me that she was just a friend. The type of friend you intend to marry, obviously.'

'I believe there was some pressure from his mother and hers. Chris is usually as tight as a drum but he let that slip.'

'That makes it even worse,' Lucy said. 'I think it is a very feeble man who marries a girl because his mother tells him to, and not a man I would want to spend the rest of my life with if he had been free. In America, I would have been able to forget all about him and I thought it would have helped that I had told no one there about Clive, so they wouldn't know what a fool I had made of myself.'

'But you didn't go to America in the end.'

'I saw it as sort of running away, and I also thought of all those who had believed in me, right back to old Lady Heatherington, who left money in her will so that I could follow my dream. But my dream would have come to nothing if Chris hadn't tutored me so tirelessly, and you let me lodge with you, so I could pick up valuable experience in the Cottage Hospital, which Chris also organised. I owed you all so much and I knew I couldn't turn my back on that. I thought Clive had ruined my life, but I realised he could only do that if I allowed him to.'

The words were brave ones but Gwen knew Lucy well enough now to realise she was holding her emotions in check and she saw tears brimming in her eyes. 'You must still miss him, my dear,' she said with sympathy.

'I did,' Lucy admitted, as two rogue tears tumbled over her eyelids and trickled down her cheeks, but she continued resolutely. 'I missed Clive because I loved him so very much, but passing those exams means that that part of my life is now over. So I am going to draw a line under it and I've decided I don't need a man to determine my future. I will make my own.'

Gwen took hold of her hands. 'You are a wonderful young woman, Lucy, and one it has been a pleasure to know. I believe, as my son does, that you will make a first-rate nurse and you should go now and tell your mother in America what a clever daughter she has.'

Lucy was too choked to speak but, as she hugged Gwen before she left the house a few

376

minutes later, she realised how fond she was of her.

At the Cottage Hospital such a fuss was made of her, and she was hugged and kissed by patients as well as staff. She knew what a debt she owed Chris, though, because he had tutored her so well, but when she thanked him sincerely for what he had done for her, he waved her gratefulness aside.

'It was a pleasure, my dear, a great pleasure,' he said, taking her in his arms and kissing her gently on both cheeks. Though it was just an innocent kiss she still blushed slightly at the unusualness of it.

After work she took the bus down to Aston. Clodagh was so delighted at her news that she danced her around the room, much to the amusement of Hazel's family, who all congratulated her warmly. Clodagh readily agreed to going with her into town, especially when Lucy showed her the list, for she declared that she would never carry all the parcels herself. 'Anyway, it's always a gas when we are together,' Clodagh said, and Lucy agreed.

And the icing on the cake that wonderful day was when she arrived home to find five telegrams waiting for her, one from each of her siblings and one from her mother and Declan. Even through the stark words of a telegram she read of their pride.

The following day, Lucy met Clodagh in the town by Lewis's. The first thing she did was draw a lot of money out of the Post Office before they made their way to Jenner's, where the nursing uniforms could be bought. Clodagh thought it totally unfair that Lucy should have to buy her own uniform. Each dress she was measured for cost thirteen shillings and four pence, and she was expected to have at least two of these. The compulsory twelve aprons were three shillings each, four caps costing one and four pence each, and a cape that was sixteen shillings and eight pence. In addition to these were six pair of lisle fawn stockings and Benduble brown lace-up shoes.

'That's an awful lot of money you paid there,' Clodagh said as they left the shop weighed down with their parcels.

'I know,' Lucy said. 'But it's only what I expected. I got good wages when I was looking after the old lady and could save a lot of it, and then she left me all that money. You don't go into nursing for the money – well, at least not when you're training.'

Clodagh shook her head. 'Then I don't know what you do it for,' she said candidly, leading the way down the road. 'S'pose you want to look at the nursing hospital now we're here?'

'Yes. Do you mind?'

'Why should I mind?' Clodagh said. 'I expected you to say that.'

So just minutes later she was looking at a huge and imposing structure built with light bricks. It was much bigger than the Cottage Hospital.

'Looks sort of intimidating, don't you think?' Clodagh said.

'Mmm, I do see what you mean,' Lucy said. It's probably because it was built as a workhouse; Gwen told me. Still, Chris told me it's a fine hospital.' She clasped her hands across her chest as the thrill of excitement began in her toes and spread through her body. For a moment or two she remembered her earlier, spartan existence in Mountcharles, and now she was here and about to embark on a career in nursing. It was unbelievable and very exciting.

Clodagh watched her friend's eyes shining with excitement and was very glad that Lucy had something else in her life. She seemed to have completely forgotten that cad Clive Heatherington. Still, she thought he would live to regret his marriage, for he was to wed a she-devil. Clodagh had seen the announcement of the wedding in the paper. Thank God, Lucy hadn't seen it, for Clodagh was sure if she had she would have mentioned it. Still, she seemed completely gone on this nursing now.

'You have to live in the hospital, don't you?'

Lucy nodded. 'Not in the hospital itself, the nurses' home, but it is connected,' she said. 'According to the map they sent, the entrance is on Whittall Street, which leads off Steelhouse Lane.'

They soon found it as they walked down the short road, and then Lucy was looking at the entrance to the nurses' home, where she would live for four years.

'No problem about you going to Mass, anyway,' Clodagh said. Just yards from the nurses' home was a red-brick church with two blue spires pointing heavenwards.

'St Chad's Cathedral,' Lucy said. 'It's a fine-looking place all right, but I always thought cathedrals were bigger than that.'

'So, how many cathedrals do you know, then?'

'Oh, you know what I mean,' Lucy said. 'You get an image in your mind's eye that a cathedral is bigger and more majestic than a church.'

'Maybe it's bigger than it looks and is magnificent inside?' Clodagh suggested.

Lucy was to find that this was so, but she said doubtfully, 'I suppose I will be let go to Mass.'

'You'd better be let,' Clodagh shrugged. 'It's a mortal sin if you miss Mass. Still, there must be some arrangement because you can't be the only Catholic working in a place that size.'

'Of course I won't be,' Lucy said. 'It's just like me to worry about something before I need to.' Her stomach gave a sudden rumble and Clodagh grinned as Lucy said, 'I couldn't eat breakfast I was so nervous.'

'I managed all right,' Clodagh said. 'But that was hours ago. Just now I could murder a plate of fish and chips.'

'Oh, me too,' Lucy said, her mouth watering at the thought. 'And my treat as a thank-you for coming with me.'

As the summer progressed, railings disappeared from around buildings, deep ditches were dug in parks and brick-built shelters seemed to be popping up everywhere. At weekends and through the summer holidays, children were drafted in to fill sandbags to pack around them. On 25 August, Britain signed an alliance with Poland, promising to go to their aid if they were attacked. A blackout would be in force from September.

Gwen and Lucy went off to the Bull Ring one day and bought yards and yards of horrid black material. Lucy thought they would spend hours sewing, for there were many windows in that house, but Chris arrived the following night with a brand-new Singer sewing machine.

Gwen was a little nervous of it, but Lucy soon mastered it and made the curtains in no time. Chris came to put them up while Lucy made more to go in the surgery and Chris's flat, and though she knew it had to be done – and there was anyway a £200 fine if a person didn't comply – it looked incredibly dismal to have black curtains. The windows beneath them were crisscrossed with tape to prevent flying glass in the event of a raid.

The next day, the *Evening Mail* showed a picture of seventy Jewish children arriving in Birmingham, where they would stay with foster families until they were eighteen. Lucy looked at the disoriented and bewildered children and felt her heart go out to them. They were coming to strange people, who spoke a strange language and had a different culture, and the older ones would be aware that it was extremely unlikely they would ever see their parents again.

'It's a monstrous thing for their parents to have to send their children away like that,' Gwen said. 'But Hitler's track record with Jews is not good. If your children were given a chance to escape that man's tyranny, wouldn't you grab it? Even if you couldn't get out yourself?'

Lucy nodded. She thought it dreadful that the parents were forced to make that choice. 'They are just innocent victims,' she said.

'Yes,' Gwen said, 'and there will be many more before this is resolved, mark my words.'

That night the broadcaster on the wireless talked of heavy troop movement fanning across the Polish borders. Gwen looked at Lucy and said, 'We pick up the gas masks tomorrow. Hasn't come a moment too soon, I think.'

'Oh, but don't you hate the thought of wearing them?' Lucy cried. 'They are hideous.'

'They are not pretty, right enough,' Gwen conceded. 'Won't smell very sweet either, I wouldn't have thought, being made out of rubber, but I remember the poor devils from the Great War with their lungs eaten away with mustard gas.' She shook her head. 'Wouldn't wish that on my worst enemy. If there is a need, I will wear that gas mask.'

However, when Lucy arrived home from the hospital that night there was more to worry about than gas masks. 'German tanks have invaded Poland,' Gwen told her. 'Three border towns were bombed before dawn and Warsaw is under heavy bombardment.'

The following day the broadcaster on the wireless announced the Poles were fighting for their lives and many towns and cities were being attacked, with heavy civilian casualties. Lucy was shocked when she heard that even an evacuation train carrying women and children had been blown up. It showed again how heartless the German armies were that were creeping across Europe.

The broadcaster went on to say that Mr Chamberlain, the British prime minister, had issued an ultimatum to Hitler to withdraw his troops from Poland or face the consequences, but that the call-up of men under forty-one would begin immediately. The only cheery bit of news was that Australian troops had arrived in Britain, New Zealand had also promised support, and Canadian troops were being mobilised. The prime minister was giving an address on Sunday morning and no one was in any doubt of what it would say.

Lucy didn't linger after Mass, but then neither did anyone else, and she had arrived home to find Chris there already. She knew his mother would be glad of his presence. Gwen had invited in two neighbours who hadn't wireless sets of their own and so there was a little crowd of them to hear Neville Chamberlain's sombre tones just after 11.15 that Sunday morning, 3 September, when he announced that because Germany refused to withdraw their troops from Poland, *'...this country is at war with Germany.'*

They had accepted the situation for so long that the news came as a sort of anticlimax to Lucy, although the women Gwen had invited in began to cry. Like Gwen, they were remembering earlier conflicts with the same nation.

Then suddenly a sound they were going to become all too familiar with rent the air, and everyone remembered what they were recommended to do in the event of a raid, but that they hadn't got round to. Gwen hadn't collected up her bank books, insurance policies, treasured photographs and, maybe, a pack of cards into a shelter bag that would go with them everywhere. Chris hadn't checked that the cellar was strong enough to take shelter in, and if it wasn't, to get it reinforced. Neither Lucy nor Gwen had filled galvanised buckets with sand, and left one on the upstairs landing and one in the attic, ready to use to prevent the spread of fire.

There was no raid – it had been a false alarm – but they knew the next time it could be real and they had to drop their laissez-faire attitude. Their country was at war and life would never be the same for them again.

Almost a week later, after a tearful farewell to Gwen, Chris drove Lucy to the General Hospital, where she would have the weekend to settle in before reporting for work on Monday morning, 11 September.

'Driving a car will probably be a thing of the past as well,' he said to Lucy. 'Petrol is bound to be rationed in some way.'

'Will it affect you?' Lucy said. 'Doctors and people like that.'

Chris nodded. 'I'll probably get an allowance, but I would guess that it will have to be accounted for. But the question might not arise because I'm still wondering what to do with myself.'

'What do you mean?'

'Well, I can enlist now and be part of the medical team for the Royal Warwickshires or I can claim exemption and stay a civilian.'

'Can you claim exemption?'

'Yes,' Chris said. 'But I wouldn't be doing it to get out of military service. I am just thinking that if there is a lot of aerial bombing, like people say, there will be casualties and some of them will probably be severe, so I might be more use here.'

'Oh, yes,' said Lucy. 'I can see your dilemma there.'

'I think the only thing to do is wait and see what happens in the next few months,' Chris said as he drew up outside the nurses' home. 'Come on, let's get you inside.'

No men were allowed upstairs in the nurses' home, and the home sister, Sister Magee, made sure that that rule was strictly adhered to. Lucy took her case from Chris at the door. He would have liked to have given her a kiss goodbye but, under the watchful eyes of Sister Magee, he didn't dare. 'Goodbye then, Lucy,' he said, putting out his hand. 'Look after yourself but don't forget where we live.'

Lucy shook Chris's hand warmly. 'I won't forget, don't you worry,' she said. 'And thank you for all you have done for me.'

He turned away as Sister Magee began directing Lucy to her room. 'It's on the second floor. Left at the head of the stair. Number eighteen.'

There were four beds and beside each one was a wardrobe and a chest of drawers. The walls were distempered cream and the floor was covered with blue lino with a mottled pattern. The only thing that spoilt the room were the black shutters fitted to the windows.

There was a girl already in the room, who looked immensely glad to see Lucy. She was a little on the plump side and had blonde hair tied up in a chignon at the nape of her neck and big blue eyes, which Lucy saw glittered with unshed tears. She introduced herself as Barbara Irvine.

'Everyone calls me Babs, though,' she added. 'What about you?'

'Lucy Cassidy,' Lucy said. 'Are you all right?

You look a bit upset?'

'It's because I was on my own in the room,' Babs said. 'I started feeling sorry for myself, and then started to feel most incredibly homesick. Mad, isn't it? I mean, I only left them this morning.'

'You haven't left home before then?'

'No. Have you?'

'Yes,' Lucy said. 'When I was fourteen.' And she told Babs the bare bones of what had happened to her. Babs was impressed by what she called her courage, but couldn't understand why she didn't go with her family to America.

'I didn't want to go,' Lucy said. 'It was really that simple.'

'Didn't you miss them most dreadfully?'

'Of course,' Lucy said. 'I missed them with an ache that I thought would never go away. But I'm over that now and looking forward to the next chapter in my life.'

Babs was so impressed by Lucy, she told their other two roommates when they arrived. Jenny Black had deep brown eyes, bright red hair she said she had tried to calm down with a Marcel perm, so her head was full of corkscrew curls, and she had a fair face peppered with freckles. Both things, she declared, were the bane of her life.

Vera Winstanley, on the other hand, Lucy thought stuck up till she got to know her better. She spoke correctly and without an accent of any sort, and her mid-brown hair was cut short. It framed her face and made her grey-green eyes stand out even more, so she was quite striking to look at. She was, in fact, one of the nicest and kindest people, Lucy was to find, but had a naturally reserved nature.

All the probationary nurses had to have an interview with Matron Turner and a medical before they were finally accepted on the nursing course. Quite a few were worried about the interview, for Matron was said to be a formidable woman who could rip a body to shreds in minutes with her tongue.

'People say that the army's loss is our gain,' Babs said, 'and that she would make a good sergeant major.'

Lucy laughed. 'Probably her bark is worse than her bite.'

And so it was proved when it was her turn to be interviewed, though it didn't seem so at first. As she entered the room she cast her eyes over the woman on the other side of the desk. She wore a dark blue dress covered with a pure white apron, and the ruff at her neck seemed as stiff as the woman herself. Her grey hair was scraped back from her head so tightly that her eyebrows arched and deep worry lines furrowed her brow and scored down either side of her nose. She wore a starched white matron's cap on her head. Lucy also noticed her eyes were the most dazzling blue and these darkened and the frowns deepened disconcertingly as she bade Lucy sit. She sat gingerly on the chair opposite the matron and felt decidedly uncomfortable.

Then Matron smiled, which transformed her face, and Lucy began to relax as the matron told her she was about to embark on a noble profession and so her manner at all times must reflect this. All student nurses, she said, must strive to show refinement of mind, clean habits and tidy ways, and then these attributes would be carried on to the ward.

'And of crucial importance is cleanliness, hygiene,' she said to Lucy. 'I am sure that this has already been explained to you at the Cottage Hospital in Sutton Coldfield.'

'Oh, yes, Matron,' Lucy said. 'They said I had to keep my nails short, and I had to scrub my hands before I went on the ward and before I dealt with any patient, and also between patients.'

Matron nodded approvingly. 'And because you have been doing this type of work for some time, I do not have to tell you that the hours are long and some of the work arduous?'

Lucy smiled. 'No, Matron.'

'And I must say I have seldom had a student here with such glowing testimonials, both from the hospital and a Dr Christopher Gilbert,' the matron said. 'If only half of what they said about you was true then you will make a first-rate nurse, because between you and me, as well as their commendations, you gained almost full marks in the exam.'

'Oh!'

'You are surprised?'

'Oh, yes, Matron,' Lucy said, 'because I left school at fourteen. It was Dr Gilbert who taught me what I needed to know. I lodged with his mother, you see. That's how that came about.'

'I would have said then that you were an attentive student because you want to nurse a great

388

deal,' the matron said.

'I do, Matron,' Lucy said earnestly. 'Very much.'

Then Matron's smile was very wide indeed as she got to her feet and said, 'Well, I will be expecting good reports of you,' and she shook Lucy by the hand. 'Welcome aboard, Miss Cassidy.'

Not everyone was welcomed as warmly as Lucy, so she kept quiet about her interview and listened sympathetically to many of the others moaning about Matron. But in the end they all got through the interview and all passed their medicals as well. Lucy felt she was on her way at last. In talking to the others, and in particular the girls who shared her room, she found she was the only one with so much experience and the only one so passionate about nursing.

Babs was there because her father was a Methodist minister and thought that his eldest daughter should be seen to be doing something useful with her life. Jenny's parents, meanwhile, had both worked their socks off at unskilled low-paid jobs in order to give their two children a future. Now her brother was an apprentice tool-maker, and she hadn't the heart to tell them that she didn't really want to nurse when they had set their hearts on it. Vera had taken it up as a sop to her mother, who had wanted her only daughter to make some sense of her expensive private education and become a doctor. She hadn't the brains, and the teachers had told her mother the same. In the end her father had suggested nursing instead, maybe to stop her mother fussing.

'And has it?' Lucy asked.

Vera shook her head. 'No. Not really.'

'I'm glad that I haven't had pressure either way,' Lucy said. 'And it is just as good as I thought it would be.'

She knew, though, with her limited time off and her shift patterns it was going to be very hard to see Clodagh. Clodagh was aware of this too because just two nights before Lucy had moved into the nurses' home, as she waited for the bus back to Sutton after a night at a cinema in Aston, Clodagh uncharacteristically put her arms around her and said, 'I'm going to miss you, Lucy.'

Lucy, a little embarrassed, had said, 'What you talking about? I'm not emigrating, you know.'

'Might as well be, according to Hazel's sister,' Clodagh said. 'She had a friend went into nursing and she said her time off was dismal.'

And it was dismal, Lucy had to agree. It put paid to her dancing lessons and her evenings at the cinema, and unless you were really passionate about nursing she doubted many would stick at it. They certainly wouldn't do it for the money, which was thirty pounds for the year, and rising in increments of five pounds a year until your period of training was over, and you didn't get anything at all for the first six weeks of the first year, and nothing if you failed your exams either. She was immensely glad of her savings, which she could dip into if she had to.

What Lucy found harder to cope with was the crippling exhaustion. Most of her off-duty time was spent trying to catch up on sleep for the first fortnight or so. She had thought she wouldn't feel it like the others, but as a volunteer in the hospital she hadn't been subjected to the same hours as the other nurses and she had had her weekends free. Now she was on duty from half-past six, when she had to help with the breakfasts, and did not finish until eight o'clock at night apart from half an hour for her dinner and two hours recreational time spread throughout the day, which had to be spent away from the wards.

She was off duty every Tuesday, from 2 p.m. until 9.30, and alternate Sundays, from 9.00 a.m. until 12.30 one week, and the following week from 2 p.m. to 9.30. Then, once a month, she was off from 2 p.m. until midday the following day. Like everyone else, Lucy found the shift patterns difficult at first.

However, she had no trouble with the training. They had lectures on anatomy, physiology and hygiene, which she found both interesting and challenging, and the basic nursing they were being shown was more or less a continuation of what she had been doing at the Cottage Hospital.

'It seems to come naturally to you,' Jenny said as they reached the room after a particularly gruelling session.

'It's just months and months of practice, that's all.'

'But that's it,' Babs complained. 'We haven't got months and months. We have an exam in a few weeks and I seem to be all fingers and thumbs at the practical stuff.'

'Me too,' Jenny said. 'And I'm not too hot on the theory either.'

There again Lucy had the advantage, for Chris

had done far more than teach her the basics that she would need to know. The nurses too had given her quite a few nuggets of knowledge, which she often found useful. Suddenly she felt very sorry for her friends.

'Do you all feel this way?' she asked. 'Vera, what about you? Are you struggling too?'

'Oh, rather,' Vera said. 'All help gratefully received down this end.'

'Right,' Lucy said. 'I'll help you all I can. I can at least teach you the basic stuff.'

'That would be great,' Jenny said.

'I would be most awfully grateful,' Vera said, while Babs put in, 'Anyway, exams aside, we need to know as much as possible as soon as possible, just in case there is going to be the aerial bombing everyone was talking about. I know that nothing has happened yet but that doesn't mean that it isn't going to.'

'I know,' Lucy said. 'Sometimes it's hard to realise we are at war. I mean, I know Poland's gone, another notch to Hitler's belt, but that was more or less expected. But apart from the loss of a couple of ships there has been nothing else.'

'What does your doctor chap think of it?' Jenny said, because they all knew about Jenny lodging with the doctor's mother and his views on claiming exemption to work with those injured from the bombing on his own territory.

'Oh, I had a letter from his mother just this week and she said he is really cheesed off. I mean, it's not that he wants people to be injured, but if the bombers are going to leave us alone he feels he might be better employed elsewhere.

Anyway, he told her that he'll leave it till Christmas and if there is still nothing, he will enlist.'

'His mother will miss him, with you gone as well,' Babs said.

'Well, he didn't live at home, anyway,' Lucy said. 'And Gwen isn't giving herself time to get miserable. She has joined the WVS and said that she is ashamed to admit that she is happier than she has been for many years.'

'Feels of some use, I suppose,' Vera said. 'Oh, I wish my mother would find something to occupy her and not worry about me so much.'

'And mine,' Jenny said. 'Always asking how it's going and if I'm working hard, as if there is any flipping chance to do anything else.'

'Oh,' Babs said, 'you have it easy. I have the entire church praying to me. What sort of pressure is that if I fail?'

'Yes, while Lucy floats through life without anyone getting at her,' Jenny said.

'At first my mother didn't even want me to stay in Britain once war was declared,' Lucy said as she remembered the passionate letter her mother had sent her.

Please, think seriously about joining us here now for there may be desperate and dangerous times ahead for Britain. I know how you feel about nursing but you could do your training here. Declan is sure they would recognise your qualifications because British nurses are well thought of over here. Please, please, consider this, my darling girl, for I will worry about you so much if you insist on staying there now that they have declared war on Germany.

The letter had arrived before she'd left for the nurses' home, and she had passed it to Gwen to read.

'What will you do?' Gwen had asked.

In answer, Lucy had said, 'I wanted to nurse to make people better, ease their suffering, and I think there might be a great deal of suffering here, especially if the bombing raids do come. This isn't the time to try and keep myself safe at all costs when I might be needed more here.'

Now, Lucy said to her roommates, 'But I must admit, now that Mammy has accepted that I am not going to hide the war out in America all she does is send me encouraging little missives.'

'Yeah, with ten-dollar bills inside.'

'Yeah, I know,' Lucy said. She hadn't wanted to accept the money, but her mother had insisted since she had learnt that she'd begun at the hospital.

I am so very proud of you, for you have done this all yourself and accepted no help, which was hard in a way for me because it is the only time in my life that I was able to help you. Now Declan puts money in the bank for me every month. It is for my own personal use and if I choose to send some to my dear daughter who I still miss so much then please don't refuse it. I know trainee nurses are not overpaid.

How could Lucy not accept money from her mother after she had sent a letter like that?

She said to the girls, 'I am getting quite a little nest egg in the Post Office because I never have time to spend it,' and the other three nodded sagely because they knew exactly what she meant.

TWENTY-TWO

In the end, with the extra work Babs, Jenny and Vera put in with Lucy's help, which was reinforced by the lectures and the time spent on the wards, the girls approached the exams at the end of October with quiet confidence, and found them not too bad at all.

There were still no raids, so they were surprised when the *Evening Mail* reported on 15 November that one hundred thousand air-raid shelters had been delivered to Birmingham.

'Makes chilling reading,' Vera said. 'Think they know something we don't?'

'Probably,' Lucy said. 'But it is reassuring that they are ordering these shelters. Better be safe than sorry, surely?'

'I'd say so,' Babs said, spreading the paper out so that they could all see the diagrams. 'Look, they come as corrugated-iron sheets that have to be bent over and bolted together. Then they're partially buried and the whole thing covered with earth and sandbags.'

'Not much use to those without gardens,' Jenny said. 'My parents will have to use a communal brick-built shelter, I suppose, 'cos we haven't got a cellar either.'

'Yeah,' Babs said. 'And I know they are sand-bagged and have no windows and that, but they don't seem much safer than a house to me.'

'No, and,' Jenny said, 'scurrying down underground and sitting out the raids in a comfortless tin shack won't be much pleasure either.'

'It isn't supposed to be a pleasure,' Lucy said. 'It's about keeping safe. We will have no say in the matter if raids threaten the hospital. You heard Matron. If we are on duty, nurses will be selected to take those who are able down to the cellars.'

'Yeah, and if they can't go down there, we have to fit those steel cages over the beds,' Babs said. 'And if the bombs are coming fast and furious I just might crawl under those cages myself.'

'What about you, Vera?' Lucy asked.

'Huh, my father didn't believe that treaty Chamberlain signed last year, so he had a big concrete bunker built. I feel a bit embarrassed about it because Four Oaks, where I live, is unlikely to be bombed.'

'How can you be so sure of that?' Babs said. ''Tisn't as if the Jerries have done a dummy run and dropped a few little ones to give us a sort of clue as to where the action is going to be, is it?'

'Well, no.'

'Look,' Lucy said, 'we cannot be responsible for things our parents do, only the things we do ourselves. Doesn't everyone agree with that?'

They did and she went on, 'So, Vera, don't feel embarrassed about any old bunker your dad has had built.'

'No, indeed,' said Babs, and continued, with a broad wink to the others, 'In fact, I have a good idea. Why don't you write your address down and if there is a humdinger of a raid, we'll all come and share your bunker? Then you might feel a wee bit better about it.'

All the girls collapsed into laughter.

Early in December the girls received word that they had all passed their exams. They were very relieved. 'It means that we can really enjoy Christmas,' Jenny said.

'Yes,' Lucy agreed, 'and I was talking to a second-year probationary yesterday, who said they always have a show like a pantomime and a concert. Everyone makes an effort at Christmas.'

'Well, it is a special time of the year,' Vera said, 'and it must be awful to spend it in hospital.'

Jenny gave a hoot of laughter. 'Don't see why,' she said. 'We have to stay here too and I don't see anyone feeling sorry for us.'

'We had an element of choice,' said Babs.

'I know,' Jenny said. 'Aren't we mad? We chose to work all the hours God sends with little time off and virtually no money, and as far as we are concerned Christmas will be like just another day.'

Lucy laughed. 'You are so right, Jenny, and yet I wouldn't want to be any place but here.'

'I feel the same,' Jenny said, 'and for the life of me I don't know why. But Mum will be pleased.'

'And mine will be,' Vera said. 'I mean, I came here originally to shut her up about my becoming a doctor, but nursing sort of gets under your skin and I like it much better than I ever would doctoring because I am more involved with the patients.'

397

'And that's what it's all about, isn't it?' Babs said. 'The patients, and the way they are so grateful for anything you do for them. It makes you want to do more.'

'So let's see if we can make Christmas a really happy time for them,' Lucy said, 'because I think if we do we will enjoy it more ourselves.'

The following day was Friday and Lucy's twenty-four hours off duty. She had written to Gwen and asked if she could see her, and Gwen had said she must come to stay the night. Lucy accepted the invitation gladly and was quite excited about seeing her again and staying once more in the cosy bedroom, but she went first to the Bull Ring to buy presents for Gwen and Clodagh. She intended stopping off in Aston to see her old friend whom she hadn't seen in ages.

She took the tram to Aston Cross, and when she alighted she saw that it was a few minutes to four, according to the big green clock. Lucy remembered that when Clodagh told her about the job she had in Rocky Lane she said they got off at four on Fridays, so Lucy decided to meet her coming home.

She hadn't gone far down the road when she heard a hooter sound. Minutes later women were pouring out of the gates of a factory and spilling over the pavements. They all looked so similar in their boots and their dark coats, the grime on their pasty faces making the scarlet lipstick seem out of place and their hair caught up in scarves worn like turbans. There was a great deal of noise too: the tramp of boots on the cobbled streets and the banter and ribaldry shouted from one to another in raucous voices, which Clodagh was to tell her later developed from having to shout above the noise of the machines.

In fact, so similar were the women in that dusky light that Lucy almost didn't recognise Clodagh. She was dressed the same as the others and was linking arms with Hazel on one side of her and Hazel's sister, Betty, on the other. Her tired face broke into a beam of happiness when she saw Lucy and she unlinked herself and threw her arms around her. Hazel knew her, of course, and her sister had seen Lucy when she had come to the house to tell them she had passed her nursing exams. They were very welcoming to Lucy and pressed her to go home with them for a cup of tea at least. Lucy had seen the fatigue etched on the three girls' faces, but they were most insistent and said they would have the house to themselves as Hazel and Betty's parents didn't finish work until half-past five. That decided Lucy, for she did want to talk with her friend.

Once they reached the house, Lucy gave Clodagh the pale blue scarf and gloves set, and though she said it was for Christmas, Clodagh ripped the paper off straight away. She was thrilled with them and said they were the exact shade needed to go with her best coat. And then Hazel and Betty came in with a tray of tea and a packet of biscuits and settled down to a good natter.

First, the three girls told her about their jobs, which were all war-related now. They said that's where the money was to be made. Then Clodagh asked Lucy many questions about nursing.

'Is it as good as you thought it was going to be?'
Clodagh asked.

'Oh, yes,' Lucy said. 'I love it. Course, I had a
good idea of what I was letting myself in for
through my work at the Cottage Hospital, and
the work is physically tough and the hours are
long, but you feel that you are doing some good,
I'd rather have it than be in service, any day of the
week.'

'Won't be any in-service work to be had after
this war,' Clodagh said. 'Have you heard what
has been happening to the Heatheringtons?'

'No, have you?'

'You bet,' Clodagh said. 'I met Cook in the Bull
Ring.'

'You met Cook in the Bull Ring?' Lucy repeated incredulously. Cook had seldom left the
Hall.

'Yes, listen,' Clodagh said impatiently. 'She's
left Maxted Hall, and Clara has.'

'Left?'

'Yes. To quote Cook, neither of them would
work for that stuck-up besom, Jessica Ponsomby.'
Clodagh grinned, remembering the encounter.
'She said Jessica was trying to order them about
and talking to them like they were pieces of shit
she's picked up on her shoe.'

Lucy had never heard Cook utter a swear word
and she said, 'Cook never said that?'

'She did,' Clodagh maintained. 'Honest, as
God is my witness, those were her very words.
She said Lord and Lady Heatherington were cut
up about them leaving, but neither felt able to
stay.'

'I wrote to Clara a few times but did wonder if something was the matter when I didn't get a reply,' Lucy said. 'And Mammy mustn't know either because she'd have mentioned it.'

'Well, it wasn't that long ago they left,' Clodagh said. 'And Clara was really upset, so Cook said.'

Lucy remembered Clara telling them that Maxted Hall had been a sort of refuge for her when she had come to England after the death of her husband, and for that she felt she owed them something, so Lucy could imagine her distress if she'd been forced to leave through the behaviour of another. No wonder she hadn't felt able to write.

'Point is,' Clodagh went on, 'Lord Heatherington didn't want them to leave and he took that Jessica to task for upsetting his staff and she took umbrage, and went running back to her mammy. I suppose Lord Heatherington thought, as he had sent Jessica packing, Cook and Clara would stay, and they did think about it. But they knew she could come back any time, married to Clive, and there was no one could stop her.'

'So where did they go?'

'Oh, they were soon fixed up,' Clodagh said. 'Lord Heatherington gave them both superb references – he said it was the least he could do – and they were both taken on at the Naafi at St George's Barracks in Sutton Coldfield, and found lodgings nearby.'

'What about Emily?'

'She's gone too,' Clodagh said. 'She just went out one day, and no one knew where she had gone, and then her father phoned and said she

401

wasn't coming back. And Jerry was called up, and that young gardener.'

'Was there anyone left?'

'Very few, but Cook said it got worse. The Master had to sell his hunters, which upset him a great deal.'

'Oh, he thought the world of those horses.'

'Well, there was no one to see to them, you see,' Clodagh explained, 'because Hilda and Bert went as well.'

'Golly!'

'Well, Hilda had a slight stroke.'

'Ah, that's a shame,' Lucy said, remembering the kindly woman.

'Oh, she was all right, Cook said,' Clodagh assured Lucy. 'But it shook her up, and she said she wanted to move closer to her daughter, wherever that is, and Lord Heatherington arranged it. Then Maxted Hall was requisitioned by the army and Lord and Lady Heatherington moved into the Lodge House with Mr Carlisle and Norah, and a local woman chars for them.'

'What changes,' Lucy said almost wistfully. 'So what's Clive doing?'

'You don't still hold a candle for him, do you?'

'Of course not,' Lucy said emphatically, trying to ignore her heart pounding and her unaccountably dry mouth. 'But you have told me about everyone else.'

'Clive is an officer with the Royal Warwickshires,' Clodagh said. 'Rumour has it that he went for it as soon as his compulsory six weeks was up, and though he had leave he didn't come home.'

'Why on earth not?'

'I think it was something to do with Jessica, who it's said was showing her true colours even before the wedding. According to Cook, he actually told Clara that he would call it off if he could but it was too late. Serve him right, I say, for the way he treated you, eh?'

Lucy found that she couldn't think vengeful thoughts of Clive but just sadness at the waste of two young lives. Clive married Jessica Ponsomby because they needed money to repair and refurbish the house and allow their lives to go on as before. But war was declared and the staff either left or were called up, the fine house was taken by the military, the hunters were sold and, if Chris was right, the fine car wouldn't be used much because there would be no petrol. Clive's parents, far from being saved by his marriage, were reduced to living in the Lodge House.

'Anyway,' Clodagh said, 'no one knows where the hell he is, but could well be "somewhere in France" because of what some of the girls in the factory are told about their blokes away fighting.'

'Well,' said Lucy, 'wherever he is, he will be in the regular army and at least able to write to his parents this time.' She glanced at the clock over the mantelpiece and exclaimed, 'Goodness! Is that the time? I must be on my way. Gwen will think I am not coming. You've given me plenty to think about.'

'And talk about,' Clodagh said, 'because from what I remember, Gwen used to love a good gossip.'

'Oh, she still does,' Lucy said, smiling fondly.

'One of the trials of her life is that Chris won't talk about his work.'

'Well, he can't, can he?'

Lucy shrugged as she got to her feet. 'It wouldn't really be ethical for him to discuss people's personal ailments with his mother, or anyone else, come to that. She'll make a meal out of all this.'

'I'm sure,' Clodagh said. 'And you hold your hand a minute because Hazel and I will walk you to the bus stop.'

'There's no need.'

'There is every need with the blackout the way it is,' Clodagh said firmly. 'A chap at work who seems to be able to get his hands on anything got me one of those shielded torches they have just started allowing us to use, but it isn't much good.'

'Better than nothing at all,' said Lucy.

Outside, the night had definitely got colder and Lucy was glad of the girls' linked arms as they sallied forth, and she was cheered too by the fuzzy torchlight shining through the gloom.

'So you ain't got a torch?'

'No,' Lucy said with a sigh. 'As soon as that directive came on the wireless, torches and batteries disappeared from the shops faster than the speed of light, it seemed to us. Not many of the nurses got their hands on one.'

'Shall I see if this bloke can get you one?'

'Oh, that's nice of you, Clodagh,' Lucy said. 'But my time off is so limited I wouldn't know when I will be round this way again.'

The bus came then and Lucy climbed aboard, a bit concerned how she would find her way to Gwen's in the pitch-black because any helpful moon or twinkling stars were effectively hidden by the low, leaden clouds.

How relieved she was then to see Chris with a torch standing by the bus stop when she alighted.

'Chris!' she cried in delight. 'What are you doing here?'

'Waiting for you, of course,' Chris said. He didn't tell her that he had been waiting the best part of an hour and it was a wonder he hadn't stuck to the ground. Lucy wasn't able to say anything either for suddenly a gust of wind cannoned into her, nearly lifting her off her feet. Chris prevented her falling and then, putting an arm around her shoulder, he advised, 'Lean against me. This wind is enough to blow you over.'

Lucy was glad to do as he suggested, and as Chris's arm tightened around her, he thought that despite the awful weather he wished the journey to his mother's house three times as long because it would give him more time to legitimately cuddle Lucy, as he had longed to do for ages.

'It was really nice of you to meet me, Chris,' Lucy said as they walked, welded together. 'I was worried enough making my way to your mother's in the blackout. I never gave a thought to coping with the wind as well.'

'So you haven't managed to get hold of a torch, then?'

'No, and I have tried everywhere.'

'They are devilish hard to get hold of,' Chris said, 'but necessary in the blackout.'

'I know,' Lucy said. 'All of us keep trying. We'll probably get one eventually.'

'Well, here we are,' Chris said, opening the

front gate. 'Home without incident.'

Gwen fussed over them when they came in, delighted to see Lucy, though when she said she thought Chris had got lost, Lucy realised he had probably been waiting a long time at the bus stop and although there was no time stated for her to arrive she still felt guilty.

'I'm sorry,' she said to them both. 'I called to see Clodagh, for we haven't seen each other in an age, and we quite forget the time.'

'Understandable, my dear,' Gwen said.

'I have a present for you.' Lucy gave Gwen the parcel.

Gwen showed more restraint than Clodagh, though she did have a good feel round the thin paper, which was all Lucy could find to wrap things in, and she could probably guess that they were leather gloves.

'I haven't a present for you, I'm afraid,' Lucy said to Chris.

'I would have been cross if you had bought me something,' Chris said with a smile. 'It is not for penniless student nurses to buy presents for rich doctors.'

'I'm not exactly penniless,' Lucy said. 'My mother sends me money from America.'

'Yes, to spend on yourself, not others,' Chris said.

'I suppose when you are given a gift of money you can spend it as you wish,' Lucy said with a wide smile, for she enjoyed sparring with Chris.

'Touché,' Chris said, with a bow, which made Lucy giggle. The sound of her laughter brought such a rush of love inside him that it was ap-

406

parent on his face for just an instant. His mother saw and knew what it meant, and because she knew and loved Lucy like a daughter she was delighted.

Nothing more was said then, though, for the meal was ready to be served. It was a meal that Gwen said they should relish because rationing was being introduced in the New Year, which, though it would probably prove to be a nuisance, had to be a much fairer system than the free-for-all of the Great War. The roast beef dinner was delicious, and as they ate, Lucy regaled them with the things Clodagh had told her. She was staggered that Gwen was aware of a lot of it but, when she commented on this, Gwen said with a smile, 'Oh, I have the WVS now. It's a hotbed of gossip, that place is. Mind, I didn't know a lot of what you told me, not for certain, but I sort of surmised it from the bits I did know.'

'Don't see why you are so interested in the Heatheringtons, anyway,' Chris said gloomily.

'That's because you're a man,' Lucy said. 'You'd never understand such things.'

'Oh?' Chris said, his eyebrows raised enquiringly. He added sardonically, 'And of course, you are such an authority on men.'

'Might be,' Lucy said, with such an impish look on her face that he had the urge to pull her into his arms and cover her with kisses. He knew at that moment that he didn't just care for Lucy, he truly loved her and probably always had. But he was ten years her senior, which she probably saw as a great age difference. She deserved someone as young and as full of vitality as she was herself.

Such a gamut of emotions crossed his face that she was looking at him quizzically, and probably wondering why he wasn't coming back at her with some quip, but Gwen understood what had seemingly rendered her son incapable of speech. To help him, she said, 'I'm sure that Lucy knows plenty about men, and about people in general, for she wouldn't be such a good nurse if she didn't understand them. But you are right, Chris, we don't want to be discussing the Heatheringtons ad infinitum when so much is happening in the world that is affecting us.'

'But nothing is happening yet,' Lucy said.

'Oh, things are,' Chris said. 'Because though there has been no bombing of the cities, I think Churchill was right when he said that Hitler is using a siege tactic.'

'Oh, you mean with the ships he keeps bombing?'

'Exactly that, Mum,' Chris said. 'Being an island makes us moderately safer than countries near or bordering Germany, but because we are nowhere near being self-sufficient, we have got to bring in a lot of our foodstuff. If he can stop those ships reaching us, he could starve us into submission.'

'Golly!' said Lucy. 'I never thought of that. I just thought of the poor sailors who lost their lives when I heard of ships sunk. I didn't think of the cargo the ship was probably carrying. I suppose that's another reason to introduce rationing.'

'I should say so,' Chris said. 'And so will trying to produce what we now have to import.'

'Mmm,' Gwen said, 'we might have to put up with very strange meals.'

'Ah, but no meal at all is infinitely worse,' Lucy said.

'I don't think it will come to that,' Chris said. 'But I'm pretty sure things will be in short supply. I was talking to a man the other day and he said that thousands of hens have been killed to save on their feedstuff, so the days of a nice boiled chuckie egg for breakfast will be a thing of the past.'

'I know,' Gwen said. 'Shame, isn't it, but we will just have to cope with it like we do everything else.'

'And,' said Lucy, with a wide smile, 'there is no good complaining, for don't you know there's a war on?'

'Get away,' Chris replied with a sardonic grin. 'You know, I never noticed that.' And they all laughed gently together.

Chris left soon after that, as he said he had a couple of early-morning visits before surgery the following day. Lucy thought that when he left it was as if the sun had gone behind a cloud.

She washed up with Gwen and they chatted amiably together as they always had, but it was as if some of the essence had gone. Lucy couldn't really understand why she should feel that because she had never seen that much of Chris to talk to. When he had visited the house before she moved to the General, he mainly spoke to Gwen, but he had seemed different this evening. It was all very confusing, and it was only much later tucked up in bed that Lucy realised that she hadn't even wished Chris a 'Happy Christmas'. That was a shame because she knew she probably wouldn't see him again for some time.

It was the heartfelt and genuine enjoyment of the patients that made Christmas for Lucy that year. On Christmas Eve, nurses helped some of the patients into the dining room, where a makeshift stage had been set up. Others came under their own steam, and a couple were on crutches. Then there were those in wheelchairs, and even some of the bed-bound were wheeled in by the nurses. They all settled down to watch the show.

They seemed to forget their aches and pains, and laughed as uproariously as the nurses at the funny sketches. Lucy was astounded that their stiff and starchy doctors and surgeons could don a myriad of silly costumes or go cavorting around the stage using the guise of Christmas to raise a smile on patients' faces. Everyone joined in with the music-hall songs and then they began singing Christmas carols. Lucy kept her eye on the clock because she had been given special dispensation and a late pass so that she could attend midnight Mass at St Chad's. She slipped out into the black icy night as the audience were singing 'Good King Wenceslas' with gusto, and felt her feet slide on the ice, which the blackout made impossible to see. Picking her way gingerly, she was glad that she hadn't far to go.

The familiarity of the midnight Mass interspersed with carols seemed to soothe her very soul. As Lucy had become a familiar face to many, she left the church at the end of Mass with Christmas greetings ringing in her ears. She nearly cannoned into a man standing in the doorway, but it wasn't until he turned on his torch that she saw who it was.

'Chris, what are you doing here?'

'Waiting for you,' Chris said, taking her arm and shining the torchlight in front of them so they had a chance of seeing the ice patches.

'At this time of night? Don't be so silly.'

'Doctors don't work normal hours, you know that,' Chris said. 'Tonight I was called out to a woman with breathing problems. Didn't like the sound of her chest, so I called for an ambulance and they took her to the General, and I followed to keep a check on her. There were very few people about. The nurse on duty said that they were all at the show, which should be finishing any minute. But when I asked were you there she said that she thought you had gone to midnight Mass, so here I am.'

'Yes, but *why* are you here?'

'Well, first and foremost I wanted to see you,' Chris said. 'I have a present for you,' and he pressed a bag into her hand as they reached the door of the nurses' home. 'Sorry I couldn't wrap it up all fancy for you.'

'Don't be so silly,' Lucy said. 'Thank you very much, Chris. Can I peep?'

Chris gave a shrug. 'If you like. It is after twelve, and so officially Christmas Day now anyway.'

Lucy gave a squeal of delight when she looked in the bag. 'A torch! Oh, Chris, you angel. And spare batteries too.'

Chris smiled. 'Glad you're pleased. Came from one of my patients. Seems able to lay his hands on most things. I didn't ask many questions because I really thought you needed a torch.'

'I did,' Lucy said. 'Thank you so much.'

'It's a pleasure,' Chris said. 'But I have another reason for wanting to see you – as well as wishing you a very Happy Christmas. I have enlisted and must join my unit the day after Boxing Day. It is unlikely I will get down again and I wanted to ask a favour.'

Lucy smiled. 'Ask away.'

'Lucy, will you write to me?'

It was the last thing Lucy was expecting Chris to say; and so when she didn't answer immediately, he said, 'Please, Lucy. It will mean the world to me if you say yes.'

'But of course I will, Chris,' she said. 'I'm sorry I didn't answer straight away. It was just that I was surprised.'

'You don't mind?'

'Not at all.'

Chris's sigh was one of relief and he drew her towards him and kissed her cheek gently. 'Happy Christmas, Lucy.'

Lucy felt the spot Chris had kissed burning into her cheek, and she said, 'And you, Chris, look after yourself.'

'Don't worry, I am not a fighting man. I am just there to patch up the rest. But you had better go in now. It's freezing and we will both stick to the ground if we stay out here much longer.'

'Yes,' Lucy said, 'and though I have got a late pass, I will get it in the neck if I am too late.'

She watched Chris melt away into the darkness. She was glad he had asked her to write because he was a good, kind man and she liked him very much. She would pray that he would come back safe and sound.

TWENTY-THREE

Lucy hadn't time to miss Chris, or indeed to miss anyone, because on 1 January the four girls began their three-month stint on nights, which all nurses had to do every year. This first involved packing all their belongings and moving to rooms above Matron's office, as they were quieter and they would need to sleep in the day. They would be on duty for twelve nights from 11 p.m. until 8.15 a.m. and then have two nights off.

'I'm not looking forward to this,' Lucy said to Babs as they surveyed their new accommodation. 'I've never been very good at night.'

'Nor me,' said Jenny. 'I need my sleep, I do.'

'Yeah,' Babs said, 'we've noticed. You would have missed breakfast a few times if it hadn't been for us.'

'And then fainted on one of the wards from starvation, like as not,' Vera said. 'I am always ravenous for my breakfast.'

'I can't help being sleepy,' Jenny complained. 'What I'm afraid of is that on night shift you will find me in a corner somewhere fast asleep like a dormouse.'

'You'd make a flipping big dormouse,' Lucy said. 'And don't worry about falling asleep, Jen, we'll pinch you awake.'

'Yeah, and take pleasure in it,' Babs said with a grin.

413

'Sadistic tendencies are not one of the attributes a nurse should aspire to,' Jenny retorted.

'Neither is being asleep on duty,' Vera added.

'Come on, girls,' Lucy said. 'Whatever we think of night duty we have to get used to it because it is part of the job, and that is that.'

'You sure your second name isn't Pollyanna?' Jenny asked Lucy derisively.

'No, surely, it's Florence Nightingale?' Vera said.

'Give over, you lot,' Lucy said, but she was laughing herself because the ribaldry between them was always good-natured.

'So we have got a day off,' Babs said. 'What are we going to do with it?'

'Look,' Jenny said, 'the day might be cold but the sun is shining so let's take a gander into town, have a bite to eat at Lyons in New Street, and come back here. That will be long enough to get a bit of shut-eye before we have to go on duty.' There was a chorus of agreement to this plan.

Lucy thought it very strange to begin work when normally she would be tucked up in bed, and the others all said the same. The senior nurse in charge, Nurse Pat Cornley, told them she had felt the same at first, but that they would soon get used to it.

The first thing they did was walk around the ward, introducing themselves to any of the patients that were awake and checking they were comfortable. They might only need a drink or a warm hot-water bottle or a bedpan fetching, or asthmatics might need adrenalin administered. However, those in distress or discomfort had to be

414

seen first. And when the initial patients' needs had been met there was stock to cut and fold, the dressing drums to pack, bandages to roll, columns to draw in the book to record each patient's temperature, pulse and respiration function, and sulphonamide to be spread on lint and stored for future use to prevent the spread of infection.

Doing all this, plus checking the patients, did help the time pass quite quickly, but Lucy was still pleased when Nurse Cornley sent her off for something to eat at three o'clock. 'I'm starving,' said Babs as they trotted down the corridor to-wards the canteen. 'Can't understand it. I mean, I'm not usually hungry at three o'clock in the morning.'

'Yeah, but you're not running about then either,' Lucy pointed out. 'And if I were you I'd have a good feed because it's still a long time until quar-ter past eight.'

They had a bowl of soup each, followed by cheese sandwiches, a slab of cake and two cups of tea. Lucy sat back contentedly as she drained the second cup of tea.

'Oh, I feel better for that,' she said. 'You know I didn't feel that hungry until I started eating.'

'It's like that sometimes,' Babs said. 'The thing about eating a big meal, though, is it can make you sleepy. I mean, I could drop off lovely now.'

'Not a chance,' Lucy said with a smile. 'In fact, we'd better head back. Nurse Cornley said half an hour, and anyway, Vera and Jenny must be just as hungry as we were.'

They were, but they were back on the ward again when they had a visit from the night sister,

415

who quizzed the younger probationers on the names of the patients and what they had wrong with them. Fortunately, they were able to answer every question correctly and as the ward was clean and tidy she could find nothing to criticise.

After her inspection it wasn't that long till the day staff started. Then they helped with breakfast, making drinks, buttering bread or feeding those unable to feed themselves, while the day nurses got those who had eaten ready for the doctors' rounds.

By the time the girls had worked on nights for twelve days they were so weary that they spent most of their two days off sleeping. Lucy had kept up with her letter writing, though, because she knew that people looked forward to receiving letters from her telling them she was all right, and, though she told her mother she was doing her spell of night duty, she didn't stress her tiredness.

She also wrote to Clara. It was her second letter since Clodagh had told her where she and Cook had moved to, her first she had received a lovely letter back inside a Christmas card. Clara had written that she was sorry that she hadn't told Lucy of her plans but in the end it had happened in a rush and she had felt quite numb at the time.

I am fine again now and realise that I was holding on to Maxted Hall like some sort of security blanket, afraid to move. Ada said she felt the same, but in the end, having been almost forced into leaving, it is the best thing we have ever done. We get on as we always have and we both have the freedom to do whatever we

*choose when our work is done. We often talk of you
and would love to know how you are faring.*

Lucy sent Clara a reply similar to the one she had
sent her mother, but in the letter to Chris she was
much more honest. She told him that though she
was thoroughly enjoying nursing, night duty had
come as a shock. She was more than tired, and
felt as if sheer fatigue had seeped into her bones.
She knew he would understand that better than
anyone else.

At last, night duty was over and the young nurses
celebrated by heading off to the Bull Ring to get
themselves some clothes for the coming spring,
for they had spent very little while they had been
on night shift. Lucy looked around the cobbled
streets and contrasted this visit with the one she
had made with Clara and Clodagh when she had
first arrived in Birmingham, as a callow and naïve
girl who knew nothing about anything.

   Now there were no flower sellers grouped
around Nelson's Column or in front or St Martin's, and, as the girls began weaving their way
between the stalls, Lucy noticed there was
precious little fruit on the barrows that once had
been heaped high, and no eggs or butter and only
a couple of sad lumps of cheese for sale on the
barrows selling dairy products. The butchers'
barrows were worst and housed only bloody trays
of offal, though most had rabbits hanging on the
rails above them.

   Lucy had no problem eating rabbit, which she
viewed as pests to the farmer, and Minnie had

always been grateful for any person passing a rabbit her way. Rabbit was what they had usually had for Christmas because it was the cheapest meat. In fact, it had surprised her that in Britain rabbits had been sold as pets to be kept in hutches in suburban gardens, and she had never seen dead ones hanging up from stalls in the Bull Ring before.

'Probably because of meat rationing,' Jenny said when Lucy commented on this, and she realised that despite Gwen mentioning that rationing was being introduced in January, being on the night shift had sort of inured her to the war, and, though by the end of March, bacon, ham, sugar, butter and meat were on ration, food always seemed plentiful in the hospital.

'Our mum nearly bust a gut about it,' Jenny went on. 'I mean, she just about coped with four ounces of butter and bacon, and twelve ounces of sugar in January, though our dad used to moan 'cos he used to like three heaped teaspoons of sugar in his tea. He will really have something to moan about now, though, 'cos you can only get meat worth one shilling and eight pence. I mean, what can you get with that? Our old man could eat that much at one sitting and still not be full.'

'So could mine,' Vera said, 'but he is partial to a bit of rabbit.'

'Is he?' Lucy asked, surprised that Vera's father, so obviously well-heeled, was keen on something so lowly.

'Oh, yes,' Vera said. 'Nothing pleases him more than when a man arrives at the door with a brace of rabbit. They are normally poached, you know, from someone's private land but, in my father's opinion, ridding the place of rabbits, which he considers vermin, can only be good, so he asks no questions. He wouldn't have partridge or pheasant or even venison, though he has been offered them, but rabbit, he thinks, is fair game, which anyone should be able to shoot or trap.'

'Oh, what it is to have connections,' Babs said, rolling her eyes to the sky, and the girls fell about laughing.

'The rest of us will have to make do with liver or something similar,' Jenny said, ''cos offal isn't counted. How would you fancy brains on the canteen menu?'

'Ugh!' said Babs and Vera together, but Lucy had a broad smile on her face as she said, 'I wouldn't mind brains, especially if by eating it I contributed to my own bit of grey matter. We are starting those series of lectures come Monday, remember, by senior doctors who are so lofty they'll probably use high-falutin' terms and words that I won't know the meaning of. Any help in the brain department is fine by me. I need all the help I can get.'

'You and me both,' Babs and Jenny said in unison.

Vera said, 'Don't know about you lot, but all this talk of food is making me hungry. Why don't we get what we came for and then pool our money and see if we have enough for a bun in the Market Hall?'

Everyone was agreeable to this, so they headed down past the old lady outside Woolworths and her constant cry, like a litany – 'Carriers! Handy

419

carriers!' – to where a lot of the stalls selling clothes had positioned themselves.

Lucy was able to buy herself a flowery dress, a red spotted skirt, a pair of sandals and a light-weight coat from the rag market and still have money left. She was, however, a bit disappointed to find that the stalls inside the Market Hall sold similar things to the stalls outside.

'Never mind,' Jenny said to Lucy as they carried the buns to the table, 'we've still got the clock.'

'What clock?'

'That one. Look up.' Jenny was pointing and Lucy saw a magnificent and elaborate structure made of solid oak, which showed three knights and a lady. It was very nearly four o'clock, she noticed, and suddenly a hush fell as many shop-pers stopped in their tracks as the tinkling tone heralding the hour began, and the knight and lady emerged to strike the bell four times.

When it was over and the babble of voices began again, Vera said, 'My father used to say there was a curse put on that clock by the man who made it because he said he was never paid in full.'

'Bit of a swizz if that's true,' Jenny said.

'Yeah,' Lucy said, 'because it must have taken him hours to make it, but I don't believe in curses really. I think it's just something he said 'cos he was so cross.'

'Isn't there a lot of unfairness in the world?' Jenny said.

'There definitely is,' Babs replied. 'My dad gets mad about it sometimes and he hates to see those poor beggars on the Market Hall steps with trays round their necks. He says they fought in a war to make this a land fit for heroes, and just look at them.'

'I hate it too,' Vera said, 'but we must keep our peckers up because we have patients relying on us. Hard though it is we must try and leave our troubles behind us when we go on the ward. So let's treat ourselves to the pictures. *The Philadelphia Story* is on at the Odeon, with Cary Grant and Katharine Hepburn.'

Jenny groaned. 'Oh, I'd love to, but I haven't enough money left.'

'Nor me,' Babs said.

'Ah, but look what I have,' Vera said, pulling something out of her bag and holding it aloft.

'Cinema tickets!' Lucy cried. 'Where the hell did you get cinema tickets?'

'My dad,' Vera said. 'He sent them a few days ago and said they were for us to use when we finished night shift, and goodness knows when we will have a Saturday night off all together again.'

'Your dad is lovely,' Lucy cried. 'And it will be a fitting end to the day.'

'Yeah, it isn't as if it's worth hanging around the Bull Ring any more on a Saturday, like it used to be before the war.'

'Why would it ever be worth hanging around after the shops shut?' Lucy asked.

'Oh, Lucy,' said Babs, 'Saturday night, the Bull Ring was *the* place to go.' She linked Lucy's arm and went on, 'Come on, we'll tell you all about it as we make our way to the cinema.'

So Lucy heard all about the pre-war Bull Ring when, on Saturday nights, it was lit up by gut-

421

tering gas flares.

'It was magical,' said Babs.

Jenny nodded agreement. 'It was like fairyland, and there were these two fellows on stilts. No piddling little ones but great big tall ones, and they weren't holding on or anything, and all dressed up in like circus clothes with top hats and everything.'

'I remember the first time I was taken,' Vera said. 'There was an Indian gentleman with very few clothes on, lying on a bed of nails just as if it was a feather bed, and inviting the young women around to stand on him. One did, and I saw the nails go right into his skin and I felt sick. I had nightmares for ages.'

'Not surprised,' said Babs with a giggle. 'You'd think when he got up he would be all over holes but he never was. There was a big bruiser of a boxer too, and if anyone knocked him down they got a fiver.'

'And did anyone?'

Babs shook her head. 'I never saw anyone.'

'Nor me,' said Jenny, 'though I saw a good many try, especially when they had sunk a good few pints in the pub. We had Birmingham's own Houdini as well.'

'Who's he?'

'An escapologist,' Jenny said. 'He used to get trussed up in chains and that, and you could check the chains. I did check them lots of times, and my brother did, and his mates, and I can't see how it could be a swizz. And however well he was twisted up with all these chains, when the money in his hat reached a pound, he would free himself.'

'How did he do it?'

Jenny shrugged. 'No one ever knew because he used to be in a cage-type thing and the assistant used to put a curtain over it.'

'I wish I'd seen it.'

'And I do,' Vera said. 'Because after this war I don't think things will ever go back to the way they were.'

The others nodded in agreement.

On Monday morning the probationers lined up to attend the lectures. Senior doctors gave talks on the theory of nursing in their own specialist subjects, and so they learnt about ear, nose and throat treatments and ophthalmic problems; and those in gynaecology, midwifery and paediatrics. Lucy took copious notes, feeling sure they would be asked questions relating to these talks in their prelim papers.

The following week, lessons were taken by a staff nurse. This was far more hands-on. She showed the girls how to nurse a postoperative patient, and a frail elderly one. The next day they were taken to a kitchen in Oozel's Street School, where they learnt about the special diet some patients might need and got the chance to cook some of the food in the school kitchens. They all enjoyed the day and thought what they had learnt a very important part of nursing care. They were still chatting about it when they reached the nurses' home.

Barely were they through the door when they heard a clamorous hubbub swelling out of the dining room.

'What's up?' Lucy asked a passing girl.

'Haven't you heard the latest?' the girl said. 'Hitler has taken over Denmark and invaded Norway.'

The four girls looked at one another in dismay. The girl went on, 'Denmark gave up without a fight, it seems, according to the announcer on the wireless, and Norway hadn't even mined the fjords. I mean, how daft is that? They say they will make for Holland and Belgium next.'

'No one seems able to stop this man and his bloody armies,' Vera said later as they ate their dinner.

There was no way you could get away from what was happening – even the patients were talking about it – and Lucy longed for a letter from Chris. He could tell her nothing, she knew, but she would know he was still alive. There had been gaps before and then two or three letters would come together, but it had been some time since she had heard from him and she hesitated to drop a line to Gwen, for if she hadn't heard either it might cause her to worry more and wouldn't help Lucy.

There seemed greater urgency in the training of the probationers and they could all understand why. In the wards each staff nurse had to fill in an experience sheet for the probationer nurse she had assigned to her ward so that Matron could see the progress at a glance. Lucy had been assigned to work with Staff Nurse Hammond, and she liked the look of her straight away. Her grey eyes were kindly looking and she had a lovely smile.

Lucy had already had ticks for the cleaning she had been doing since she entered the hospital. She had thought she knew how to make beds, but the bed had often to be made in a different way, for example, an amputee or a person with renal or cardiac problems.

She knew how to lift patients, take care of pressure points, give a blanket bath, use a thermometer and apply various types of dressings. Now she was learning how to test a person's urine, give them an enema and administer intramuscular injections into the thigh of a patient to ease the pain of sciatica. Each time the hypodermic needle was used their sharpness was tested by running the point through a pad of cotton wool. Any snag and the needle would be put aside for resharpening, so Lucy had never to forget to do that.

She could see that her experience chart had a respectable number of ticks on it and yet there were areas she had yet to touch on. She had a dread feeling that all her nursing skills would be tested very soon and she hoped that she would be able to cope.

TWENTY-FOUR

Despite Vera's very wise words about leaving troubles behind when nurses were on the wards, as the weeks passed with no news from Chris, Lucy found it hard to lay her despondency aside and put on a brave face. Her three roommates tried to jolly her out of it, by bullying her into doing the beetle drive organised at the hospital, and taking her to see *The Flying Deuces*, with Laurel and Hardy, at the Odeon, but even that hadn't raised a smile.

Eventually, Vera became exasperated enough to tell Lucy that she obviously enjoyed being miserable.

'How can you say that?' Lucy demanded.

'Vera has a point,' Jenny said. 'I have a brother in the Forces that I worry about.'

'And I have two cousins,' Babs put in.

'You don't understand.'

'We understand all right,' Jenny said. 'But moping around the place is not going to help.'

However, they couldn't seem to get through to Lucy, though even she could see that it wasn't doing the patients any good, for they had become used to her happy face and ready smile and were confused by her moroseness. Eventually, Staff Nurse Hammond asked her to stay behind one night at the end of her shift. When she took her into her office and asked her what was wrong, the sympathy in her voice broke through Lucy's reserve. She wept as she spoke of Chris Gilbert and explained that he was a doctor and that he had joined the medical corps of the Royal Warwickshires and she had not heard from him for weeks.

'It's happened before,' Lucy said, 'though not for such a long time, and then I have had a bunch of letters.'

Lucy was not the first probationer who was suffering this way, Staff Nurse Hammond re-

426

flected, nor would she be the last, especially as Sister had told her she had received notification to expect heavy casualties in the next few days. Junior nurses had been deployed opening and cleaning unused wards for the military to use. However, Lucy was a first-class nurse and her skills might be called upon shortly. If this Chris did not come back, then Lucy would have to learn to deal with it as others had.

'Tell me, Lucy,' she said, 'has this man a special place in your heart?'

'Oh, no, Nurse Hammond, nothing like that,' Lucy said. 'Chris is just a friend.'

Staff Nurse Hammond had been watching Lucy's face and knew the man was far more than just a friend, but if Lucy herself was unaware of it that was perhaps all to the good if the man wasn't going to return. In the meantime, Lucy's mood was affecting morale in the ward and yet she could hardly order her to be cheerful. A change of scene was what she needed. She had not done any work in theatre yet. She would have to do it sometime, so now might be as good a time as any. She would have to clear it with Sister first, though, so she said, 'All right, Lucy. Go on and have your meal now, and tomorrow come straight to me instead of going on to the ward.'

'Yes, Nurse Hammond,' Lucy said. 'And thank you for listening.'

And so the next morning Lucy found herself going to the operating theatre. She knew it was because Staff Nurse Hammond didn't want her upsetting the patients, and that knowledge hurt.

427

She resolved to try as hard as possible to please Staff Nurse Perryman, who was in charge of the operating wards and who understood just how nervous and apprehensive Lucy was. All student nurses had to work on the operation wards some time, for experience, but she told Lucy that few made the grade to full theatre nurses because they were very special people.

'So what qualities do you look for in a theatre nurse?' Lucy asked, intrigued.

'Well,' Staff Nurse Perryman said, 'I suppose a nurse who can work well under strain, who can think quickly and yet work harmoniously with the group. Teamwork is essential in any ward situation, but never more so than in an operation, when a minute's delay, unnecessary questioning of orders, may mean the life of a patient.'

'Oh, gosh,' Lucy gasped. 'It sounds a terrible responsibility.'

'It is,' Staff Nurse Perryman said. 'But what a privilege, too, to be instrumental in saving the life of someone who might have died without an operation?'

'Yes,' said Lucy, inspired. 'What do you want me to do?'

'For now, just familiarise yourself with our sterilisation methods, the steriliser itself and the water boiler,' she said, pointing to them in turn, 'and of course the steam cleanser, the autoclave. Watch and learn, and remember that what you have learnt so far in hygiene has to go up a notch in the operating theatre. Infection can most easily enter the body through an incision in the skin so anything used on or near the open wound has to be completely sterile.'

Lucy understood that, and Staff Nurse Perryman showed Lucy how to use each one of the machines over and over till she was satisfied that she had understood.

'How do you sterilise the needles and knives and things?' Lucy asked. 'Have you a special place for them?'

'No, they go into the water boiler too, with a fairly hefty dose of Lysol,' Staff Nurse Perryman said. 'That's horrible stuff, stinks to high heaven and is very caustic, but does the job. And let's face it, I would not like a doctor to make a cut on my body with a knife not properly cleaned, or inject me with a dirty needle.'

'No, nor me.'

'Now, I'm going to teach you the correct way to lay out a surgeon's tray,' Staff Nurse Perryman said. 'That is another valuable skill a theatre nurse needs to know. Though certain things will vary according to the operation being carried out, there will always be a sharp knife to make the incision, and scissors, clamps, gauze dressings and sponges. Sutures will nearly always be used and needles, of course, though the surgeon will specify what type of needles he requires. I'm sure you know how to test needles for sharpness?'

Lucy nodded. 'Run it through a pad of cotton wool.'

'Right, and put by for sharpening any you are not sure about,' Staff Nurse Perryman said. 'The surgeon will tell you what he needs to stitch the wound. Again, this depends on the operation. An experienced nurse will know this herself but the student nurse must familiarise herself with the options so that the thread can be added to the tray with as little delay as possible. And each item must be laid on a clean towel and in the same order so that the surgeon can put his hand straight on it.'

'Oh, I do see that,' Lucy said.

'You've probably had experience in packing the drums we use in the autoclave?' she asked Lucy.

'Yes,' Lucy said, 'I did a lot of that on night shift. The staff nurse there was so particular about the gowns for the theatres and wouldn't let us touch them until she was sure we were folding them the right way.'

Staff Nurse Perryman nodded. 'That's so that the surgeon can put them on without touching them. Risk of infection, you see, and also because he has usually scrubbed up by then and has his surgical gloves on. Oh, and talking of gloves, after each operation they have to be washed in soapy water and then checked for leaks, and if there are any they are repaired. You will be shown how, and then each pair is put in a linen bag with a talcum powder ball and put into another drum for auto-claving with the drapes, the towels, hats and the face masks.'

Lucy's head was swimming with all the inform-ation Staff Nurse Perryman had given her, yet she thought the theatre would be a terribly inter-esting place to work.

'Tell me, Lucy, are you tickly stomached?' Staff Nurse Perrymen asked her suddenly.

'Mmm, not especially, Nurse Perryman.'

'Would you like a spell working down here in the theatre or would you faint away in the middle of an operation?'

Lucy forced a smile on her face, though her stomach was tied in knots in nervousness as she said, 'I would do my level best to stay upright, but as I don't know what I am doing, wouldn't I be a bit of a liability?'

'No,' Staff Nurse Perryman said. 'See, there are normally four nurses for any major op and three have got specific jobs, but one nurse will be a circulating nurse and she does everything else. Basically, she makes sure that the nurses have the supplies needed, keeps the steriliser filled with boiling water and the operating room clean and tidy. We have an operation scheduled for two o'clock this afternoon and you could assist as the circulating nurse.'

What could Lucy say? She was nervous, but she realised what a marvellous opportunity she was being given, and she nodded. 'I'll do my best.'

Staff Nurse Perryman was pleased, she could see. 'You have taken in a lot today already. I expect you're feeling a little punch-drunk, aren't you?'

Lucy grinned a little ruefully. 'I am a bit, Nurse Perryman.'

'Well, go and have a bite to eat and let it all sink in,' Staff Nurse Perryman said. 'I want you back here just after one. And don't worry about not remembering everything. I think people learn more by doing than by just listening.'

Lucy never forgot her first operation. The atmosphere in the room changed with the arrival of the surgeon, Mr McAllister and, it was so charged

431

with tension, Lucy felt she could almost touch it. He was totally focused on the opening he had made in the side of the man's stomach and though it was gruesome – and she saw Staff Nurse Perryman watching her – Lucy didn't feel nauseous, just interested. She was also fascinated by the way the nurses seemed to anticipate exactly what Mr McAllister wanted, and when the sweat stood out on his forehead, Staff Nurse Perryman would wipe it away before it dribbled into his eyes.

It was over an hour before the young man was taken from the operating table to the recovery ward by stretcher, and the operating theatre was cleaned and sterilised again for a second operation. Altogether there were four operations performed that afternoon, and Lucy could not understand her total exhaustion until the nurses admitted they had felt that way too in the beginning.

'You did well,' one of the nurses said, and the others agreed. 'Did you enjoy it?'

'"Enjoy" is probably not the right word,' Lucy said, 'but it was riveting watching Mr McAllister at work. I know all nursing is special – that's why I wanted to go into it in the first place – but this type of nursing is sort of extra special somehow.'

'Well,' said Staff Nurse Perryman, 'as the girls said, you have done well today, but one day is not going to give you much in the way of experience, so I'll have a word with Staff Nurse Hammond and see if she minds if you work here for a week or two. Would you like me to do that?'

'Oh, yes, please, Nurse Perryman,' Lucy said. 'I would love that.'

While Lucy continued her work in the operating theatre, the rumblings in Europe continued more worryingly than ever. Lucy had to try to put the war news from her mind while she worked in the theatre, but it was the main topic of conversation in the canteen, and in the student common room where most of the young nurses began to gravitate after the evening meal. The wireless was in there so that they could keep up with the news. No one was really surprised when Chamberlain resigned.

'I suppose we've got old Winnie now?' Lucy said.

'Yeah,' Babs said. 'Why, don't you like him? Everyone else seems to.'

Lucy shrugged. 'I don't dislike him, but he looks and behaves like a bit of a grump, and what is he good at really but delivering speeches that someone else has written?'

'Maybe that's what we need when we are at war.'

'Maybe it is,' Lucy said. 'Everyone talks about keeping up morale and all, so I suppose only time will tell.'

'We do need something,' Vera said. 'The news is bad enough but the map in the *Evening Mail* frightens me to death because there are bloody swastikas all over it.'

By the second week in May, Lucy had finished her time in the operating theatre. She was very tired and she was relaxing with her three room-mates in the student common room after the evening meal. Vera was skimming through the newspaper when she suddenly exclaimed, 'I say, I don't think much of the Belgium idea of something being impregnable.'

There was a murmur of agreement. The Belgians were supposed to have an impregnable fort that guarded three important bridges and, just the day before, the Germans had landed paratroopers on it, and it was in German hands within twenty-four hours.

'Don't think much of them destroying the Dutch Air Force either,' Lucy said. 'According to the paper only twelve planes are operational.'

'Yes, and there was a reason for them doing that,' Jenny said. 'Mark my words, Hitler has something nasty up his sleeve for Holland.'

Barely were the words out of Jenny's mouth when the band music emanating from the wireless was suddenly interrupted by a newsflash.

'This evening the Luftwaffe launched an attack against Rotterdam, which went on for two and a half hours. It is estimated that there were as many as one thousand people killed. Many thousands more were injured and fifty thousand people are without homes.'

'Oh, God,' Jenny cried. 'A thousand people killed. It's hard to even visualise so many, and how was it possible to kill and injure so many in just two and a half hours?'

Lucy tried to imagine what it would be like to be in a city being pulverised by bombs indiscriminately, killing and maiming men, women, children, babies, the elderly and frail, and the sick in hospitals like the General. Whole families could have been destroyed that night, not to mention their homes blown to bits. She thought the poor Dutch people must have been in despair. She felt sick to the pit of her stomach and she saw that her friends were similarly affected.

Eventually, Babs said rather shakily, 'They are a barbarous country that we have waged war on, and they are also crafty and clever.'

'Hush,' said the girl nearest the wireless. 'There's another broadcast.'

'It is understood from reports coming in that the Germans have breached the French defences.'

It was a blow, no doubt about it. France was just too close.

Later, up in their room, Babs spread the map out on the bed and said, 'What about that Maginot line the French were always going on about?'

'I don't know,' Lucy said, 'but that might prove to be another impregnable obstacle that doesn't hinder this German army creeping over Europe like some sort of unstoppable monster.'

'Point is,' Vera said, 'that raid on Rotterdam was on a country that had done Hitler no harm – I mean, not declared war or anything.'

'Like we have, you mean?'

'Just like we have,' Vera said. 'So if France is defeated, what has Hitler got lined up for us?'

No one answered because there *were* no answers. Lucy wasn't surprised when her sleep that night was broken by terrifying and lurid nightmares.

Things seemed to escalate from there. No one was surprised that Holland had surrendered and everyone knew it was only a matter of time until

Belgium admitted defeat. A call went out from Anthony Eden for those below the age of conscription or over it, or not going into the services for any other reason, to register at the local police station to form a new civilian force called Local Defence Volunteers. In Birmingham, so many men turned up that the police stations were unable to cope. Everyone wanted to do their bit.

Though Lucy still had a niggle of concern for Chris, she was far too busy to let this surface during the day because she was back on the ward. The first military casualties had begun to arrive and it was very upsetting, Lucy thought, to see such dreadfully bruised and battered young men peppered with bullets or with shrapnel pellets embedded in their skin, or with missing limbs, or their bodies sliced into with bayonets. They were still caked in mud, in matted tattered uniforms, and blood from their wounds and pus from the infections had seeped on to their uniforms. The smell was often appalling, and peeling the material off without taking skin with it was very difficult. Lucy, along with her fellow nurses, worked from 6.30 a.m. to 9 p.m. day in and day out because there was so much to do.

They were the lucky ones. With the German armies conquering all before them, the British Expeditionary Force, or BEF, were given orders to retreat to the beaches of Dunkirk, destroying or disabling military equipment and vehicles en route. There the men had to use any discarded materials to build makeshift piers because the naval rescue ships couldn't come close to shore and some troops had to be lifted off the beaches in smaller boats and ferried to the waiting ships.

The survivors had nothing belonging to them but their tattered and torn uniforms. A call had gone out for clothes and *toilettes* for these men, and the people of Birmingham responded brilliantly. They sent underwear, pyjamas, dressing gowns, soap, brushes, and combs, writing paper and stamps, books and cigarettes. The young soldiers seemed overcome with the generosity shown to them by the people of Birmingham, but then, as Lucy said, they were grateful for anything done for them.

'They feel betrayed, I do know that,' Jenny said. Her brother had returned in one piece, but Jenny said he was terribly angered by the way it was all handled. There had been no plans to get the BEF out once they were in there. 'He says it was a rout, and he felt let down by the other European nations saying they had defences in place that turned out to be worse than useless.'

'I can see why he thinks that way,' Babs said. 'I mean, that Ardennes Forest isn't as impassable as the French said it was. The Germans drove their tanks right through it.'

'It probably was a barrier years ago,' Lucy said, 'Like that Maginot line and the fort, Eben-Emael. They were put up after the Great War, but since then everything has changed. Germany has invested in armaments and the like for years.'

'Yeah, you're right,' Babs said. 'I mean, in the Great War they weren't able to lay waste a city in hours.'

'It was a grave mistake, I think,' Vera said, 'and one France will pay a heavy price for.'

437

'And so might we, if France falls,' Babs said. 'For then Hitler will be bent on invasion, mark my words, and however keen they are, that motley bunch of Defence Volunteers practising with broom staves, like we saw in that picture in the *Evening Mail* the other night, will be no match for a German army that has goose-stepped over more than half of Europe.'

'I think no country so far has been prepared for the might and precision of the German armies,' Vera said.

'Are we?'

'Who knows? But we are an island and that has got to help.'

And that was all the hope they had, which wasn't much comfort, Lucy thought, when you remembered the way the Germans had invaded Denmark and Norway.

The evacuation from Dunkirk was known as Operation Dynamo. It was officially over by 4 June, though the casualties came in thick and fast for many days afterwards. By the time the French government fled to Bordeaux on 13 June, Lucy had faced the fact that Chris was dead and gone. She knew that Gwen had received no official notification of his death by telegram or by some other means, but that didn't surprise her because after the débâcle at Dunkirk she imagined it would take the authorities some time to find out what had happened to every serviceman involved, and then to inform the relatives. She knew that if Chris had survived, even if he was injured, then he would have got a message to them by now.

Although she felt the pang of his loss, which would sometimes catch her unawares by its sharpness, she felt guilty that she had not grieved properly for that good, kind man, for whom she now realised she had deeper feelings than she had thought. It was just that with so many needing her attention she was working such long and arduous hours that she had no time to think in the day and fell into bed each night to sleep the sleep of the totally exhausted. She often dreamt of Chris, though, and sometimes, when she woke, her pillow was damp.

She knew that Gwen would have come to the same conclusion as she had, for she was no fool. In fact, she had spoken about it in the many letters they had exchanged. She didn't know how she was coping with the loss of a dearly beloved son and wished she had time to go and see her and both take and give comfort, because she had got to know Chris better through his letters, and the genuine liking she had always had for him had turned into loving without her really being aware of it. Now it was hard to think that she would never see him again, and there seemed a constant ache in her heart.

With the Germans in Paris and steadily occupying France, Britain was staring the threat of invasion in the face. People were told to hide maps and disable cars and bicycles not in use, and signposts and station names had been painted over to confuse the potential invading enemy. It confused many Brummies too, but if you complained about anything, people would remind you there was a war on, as if you had dropped in from another planet and were taken unawares.

Lucy wasn't thinking of that one beautiful Sunday morning in late June. She wasn't thinking of anything much except how wonderful it was to have such lovely weather when she had the whole day off and wasn't on duty again until midway through the following day. She hadn't had to scurry about going to early Mass at half-past six either, but, she decided, as she gave a delicious stretch, she would go to the one at nine o'clock, for she wanted to have the rest of the day to herself.

She would go and see Gwen because she had been forced to neglect her a little and felt bad about it. She had worked fourteen days without a break, and so had Babs, hence the Sunday off, and before that, there had been so much to do their time off had been severely curtailed. Lucy had been forced to settle for writing little notes to Gwen, but she really needed to see her and maybe talk, if Gwen wanted to, about the man they had both loved and lost.

When there was a knock on the door, both Lucy and Babs groaned, for the other two girls were at work.

'You go,' Babs said to Lucy. 'You'd have had to get up in a minute anyway, to go to Mass. I want at least another hour.'

Grumbling, Lucy got to her feet and wrapped a robe around herself before opening the door to find Sister Magee outside.

'There's a man waiting for you downstairs, Nurse Cassidy.'

'A man?' Lucy cried. 'Who is it?'

'I didn't ask his name.'

Lucy hid her impatience. 'I'd better come down then.'

'More suitably attired, I hope.'

Lucy didn't bother answering that. 'Please, could you ask him to give me a minute?' she said.

'What did she think?' Lucy said to Babs as she threw on clothes. 'That I would go down there in my birthday suit?'

'Oh, that I would like to see,' Babs said.

Lucy slipped out of the door and along the corridor quickly, anxious to see who her visitor was. As she leant over the banister for a look she felt her heart actually stop beating for a moment. Then she was running down the stairs like the wind, and not giving a minute's thought to whether Sister Magee would approve or not, she threw herself into the man's arms.

'Chris! Oh, my darling, darling Chris, I thought you were dead. I thought I would never see you again.'

Chris felt almost light-headed with joy. He was holding Lucy tight as he had fantasised about many times, and she was saying words that he had longed to hear. He knew that it was mainly relief talking, but still, he reasoned, she must have some feelings for him to react as she did.

Lucy was thinking that it felt so right to be held in Chris's arms, but she didn't know what he thought of her just throwing herself at him the way she had, and she pulled back a little. 'You're clean-shaven,' she said, running her finger across Chris's slightly stubbly chin. 'It's nice. Suits you.'

'Army regs,' Chris said. 'Even in the Medical

Corps we have to obey orders. But none of that is important. Lucy, did you mean the things you said?'

'What things?'

'You called me darling, seemed more than just relieved to see me. You acted as though you really cared.'

'Chris, of course I care,' Lucy said. 'I have always. I nearly went mad when I thought I had lost you.'

'I'll say she did,' Babs said from the stairs, and Chris turned to find Lucy's roommate staring at Chris accusingly. 'Soaked in misery for weeks, she was.'

'Oh, God,' Chris said. 'Is this true?'

Lucy nodded, and Babs said, 'Couldn't you have found time to write a note to say you were all right?'

'It was hell on earth back there. You have no idea.'

'But when you got back?'

Lucy looked at the slightly panicky look in Chris's eyes and heard the not-so-discreet cough from Sister Magee, and knew that she would disapprove of such an open display of emotions played out in the entrance hall. So she said, 'Look, Babs, thanks for the support. I really do appreciate it, but I feel I need to talk to Chris on my own.'

'Thought you were going to Mass?'

'I was,' Lucy said. 'But there are a few things more important to me than Sunday Mass, and talking to Chris now is one of those things.'

'Thank you,' said Chris when they were outside

442

the nurses' home. 'I thought I was on trial.'

'Good job they weren't all there,' Lucy said with a smile. 'Might have resembled the Spanish Inquisition then.'

Chris gave a slight chuckle, then asked, 'Lucy, is it all right if I hold your hand?'

'Perfectly all right,' Lucy said. 'In fact I would like it very much.'

A tingle went through Lucy's hand as Chris enfolded it with his own, and seemed to run all through her body. Her mouth felt suddenly dry as she looked at him, almost as though she was seeing him for the first time.

'I love you, Lucy,' he said. 'I can scarcely re-member a time when I did not love you, only I dared not speak of it, for you were too young.'

'I am a child no longer, Chris,' Lucy said. 'And I know now I love you too.'

'Lucy, I am ten years older than you.'

'If you were twenty years older you are still the only man for me,' Lucy said determinedly.

'Oh, God, Lucy, do you mean that?'

'Every word,' Lucy said and, giving his hand a squeeze, urged, 'Please, tell me what happened to you. I was beside myself hearing what was hap-pening in Europe and not knowing if you were there or not.'

'I was there,' Chris said. 'I'll not explain Dunkirk or of the days leading up to the order to retreat. It would take too long. Suffice it to say that I had sick men to see to and couldn't just think of myself, so I was one of the stragglers. The noise and mayhem when I reached the beaches was incredible: the barrage of guns, and the bombs and the screaming

443

Stukas, and the rat-tat-tat of machine-gun fire, and the field guns the Allies set up on the beach spitting bullets into the air. Soldiers were blown up before my eyes and the smell of the stinking black smoke was swirling in the air mixed up with the acrid reek of cordite and the pungent stench of blood. You were afraid of trying to slither your way across the sand, but more afraid not to.

'I never thought I would make it out alive, but eventually I joined the soldiers queuing on a makeshift pier to get into the yachts, pleasure boats, fishing smacks and the like. You must have heard of the flotilla of boats that ferried the rescued soldiers to the naval ships anchored in deeper water?'

Lucy nodded. She remembered hearing about these little privately owned boats, once the veil of secrecy was lifted. There were pictures of the boats in the papers too, setting sail as if they were off to some jolly regatta. 'I thought the owners of those boats so brave because they were just ordinary civilians with no protection whatsoever.'

'You're right,' Chris said, 'They were extremely brave. Many of those boat owners never made it back. Anyway, there I was, waiting with countless others for the last boat leaving Dunkirk. We knew we wouldn't all get on but we shuffled forward hopefully, keeping a weather eye on the bloody Stukas, and then the man in front of me boarded and I was prevented.'

Chris stopped and his eyes were dark and brooding. Lucy felt immense pity for him, for she knew that he was back there again. She gave his hand a slight squeeze and it seemed to give him the strength to go on.

'I pleaded with the skipper but he said if one more got on then all would be drowned, and he was about to push off when suddenly there was a shout from an officer at the back. He jumped out of the boat, shook me by the hand and insisted I take his place. He said particularly at the moment Britain needed doctors and I would be more use to the human race than he was.

'I remonstrated with him but not for long, for the man behind me said he would take the place of both of us if we were not quick, and those in the boat urged me to hurry as the skipper cast off. The officer said not to waste the chance, and he pushed me, but the boat had pulled away a bit and I landed in the drink. Then the others hauled me into the boat. I looked back once and the man gave me the thumbs up sign and then disappeared. We were only just in time because the Germans were on the beaches in minutes. They took a few shots at us but they were just too far away. Now, guess who that man was.'

'Well, the only one I know going for officer training was Clive Heatherington,' Lucy said uncertainly.

'And that's who it was,' Chris said. 'He gave his life to save mine because he would have been mown down on the beaches like everyone else. When I got home, I felt I had to make Clive's sacrifice worth it. Can you see that, Lucy?'

'Absolutely, Chris.'

'I didn't think of you, or my mother at the time,' Chris admitted, 'just Clive and the ultimate sacrifice he had made. So I volunteered for

445

everything going, though by then I hadn't slept for days. I was sent to Portsmouth, where all the severe medical cases were treated, and I found that I couldn't sleep at all, even before the bombs began falling.

'One day I finished my shift in theatre and pulled off my gown and mask, and just walked out of the hospital. I have no recollection of this; I was told later by colleagues. The first thing I remember is waking up in a hospital in Portsmouth, where I'd lain in a coma for three days after walking in front of a bus that was fortunately going slow enough to avoid running over me.'

'Oh, Chris!'

'It was sheer and absolute exhaustion,' Chris said.

'Oh, Chris,' Lucy said again, 'how you have suffered. Does your mother know all this?'

'She knows nothing,' Chris said. 'I came first to explain everything to you.'

'How did you know that I would be off duty?'

'I didn't,' Chris said. 'I just came. When do you need to go back?'

'Not till tomorrow lunchtime,' Lucy said.

'How wonderful then that your day off coincides with my time off,' he said in delight. 'What will we do with ourselves?'

'See your mother first and show her you are in the land of the living.'

'And then tell her how we feel about one another?'

'That too,' Lucy said, 'but if I know your mother as well as I think I do, we may not have to tell her much about that at all.'

TWENTY-FIVE

Gwen nearly had a heart attack when she saw the son that she had been mourning for days standing hale and hearty outside her door. Lucy wished she could have prepared her in some way as she watched the blood drain from her face, leaving it the colour of lint. Next minute, though, the tears gushed from her eyes, she had pulled Chris into the house and he had held her tight. Eventually, her hiccuping sobs changed to a sigh of contentment and he led her into the living room and sat her in the easy chair. Then he sat beside her on the settee. And all the time, Gwen never took her eyes from her son's face. The love that Chris and his mother shared was almost tangible and beautiful to see. Yet Lucy wished that, at that moment, she had her own mother beside her. She gave an imperceptibly small sigh and took herself off to the kitchen to make tea for the three of them. After that she intended to take herself somewhere and leave them alone to talk.

When she went back in with the tray a little later, Chris was telling his mother a diluted version of what he had told her, including the sacrifice Clive Heatherington had made. When Lucy suggested leaving Chris and his mother alone, however, he wouldn't hear of it. 'I want to talk of us and you need to be here,' he said.

Gwen smiled at Lucy. 'It's no surprise how

Chris feels about you, my dear, but I had no idea that you felt the same.'

'I didn't,' Lucy said. 'I was all bound up with that silly infatuation with Clive Heatherington. How stupid was that?'

'Don't be so hard on yourself,' Chris said. 'The self-centred boy that he was then was also very charming and persuasive, and you were young and I believe he took advantage of you.' Chris put an arm around Lucy and gave her a squeeze, as he said jocularly, 'In matters of the heart, you, my darling girl, were a mere infant, but I think I began to love you when I saw the way you dealt with the little old lady.' He glanced across at his mother. 'I have never told you this.'

'Well, that's nothing new,' Gwen said. 'You never discuss your patients.'

'It wouldn't be right,' Chris said, 'but it won't hurt for you to know this. Lord Heatherington's mother was a real termagant of a woman, but also old and ill, and so was brought to live with the Heatheringtons. Only Lucy could handle her and she was such a dot of a thing. I mean, she is not all that big now but she was smaller then, and that is when I fell in love with her.'

'No, you didn't,' Lucy said disbelievingly.

'Yes, I did,' Chris insisted. 'I couldn't speak of it because you really were only a child then.'

'So, what did you think of my son then?' Gwen asked.

Lucy considered this. 'I thought him a nice, kind man who was considerate to an old lady who really didn't want to be old and infirm.'

'You've spoken of the old lady sometimes and

with affection,' Gwen said to Lucy. Then she turned to Chris and said, 'And you think you are telling me news, Chris, but let me tell you that old lady was well known for her tempers and the rages she would fly into. Servants talk, and the two nurses Lord Heatherington employed lost no time in telling all and sundry why they had walked out. In fact, one of them, I believe, needed medical attention.'

Chris nodded and smiled ruefully. 'She needed stitches for the cut above her eyes caused by a thrown pepper pot. I am surprised you didn't know that as well.'

'I probably would have, given time,' Gwen said.

Lucy laughed. 'Oh, you would have, Gwen. My father used to say the three quickest ways to send news of any description were telephone, tele-graph or tell a woman.'

'And he wasn't far wrong there,' Gwen said. 'But, my dear, were you not nervous about dealing with such a woman?'

Lucy shook her head. 'I was too angry to be nervous because as well as attacking the nurse she threw a paperweight at a very dear friend of mine and could have killed her, and so I went up and told her in no uncertain terms that if she lobbed the paperweight she was holding at me then I would throw it right back at her.'

Even Chris was looking at her open-mouthed as his mother said, 'You never did?'

'I did,' Lucy said. 'And when she lowered the paperweight, I put her straight about what I would not tolerate, which included having things thrown at me and being pinched or slapped or being

449

bawled at.'

'And she capitulated just like that?'

'More or less,' Lucy said. 'She was old and frail, and hated the way her body had let her down, as well as being worried about Clive. I felt sorry for her at first and then became fond of her. I told her I would love to nurse and that's why she left me money in her will.'

Chris then told his mother of the nest egg the old lady had left Lucy.

'It was lovely of her,' Lucy said. 'And yet nursing might have remained a dream if Chris hadn't sorted out my job at the Cottage Hospital, lodging with you, and the bursary to pay for it, and offered to tutor me for the nursing exams I needed to pass to be accepted.'

Gwen looked across at her son, aware there was no bursary because she had been told a little about the plan her son had cooked up with Lord Heatherington.

Chris caught his mother's eye and gave a slight shake of his head, but Lucy caught the movement and looked from one to the other. 'What?'

'Tell you later.'

'Oh, but–'

Chris bent his head to kiss her gently on the lips. A tremor ran through Lucy and she wondered why she had been so slow to recognise the love she had for him. Now, to find that he felt the same, was wonderful, simply wonderful.

An hour or so later, Chris and Lucy were on their way to Streetly because Chris had to see the Heatheringtons and tell them about their son.

450

When they were seated on the bus, Lucy said to Chris, 'Why is it so important for me to come with you? I could have helped your mother with the dinner.'

'She didn't want help,' Chris said. 'She said so.'

'Even so, Chris, the Heatheringtons won't want to see me,' Lucy said. 'I'm not really Lady Heatherington's favourite person. You know that.'

'Lord Heatherington might want to see you, though.'

'Why on earth should he?'

'Lucy,' said Chris, 'I think it's time you knew. There never was a bursary.'

'What are you on about?'

'There never was a bursary,' Chris repeated. 'It was a figment of my imagination.'

'But why lie like that?'

'Because of your stiff-necked pride, your longing to be a nurse, and a dilemma that Lord Heatherington couldn't find a solution to.' Chris told Lucy of his meeting Lord Heatherington in the club and the plan they had cooked up between them to help her. At first, she was inclined to be angry but then reminded herself that she wouldn't be training to be a nurse at the General Hospital if they hadn't done that.

'I suppose I must say thank you, to you, your mother and Lord Heatherington. I know why you did it, and I am glad that you did, but, really, I can't have Lord Heatherington pay me money every week for nothing. I will work out how much I owe him and start paying him back.'

'No, you won't,' Chris said. 'Because it's only what he owes you.'

'How d'you work that out?'

'How much do you think it would have cost him to get two qualified nurses in to look after his mother, which you did virtually single-handed? And because you did them a favour and looked after the old dear, a chain of events were set up against you. None of it was your fault, but the old lady gave you a birthday present of a sapphire pendant and left you a sizeable amount of money in her will, and so sealed your fate.'

'What do you mean?'

'Look,' Chris said, 'though Lord Heatherington promised you would always have a position with him, there was really no job for you and, because of the money and the necklace, he knew it would be difficult, if not impossible, for you to get a job elsewhere because people would think that you coerced the old lady into giving you the pendant and leaving you the money. Lady Heatherington, so I believe, was helping that rumour along as well.'

'I wouldn't put it past her,' Lucy said. 'But that wasn't how it was. You knew the old lady, Chris. You know no one could coerce her into anything.'

'You're right. Ill as she was, she was no pushover,' Chris said.

'Yes, it's just so unfair to spread rumours about me,' Lucy burst out.

Chris nodded. 'It is, I agree, and so I told Lord Heatherington that you didn't want a life in service anyway,' he said, leaping to his feet. 'Come on, this is our stop.'

Once on the pavement, he warned, 'If Lady

Heatherington is there, don't breathe a word of this unless you can get Lord Heatherington on his own. I don't want to see the old codger nagged to death.'

Lucy giggled at Chris calling such a titled and important man a 'codger'. But then the Lodge was in front of them and, in spite of herself, it was hard for Lucy to imagine Lord and Lady Heatherington in a house as small as this one. Not that it *was* a small house – far from it – and a very pretty one too, but tiny compared to Maxted Hall.

Mr Carlisle was as stiff and correct as he ever was, and though he greeted them both, Lucy saw that he was surprised to see her.

Mr Carlisle informed them that Lady Heatherington was at church, and Lucy gave an inward sigh of relief as he went on to say that he would see if his lordship was at home, which they both knew was gentry speak. If someone was 'not at home', it meant that they didn't want to see you.

Fortunately, Lord Heatherington was very much at home, and he strode across the room with his hand outstretched as they entered. He hadn't seen Chris Gilbert for some time, but he was bowled over by Lucy, astounded that the little undersized girl who had begun in his household as a scullery maid almost five years ago had grown into such a stunningly beautiful girl with such a radiant smile. And that smile was very much in evidence at the way Carlisle ushered them in with as much aplomb as if he was still at Maxted Hall. Lord Heatherington asked him if he would organise tea.

As the door shut behind him, he said, 'Poor Carlisle, the move here upset him more than me. Mind you,' he went on, 'I am seldom here. War work, you know. Hush-hush, and all that. It was just that, when Amelia got the telegram about poor Clive, I knew I needed to be home. They gave me three days' compassionate leave. I go back tomorrow.' He sighed, and said, 'And I will be glad. I do too much thinking here.' Lucy plainly saw the pain in the eyes he turned on them as he said, 'Don't think I am not heartbroken about the death of my youngest and only son because I am, but thinking about him all the time will not bring him back.'

'I am here to speak of Clive, sir,' Chris said. 'We were together in Dunkirk. But first, Lucy has something to say to you that is better said before your wife returns.'

'I am intrigued, my dear,' Lord Heatherington said.

But then Carlisle came in with tea and scones and, as he arranged them on a small table, Lord Heatherington found himself studying Lucy again. No wonder Clive had been smitten, had wanted to marry her, no less. Not that he thought that a good idea. Marriages seldom worked when people were from such dissimilar backgrounds. They'd be like chalk and cheese. But then, he mused, she might have made him a damn sight happier than the she-devil he had married. Clive had looked quite haunted when he sailed to France, and never came home again.

'Would you like me to pour, sir?' Carlisle said.

'No,' Lord Heatherington replied, jerking back to the present. 'We'll help ourselves.'

454

'Very good, sir.'

As the door closed behind Carlisle, Lord Heatherington poured the tea and handed around the scones before saying to Lucy, 'What is it you want to say that is not for my wife's ears?'

'The bursary,' Lucy said. 'I have just found out that the money was not from any bursary, but from your own pocket.'

'Ah, but my pockets are very deep, Lucy.'

'I am very grateful, sir,' Lucy said.

'And you are a nurse now?'

'Not yet, sir.'

'She is a very hard-working probationer,' Chris said. 'To get this Sunday off, she has worked for a fortnight without a break.'

'Is that so?'

'Oh, yes, sir,' Lucy said. 'But it had to be all hands on deck because we had a lot of injured servicemen from Dunkirk. You can't just go off duty when there are patients that need care. It's never going to be that sort of job.'

'But you enjoy it?'

'Much more than that, sir,' Lucy said. 'It's more like I was born to nurse, and I have you and Chris and Chris's mother, Gwen, to thank for making it possible.'

Both Lord Heatherington and Chris felt choked at the sincere way in which Lucy had spoken.

And then she said, 'And I have been here a little time and not told you how sorry I am about Clive, and also sorry for you and his mother dealing with the loss of him.'

'Thank you, my dear girl,' Lord Heatherington said huskily, leaning forward and grasping Lucy's hands. 'But how did you learn about Clive?'

'I told her,' Chris said. 'And now I must tell you about your brave and selfless son.'

Lucy excused herself because she had the feeling Lord Heatherington might get upset, and she knew he would not like to get upset if she was present. Sometimes she felt sorry for men. In the midst of grief some were unable to cry, possibly thinking it unmanly. Having a stiff upper lip was all very well, but Lucy thought it might be healthier if it was allowed to wobble a bit now and then.

When she had asked to be excused, Lord Heatherington had directed her upstairs where he said she might 'powder her nose'. But Lucy didn't want to powder her nose, or do anything else either, and she lingered at the landing window. From there she could see the gravel drive and the imposing front of Maxted Hall. Only now, the drive was full of army trucks and soldiers milled everywhere. Some, obviously off duty, sprawled on the lawns. It looked very strange to see the Hall that way.

She was still studying the Hall when she heard an anguished cry and heart-rending sobs, and then the sound of Lady Heatherington returning from church. Not long after that, Chris came up to find her.

'Lady Heatherington is home now,' he said. 'And Charles will tell her why he is so upset. They need to be a support for one another, and we should go home.'

'Yes,' Lucy said. 'But should we not say good-bye?'

'There is no need,' Chris said. 'They will understand.'

Later that same day Lucy wished for just a short while that she could stop the clocks, hold back the minutes, knowing that when she kissed Chris goodbye, they might not meet again for many months. That afternoon, after one of the nicest meals Lucy had had in ages, she and Chris strolled the parts of Sutton Park the civilians could still use. Chris was very quiet, but he had been that way since he'd spoken to Lord Heatherington, even through dinner. And eventually, he said to Lucy, 'When I think about the chaps we both patch up, and remember the poor sods left behind on the beach at Dunkirk, it makes me realise that we have got to make every minute count.'

'Yes, I agree,' Lucy said, remembering a time she had said similar words to Clive.

'Oh, Lucy,' Chris cried, and his arms went around her and he was showering her with kisses on her face, her throat, her eyelids and lastly her lips. 'I want to marry you when this damned war is over. Will you marry me?'

'Of course,' Lucy said. 'Isn't that what people who love each other do?'

'Will you wear my ring?' Chris asked. 'Get engaged properly? Make it more official?'

Lucy nodded. 'I would be honoured to wear your ring, but you don't have to go to the expense. My words should be enough.'

'It is enough, but I want you to have a ring.'

'A ring it is then,' Lucy said. 'Shall we go and tell your mother?'

'All right,' Chris said. 'But I don't think she will be surprised.'

'Mine will be,' Lucy said. 'I must write to her at the first opportunity and tell her everything.'

As they had anticipated, Gwen was delighted for them and kissed Lucy soundly. She said that she couldn't have chosen a better person than Lucy for her son and that she would gladly welcome her as a daughter. Her words set Lucy's mind at rest, for she knew between a mother and son, especially when they are so obviously close, the mother can sometimes resent the fact that another woman comes first in her son's heart. Gwen, however, wasn't a bit like that.

'But what of your own mother, my dear?' she said.

'I think that she will understand that we have to grasp our opportunity while we still can,' Lucy said. 'She married Declan when my father had been dead less than two years. It was circumstances dictated that and I didn't understand then the power of love.'

'Shall she think you too young or my son too old for you?'

Lucy smiled. 'Knowing my mother she might see it as a good thing,' she said. 'Someone steady who might calm me down.' Then she glanced at Chris, laugher in her eyes as she said, 'You know, someone to curb my youthful exuberance.'

Chris laughed with her. Then he crossed the room and put his arm around her as he said, 'If that's what she hopes, she will be disappointed because I wouldn't dare try. Anyway,' he added, planting a small kiss on her lips, 'it's what I love about you.'

Gwen saw the love sparkling between the young couple and she said, 'Lucy said you must seize the moment and she is right and let us also capture the moment.'

She produced a Brownie box camera and took pictures of the young couple. There were photographs of Lucy and Chris, and another of Gwen with Lucy, and eventually she called a halt. 'There is one left and that is for the ring,' she said. 'If you pop in and show it to me on your way back to the hospital, I'll take a picture of it and that will be the end of the film. I'll get them developed and send you some, Lucy. It will help us remember what Chris's ugly mug looks like,' she said, jerking her head towards her son.

Her words were brave, but her voice was choked at the end, and her eyes were very bright. Lucy quite understood how she felt and she would do anything in the world if she didn't have to be parted from Chris the following day, God only knew for how long. She knew that would happen, however, and she would have to cope with it because it was the only thing to do.

TWENTY-SIX

Lucy couldn't hold back the tears when she bid goodbye to Chris the following day. She knew that he was returning to Portsmouth later, and with their heavy schedules, limited time off and

459

the distance separating them, she knew they would be unlikely to meet for ages. But, she told herself firmly, many were worse off. Still, she was glad to find her room empty and so she was able to bathe her eyes to relieve the puffiness before she put on her uniform.

Babs had already filled the others in about that doctor chap, who Lucy had seemed so keen on, arriving unexpectedly Sunday morning, and that Lucy seemed more than pleased to see him. However, there was no time to discuss it further while they were working on the wards. If you tried to exchange more than the odd word you were likely to get your ears scalded by the staff nurse or, even worse, the ward sister.

Vera and Jenny finished their shift at half-past seven, but Babs and Lucy had another two hours to go as they hadn't started until noon.

When they did leave the ward together, Babs said, 'Don't say anything to me about your day off unless you want to repeat it all in a few minutes. I do want to know, but Jenny and Vera are positively agog.'

Lucy laughed. 'I'll save my breath for now then. What was yours like?'

'Not bad,' Babs said. 'My dad's bowled over that I like nursing so much. I mean, it was him who really pushed me into it.'

'What about your mother?'

'Well, she goes along with whatever my father wants, but I think she thought that nursing might not be the right sort of job for a clergyman's daughter. So I told her all about nursing the young soldiers injured in Dunkirk, and the type of things we had to do with them, and the hours we had to work because there was just so much to do, and she was quite impressed. And she realised maybe for the first time the invaluable job we do. I told them both that I wouldn't wish to do anything else.'

'Nor me,' Lucy said, as they reached the stairs.

Babs, with a grin, said, 'You ready for this?'

'Oh, I suppose as ready as I ever will be,' Lucy said with an answering smile, and, despite the fact that they had been nine hours on their feet, they bounded up the stairs.

Vera and Jenny were waiting for Lucy, and began firing questions at her before she was through the door. She told them all about Chris and how they had discovered their deep friendship had developed into love. They could accept all that and even thought it romantic. But they could hardly credit that she had become engaged.

'Why wait?' Lucy said. 'It isn't as if I don't know the man.' She got off her bed where she had been reclining and went to her drawer to get the ring to show them.

'It is a terrific ring,' Babs conceded. The large central diamond was encircled by four smaller ones, and it was truly beautiful. It sparkled and glistened in the light. 'But I still say that you are a quick worker.'

'Yeah,' said Jenny, with a wry smile. 'Nabbed a doctor without even trying. You will be the envy of the whole probationary year. Think a lot of them come into nursing with that in mind.'

'Surely not.'

'Oh, yes,' Jenny said. 'I don't mean that they

461

don't want to nurse, just that if they manage to catch the eye of a doctor they'd count that as some sort of added bonus.'

'It would be very difficult for a probationary nurse to catch the eye of any doctor here, I'd say,' said Vera. 'Anyway, there are more and more woman doctors now, and we are not encouraged to fraternise or even talk to the few male doctors that are still working here. It's like they have two heads or something.'

'Yeah, and one breach of hospital regulations and you're out on your ear,' Jenny said.

'Yes, but I saw a lot of Chris when I nursed the old lady, and, when she died, he taught me what I needed to know to pass my nursing exams,' Lucy said. 'And that's something else I found out yesterday. You know that bursary that I was supposed to get because I was doing a pre-nursing course at the Cottage Hospital that you lot had never heard of?'

'Yeah,' the three girls said collectively.

'Well, you hadn't heard about it because it didn't exist,' Lucy said. 'That was Chris again cooking up a plan with Lord Heatherington, who I used to work for. The money came out of Lord Heatherington's pocket.'

'Golly,' Jenny said. 'I didn't think the gentry did things like that.'

'They aren't known for it generally,' Lucy said. 'And then Chris's mother let me stay with her free of charge, though I didn't find that out till yesterday either. But it does mean that neither Chris nor his mother are exactly strangers. Anyway, with him working long hours in Portsmouth and me working long hours here, God knows when I'll see him again, and that's not even taking into account that he might be sent abroad again.'

'Yeah, but you said you had only just found out that you loved one another, but getting engaged makes it sort of permanent.'

'I know, but Chris said he has loved me for years, and I think I must have loved him too. It was staring me in the face and I didn't recognise it for what it was. It was when I thought he had died and then saw him standing there in the hall, the knowledge that I loved Christopher Gilbert hit me like a sledgehammer.'

She was silent for a moment and then went on, 'And don't you get the feeling that you sort of have to make every day count, that if you wait for something you might not get it, that our lives might change beyond recognition?'

'You're thinking of invasion,' Vera said.

'And you could have reason,' Jenny said. 'Don't know if you or Babs got near a wireless yesterday but me and Vera did.'

'And?'

'And Italy has declared war on France and invaded through the Riviera. Pétain, who is the leader of the government there, apparently, has applied for an armistice with Germany.'

'So we are definitely on our own now?'

'Yeah. That's about the size of it.'

The following evening, Lucy listened to the speech that Churchill had delivered in the House of Commons that day, saying, 'The Battle for

463

France is over and the Battle for Britain has begun.'

Germans, Austrians and others thought to have Nazi sympathies had already been interned or had their movements restricted, and now Italians too were rounded up. Any schools or children evacuated to the South Coast or even southern counties like Kent or Sussex were moved further north because invasion seemed inevitable. Everyone knew that Hitler had amassed an armada of barges, cargo ships, motorboats and even tugs, all capable of crossing that small stretch of water, and everyone was gearing up for it.

Everyone wanted to do something. Each day in the paper the young nurses read of people becoming ARP wardens or joining the Auxiliary Fire, Police and Ambulance Service, or signing up as fire watchers. The Red Cross and St John Ambulance were swamped by people wanting to learn first aid, and Gwen said the WVS were overwhelmed by the women wanting to get involved.

'I read in the paper that Hitler has to destroy the RAF before he will risk an invasion,' Vera said one evening towards the end of summer.

'Yes, 'cos the boys in blue would just blow him out of the water,' Jenny said.

'So I suppose that's why the Luftwaffe are attacking shipping,' Lucy said. 'Every time I hear of another stricken ship it makes me feel sick to think of all that food on the seabed and the poor merchant seamen drowned.'

'That's why the RAF are trying to stop them,' Jenny said. 'Some of the people who live by the coast were on the wireless the other day describing the dogfights they have seen over the Channel.'

'Yes,' Lucy said, but it was the attacks on the coastal ports that worried her most. Dover had been bombed consistently since the end of May, but now Portsmouth was getting a hammering along with Plymouth, Ramsgate and Folkstone. Afterwards, the newspapers would be full of pictures of the destruction wreaked and accounts of the numbers of civilians killed and injured. Hospitals were not immune from attack, and whenever she heard of a raid on Portsmouth her heart would be in her mouth. Chris wrote when he could, sometimes just a scribbled note, but she would read the estimated casualty figures and knew that he would be working flat out.

When the first bombs fell on Birmingham, on 9 August, the girls were almost unaware of it. No sirens had sounded and the attack was from one plane, which dropped three bombs in a district of Erdington. The nurses looked at the pictures in the *Evening Mail* and read that, despite the fact that the houses had been reduced to mounds of rubble and that some of the occupants had to be dug out, the only death was that of a young soldier. It seemed particularly poignant that he was home on leave after being rescued from Dunkirk.

'They say the bomber was probably making for Dunlop's,' Vera read out of the *Evening Dispatch* the following day.

'Good job the canals were boarding, then,' Lucy said, though she hadn't seen the thinking behind it at the time and it had been Jenny who put her right. 'I asked my dad why they were doing that,' she said, 'and he said in the past lots of the factories were built backing out on canals so that they could throw their waste into it.'

'Which is why they can stink to high heaven and are dirty and oil-slicked,' Babs said.

'Right,' Jenny said. 'And they are threaded all over the city.'

'Yeah,' Vera said. 'Someone told me once that Birmingham had more canals than Venice.'

'Don't know about that,' Jenny said. 'I've never been to Venice, but there is a canal that runs from Gas Street Basin all through the town, down behind all the workshops and small factories in Aston and the ones all the way up the Tyburn Road, all making war-related stuff, and on to Dunlop's.'

'Yeah, and it curls round at Dunlop's,' Babs said, 'and goes on to the Vickers factory opposite Castle Bromwich aerodrome, where they are making all the Spitfires. And if a bomber caught the gleam of water in his headlights...'

'Oh, he could make a killing,' Lucy said. 'I see now how sensible it was to get the bargees to board them every night.'

'Mind, Dunlop's uses them Smokey Joes as well,' said Jenny.

'Smokey Joes?'

'Yeah. I have a cousin living up that way and she was telling me all about them. They're oil drums filled with black oil that are lit every night. There's two of them just outside the main gate and the stench from the dense black smoke nearly chokes you, my cousin said. And the grey

466

smut particles settle on everything. It is the very devil to get off clothes.'

'Well, it's no good moaning,' Vera said. 'Don't you know there's a war on?'

There was a raid the next night and the next, and though in the main they were light skirmishes compared to the blanket bombing they had been expecting, no sirens heralded these raids, or they were sounded too late and so didn't give people time to take cover.

'Apparently, a policeman rides round on a bike blowing a whistle,' Vera said.

'That's what a lot of the patients are saying.'

'Doesn't hit you with the same sense of urgency, does it?' Babs said. 'A copper on a bike, blowing a whistle.'

'No, it flipping doesn't,' Jenny agreed. 'The way I see it is, a bomb is a bomb whether it falls in a large prolonged raid or a short sporadic one. If it hits you it will kill you, and there is no getting away from that. Bombs are not the friendliest buggers to have any sort of close encounter with.'

Jenny was right, and as they coped with the many injured brought in after a sustained raid on 19 August, and another in Aston on 23 August, the bombs were falling before the sirens even sounded. The nurses went into bomb-raid mode, some helping to the basement those who could walk or use a wheelchair, others placing cages over the bed-bound while others would be filling up the baths and sterilisers with water. The raid lasted seven and a half hours, and Lucy was one of many nurses brought out of the basement to

467

tend to the injured being brought in. Lucy felt so sorry for the people, particularly the bewildered children, often covered in brick dust, their clothes in tatters, and sometimes keening in fear and distress. They had been made even more vulnerable because they were not warned in time to take shelter.

'Why aren't those sirens sounding in time?' Lucy asked angrily that evening as she returned to the room after tending a young boy who had had to be dug out of the rubble of what had once been his house. His face and remains of his clothes were grey-red with brick dust, and his eyes were red-rimmed and glazed with fear and pain. The brick dust didn't quite hide the lacerations all over his small body, or his leg twisted at a very odd angle, or the mangled right arm that doctors didn't think they would be able to save.

The following day the *Evening Mail*, in response to the many letters of complaint, decided to find out how the sirens were supposed to operate. Lucy, Babs and Jenny were in the common room waiting for Churchill's speech to be broadcast on the wireless, and Babs was leafing through the paper when she suddenly said, 'Hey, listen to this. It says here the lookouts for the planes are volunteers from the Royal Observer Corp.'

'Oh, God,' Jenny cried. 'There is no hope for any of us. Did you say Royal *Observer* Corp? Can't be much cop at it, that's all I can say, if they can't see dirty great planes coming till they're directly overhead.'

'Shut up,' Babs said, but she was laughing too.

'Go on,' Lucy said. 'We're all ears.'

'Yeah, well, these Observer Corp people are based in one thousand four hundred locations all over the country, and when they see planes approaching they are supposed to relay that information to Fighter Command and ARP Headquarters.'

'How are they informing them?' Jenny asked. 'By carrier pigeon?'

All the girls were giggling now and Lucy said, 'You are an idiot, Jen.'

'I think that was a perfectly reasonable question,' Jenny said. 'And when the carrier pigeons get to Fighter Command or the ARP Headquarters what happens then?'

'Then the message is relayed to the schools and factories where the sirens are placed.'

'Not terribly efficient, is it?'

'Ssh,' someone said, and the wireless was turned up. Lucy listened to the confident and inspiring words of Churchill and knew the country needed a man like that. She remembered once decrying Churchill, when he took over after Chamberlain resigned, saying he was only good for speeches others had written, but she knew that few men could have delivered those speeches as well. Their backs were to the wall, there was no doubt about it, and the enemy was at the gate. Yet Churchill could almost make you believe that victory was within our grasp. He paid tribute to the brave pilots who risked their lives daily, some paying the ultimate price, and a phrase stuck in Lucy's head that seemed so apt: 'Never in the field of human conflict was so much owed by so many to so few.'

It was so true, and yet so scary, that the future of the entire nation rested on the slim shoulders of those very young men who fought their battles in the air.

The sirens wailed out in plenty of time just the day after Churchill's speech. This time there was more of a drone in the air and Lucy guessed that this raid might be more severe and sustained than previous ones. She reckoned she wouldn't be in the basement long. The first crumps and crashes were soon heard, though slightly muted, Lucy being underground. Despite this some of the more elderly or anxious were giving little yelps of fear, and Lucy found consoling them helped to keep her calm as well. After an hour or so, Lucy was one of the ones selected to go back to the hospital to deal with the wounded.

The raid went on hour after hour, and the noise seemed all around them, yet muted in the wards. Though nothing could be seen through the blackout shutters, she could plainly hear the whistle of a descending bomb and the resultant crashes and blasts and sounds of falling masonry, and then the ack-ack guns barking into the night.

As people were patched up they talked about the raid and so did the ambulance drivers. Lucy learnt that the Bull Ring took the main force of it. St Martin's was damaged, and the shops on the slope leading down from the High Street reduced to rubble.

'In fact, the whole Bull Ring is one unholy mess,' one man said as she dressed his wounds.

'Whole roof is off the Market Hall. The place is just a shell now, and that clock burnt to a cinder. Good job the night watchman released the animals from Pimm's Pet Shop.'

'Oh, yes, indeed,' Lucy said, for though she doubted many of the animals would survive, she couldn't imagine anything worse than being burnt to a crisp.

The next night the sirens went off at midnight and all the girls were jerked suddenly awake. 'Oh, God!' groaned Babs. 'I feel as if I haven't really gone to bed.'

Lucy yawned. 'I know what you mean but we had better get up just the same.'

So, grumbling, they all dressed. It was so hard to rouse all the sleeping patients. Many were confused and reluctant to leave the wards, especially as they could hear the raid going on some way away. However, the nurses were well aware how fast planes were and knew they could be on top of them in minutes. And sure enough, three hours into the raid they heard the drone of the planes coming closer.

'It's not the Bull Ring,' said Lucy, listening intently, 'but it's somewhere close.'

'We'll know soon enough,' Babs said, as the bells of the emergency services were heard.

Shortly after that a party of them were sent upstairs. This time many of the injuries were burns. One ambulance driver told them of the sea of fire that stretched from Snow Hill Station on Colmore Row to St Paul's Church and the start of the Jewellery Quarter.

'The Jewellery Quarter?' Lucy repeated.

'Nearly all the warehouses and workshops there are wood.'

'Don't I know it?' the ambulance driver said. 'Tell you, them firefighters deserve a medal. You should have seen it. Everything was ablaze and they were fighting to try to stop it spreading or the whole lot would have gone up. Christ, even roads had melted, and the burning tar was running like liquid fire, setting light to more and more buildings in its path.'

Ninety crews were involved in fighting the blazes that night and many of them had to receive hospital treatment of one sort and another, especially the young man on the turntable ladder who had become engulfed with flames before they could get him down.

'All these people so badly hurt,' Lucy said that night as she got into bed. 'I know Staff Nurse said it's best not to get involved, but it's hard not to.'

'I agree,' Jenny said. 'And you know what, I don't think we'd make as good nurses if we didn't care.'

There was a murmur of agreement, but really the girls were too tired to talk, and soon the only sound in the room was their even breathing.

The raids continued, some lasting as long as five hours and some lasting only two or three, and while some were in the distance one, in late August, destroyed the C & A Store in Corporation Street. All the nurses mourned that because C & A had some reasonably priced clothes and beautiful hats for special occasions at a fraction of the price of those in more salubrious establishments.

Many of the raids, though, were too far away for them to worry too much about. However, because they had patients in their care and it took time to organise them all, they could never take the risk of waiting to see, and every time the sirens went off it had to be taken seriously. It played havoc with the girls' sleep patterns. They had been tired before, but they had never experienced this whole body weariness that affected them now.

They were all buoyed up, though, by the major battle the RAF won over the Luftwaffe towards the end of September, because it meant Hitler's invasion plans had to be shelved. The pilots had not just won a major air battle, they had won the Battle of Britain, and that gave everyone the boost they needed.

The next day the Luftwaffe started a series of daylight raids, which worried mothers to death, having their children apart from them with a raid in progress. They also strafed people with machine-gun fire. That appeared to be totally indiscriminate: men and women waiting for trams or buses, or the vehicles themselves attacked, or people just walking down the street. It lasted only a few weeks but there were deaths and injuries, and the unpredictability of it played havoc with people's nerves.

And then, as suddenly as it began, it stopped. No night-time raids, no daytime raids. Lucy thought how much better life looked when a person had a good night's sleep. She caught up with her sadly neglected correspondence, writing a long and loving letter to Chris, and another to his mother, thanking her for the photographs she had sent. She selected a few nice ones to send to her mother, and others she had framed and set on her chest of drawers. She also wrote to Clara and Cook, telling them of her engagement.

She could answer none of her own mother's questions about the war, but thanked her for her warm and sincere congratulations on the announcement of her engagement. Minnie had no issue with the age of the doctor and wrote that she wasn't totally surprised at the news, for when Lucy had been nursing the old lady she had mentioned the doctor more often than she probably realised. Lucy blushed when she had read that, for she hadn't known.

So she had probably loved him for a long time, and long before she had been aware of it herself. She felt a warm glow just thinking about him and longed to see him again.

TWENTY-SEVEN

On 14 October, Clementine Churchill, the Prime Minister's wife, visited the city to see for herself the effects of the bombardment by the Luftwaffe. There were pictures in the paper of her talking to the homeless and dispossessed in the emergency shelters hastily set up for them in church halls and such like. Some of the women were able to point out where their houses had been and put Union Jacks sticking out of the mounds of rubbish.

'Our houses may be down, but our spirits are up,' one old woman told her, and in the paper it said that Clementine Churchill had been impressed with such unflinching courage.

And unflinching courage was needed. That night, just an hour or so after Lucy and her roommates had started their three months of night duty in a women's surgical ward, the sirens blared out again.

'Oh, God, I hope we're not getting another spate of it,' Babs said.

Lucy said nothing. She hoped the same, like anyone in their right mind, but thought realistically that this would not be an isolated attack. London and a great many other cities were really going through it.

'No good worrying about something you can't do anything about,' Staff Nurse Cornley said quite sharply, but in a quiet voice. 'The patients seem to be unsettled enough as it is.'

The staff nurse was right, Lucy thought. Many of them were fairly new admissions to the hospital and so wouldn't have any experience of the hospital's procedure in the event of a raid. Now thoroughly jerked awake because of the sirens, they were, in the main, distressed and frightened.

'You're all right,' Lucy told them as she helped them into dressing gowns and slippers. 'You'll all be going down into the basement.'

'What about me, Nurse?' a woman called Mrs Lancaster cried in sudden alarm. She had had an

475

operation the previous day and couldn't be moved.

'It's all right,' Staff Nurse Cornley assured her. 'We have a special cage to put over the bed to protect you.' She looked at Lucy, who was beside her at the time, and Lucy knew what that look meant. Then the older nurse continued, 'And Nurse Cassidy will stay with you, don't fret.'

Mrs Lancaster looked at the slight, very young nurse and she said, 'You promise?'

Lucy saw the fear on the woman's face and her voice was very gentle but determined as she said, 'I promise, Mrs Lancaster.'

'Won't you be scared?'

'Quite possibly,' Lucy answered candidly. 'But I will still stay.'

And she did stay, and held Mrs Lancaster's hand through the cage, and encouraged her to talk about her family and her life as they listened to the drone of the planes, the whistle and scream of the descending bombs, the crump and crash of explosions and the ack-ack guns' barking response, and, eventually, the ringing of the bells of the emergency services. Occasionally, when a bomb fell very close, Lucy would give an involuntary shudder, but her sharp intake of breath she hid from Mrs Lancaster, who would cry out at times and seemed to be just waiting for the hospital to be hit. Lucy was as pleased as Mrs Lancaster to hear the reassuring strain of the all-clear blasting out.

Much later, when all the girls were eating a well-earned breakfast in the canteen, Babs said, 'Pity Clementine Churchill didn't stop longer.

She said she wanted to see an area badly affected by the bombing. I thought at the time she had plenty to choose from, but if she had hung on a bit longer she could have seen one first-hand.'

'Well, we have had almost a fortnight free of bombing,' Lucy said. 'I made the most of that bit of peace, didn't you?'

'I suppose,' Babs said. 'Not to start with, though. At first, I lay awake waiting for the raids to start. I was a bag of nerves.'

Lucy smiled. 'So was I, at first,' she said, 'but I had to get a grip on myself because I went to see Chris's mother on my first full Sunday off and I didn't want to arrive like a gibbering wreck. I'd also arranged to see my mother's old friend, Clara O'Leary, who used to be housekeeper in the house I worked in, and Ada Murphy, who used to be the cook. It was really tremendous to see them again and we couldn't think why we had never done it before. We don't intend leaving it so long to meet up next time. We went to the Royal Hotel for lunch because Clara had eaten there before when she had been interviewing for staff and she said the food was good. Mind you, that was pre-war days. It was like a different world then. I mean, Gwen had offered to cook lunch, and she is a grand cook and loves having people to eat with her, because I don't think she bothers much when she's by herself.'

'Why didn't you take her up on the offer then?' Babs asked.

'Because Gwen would either have queued for hours at the Bull Ring for rabbit or something – time she can ill afford now that she is putting in so many hours at the WVS – or else used her entire meat ration to put something edible on the table other than what we did get, which was a variation on Spam.'

Vera laughed. 'I reckon the government have shares in all the Spam factories.'

'You got a chance on that,' Lucy said. 'And if that is the case they must be making a fortune.'

'Yeah,' Jenny put in, 'because, however awful and tasteless it often is, if that is all there's on offer you eat it.'

'Yes,' Babs said. 'I think as far as rations go we are cushioned here. My mum is always complaining about it.'

'And mine,' Jenny said.

'My mother has a cook that has been with them for years, who she says is a marvel for stretching the rations,' Vera said.

'You got a flipping cook?' Jenny said incredulously.

Vera was embarrassed, but she fought back. 'Yes, we have, but she is more an old retainer than any sort of servant. I can't remember a time when she wasn't there, and what would she do and where would she live if she left?'

'How the other half live, eh?'

Lucy felt sorry for Vera, who couldn't seem to see that Jenny was just winding her up, and so she said, 'Put a sock in it, Jen. We agreed we're not responsible for our parents or how they live, so stop giving Vera a hard time over it.'

Jenny felt bad when she saw how red Vera was. She didn't seem to have the same sense of humour as the others and took things to heart more and so she was easy to torment, but that wasn't her fault either, and so she said, 'Sorry, Vera. I was only teasing you. No hard feelings?'

'Course not.'

'Tell you what,' Babs said. 'If I had to get my rations every week and try and live on them I would be going mad. Last time I was home my dad said we just might end up beating Hitler but it will do us no good if this is a long war because by the end of it we will all be bored to death.'

'My father seems unable to understand that he can't have bacon and egg for breakfast every morning like he used to,' Vera said. 'Or have a cup of tea when he likes. He complains far more than my mother.'

'Yeah. Women cope better, don't they?' Jenny said. 'My mum listens to the *Kitchen Front* on the wireless after the eight o'clock news and it gives out recipes that she tries out on my dad.'

'Like what?'

'Well, Vegetable and Oatmeal Goulash was one. No meat in that at all, just meat essence.'

'Was it nice?'

Jenny smiled as she shook her head. 'Dad said it was bloody awful, but he didn't blame Mum because she was doing her best; so then she tried sardine fritters, and then something called Poor Man's Goose that's never even had a whiff of a goose. It's made with liver, and not much of that. But whatever Mum puts in front of my dad he eats because he knows there is nothing else. And,' she added 'it's set to get worse in the New Year, so Mum says.'

'What's left to ration?' Babs said. 'They already

ration butter and sugar and bacon and meat.'

'Yeah,' Jenny said. 'And don't forget margarine, lard, cheese and tea, and I would say that you need most of those to make a meal and drink afterwards.'

'It must be a headache for mothers with hungry children to feed,' Lucy said. 'Like Babs said, at least we are well fed here.'

'Yeah,' said Vera. 'Even if they do run it all off us.'

'Well, there is that,' Lucy said.

And then Jenny said, 'Tell you something, though. I have done all the running I intend to do for now and I am going to try and get my head down for a few hours.'

No one disagreed with her for they were all worn out.

After that the raids went on night after night, some were heavy, leaving many dead or injured and much destruction in their wake. The General Hospital was always able to cope, in part because of the night staff staying over to help in the morning. They couldn't not, for, as Lucy said, how could they just walk out and leave the day shift tending the injured still coming in, or those admitted through the night, and still cope with regular patients? So they would help with breakfast and bringing bedpans or taking patients to the bathroom as necessary.

The night of 24 October, the city was pounded mercilessly. The staff took everyone they could down to the basement, but not long after the raid began they'd heard the ambulances bringing the injured in. Nurses then left the relative safety of the basement to work alongside the doctors through the teeth of the raid to help in any way they could. Sometimes it just wasn't enough, and that was upsetting for all of them. Lucy wept bitterly when a little girl with the sweetest smile died in her arms before the doctor had even had a chance to look at her.

Then there was the baby boy who was un-injured though he had been buried in the ruins of his house, and when he was found he was still suckling at the breast of his dead mother. And the man battered and bruised, with badly burnt hands and haunted eyes, who claimed he had killed his wife and three children.

Lucy carried on dressing his hand as she said gently, 'I am so sorry for your loss and I can only imagine what it is like for you. But it wouldn't have been your fault.'

'Ah, but it would, do you see,' the man said, his voice shaky with emotion. 'The raid had begun when I arrived home from work and found my wife and children hiding under the stairs. I insisted that they come out of there and we all went to a solid sandbagged brick-built shelter because I said it would be safer.' The eyes he turned to Lucy were awash with unshed tears. 'You would think it would be safer. It's what they tell you, isn't it?'

Lucy agreed that it was, but wasn't sure if the man heard her or not, for he was talking again. 'We'd been in there about two hours when I was asked to help get people out of this building before they were roasted alive because it was blazing like crazy. That's how I got my hands so burnt. It took a long time because the bomb and then the fire had made the place so unstable. It was liable to cave in any minute, and so it was a few hours later before the last person was out, the injured packed off to hospital and the all-clear was sounded. As I was turning the corner where the shelter was I saw nothing, just this gigantic mound of rubbish. My wife and three kiddies who never had done any harm to anyone, and every other person in that shelter too, had been blown into a million pieces.'

The tears came then, a great outpouring of grief, and Lucy felt prickling behind her own eyes at the man's distress. 'It must have been terrible for you,' she said, putting her hand on his arm, 'but you mustn't blame yourself.'

'Oh, yes, I must,' the man said, his voice husky. He wiped the tear trails from his cheeks with his bandaged hand. 'The house still stands. I went to check. If I had left them under the stairs they would still be alive, and I can't live with that.' He got to his feet, and though Lucy called after him he didn't stop. In seconds he was lost among the people milling around waiting for treatment.

Lucy couldn't go after him, there were so many others needing attention. Nearly everyone had a tale of loss, of tragedy, and yet she couldn't get the man's face out of her mind. His eyes had been full of absolute despair.

Much, much later, Lucy and Jenny trudged up to their room to try to grab at least a few hours' sleep before they would begin the night shift. Lucy said she felt as if she had been through an emotional wringer.

Jenny sighed. 'Me, too. When you hear what they have gone through, it breaks my heart.'

Lucy nodded. 'Did that to me too at first,' she said, 'but now I just feel angry, really blisteringly angry. I mean, they have done nothing to deserve this.'

'One of the ambulance drivers was telling me that a whole corner of New Street has been knocked out and there are dirty great craters in the middle of the road,' Jenny said. 'He told me buckled tramlines are all over the place, and Marshall and Snelgrove's just one gigantic mountain of rubbish with iron girders sticking through it and the pavements covered with glass.'

'That was one of the posh shops Clara took Clodagh and me to see when we first came over to England,' Lucy said. 'Not that I could ever have bought anything there – it was far too pricey for me – but it was nice to see it, and now it is gone the same as C & A.'

'And the Empire on Broad Street,' Jenny said in a whisper, because the room was in darkness. When they turned on the light they saw the other two were in bed. The light woke Babs.

'Turn the light off, can't you?' she said.

'Not likely,' Jenny said. 'We have got to see to get undressed.'

As Lucy settled herself into bed, she thought of the city she had chosen to live in, and the destruction wreaked on it, and felt totally depressed. Sleep refused to come, despite her exhaustion, as she relived the hours on the ward after the raid. Those already dead or dying, the mutilated or seriously injured – particularly distressing if it was a child – the images went round and round in her head and drove away the sleep she desperately needed before she had to report for night duty.

Lucy was still awake when the sirens went off, and it was the same the following night. By this time, Lewis's department store, seeing the dilemma of the General Hospital, had cleaned out their basement for use as overspill and some medical teams had already been assigned there. Matron noted Lucy's grey face and the blue smudges beneath her tired eyes, but had no option except to ask her if she would work with the medical teams in Lewis's for an hour or two as the situation there was desperate. They had been overwhelmed by the number of casualties brought in that night, the hospital itself was bursting at the seams, and she couldn't spare any of the day staff.

Lucy felt a little like a zombie but she knew she couldn't refuse, and Jenny elected to go too. As they crossed the town, wearing their regulation steel helmets, Jenny said two sets of hands were better than one, and if she helped they might get away and back to bed quicker. Lucy was glad of her company.

There was a terrific smell of burning and the sky was glowing orange from the many fires still blazing. To the black sooty smell of the swirling smoke was added the stink of cordite and a whiff of gas. However, all this was wiped from Lucy's mind when she stood at the top of the wide stairwell leading to Lewis's basement. The steps were covered with blood-soaked clothing and stretchers covered the whole of the basement floor. Only the faces were visible, and all were a reddy-brown colour from the brick dust. A feeling of deep pity stole over Lucy, and when her eyes met Jenny's she saw she felt the same.

In the end they could do little but sponge the dirt from hands and faces, make the injured comfortable, give them water and so on, while they waited for the doctor to examine them, but she guessed medical attention would be minimal, and for a great many it was far too late to help them.

And it was while Lucy was going down a row with a fresh warm bowl of soapy water that she suddenly came to a dead stop. The young woman she saw was covered in dust, even her hair, and her eyes were closed, but the resemblance...? 'Clodagh?' Lucy said hesitantly, and the young woman's eyes fluttered open. 'Lucy?'

Lucy had the desire to lay her head on her friend's chest and weep, but she knew that would never do. 'I'm so sorry to see you like this,' she said. 'Is Hazel here too?'

She saw even the slight shake of her head that Clodagh made hurt her as she ground out, 'Hazel's dead!'

Lucy recoiled in shock.

Clodagh continued, 'They are all dead: Hazel's sister, Betty, and her parents, and even her grandparents, who had been living there since they were bombed out last month.'

Lucy felt her eyes fill with tears but she refused to let them fall and resolutely swallowed the lump in her throat as Clodagh said, 'We were under the stairs. When the bomb hit I was thrown across the room. The rest of the house collapsed on them.'

Lucy was too choked to speak as she gently washed Clodagh's face.

Clodagh sighed. 'That's good,' she said. 'The dust went everywhere, even into my eyes. They still sting.'

Lucy heard the slur in Clodagh's voice and she said, 'Stay awake, Clodagh. The doctor will be here soon.' But it was as if her eyelids were too heavy for Clodagh to keep open any longer.

'Clodagh!' Lucy cried in anguish.

Suddenly another nurse was by Lucy's side. 'What is it?' she asked.

'S-she... Clodagh is a good friend of mine,' Lucy said, and the nurse didn't speak as she lifted Clodagh's hand and felt for her pulse.

She looked at Lucy with great sympathy as she let Clodagh's hand fall, and Lucy cried, 'No! No! She can't be dead! She was talking to me just a moment ago.'

However, she knew that was how it was sometimes. She was no stranger to death, but didn't want to accept it for her friend – and she so young – and she sobbed uncontrollably. The nurse alerted Jenny and told her to take Lucy back to the General and for them both to try to get some sleep. Lucy allowed herself to be led away, tears still streaming from her eyes, and Jenny helped her as if she was a child.

She didn't expect to sleep. Memories of Clodagh flooded into her mind and she was filled with immeasurable sadness. And yet extreme exhaustion claimed her and when her head touched the pillow she fell almost immediately into a deep slumber.

The next day they heard of the extent of the bombing that had destroyed the city centre, wrecking department stores, smaller shops, office blocks and factories. Residential areas had also been flattened, and hundreds of fires burnt in and around the city centre. But it was the injured Lucy felt sorry for. She found it very hard to get over Clodagh's death and though she knew Clodagh's parents would probably have been informed by the authorities she wrote to them, describing her as a very good friend. She also wrote to her mother and Gwen, and to Clara and Ada, telling them what had happened. She shed further tears when she remembered the friendship they shared in Letterkenny and then in Birmingham, and she was sorry that circumstances had forced them apart.

Her roommates thought that was part and parcel of growing up. 'Your lives took different paths, that's all,' Babs said. 'Later, you could have married and moved to different parts of the country. I think that from what you say, Clodagh still thought of you as her good friend and so wasn't it lovely for her that she was with you at the end.'

'I never thought of that.'

'Well, I think death's a lonely path to tread,' Babs said. 'You say she was conscious to the end and so how comforting to know someone you care about is right by your side when you start on that journey.'

Babs' words made Lucy feel better then but, a few days later, Clodagh's sorrowful parents attended her sad little funeral. Lucy was glad to see Clara and Cook had come because it helped her cope when Clodagh's parents spoke so kindly to her, saying they had heard all about her from Clodagh, and she was able to shake them by the hand and said Clodagh had been a great girl altogether. It was when they said it eased their pain to think she was with her at the end that Lucy broke down completely and cried in Clara's arms.

But life, especially in a hospital, has to go on, and everyone was glad that the intensive bombing had eased a little. As November began, there were only light skirmishes. However, halfway through the month, the news on the wireless was of a raid on Coventry by the Luftwaffe that was so heavy that within a square mile eighty per cent of buildings had been destroyed and well over five hundred people killed. Coventry, like Birmingham, had suffered many raids, but everyone was stunned by the savagery of that one, dubbed by the *Birmingham Gazette* 'our Guernica'. It was said that a new word had entered the German language and that was *Koventrieren* or Coventration, which meant a razing to the ground of a place.

Birmingham waited, aware that what had been done to Coventry could quite easily be done to them because they made so much for the war effort. Five days after Coventry's ordeal Birmingham's began. At quarter-past seven the first planes dropped flares and incendiaries to light up their targets. Even in the hospital basement the roar of the planes was louder than anything they had heard before, the bombs falling in clusters so that it was hard to distinguish between them. Some of the explosions were so close and loud that the tremors were felt in the basement. Even Lucy wondered if the basement would hold if the hospital was hit, or if this place they thought was safe would turn out to be their tomb.

Lucy knew that she could not show her own fear in any way, for many of the patients were terrified, some giving little yelps of fright, others keening in a long low moan and others praying, their lips moving constantly. She was even slightly relieved to be called out of the basement because she knew the only way to keep a cap on her fear was to keep busy.

Nothing that she had experienced before, though, could have prepared her for what she saw in the hospital that day. Despite the overspill at Lewis's, people were still coming in, though the hospital was chock-a-block and the injured lay on stretchers or sat on chairs waiting attention, and others milled about aimlessly. Nearly everyone there was covered in a film of brick dust, either grey or brown, that was ingrained in their hair and their faces where it gilded their eyebrows and eyelashes and rendered eyes red-rimmed and bloodshot. The air stank too, the smell of the brick dust, smoke and cordite mixing with the stink of vomit, blood, charred flesh and intense fear.

The noise too was almost deafening, some weeping with despairing sobs that tore at Lucy's heart, others shouting and screaming. The nurses didn't even try to keep any sort of order, but moved amongst them, trying to soothe and reassure. A good few patients died before they even had the offer of help, and then the nurses would cover their eyes and move on.

Doctors and nurses who should have finished their shifts stayed on, and others came in regardless of shift. They all worked as hard as possible but there were so many to see to, and more arriving all the time. Lucy was assigned to help one of the doctors and she was glad to be doing something. She stood to one side as he examined one after another. The courage and stoicism portrayed by many of the people, especially the children, could have reduced her to tears, but there was no time for that. She knew that though the doctor tried his best, and so did she, if the lacerations were deep enough, the burns intensive enough, or there were internal injuries as well, their chances of survival were remote.

She thought as the all-clear went off at half-past four that she had dealt with more deaths than she had done in all her years on the wards, and many of those had not been any sort of peaceful passing, but often people in the throes of agony or despair. The injured kept coming, and others uninjured: traumatised, wailing children needing their mothers, distraught women frantically searching for their children, elderly parents or any other missing family members. Most couldn't go home for they had no home nor any clothes other than those tattered and torn that they had on, and no idea what to do.

On Thursday night, Lucy was just finishing her

tea when the sirens sounded, and though there was a collective groan, in the canteen everyone sprang into action. To start with, it was a repeat of Tuesday's air raid, but there were more land mines dropped and a large number of low-level attacks, which caused more death and desolation until six hundred fires were blazing.

The hospital was soon bursting at the seams. Ansells Brewery at Aston Cross opened up their cellars to try to ease the crisis, and some doctors and nurses were drafted there to help. Lucy stayed at the General, where the scale of the human tragedy almost overwhelmed her. She worked alongside many others through the raid, doing all she could for the distressed and injured. She tended a fireman who had been caught by the bomb blast in Bristol Road that had fractured three trunk water mains. The city was then without water, and the many fires had to be left to burn.

The following day fires were still blazing. Most people knew that if there was another raid that night, Birmingham would burn to the ground. Thankfully, there was not another raid for many days. Then, on 3 December, fifty bombers attacked the city. There was a lull after that, and Lucy was not the only one to hope that the massive raids were over. However, on 11 December, two hundred bombers attacked the city for thirteen hours. Later, when Lucy read in the paper that two hundred and fifty people had been killed and two hundred and forty-five were gravely injured, she knew a great many of those had arrived at the General and she had been so busy dealing with them that the unprecedented visit from King George passed her by completely. Lucy looked at the pictures in the paper and said, 'It's like when Clementine Churchill came. They can't do anything.'

'They raise morale,' Babs said. 'And you can't deny it does. Look at them lining the roads and cheering.'

'Well, if it does that for them it's got to be a good thing,' Lucy said. 'Because many of those poor souls have lost everything. It's tragic.'

'Yeah, 1940 has been an awful year,' Vera said.

'Well, it is nearly the end of it,' Lucy said. 'But I don't know that 1941 will be any better.'

TWENTY-EIGHT

It really did seem as if 1941 might be a bit quieter than 1940 to start with because in the first three months of the year there were only three raids spread a month apart. They were light, and as bombs fell in Handsworth, Selly Oak and South Yardley they were too far away for anyone at the General to worry about.

Lucy, now back on the day shift, was glad of the respite, for they had their prelims coming up the Wednesday before Easter. They had been going to sit these exams early in the New Year but with the concentrated bombing and the long hours all the student nurses had had to put in because of the raids, Matron had made the unprecedented step of postponing them.

Lucy was fairly certain that she would pass, for, after all her experience dealing with victims of the bombing, her confidence had improved enormously. They'd all had to do procedures that student nurses wouldn't normally be expected to do at that stage in their career. Often there had been no one around to show them how to do something and they had had to rely on gut instinct. It had sometimes been a scary experience and often very sad, dealing with the badly injured victims, but it had all added to her experience.

Chris was sending her regular letters and each one stressed how much he missed her. He urged her to take care, for she was precious to him. The letters, even though they were sometimes brief, always gave Lucy a warm glow inside. She did miss Chris most dreadfully, but she didn't say anything because it did no good, and anyway, she wasn't the only one going through such separation.

All the girls had a week off just before the prelim exams. As Lucy couldn't go home she took up Gwen's invitation to spend the time at her house. She was looking forward to it because she loved Gwen anyway, and also because she knew that she could talk about Chris to her heart's content there.

Gwen loved reminiscing about her son, and she also knew that Lucy had gone through the mill with the terrifying raids. She wanted to give her a complete rest so she took a week off from WVS, which was a little easier to do with the Luftwaffe giving them a bit of a break. The weather was kind to them and so she took Lucy on jaunts out on the bus to pretty little villages where it appeared the war had never happened, and, nearer to home, to the areas the public could still go to in Sutton Park

She sympathised with Lucy about Clodagh's death. Lucy admitted how hard she had found it. 'It seemed so tragic,' she said. 'Mind you, I feel that about all the deaths I've had to deal with, but when it's someone you know, a friend... Oh, I found that very difficult.'

'It must have been, my dear,' Gwen said. 'But you will always have a part of your friend with you in the memories you shared. No one can ever take those from you.'

Lucy had never thought of it that way before and she felt a little easier in her mind. Each day she felt more of the tensions, which she hadn't even been aware she was carrying, begin to seep out of her. But much as Lucy loved her days out she also enjoyed sitting with Gwen in the evenings before the fire with the meal over and all the jobs done, and encouraging her to talk about Chris.

Gwen would tell her what he had been like as a child growing up, the funny things he had said and done, the places he liked to go to, the games he enjoyed and his favourite food. Lucy lapped it up. She was anxious to know everything there was to know about the man who would be sharing her life when this war came to an end, and Gwen made him come alive for her.

'He is a lucky man indeed,' she said to Lucy

494

one evening, 'to have the absolute love of two women.'

'Oh, no, I think I am the lucky one,' Lucy said, and she meant it. He was a wonderful man, and even in his letters he managed to wrap her in his love.

Another time, Gwen said, 'If I have any regrets it is that Chris's father didn't live to see him make it as a doctor. He was always so proud of him and he would have loved you, my dear.'

'My father would have been astounded to see me too,' Lucy said, knowing that her father would have been stunned enough and very proud at her becoming a nurse, let alone engaged to a doctor. In Ireland, things like that didn't happen to people like the Cassidys. You were set in the life you were born into, though it couldn't be the same in America because her mother had expressed no surprise, only delight when Lucy had written to tell her of her engagement. 'But if my father had lived,' she went on, 'my future would probably have been very different. I doubt I would have left Ireland and probably be married to some burly farmer with three or four weans hanging on to my skirts.'

'And would you have liked that?'

'No,' Lucy said. 'But there ... I don't know ... it's what you do over there. It's what most girls aspire to. But I like being a nurse, doing something for myself, though I would love children one day.'

'So if your father hadn't died, the chances are you would never even have met Chris?'

'Oh, no, I probably wouldn't have,' Lucy said.

'Isn't that a dreadful thought? But I didn't want my father to die. I loved him dearly and missed him for ages.'

'Oh, Lucy, I don't doubt that for a minute,' Gwen said. 'I have heard you talk of your father before with love in your voice, but when he died you did what you had to do and that has led you here.'

'Yes,' Lucy said. 'Life's funny, isn't it?'

'It can be,' Gwen said, 'but it's very precious and not something to be squandered because you only have one go at it.'

'And that is why you should grasp every opportunity and make the most of every day,' Lucy agreed.

Lucy returned to the hospital feeling more rested and optimistic about the future than she had felt in a long while, even about the prelims that her roommates seemed to be sweating over.

'You'll be fine,' she said to Vera, who she found was still awake and frantically reading a textbook a long time after the others had gone to sleep. 'Honestly, a good night's sleep will do you more good than any last-minute cramming.'

'Oh, it's all right for you,' Vera said. 'You have an understanding mother, and even if she wasn't totally understanding she lives on another continent. What did you do on your week off?'

Lucy recounted some of the things and Vera said wistfully, 'That sounds lovely.'

'It was,' Lucy maintained. 'So what did you do?'

'I worked.'

'Worked for your exams, you mean?' Vera gave a brief nod and Lucy went on, 'All of the time?'

'More or less,' Vera said. 'Even my father told me to do my best for my mother's sake. And my mother said that if I had chosen nursing instead of going on to train as a doctor – which incidentally she calls a second-rate career – the very least I can do to try to repay the money spent on my private education is to get top marks. She won't accept that I'm not very bright. She just says I don't try.'

She looked at Lucy with bright glittery eyes and went on, 'Dad says that's half the trouble, because my mother *is* clever, and in her day and in her family that was frowned on. Clever girls weren't good in the marriage stakes so there was no secondary education for them, never mind university. Instead, she was taught accomplishments: how to embroider and sketch, sing and play moderately well on the piano. And then she was told to go and hook herself a nice rich husband and not to bother her pretty little head about mathematics, science or politics, the three things she seemed to be most passionate about. She was advised to leave that to the men.'

'But none of that is your fault,' Lucy said. 'Your mother is trying to live her life through you, but you are not her so you mustn't let her.'

'Oh, you don't know her,' Vera said. 'She is very forceful.'

'Only with you,' Lucy said. 'If she was really that forceful she would have fought for what she believed in at the time, not bring resentment into the marriage she probably didn't want and load it all on her daughter.'

Vera looked at Lucy with admiration. 'Do you know, Lucy, I have never seen it that way before.'

'That's because you were too close to it,' Lucy said. 'And brought up in that way without even a brother or sister to knock the corners off you. But you are not your mother. You have to live your own life and follow your own dream, and it is about time you told her so. Write it all down if you really can't face her. And anyway, if she is so bright, why isn't she offering her services somewhere now and doing something for the war effort?'

'Oh, she always prided herself that she never needed to go out to work.'

'Then she is very lucky, but that doesn't mean that she can sit on her backside and let the rest of us graft now we are at war. And if she had more to do with her time, just maybe she wouldn't be quite so concerned with you.'

Lucy saw that she had got through to Vera, who until then had just accepted that's how things were and questioned none of it.

'And that's another thing, while we're about it,' Lucy said. 'Stop saying you're not bright. All right, so you are not Brain of Britain, but who is? You are at least as bright as the rest of the nurses here and your marks reflect that.' Then she added, 'You can't be top of the class every time, you know. It's only fair to give other people a chance. Now put that bloody book away and go to sleep. I need my beauty sleep even if you don't.'

Vera obediently turned the light off but, when Lucy's even breathing indicated that she was asleep, she withdrew a writing pad from the top drawer of the cabinet beside her bed and, by the light from her torch, wrote a letter to her mother, knowing that she had to write it while she was still fired up with Lucy's enthusiasm and before her confidence ebbed away.

None of the girls found the prelims that hard. Afterwards, they talked about the exam in their room together and then fell to discussing the raids. 'There were so many with really serious conditions and you had no time to think what to do,' Jenny said.

There was a murmur of agreement and Babs said, 'We can only do our best and remember that we're not flipping robots.'

'Fat lot of good we would be if we didn't care,' Vera said. 'And some get to you more than others. I'm not talking here about seeing friends in such a dreadful condition that you can't help them, like you did, Lucy – I can barely imagine how really distressing that must have been – I mean, when I see people who aren't going to make it, especially the young or very old, I can get upset. Personally, I would be more worried if a person didn't react in that way.'

'And I would,' Jenny said. 'Anyway, apart from the odd skirmish here and there, those raids seem to be a thing of the past. We can go back to standard nursing again, and the only blot on our personal horizon will be Matron.'

The girls laughed together and Lucy gave Jenny a push. 'What planet are you from, Miss Jennifer Black?' she exclaimed. 'Because it certainly isn't the same as mine. The war is still going on; Hitler might have any number of surprises in store for us yet. Doesn't do to get complacent.'

Lucy's words were prophetic, for the girls were all in their room the following night when the sirens went off at about half-past nine. When the sound died down, Lucy could tell by the rumble in the sky that there were a great many planes approaching and she felt her stomach lurch. Her mouth was suddenly very dry, yet she said with determination, 'I'm not bothering going into the basement. We will only be brought out again. This is another biggy and it will be all hands on deck, if you ask me.'

'I agree,' Jenny said, and the other two said the same.

'We'd still better see if anyone needs a hand getting the patients down to the basement first,' Babs suggested.

They were in the throes of doing this, the crump and crash of explosions in the distance, when they were approached by a staff nurse from Women's Surgical who asked if one of them would volunteer to sit with the bedridden as two of the probationers had been taken to the sickbay. As she didn't intend to take shelter anyway, Vera readily offered to do this and the girls parted.

The onslaught was directly over them: the roar and drone of many planes, the clatter of incendiaries hurtling down, closely followed by the scream of descending bombs and the boom of explosions, one after another with no space between them. Soon the ambulancemen were carrying in the wounded and describing the carnage.

'The Midlands Arcade is just a wall of flames from High Street to New Street,' one said. 'The road is ablaze too: a molten stream of blazing tar running down towards New Street Station. Dunno what they're going to do about it. Have to blow summat up, like, to make a firebreak.'

'The oldest pub in the city, the Swan, has gone too,' another said sadly. 'And the Prince of Wales Theatre has been burnt out.'

Lucy was sorry about the destruction of old buildings, but patients were coming in with the most horrific injuries and to her they were far more important.

Suddenly there was an enormous crash, a whooshing sound, and Lucy was flung to the floor. For a split second it was as if all the air had been sucked from the room, and the lights flickered and went out. People began to weep and scream hysterically.

Lucy was just as frightened as all the rest. She knew a bomb had landed very close and the hospital had been caught in the blast. She stretched out her limbs one by one, gratified to see she had no obvious injury, though her head ached quite badly. When she ran her fingers along gently, she felt the jagged cut to the right-hand side of her head and blood that had seeped into her hair. She sat up gingerly, but it was when the dim emergency lighting came on that she discovered the scale of the tragedy. An entire corner of the hospital was just missing. 'Oh, my God!' she breathed incredulously. 'Oh, my God!'

Ignoring the wailing around her, she tried to stand, to find out exactly what had happened.

However, as she got to her feet, the room listed and tipped, and she knew she was going to fall and could do nothing to stop it. Before she hit the floor she felt herself enveloped in a cloak of blackness.

The next thing Lucy remembered was waking up in a comfortable white bed. It was silent so that meant the raid was over. She gave an involuntary sigh of relief and let the memories seep into her brain slowly. As she forced her heavy eyelids open she saw Jenny sitting beside her in a chair.

Jenny noticed the slight movement Lucy made. 'How are you feeling?'

Lucy gave a slight shrug. 'All right, I suppose. Where am I?'

'The infirmary,' Jenny said. 'They stitched your head. Don't you remember?'

Lucy lifted her hand and felt the bandage encircling her head. 'Nothing much after the bomb. The hospital was hit, I remember that. Was there much damage?'

Jenny nodded. 'But it's worse than damage to bricks and mortar. 'It's ... it's ... oh, God, Lucy ... Vera is dead.'

'Dead?' Lucy echoed incredulously, and it felt like a lead weight had landed in her stomach. Vera ... dead! It didn't seem possible.

'They all copped it,' Jenny said. 'Well, the people that end, anyway: a couple of doctors and nurses, including Vera, and four bed-bound patients.'

'Oh, God!'

'Awful, isn't it?' Jenny said. 'Me and Babs, well, we haven't really come to terms with it, but

502

Matron said it would be a real shock to you, and she gave me and Babs leave to sit with you till you woke up. We've taken it in turns.'

'I just can't believe it,' Lucy said. 'And yet why should I be so surprised? Every raid delivers death, and bombs do not discriminate. But poor, poor Vera. How perfectly awful.'

'And you didn't get away scot-free either,' Jenny said. 'That was a really nasty crack on the head you had.'

'Hardly in the same league, though,' Lucy replied. 'What's a crack on the head balanced against a life?'

'Ah, yes, you're right,' Jenny agreed. 'And there were so many killed and badly injured last night. It was carnage, just like the raid in the autumn of last year.'

'Hope this isn't the start of another blitz then.'

'And me. But if it is there is little we can do about it.'

Lucy suffered no ill effects from her head injury. Two days later she had the bandage removed and insisted that she was fit for work again. She found her roommates in something of a dilemma. As her father, Mr Winstanley, had asked, they had packed all Vera's things in the suitcase she had brought, and in doing so had found a letter she had written. She'd put it into an envelope addressed to her parents but without a stamp on and not sealed.

'We read it,' Babs said, 'because it can sometimes be really upsetting to receive a letter after a person dies.'

'So what did it say?'

'You'd better read it for yourself,' Babs said.

So Lucy read a letter detailing almost everything she had talked about with Vera the night before their prelims. She told her mother straight that she was her own person and it was her life and that she should not be demanding such a large piece of it. She had even suggested that her mother should take up some form of war work, and went on to say that she felt strongly that everyone should do their bit.

'I never knew Vera felt like that, did you?' Babs said.

'The night before our prelims, when I came up to go to bed, you and Jenny were bringing the pigs home,' Lucy said. 'And Vera had open a textbook, trying to cram in some last-minute revision. She told me that her mother had had her working all through her week off.'

'Why?'

'Well, it all came out that her mother, despite being very intelligent and wanting to be a doctor, was denied the chance to go to university because she was a woman. She wanted Vera to live that life for her. So I told Vera that it wasn't her fault that her mother couldn't fulfil her ambitions, that she wasn't her mother and she should stand up to her more.'

'Seems she took what you said to heart.'

Lucy nodded. 'Seems so. She must have written it that night because she had little time after that, but she never posted it.'

'Maybe she never intended sending it?' Babs said.

'Maybe,' Lucy conceded. 'But then why go to the trouble of putting it in an envelope with the address on the front? And whether she intended sending it or not, is there any point in even letting her parents see it when she's dead?'

'You see the problem, Luce?' Jenny said.

'I do certainly. But I don't feel right getting rid of it.'

'Nor did we,' Babs said.

'Well, it is her mother's attitude that she is complaining about,' Lucy said. 'And with reason, I think, so I suggest we seal the letter and give it to her father – she got on better with him – and whether he lets her mother see it or not is up to him. There will probably be an opportunity to hand it to him at the funeral.'

'We are not invited to the funeral,' Jenny said. 'Mrs Winstanley phoned Matron and was quite clear, she said. Nor does she want any commemorative service held for her here, and she added that she had never wanted Vera to go into nursing but Vera, aided by her father, had defied her.'

'She sounds a very objectionable woman,' Lucy said. 'I didn't like the sound of her when Vera was telling me about her. She had Vera convinced she was stupid. You must have heard her say that.'

The other two nodded, and Jenny added, 'Her marks don't reflect that. I wish I'd done half as well.'

'Me, too,' said Babs.

'Well,' said Lucy, 'I think Vera's parents, particularly her horrid mother, need to know just how bright she was. If I have a word with Matron, I'm sure she would agree. And if we're not to go to the funeral of someone we have shared a room with for going on for two years then I'm going to write about her.'

'What, like a sort of eulogy?'

'Exactly like that.'

'Good idea,' Jenny said. 'I will do the same.'

'And so will I,' Babs said. 'I hate the thought of her going from here and disappearing without trace because we are not allowed to commemorate her life. Well, at least we can let her parents know of the great girl we thought her.'

Mr Winstanley, who came alone to fetch his daughter's things, was very tall and thin, and quite haughty-looking. He seemed a very cold sort of person, or at least very emotionless about his young daughter's death. Lucy couldn't help feeling sorry for Vera and very glad they had written the letters.

'These are really to say how sorry we are that this terrible thing has happened,' Jenny said.

'Yes,' said Babs, 'and to remind ourselves, not that we will ever forget, what a wonderful girl Vera was. She would have made a superb nurse and was a terrific friend.'

'I endorse that,' Lucy said. 'We will all miss her so very much.'

'Thank you,' Mr Winstanley said flatly. 'Vera's death is a great loss to us, a very great loss, and it's nice to know of the good kind friends she had.'

When the man was packed and ready to go, Lucy said, 'There are just a couple more things.

The first is that we found a letter Vera had written to you but hadn't had time to send,' and she passed the letter to him.

'Oh,' he said. 'She used to write on Sundays.'

'Maybe she wrote an extra letter because of the prelim exams,' Lucy said. 'She was very worried about them. For some reason she thought she wasn't very intelligent.' She fixed Mr Winstanley with a steely glare in her eyes as she said, 'A lot of bunkum, of course, as you will see from her results.'

'Results?'

'Yes,' Lucy said. 'Matron said you might like the certificate and so she has included her certificate in with a letter from the hospital expressing condolences to both you and your wife, signed by her and by a great many more in the hospital because Vera was well liked and respected.'

'And you say our Vera did all right in this exam?'

'Oh, much better than all right, Mr Winstanley,' Lucy said. 'Vera achieved ninety-seven per cent and she was second in the year.' She had the satisfaction of seeing Mr Winstanley's mouth drop agape with astonishment.

Vera's mother might not have wanted her nursing friends to go to her daughter's funeral but she was not the only one who had died that Good Friday, and Lucy, Jenny and Babs went to many other forlorn funerals with sorrow-laden relatives in the sad days that followed. Lucy could go to none of the services, however, because she was a Catholic. None of the other girls could understand what difference it made, and Lucy had to admit neither did she.

'Why don't you ask the priest as St Chad's, the one you said was so approachable?' Babs suggested.

'I will,' Lucy said, 'because I want to know why, myself, but the Church was quite damaged in the last raid and they are a little distracted so I'll wait a few days – as long as things are still quiet.'

'Things have been quiet before, and then wallop,' Jenny said.

'I know, but Hitler has Russia in his sights.'

'Well, he has had other countries in his sights before and still attacked us,' Babs pointed out.

'I know, but this is Russia,' Lucy said. 'I don't think it has ever been conquered. I think the man has bitten off more than he can chew.'

'I hope he has,' Jenny said. 'And I hope it bloody well chokes him.'

Lucy didn't forget the rule that forbade her from attending the funerals of her colleagues and patients, and forced her to skulk around in the cemeteries. She asked Father Donahue about it after Mass one Sunday a fortnight or so later and was surprised at his answer.

'It's to do with their beliefs and ours, Lucy. Attending such a service in a non-Catholic church is affirming things we know not to be true. Such a service is seen as heretical and to take Communion in such a church compounds the sin.'

Lucy thought that none of her many non-Catholic friends would take kindly to being called heretics and said, 'But, Father, we worship the same God.'

'Yes, but in different ways and with different beliefs.'

'So what reason did he give?' Jenny asked on Lucy's return.

'Oh, some mumbo jumbo I could hardly understand,' Lucy said. 'Something about believing different things and worshipping in different ways. I can't see any problem myself, for, as I told him, we all worship the same God.'

'I think it's all eyewash anyway,' Jenny said. 'We are praying that we beat the Germans and they are sitting in their churches praying to beat us. If I was God, I would get really confused.'

'Good job you're not then,' said Babs.

'Fine chance of it, anyway,' Lucy said. 'For if ever the position became vacant you wouldn't even make the short list.'

'Good,' Jenny said. 'I want nothing to do with any of it. I will just battle away on my own without any appeals to a higher authority.'

'And you could do worse,' Lucy said.

The sporadic small raids ceased completely, though of course the Birmingham people weren't aware of that. They'd had lulls before. Eventually, though, they began to believe that the bombing raids were over. People were still living in temporary accommodation – church halls, school halls or even warehouses – and they'd had to bully the city to provide even that much.

Food was another problem, and although the WVS did their best they could only do so much. Back in December, destitute people, supported by the Lord Mayor, the Labour Party and the Cooperative Society, had begun demanding mobile canteens, clothes, blankets and specific organisation to deal with the homeless, so now at least the homeless could buy soup and a chunk of bread for three pence, and, between the hours of twelve and two, a two-course meal could be bought for eight pence.

'But that is only the tip of the iceberg,' Lucy said. 'I mean, people who have lost everything need more than a bowl of soup.'

'Yes,' Jenny said, 'but it takes time, doesn't it?'

'There are so many homeless, it will take years for them all to be dealt with adequately.'

It was a depressing thought, yet life went on and people learnt to cope with deprivation. Often through the most trying conditions, children went to school and mothers and fathers went to work.

To add to people's problems, clothes were now rationed based on a points system. Everybody had sixty points for the year, which was not a lot when a coat was 14 points, a dress 7 to 11, according to the material used, a cardigan or jumper 5, and for a pair of stockings 2 points. Every article of clothing, or even other textiles like bedding, had to be exchanged for the relevant points as well as the money.

Although they acknowledged that it must be very hard for families, the girls took clothes rationing on as a challenge. They had already been pooling their clothes to ring the changes, and as the government urged everyone to 'Make Do and Mend', and to be a squander bug was regarded as the worst thing in the world, the girls had become very adept with a needle. It was heartening to see how a new look could be achieved with the addition of a collar, or false hem, or lace around the sleeves of a jaded blouse, or the odd bow here or a set of beads there.

The point was they had to have things to make do and mend with. Gwen had been useful there because of the jumble sales run by the WVS. As soon as the raids ceased and the hospital was more or less running as it had been, Lucy saw Gwen at least once a month, when she hadn't had to be back at the hospital till noon the following day, staying the night with her, and sometimes seeing her too on the alternate Sunday when she was off duty from 2 p.m. Gwen would often have some old and dated little gem waiting for her that they could adapt to wear, or take apart to revamp. Gwen was glad to help, for she knew how hard the nurses worked and what little free time they had, and she felt gratified that Lucy used so much of it to spend with her.

As Christmas approached there was even less in the shops to buy to put in a child's stocking and little in the way of festive food either. In the hospital, wards were just beginning to be decorated. Garlands and streamers and papers lanterns were brought out of storage, and the Christmas trees installed, ready to be festooned with tinsel and shining glass baubles, and with a star on the very top. In the children's ward, nearer to Christmas Day, tantalising parcels would surround their tree. Most of these would be gifts from America, but some were from local well-wishers who wanted to make Christmas in hospital as pleasant as possible for children who had often already suffered enough.

Then, on 7 December, the Japanese attacked the US naval fleet in Pearl Harbor, and invaded Malaya and the Philippines, pulling America into the war. Some said it was about bloody time, but Lucy viewed it with dismay because whatever way you looked at it, it was an escalation of hostilities, and that filled her with despondency.

TWENTY-NINE

The news of the Japanese attack shocked many people and the speed of the Japanese advance through Malaya, as Christmas approached, stunned the world. Lucy was spending Christmas Day with Gwen, though she had to be back at the hospital the following morning, and, as they ate dinner together that day, Lucy expressed concern about the Japanese.

Gwen told her not to worry too much. 'They will be soundly repulsed when they reach the borders of Singapore. We have a heavy army presence there and Singapore itself is said to be impregnable.'

'You know, Gwen, I've already been told two things were impregnable in this war and they turned out not to be,' Lucy said. 'But I really do hope you are right about Singapore.'

'And so do I,' Gwen said gravely.

512

'Oh, let's not talk about it any more,' Lucy said suddenly. 'I know the news is bad, but let's forget it just for today.'

'You're right,' Gwen said. 'If we talk about it from now till the cows come home it will make no difference and only make us feel gloomy.'

'And we don't want that, today of all days,' Lucy said. 'After all, it is Christmas.'

'It's supposed to be the season of goodwill to all men,' Gwen said with a smile. 'Funny that I seem unable to extend that to the Germans or the Japanese.'

'Not funny at all,' Lucy said. 'Sensible, in fact. I think there are limits, even to this "goodwill to all men" caper.'

As New Year unfolded, Lucy was hoping and praying that Gwen was right and that for once impregnable meant impregnable. She tracked the Japanese advance with the help of a map from the *Evening Mail,* which she pinned to the door of her room, for Babs and Jenny were as interested as she was.

Each day the news was worse. The Japanese were taking no prisoners, and in their wake, as they pushed their relentless way forward, she read with horror about the murdered British soldiers, the mutilated bodies of Malayans who may have tried to help them, and the Australian soldiers chained and burnt to death.

What was the army in Singapore against such a savage force? Certainly not impregnable, though they fought hard and valiantly, spurred on by Churchill, who stated before the final assault,

'There must be no thought of sparing the troops or the population; commanders and senior officers should die with their troops. The honour of the British Empire and the British Army is at stake.'

However, despite Churchill, the final battle for Singapore was brutal and very, very bloody. So many men were killed that the army had no choice but to surrender to the Japanese on 15 February. Once established, they proceeded to torture and then slaughter any people of Chinese origin, and took 100,000 Allied soldiers prisoner. Churchill announced that he considered it one of worst defeats of the British Army.

One day in late February, Lucy had just come off duty and noticed that either Babs or Jenny had picked up the post and put it on the little table by the door, but, before she'd had a chance to look at the envelopes, Sister Magee came to tell her that a Mrs Gilbert was in reception and would like a word.

Lucy flew down the stairs. 'Gwen, what is it?'

Gwen said, 'Have you had a letter from Chris today?'

'I don't know,' Lucy said. 'I have post certainly, but I don't know if there's a letter from Chris.'

'Will you look?'

'Why?' Lucy said. 'What is this?'

'Please?' Gwen said.

At the look in her eyes, Lucy said, 'Come with me then.' She glanced across at Sister Magee. 'That's all right, isn't it?'

The nurse nodded grimly, for though women weren't banned from the nurses' home visitors weren't something she encouraged.

'But you share with others?' Gwen protested as she reluctantly followed Lucy up the stairs.

'No one's here,' Lucy said as she opened the door. 'They are either having something to eat or are in the common room. We will have the place to ourselves for a while at least.'

She rummaged around on the hall table as she spoke and picked an envelope out. 'Yes, here's one from Chris,' she said, and she plonked herself on her bed, pulling Gwen down beside her. 'Come on, what's all this about? I won't wait a minute longer.'

'I think Chris is overseas,' Gwen said.

'What makes you say that?' Lucy said, ripping open her envelope as she spoke. 'And if he was bound for foreign climes, wouldn't he have been given embarkation leave?'

'Don't know about embarkation leave,' Gwen said. 'Maybe it's different for the medical teams, and I'm not sure he is overseas. I wanted to see if he said anything to you.'

Lucy scanned the letter and gave a sudden gasp. 'What did he say to you that you thought odd?' she said.

'Just this,' Gwen said reading from her letter: '"Sea very choppy today. But then I was never a good sailor."'

Lucy nodded. 'Mine says, "On the move, but at least this time I might get a good tan." Put together, I would say that he's abroad and somewhere very hot, wouldn't you?' Lucy said. 'And he is trying to tell us.'

'Yes,' said Gwen. 'I just hope that he isn't mixed up in this little lot in the Pacific.'

'No, why would he be?' Lucy said, but fear gripped her at the thought of Chris in the hands of the Japanese.

The girls felt as if they had been dealt a double-edged sword as spring began to take hold, for they had a very welcome pay increase to £50 per year, almost a pound a week, and the knowledge that when they took their State examination in July, provided they passed and became junior staff nurses, they would receive £60 a year. At more or less the same time, though, the clothing coupon points were reduced to 48. 'Well, all I can say is, thank God for Gwen,' Jenny said. 'Or we'd all be going about in rags.'

And no one would want that, especially as American troops had begun arriving in Birmingham. They were a great attraction to the young girls, including nurses, for the city had had few young men in it for some time. They loved to go to the cinema, which they called 'the movies' and to dance. Lucy hadn't gone to a dance, but Jenny and Babs had, and they described it to her. It was very far removed from the dances she had learnt with Clodagh.

'They are wild,' Babs said. 'They dance this dance called the jitterbug to big-band music like "In the Mood", and stuff like that.'

'What on earth is a jitterbug, when it's at home?'

'It's this crazy dance where the American boys swing you round so fast you can sometimes show your knickers,' Babs said.

'Yes, and they shoot you between their legs,'

Jenny said, 'and spin you round until you're dizzy, and when the music stops you want to do it all over again.'

Babs nodded enthusiastically. 'Yeah, it is the most tremendous fun. You should come, it's such a laugh.'

Lucy shook her head and pointed to her chest of drawers. 'There is a ring in that drawer there that says I'm spoken for.'

'Just because you're engaged doesn't mean you have to live like a nun.'

'Oh, come on, Jenny,' Lucy snapped. 'I'd hardly like it if I heard of Chris swinging some random girl between his legs or smooching in the back row of a cinema.'

'You never know what some of the soldiers get up to,' Jenny said.

'Fighting mostly,' Lucy said quietly. 'And my Chris does his level best to patch those soldiers up so that they can go back to do it all over again. He can't tell me where he is, but that hardly matters because similar scenes are being enacted everywhere. Chris said some of them take some patching up and others he can do nothing for.'

No one said anything for a moment or two. Lucy's words dripped into the stillness. 'I'm sorry,' Jenny said. 'That was terribly wrong and insensitive of me.'

'It's all right,' Lucy said, and it was. Jenny spoke without thinking, that was all.

Though they continued to go dancing they never asked her to go again, but the three of them did have regular trips to the cinema.

Like many girls, both Babs and Jenny were taken

517

up with the Americans, and no wonder really. They were so exotic. Their accents had only ever been heard on the silver screen, for a start, and then GIs' uniforms were so much smarter than the average British Tommy's. They seemed to have more money than the average British Tommy too, and chewed gum, and had chocolate and nylon stockings for the chosen few.

More importantly they were not yet war weary, but still filled with the exuberance of youth, which had nearly been sucked out of the young people of Britain. But they were no fools, these Americans, and knew they were in Britain for a short time before they had to face the enemy. Some would not return, so they were living life to the full, and who could blame them?

Certainly not the girls, but Jenny and Babs had to pull in their wings a bit because their final exams were looming. Barely were the exams over than there was a rumour running round the canteen of bombs dropping over near the Rover car factory in Solihull. Many didn't believe that because it had been a year since the last raid. However, that night many planes pummelled Birmingham, mainly in and near Handsworth, although bombs were also dropped in Duddeston, and in Lancaster Street, right outside the fire station and very close to the hospital. Lucy felt quite panicky at the thought that it might be the start of another blitz but there was only one more raid and that was an incendiary attack that was concentrated in Yardley, far too far away to have any impact on the hospital.

Quiet night followed quiet night, and Brummies began to emerge cautiously on to the streets again. They resumed their visits to the cinemas, and Babs and Jenny started going to the dances again after they found out that they had all passed their exams.

They were now junior staff nurses and for the next year they would be learning and practising the techniques of ward management so that they could take charge of a ward the following year. To show their rank they each had a new and longer cap of white starched organdie folded into three, held in place with gold safety pins and fastened to their hair with white grips. Lucy couldn't remember ever being so proud in the whole of her life.

Gwen was almost as proud and took three photographs, one to send to Chris, one for herself to frame and stand on the sideboard, and one for Lucy to send to her mother. The sincere and heartfelt congratulations from Lucy's family in America in response to that photograph moved her to tears.

As the autumn wore on the tide of the war was turning, and for the first time in a long while Lucy looked forward to 1943. However, halfway through January, Lucy was working on the ward when she was told that a Mrs Gilbert was waiting for her in the reception of Outpatients. With great trepidation, for neither had heard from Chris since well before Christmas, she hurried to see what she wanted.

Gwen had tears streaming from her eyes as she watched Lucy approach, and yet she seemed to be smiling, which unnerved Lucy totally. She felt as if her own heart was splintering into pieces for she knew only something of great importance would have brought Gwen to seek her out at the hospital. She could guess what that something was so, as she put her arm around Gwen's shoulders, she led her gently to a seat and sat beside her. Lucy was shaking herself as she held her hand and Gwen felt the tremors running through it.

'Tell me,' Lucy said. She said it because she knew she must, though her heart screamed denial and her heart thumped so hard she knew Gwen could probably hear it.

Gwen gave a sniff and dried her cheeks with her handkerchief as she said, 'You had to know straight away, my dear. These are tears of joy because Chris has been taken prisoner by the Germans.'

'Taken prisoner?' Lucy repeated

'Yes,' Gwen said. 'He is a POW. My dear, isn't it wonderful news?'

'Is it?'

'Of course it is,' Gwen said. 'The war is over for him. He can sit out what is left of it in comparative safety.'

Gwen passed her the telegram so that Lucy could read it for herself and she realised that Gwen was right. Short of coming home, this was the best outcome all round. Her heart felt as light as air. They would find out where he was and they could write to him and send him parcels. They must send parcels. She wasn't sure how well men were fed in these places.

She leapt to her feet, pulled Gwen up and

hugged her delightedly. She felt so happy, so relieved, that if she hadn't been a nurse she could have danced a jig. Still, if she had done that, she thought with a wry smile, she'd probably be found a bed in the mental block.

'Oh, Gwen,' she said, 'I was so afraid when I saw you standing there in tears.'

'My dear,' Gwen said, 'when the boy came with the telegram I felt my heart had stopped beating and I could barely open it, my hands shook so much. And when I read it I felt such an ease in my heart and I had to come and tell you. I wouldn't disturb you normally. I know you are working.'

'Yes, and I must return to the ward,' Lucy said. 'But thank you for coming to tell me. I didn't recognise the worry I carried around with me until it was gone. But I shall not really feel at ease until I get a letter from Chris and know that he is all right.'

'I feel the same,' Gwen said.

However, Lucy's lightness of spirit could not be hidden from the men in the male surgical ward she was working in. 'By, lass,' said one eventually, 'you look like the cat that got the cream.'

'Oh,' said Lucy, almost hugging herself in delight, 'It's much, much better than that.'

The first letter from Chris was the icing on the cake for Lucy. Though he couldn't say where he was being held, he did assure her that he was being well treated. Even better news was that when they knew he was a doctor they sent him to the camp infirmary where the German doctor, who had been coping single-handed, was delighted to see him. Lucy felt utter relief flowing through her as she read that. Her own training was going on apace and it was already arranged that when this, her final year, was over she would leave the nurses' home, move in with Gwen and wait for Chris to come home. She was looking forward to it. She knew she would miss Jenny and Babs a great deal, though they too would be moving on.

Nothing seemed able to upset her equilibrium, for the writing was on the wall as far as the war was concerned. Rommel had been defeated in North Africa after the British victory in El Alamein, the Soviets had forced the surrender of the German Sixth Army at Stalingrad, and the surrender of Italy seemed imminent.

Then America halted the Japanese expansion in the Pacific at the Battle of Midway in early June, and about this time the hospital began admitting injured German soldiers.

'Wonder what the wounded officers will make of that when they arrive next week,' Lucy mused, for they'd had a special ward reopened for them that hadn't been used since the Blitz.

'Not a lot, I suspect,' Babs said. 'But if they have got any sense they'll keep them well apart.'

'Well, I'm looking forward to it,' Jenny said. 'Matron said that the operations and so on will all have been done, and it is postoperative care the officers need now. Tell you, I wouldn't mind giving a bit of TLC to some handsome officer.'

'You'll never change, Jenny.'

'Good,' Jenny said. 'But all joking apart, a girl has to look to the future. It's all right for you, Lucy, because you have a fellow. The way I see it, when this war finally grinds to a halt there might be precious few men left for the rest of us.'

'She's right, you know,' said Babs.

'Course I'm right,' Jenny said. 'So I'm not letting any opportunity of meeting eligible chaps slip by. A ward full of officers seems just the job for me.'

The others had to laugh at many of the things Jenny said, though this time she had a valid point. However, it was Lucy who was put in charge of the officers' ward and she was there to greet them all as the fleet of ambulances pulled into the hospital grounds and started to unload the men. Some were on stretchers and some in wheelchairs, and she was filled with pity to see these young men with missing limbs or bad burns.

She was helping the porters and a probationer nurse transfer a burns victim from the stretcher to bed as painlessly as possible, half aware that a man with a heavy plaster cast on his right leg and another on his left arm was being transferred from the stretcher into the adjacent bed. When she straightened up and saw who the man was the shock for both of them was palpable, for it was Clive Heatherington. His eyes were red-rimmed and glazed with pain and fatigue, and his face was far more creased than she remembered but there was no mistaking him.

'Lucy?' Clive said. 'Is it really you?'

Lucy recovered herself enough to say, 'It's a tremendous shock to see you here, Clive. I thought you dead because the last I heard was that you gave up your place to Chris Gilbert on the last boat leaving Dunkirk.'

'He told you that?' Clive asked in mild surprise. 'I didn't know you were that pally.'

'We are more than pally,' Lucy said. 'We are engaged to be married.'

She could see that she had given Clive a shock, and an unpleasant one at that, though she couldn't understand why. He lifted her hand and said, 'You wear no ring.'

Jewellery is not allowed on the wards,' Lucy said. 'Chris always thought what you did that day on the beach was a magnificent and completely selfless thing to do, and so do I. The fact that you are still alive does not detract from that.'

'I can tell you how I managed to survive, if you like.'

'Yes,' Lucy said. 'I would love to hear it, but not now. I can't neglect the other patients. I will be off duty at half-eight so we can talk then.'

Lucy was immensely glad that with so many new admissions she was kept very busy right till the end of her shift. All the time she worked she felt Clive's eyes almost boring into her. It unnerved her a little, but then everything about the man unnerved her. She couldn't explain, even to herself, how his nearness was affecting her, and how his big, blue eyes still had the power to turn her insides to jelly.

Part of her didn't want to go near Clive, yet part of her really wanted to know how he had managed to survive because Chris had been convinced he faced certain death.

'I hid myself under the dead bodies of other soldiers,' Clive told her when she eventually had time to sit by him. 'I wasted no time about it because I could hear the Jerries coming. Some of the soldiers ran when they saw them, but there was nowhere to run to and they were gunned down. The same fate awaited others who surrendered so I reckoned I had nothing to lose by playing dead.

'That night I sneaked off the beach but I had no plan of action other than to make for the South, and when I could walk no further I slept in a barn. I thought it was all up with me when the farmer found me the next morning. But it turned out he hated the Nazis and so did his wife, and they were very pro-British. So at great risk to themselves they found civilian clothes for me, disposed of my uniform and hid me away for nearly a week. Then the man said they had found someone to help me and I travelled into the town on market day in a cart, hidden in a sack amongst other sacks holding vegetables that the farmer sold at market. There I met a man called Pierre.'

'This is like some adventure story.'

'It didn't seem like it at the time,' Clive said, 'and I was scared, not only for myself but the farmer and his wife and this Pierre. He had a boat, but Hitler was set to invade and had amassed an armada of all kinds of boats and there was a lot of activity all along the coast so it was too risky to try to get me out that way. By the time Hitler had given up his invasion plans, disbanded his flotilla and turned his attention elsewhere it was coming on to winter, and Pierre didn't want to risk his small boat in the winter gales. So I ended up staying with Pierre till the spring of 1941. Course, there was no way of getting word to anyone.'

'I see that,' Lucy said. 'And so everyone would just assume you were missing presumed dead. Just one of many left on the beaches of Dunkirk.'

'Yes.'

'I suppose your father did tell you that Chris had been to see him?'

'Yes,' Clive said. 'I thought it really decent of him, but I was recalled to my own unit before I had a chance of finding out where he was.'

'Why did you do it, Clive? Just give your chance of life away like that?'

'Do you want the absolute honest truth?' Clive looked Lucy full in the face so that she felt as if her heart was melting in her breast as he said sincerely, 'Part of the reason was because I had lost you. I don't know what you feel about me, and you have a perfect right to think very badly of me, but I would just like you to know that you were the best thing that ever happened to me. I will always love you till the day I die.'

'Oh, Clive.'

'Don't worry,' Clive said, 'I probably hurt you very badly and I have no wish to do that ever again. It's just I got to thinking about that in the boat, and how my parents have lost everything anyway because of the war, and how sterile and worthless my life was. Then I saw Chris Gilbert was going to be left behind and I thought how good he had been to my father, my grandmother and me, and suddenly thought his life was far more valuable than mine. When I was on my own, of course, survival techniques kicked in, but I never expected to leave the shores of France alive.' He gave a rueful laugh. 'Then I was shipped to

526

North Africa and copped for this lot, and nearly lost my life all over again. They said it was touch and go, but the doctor injected me with this new drug.'

'Penicillin?'

'That's the stuff.'

'We've got it in the General,' Lucy said, 'but it's just for use by the military.'

'It's bloody painful when they inject it straight into the muscle of my stomach every three hours, but the doctor says it saved my life and my limbs because initially they were talking of amputation.'

'Well,' Lucy said, 'I'm glad that wasn't necessary anyway.'

'Are you?'

'Of course I am.'

'I often wondered if you hated me,' Clive said. 'I wouldn't have blamed you.'

Lucy shook her head. 'I never hated you but you killed any love I might have had for you years ago. But there has been lots of water under the bridge since then, and I am with Chris now.'

'Where's he stationed?'

'In a POW camp.'

'Oh, bad luck.'

'Better that than lying dead somewhere.'

'Yes, you're right,' Clive said, and looked suddenly so morose that Lucy said, 'Why don't you work on your marriage, Clive? Try and rekindle the spark?'

'It never had a spark,' he replied. 'A damp squib is a better description, and I can't work on it because there is nothing there to work on.'

Lucy had spoken to none of the girls about her romance with the son of the house she had worked in because she thought they would think her stupid, so she said nothing now about knowing one of the officers, but analysed her feelings in bed that night. She really thought she hadn't intentionally been lying when she told Chris that Clive meant nothing to her because he had hurt and humiliated her, and so her emotions were all over the place.

However, she knew her intense feelings for Clive had only truly subsided when she'd heard of his death, and now that he hadn't died she faced the realisation that she still loved him, and with the same passion she'd always had. But he was a married man and she was spoken for, so those feelings had to stay hidden. She knew that that wouldn't happen if she tended to him in the hospital.

So the following morning she presented herself in front of Matron and told her about the relationship she had had with Clive, as she thought she needed to know. She said that she felt that her professionalism might be compromised if she were to nurse a person known to her so well. Matron agreed, and so Jenny was put in charge of the officers' ward, which she was delighted about, while Lucy dealt with the German patients.

There was no explanation given, but that was normal, and though Lucy longed to ask about Clive she refused to allow herself to do so. He had obviously said nothing because she knew Jenny would have mentioned it if he had. And that was how it should be, Lucy thought. Clive Heatherington was part of her old life, and however he felt and however she felt he had no place in her future.

Lucy found it wasn't so easy to banish Clive totally from her thoughts and she felt terribly disloyal to Chris when another man kept popping into her consciousness. She didn't know what was the matter with her because she had truly loved Chris when she had got engaged to him, she was sure of that. Could a woman love two men? Well, whether she could or not, she could only have one at a time.

Gwen did notice Lucy's distraction but put it down to her missing Chris, and she thought it small wonder when they'd had such little time together. Now, though, people were beginning to talk about the end of the war. Many thought that 1943 might be the last wartime Christmas, though both Lucy and Gwen thought this far too optimistic.

'It would be nice to think they're right, these people,' Gwen said as she and Lucy packed a festive parcel to send to Chris, but I think it will be another year at least.'

'So do I,' Lucy said. 'I wish I didn't, but can't see how it could be less when you look at all the countries Hitler invaded and now controls. I should say that the Allies will have to go over there and liberate each one.'

'Yes,' Gwen said. 'Course they will, and the thought of them trying another assault on Europe puts the fear of God in me after Dunkirk.'

'Me too,' said Lucy. 'I am so glad that Chris is well out of it.'

They welcomed in 1944 cautiously, and almost immediately there was a massive Soviet offensive against Germany, forcing the German Army westwards, which cheered everyone enormously. Early in May, the General Hospital was told to empty its wards of civilians, and so those still needing nursing care were transferred to other hospitals. Lucy purposely didn't ask if Clive Heatherington was one of the transferred patients. About this time people became aware that the South Coast was out of bounds to civilians and most people knew from this that the Big Push was imminent.

Operation Overlord, D-Day, began on 6 June. Almost immediately patients began arriving at the General. So many casualties were expected that it was decided that all medical staff, whatever their rank, should do abnormal shifts of eight hours on and eight hours off. Lucy found the hours exhausting, especially as they worked so hard in their hours on-duty as the casualties flooded in. In the end she applied for a bed in the nurses' home as she found she could either eat and sleep, or travel back and forward to Gwen's, but she couldn't do both. After six weeks, so many medical staff were ill with exhaustion that the plan was abandoned and normal shift patterns resumed.

Meanwhile, the Allies were reaching concentration camps. The conditions of the skeletal survivors and their accounts of what had gone on inside nauseated Lucy, and though she was glad to read that the conditions in most of the POW camps were much better, it was frustrating not knowing whether Chris's camp had been one of the ones liberated or not. Lucy was in a fever of excitement to see him again after all this time.

'I wish I knew whereabouts the camp was or, better still, what it was called,' she said to Gwen.

'I know, my dear,' Gwen said. 'But he will know that and, mark my words, he will write the first chance he gets.'

And then early one morning, just before Lucy left for work, a letter did come addressed to Gwen, although it wasn't Chris's writing. Gwen opened it with no sense of alarm. Lucy hadn't heard the postman arrive so when she heard Gwen's anguished cry she ran down the stairs to find her in a dead faint. In falling she must have cracked her head badly on the fender because blood was seeping from her head on to the hearth. Lucy was so concerned that she didn't notice the letter because it was screwed up in Gwen's hand.

Lucy fell to her knees and felt for her pulse. It was very faint, and she phoned for the doctor to come urgently. While she waited for him she lifted Gwen's head on to a cushion and then she saw the paper held in her clenched fist. She prised it from her fingers and opened it out, and as she read it her heart dropped like a stone. It was from a man called Stuart Phipps, who described himself as a great mate of Chris's. He said Chris was a grand man and there was no one quite like him and he had been a great help and comfort to so many. But tragically there had been an outbreak of dysentery. Chris had worked valiantly to save as many as possible, but there had been many deaths among the malnourished men.

531

And then Chris had contracted the disease himself and he too had been unable to fight it.

'Just two days after Chris died our camp was liberated by the Allies. I am sorry to be the bearer of such sad news.'

Lucy dropped the letter as if it had burnt her and she felt pierced to her very soul. No wonder Gwen had fainted. She rocked backwards and forwards in her distress. What was she to do? Oh, dear Christ, what was she to do? Heart-rending sobs shook her whole frame and tears dribbled through the hands she had covering her face. Her grief was compounded by guilt because of the feelings she'd had for another man, which had slipped unbidden into her mind and disturbed her dreams. But Chris she had loved too, and it was Chris she had intended to marry, and now her future lay like so much dust beneath her feet.

Gwen had been like a mother to her, and the nurse in Lucy knew that Gwen was very sick. When the doctor arrived he saw that too, and arranged for her to be taken straight to the General Hospital. He was also concerned for Lucy, but she refused medication because she felt that Gwen needed her. Instead she went to the General herself, sought out Matron and tearfully explained what had happened. She even showed her the letter and saw the sympathetic look in her eyes as she looked up from reading it and regarded Lucy.

She felt very sorry for Lucy and gave her a week's compassionate leave. The news flew round the hospital, but Lucy refused to leave Gwen's side, feeling she needed to be beside her. Because she was a nurse at that hospital rules were bent and so she held Gwen's hand and willed her to live. 'I need you, Gwen,' she'd say over and over, and she'd give her hand a squeeze. 'We need each other. Come on, you can fight this. Do it for me, Gwen. Please, please, don't leave me.'

However, Gwen's skull had been badly fractured. She never regained consciousness and died three days later.

Lucy was plunged into the gloom of a dark, dark place, where her worried friends could not reach her. She was grateful for the stalwart women from the WVS who organised Gwen's funeral, for Lucy was totally unable to. By the time the funeral took place she hadn't eaten for days and just about held herself together with difficulty. She defied the Roman Catholic Church's ruling and attended Gwen's funeral along with many mourners: neighbours, friends, Gwen's colleagues from the WVS, a contingent from the hospital. Clara and Cook came as well to support Lucy.

All that could went back to Gwen's, where the ladies of the WVS had laid out a spread. There, Clara looked into Lucy's bereft eyes in her wan face, completely devoid of colour, and said, 'What will you do now?'

Lucy shook her head. She hadn't given a thought to practicalities. 'Mammy is urging me to join them in the States,' she said.

'Why don't you consider it?'

Lucy shrugged. 'I might because I do feel very alone,' she said.

'Oh, God, Lucy, my heart bleeds for you,' Clara said, as she hugged Lucy tight.

'Don't, Clara,' Lucy warned. 'If you are nice to

533

me I am likely to weep all over you.'

'A good cry never did anyone any harm,' Cook said.

'I've had a good cry,' Lucy said. 'God, some days that is all I've seemed able to do.'

'You need your mother, Lucy,' Clara said.

'I would love her to be here right now,' Lucy admitted. 'But I don't want to go to the States just yet.'

'Why not?'

'Well, for one thing the war isn't over yet,' Lucy said. 'The Atlantic is not that safe to cross. But that apart, my emotions are all up in the air and I don't think I should make such a big decision when I feel that way. The solicitor is coming tomorrow and I will have some idea where I stand then, and we will go from there.'

The next morning the solicitor told her she had no money worries and in fact she was a woman of means, for Gwen had left everything, including the house, to Chris, and in the event of his death he had left everything to Lucy in the will he'd lodged with the solicitor when he enlisted. She was, he said, a very fortunate young woman.

Lucy didn't feel in the slightest bit fortunate. Once before, being left things in a will had altered life's direction for Lucy, and in the end she had welcomed that. But this was different. She didn't want Gwen's house or money, she wanted Gwen and things back the way they used to be as they both waited for Chris to come home. But that wasn't going to happen. Eventually, the desperate sadness and almost unbearable pain of the first few days settled down to a dull ache, which

534

seemed lodged in her heart.

She felt incredibly lonely. She had the feeling she was jinxed and that if she loved anyone too much they would be taken from her. All she could see in front of her was a big black hole. Minnie wrote over and over, urging her to go over to them, and Clara called to see how she was.

'Nothing matters any more,' Lucy said.

'Of course it does,' Clara said gently but firmly. 'You are a nurse and your skills are needed, for the Allies are still fighting.'

'You can't expect me to go back to the hospital.'

'That's exactly what I'm asking you to do,' Clara said. 'And it's what Chris would have wanted.'

'You can't know that.'

'I know that man, who went to the levels he did to get you into nursing, would not like to think of you sitting here feeling sorry for yourself.'

'I'm not feeling sorry for myself.'

'Yes, you are,' Clara said. 'It's as if you are letting life go on without you.' She caught hold of Lucy's hands and said, 'My darling child, you are not the only one to suffer a loss. Go back to the job you were trained to do, where you will be able to make a difference.'

Lucy returned to the hospital, but she was a quieter more reflective person, and her ready smile and sense of humour seemed to have deserted her. Jenny and Babs couldn't get her interested in anything, for Lucy never socialised any more, but instead volunteered for all the overtime going because once away from the hospital a well of loneliness would surround her and she looked to the future with no enthusiasm.

THE AFTERMATH

The war was over. Hitler committed suicide in a bunker and the conflict in Europe was finished. Church bells rang out the joyful news and Churchill ordered a national holiday called Victory in Europe Day, on 8 May. Street parties were organised, and bonfires had been building up for weeks, but all this gaiety just seemed to emphasise Lucy's acute aloneness. She would have preferred to have been at work, but Matron had insisted she take time off as she had worked so many hours, and she said she would be too tired to be of any use to anyone if she didn't take a break.

A break was the last thing Lucy wanted, though. She intended going into her house and hiding away until the festivities were all over. She had lost too many people to feel any sort of happiness.

So when the knock came at the door she was surprised, and even more surprised to see Babs and Jenny on the doorstep. Lucy stood and stared at them for a moment or two until Jenny said, 'You going to ask us in or what?'

'Oh, yes, yes, of course,' Lucy said, opening the door wider. 'But what are you doing here?'

'Waiting for you to put your glad rags on because we are going out to celebrate.'

'Oh, you go,' Lucy said. 'That sort of thing is not for me.'

'Don't talk so wet,' Jenny said disparagingly.

'This is the day for everyone to let their hair down. Flipping heck, Lucy, there isn't ever going to be another day like this.'

'I'm no fit company for anyone at the moment.'

'Then get a grip on yourself,' Jenny snapped. 'Crikey, Lucy, you aren't the only person who lost someone, you know. My brother, George was killed on D-Day, and you know that full well. We used to scrap, but we loved one another and I will always miss him. I felt so sorry for our parents because for all their lives they worked themselves into the ground so that we wouldn't have to, so that we both could train for good jobs. It's all they cared about, and now my brother is dead. But they are going to a street party, and do you know why, Lucy?'

Lucy shook her head and Jenny said, 'They said they were going to celebrate George's life, short though it was, and the lives of all the other young men who will never grow old, and to give thanks that the world is at peace now, and we must all go on and meet it.'

The words brought tears to Lucy's eyes, and Jenny's voice was husky as she went on, 'That's true courage, that is. You can't just curl up and die, Lucy. I know you miss Gwen and Chris, but would they want you to be like this?'

Lucy looked at her friends. They lived in different places now, and often had different shifts, so they no longer saw much of each other, but the bands of friendship were as strong as ever. They had come to find her, not just gone off by themselves, and she couldn't reject friendship like that.

'No, they most certainly wouldn't,' she said in

537

answer to Jenny's question. 'And what you have said about your parents has made me slightly ashamed. If you wait a few minutes I will get myself ready and we can go.'

They went to Harrison Road in Erdington, where Jenny's parents lived, and where a street party was in full swing. Food Lucy had never seen the like of all through the war years was laid out on trestle tables.

'Where did all the food come from?' she asked.

'Don't ask,' Jenny advised. 'Just eat, drink and enjoy.'

And Lucy really did try to get into the party mood. She ate and drank with the rest, and belted out the songs from the music halls, and laughed and joked and made every appearance of enjoying herself. But she was playing a part.

And then someone sang 'I'll Be Seeing You', and when this was followed by 'White Cliffs of Dover' and then 'We'll Meet Again', the memories of that dreadful war came tumbling into Lucy's mind and with it came sadness. She had a sudden urgent need to be on her own for a while. She glanced back, but Jenny and Babs were enjoying themselves too much to miss her and she wandered out on to the High Street. Once there she decided to go to the Abbey and say a prayer for all those who would never come back.

The High Street was full of laughing, joking people, and sounds of joy and merriment were everywhere. The weather helped the mood because it was a beautiful spring day with only a gentle breeze, the sun shining from a cornflower-blue sky, the only clouds fluffy white ones. The beauty of this was lost on Lucy, though, as she walked down the street so deep in thought with her head lowered that she almost walked into a man coming the other way.

'Sorry,' she said, lifting her head, and then the words died in her throat as she stared at the man.

'Hello, Lucy,' he said.

All the nerves in Lucy's body started to jangle. 'Hello, Clive.'

'It's good to see you,' Clive went on, and the tone of his voice sent the blood pumping wildly through Lucy's veins. 'But what are you doing here? I thought you would be celebrating.'

'I was,' Lucy said. 'I was invited to a street party and I did go, but then I just wanted to be on my own for a bit.'

'Me too,' Clive said. 'There's a lot to reflect on.'

'Yes, there certainly is.'

'Were you making for anywhere in particular?'

Lucy nodded. 'The Abbey.'

'Mind if I walk along with you?'

Lucy did mind very much because the man's nearness was making her body act in very strange ways, but she could hardly say so, and so she shrugged. 'If you want.'

She noticed the limp straight away and he said, 'If you're wondering why I'm not in uniform it's because I failed the medical. They did wonders with my leg but I will always walk with this limp. That's why I missed out on D-Day.' He sighed and went on, 'It doesn't matter now the war is over. I expect you are looking forward to Chris coming home.'

Lucy shook her head. 'Chris didn't make it. He

539

died in the camp, of dysentery, just before the Allies reached them.'

'Oh, Lucy, I am so sorry.'

Lucy nodded, unable to speak for a moment. Then she recovered enough to say, 'Chris's mother, Gwen, who I lived with, fainted when she read the letter. She hit her head, fracturing her skull and never recovered consciousness.'

'Oh, Lucy,' Clive said. 'You must have felt so alone.'

The sympathy in Clive's voice was Lucy's undoing and the tears flowed from her eyes. Clive's arm went round her shoulders and it was as if an electric current had run between them. They looked at each other in amazement and Clive pulled her closer to him as he said, 'I know what that loneliness feels like.'

'Your parents?'

Clive nodded. 'The old man had a heart attack last year and my mother just seemed to fade away without him.'

'I am so sorry,' Lucy said. 'I thought a great deal of your father.'

'I missed them more than I thought I would,' Clive admitted.

'And what about Mr Carlisle and Norah?'

'I pensioned them off.'

'And you divorced your wife?'

'No, but she was divorcing me,' Clive said. 'And she'd gone down to London with this man she was running away with, but they were both killed by a doodle bug. Rough justice or what? That was just before my parents died. It's a lonely place I am in, especially as I wasn't allowed back in the army.'

'That must have been a blow.'

'In a way,' Clive said. He paused before going on, 'I suppose in a way it was my bolt hole. Jessica was having affairs almost since the day we married, and her tempers had to be seen to be believed.'

'Huh, I can imagine that.'

They had reached the lichgate and, as they began walking through the graveyard towards the church, Clive said, 'Can I ask you something?'

'I suppose so.'

'In the hospital you said I had killed your love for me.'

'Yes,' Lucy said. 'What did you expect?'

'Nothing more, really,' Clive said. 'I wanted to apologise for the harm I did you but I never saw you after that night when I told you how I had survived Dunkirk. Where did you go? I looked for you for ages and in the end I asked the nurse in charge where you were; said we were old friends. She said you had been transferred.'

'That's right,' Lucy said. 'It is what happens in hospitals. You're drafted in where you're needed.'

'Oh.'

'What?'

'I ... I thought you might have asked for a transfer because of me,' Clive said.

They had reached the door of the church and Lucy mounted the steps, leaving Clive at the bottom before turning and saying, 'My God, you have got an inflated idea of your own importance. You Heatheringtons are all the same.'

Clive sprang up the steps and grasped Lucy's hands. 'No, really, I am not like my parents,' he

541

said earnestly. 'I know now Jessica married me for the title I have now inherited and the chance to be mistress of a big house. Well, I can't do anything about the title, though I have no intention of using it, and if anything is left of the house when the military have finished with it I will take advice on how to get rid of it because I have no intention of living in a mausoleum like that.'

'Why are you telling me this?'

'Because the very things that attracted Jessica – all the trappings of wealth and influence – were the things that made you uncomfortable. All I'm saying is that I am disposing of all I can.' Lucy looked into Clive's eyes, and he pleaded, 'Give me another chance, Lucy. I once said that I loved you, would always love you till the breath leaves my body, and that's true. Let me show you how much, and now that we haven't got to please anyone but ourselves let me try and win your love back?'

Lucy's eyes glistened and she brushed the tears away as she said, 'I have never stopped loving you, Clive. I realised that a long time ago.'

'Oh, my darling girl,' Clive cried, enfolding Lucy in his arms.

It felt so right and very, very comforting. She didn't need to speak, but as she snuggled deeper she heard his sigh. They stayed locked together on the steps of the church for some time.

'Lucy,' said Clive gently, and she lifted her head and saw his eyes filled with love for her. When Clive's lips descended on hers, she gave herself up to the kiss, and as the heat flowed through her body she knew at last she was where she belonged, and neither of them would ever feel alone again.

The publishers hope that this book has given you enjoyable reading. Large Print Books are especially designed to be as easy to see and hold as possible. If you wish a complete list of our books please ask at your local library or write directly to:

Magna Large Print Books
Magna House, Long Preston,
Skipton, North Yorkshire.
BD23 4ND

This Large Print Book for the partially sighted, who cannot read normal print, is published under the auspices of

THE ULVERSCROFT FOUNDATION